# Prophets and Bad Guys

*Richard Staples*

Eloquent Books

Eloquent Books
An imprint of Strategic Book Group
P.O. Box 333
Durham CT 06422
www.StrategicBookGroup.com

ISBN: 978-1-60911-367-4

Printed in the United States of America

Book Design: Rolando F. Santos

# Prologue

## *The year 610, Common Era, Mount Hira, Arabia*

Muhammad lay prostrate, praying, in a cave. This was not the first time that he'd come to this spot to contemplate his life. A member of the Hashim clan of the Quraish tribe of Mecca, Muhammad had seen quite a lot of the world for a forty-year-old man, and it troubled him. The Quraish worshiped Allah as the one and only God. But Muhammad, in his travels as a leader of various trading caravans to Syria, had the opportunity to meet people from over 200 different tribes. And every one of those tribes worshiped a different god. Surely there were not 200 gods! If there was more than one god, how many were there? Which one was the greatest? These were questions that Muhammad asked himself but did not have the answers to.

Muhammad's restlessness of the soul had not developed over a short period but rather over his whole life. A hard, challenging life that had brought him good fortune: his loving wife, Khadijah, wealth accumulated through barter and trade and a reputation as a respected and honest man.

One would not expect such blessings considering the handicaps that Muhammad had bestowed upon him. His father, Abdullah, had died before Muhammad was born, while returning from a trading caravan. His mother, Aminah, gave birth to him shortly after learning of her husband's unfortunate death. Unable to support her son, she sent Muhammad to live with the Sa'ad tribe, in the desert of Arabia. Muhammad spent five years with the Sa'ad, and it molded and imbued him with maturity beyond his years. Living the life of a nomadic herder, he learned the value of hard work and self-reliance and his foster family taught him manners and excellent grammar. Upon Muhammad's return to Mecca his mother, Aminah, now able to support her son and thrilled have him under her roof, decided to visit relatives in the city of Yathrb. It was during this trip that she fell ill and died of fever. His uncle, Abdel Muttahib, took young Muhammad into is home and raised him as his own. Misfortune struck again when, after two years, Abdel also died. For the third time Muhammad was an orphan.

A boy, orphaned three times, and under the age of ten, would not be expected to survive the ordeals of desert life, but Muhammad had somehow gained favor with Allah. Abdel's son, Abu Talib, assumed the responsibility of caring for Muhammad and put him to work caring for sheep near Mecca.

By his early twenties, Muhammad had earned a well-deserved reputation for honesty and integrity, unusual for someone so young. However, despite his moral character, Muhammad remained a poor man without any prospects of improving his lot in life, until Allah smiled on him again.

A wealthy widow named Khadijah required an able man to lead a trading caravan to Syria and conduct business on her behalf. His uncle, Abu Talib arranged for Muhammad to meet with the lady to discuss the job. Impressed with him, she offered him the job of leading the caravan.

Muhammad was successful and Khadijah, so impressed with the young man, asked him to remain in her employ. Eventually they fell in love and married. She was fifteen years his senior.

By the time he was forty, Muhammad's yearnings began to manifest themselves. It was one of these yearnings that caused him to travel to this particular cave in the mountain. He had questions that not only he had no answers to, but also was not sure he could put into words! They were questions that only someone wiser than himself could answer.

A brilliant flash of white light lit the dark cave, the likes of which Muhammad had never seen before. It was a light brighter than one thousand suns; a light that should have blinded him, yet it did not. For a second Muhammad thought of Moses in the presence of the Lord of the Hebrews.

An entity materialized before him, human in appearance, though Muhammad knew instantly that it was not of this earth. The face was not masculine, but not exactly feminine either. It had shoulder-length blond hair and was clothed in a white, flowing gown which hid any appendages. It seemed to float just above the cave's floor. Light seemed to emanate from its body.

It was clear to Muhammad, though no words had been spoken, that this entity, be it blessed or be it evil, had a purpose for him. Muhammad was scared of no man and, though the entity did not have a menacing appearance, it frightened him. No one knew the existence of this cave. If the entity intended him harm, Muhammad knew that he was defenseless. He could die a violent death, alone in this cave, and not be found for years; then what would happen to his beloved wife Khadijah?

"Read," the voice reverberated throughout the cave. The command was as frightening as it was compelling.

"I can't read," the illiterate Muhammad replied to the entity, not knowing what else to say.

"Read," the command was uttered again. The entity raised its right hand, which became just visible from underneath its robe, towards Muhammad and balled it into a fist.

Muhammad felt an incredible force squeezing his chest. It was as if a giant hand, directed from the entity, was attempting to force the air from his lungs. When the pressure ceased, Muhammad caught his breath.

"I can't read!"

Again, the invisible hand applied its grip. Again, Muhammad felt like he was about to be crushed.

The command came again. "READ!"

Muhammad caught his breath, but rather than suffer another attack he asked a question, "What should I read?"

"Read in the name of your Lord, who created humankind. Read, for your Lord is the most generous. He taught people by the pen what they didn't know before" the entity's voice echoed.

Muhammad ran out of the cave and down the mountain, certain that he was being attacked by a demon. Muhammad felt that the demon was just a step behind him the whole time as he ran to his home but, each time that he turned to face it, nothing was there.

What did this demon want? The thought terrified Muhammad. He assumed that his meditations in the cave had somehow conjured up the demon. It talked about the lord but who, or what, was lord? The tribes worshiped various gods. Which ones were real and which ones false? Which ones were benevolent and which ones malevolent?

As he approached his home he saw the face of the entity filling the space between the horizon and the sky.

"Muhammad, you are the messenger of Allah and I am Jibr'il," the voice of the cave uttered as Muhammad staggered over the threshold of his home. Collapsing, he called to his wife and realized that, for better or worse, his life had been irrevocably changed. What he had no way of knowing was, that the world, both now and in the centuries to come, would also be irrevocably changed.

# Chapter 1

Tortured, battered, burned, bloodied and beaten David Franks awaited his execution. Kidnapped in Iraq, he did not know how or when he would die but had made his peace with God. Bound, with ropes at the wrists and ankles, Franks had been stripped naked and, over the last several days, he had been burned with cigarettes, beaten with some sort of rubber hose and shocked with electricity. He had been forced to make a video requesting forgiveness of his, and America's, crimes against Islam and the Iraqi Nation. He knew that some outrageous demands had been made—demands that would not be met by the United States and that would be the pretext for his execution.

A New York Sun-Times reporter, Franks had been on assignment in Iraq and been kidnapped by masked gunmen in Tikrit. He was immediately forced into a car, blindfolded, bound at the wrists and thrown to the floorboard in the back, the barrel of a gun jabbed into his ribs. After what seemed like an eternity, the car stopped and he was dragged out and hustled into, what he assumed was a house. It was there that his blindfold was removed, though his captors remained masked. The leader, who spoke perfect, though heavily-accented English, examined his wallet. In it he found Frank's New York driver's license, several credit cards and some New York Sun-Times business cards, which disclosed his title—reporter—and his email address: David.Franks@NYST.com.

"A Jewish reporter or Jewish spy," the masked leader asked, though he was not really interested in the reply.

"Actually, though my father was Jewish, my mother is Christian. I was raised a Roman-Catholic," Franks said.

"Silence! You are either a CIA spy or some other lackey of the U.S. Government. In any case you are an enemy of Islam and I will find out the truth," shouted the leader.

Franks was always bound at the wrists, and usually bound at the ankles, but one particularly brutal and sadistic session he was awakened with a bucket of water to discover, to his horror, that he was tied face down, spread eagle. Pillows were placed under his waist to raise and expose his testicles and anus. Every second seemed like an hour, every minute a day, and every hour a lifetime as he was beaten with a hose and electrodes were placed on his testicles. During most of the torture Franks endured the pain with minimal screaming, though now he screamed like a banshee and cried like a baby. Frank lost track of time and begged to die. Still it continued. Finally, after he could not even moan from the pain, the punishment stopped.

The leader knelt beside Franks and whispered into his ear. "You are a courageous man David Franks. No ordinary man could endure what you have endured. Your government has not met our demands and you must die. I will allow you time to make peace with your God and you will be allowed to die with dignity. You will not be hurt anymore and your corpse will not be abused."

Franks could not even acknowledge what he barely heard.

The others gave him his clothes and allowed him to dress. Franks was so weakened that he had to be helped. He was carried to another room and tied to a bed, though he was in no condition to escape. Franks thought it was late afternoon. The room was stifling hot and the windows were boarded shut. He thought that he could hear faint noises outside but the sounds were incomprehensible to him. It was later when one of the men allowed him some food and water. He was untied from the bed, though his wrists were still bound to each other, and he ate with his fingers, the type of food unknown. The finest steak he'd eaten had not tasted better. The water was better than the finest wine.

After the meal Franks was again tied to the bed and he began to contemplate his life. He assumed that he had less than twenty four hours to live, perhaps less that twelve or even six. He thought of his wife, Isabelle, and his daughter Tori. Not an overly religious man, Franks attended Mass weekly — largely due to his wife's devout Catholic upbringing. Thoughts of his family brought him to tears and he began to pray.

"God almighty I am not afraid to die but please forgive me of my sins and please take care of Isabelle and Tori."

After silently offering his short prayer Franks, his conscience clear, fell asleep from exhaustion.

Franks was awakened roughly by one of his captors. He was unmasked and looked very much like a typical Arab, dark complexion and a beard, though somehow his face seemed flush. He definitely seemed agitated as he drew a knife.

*So this is it*, Franks thought as he prepared to die. He was speechless when the Muslim cut the ropes binding his wrists together.

"I know you are weak but can you walk?" his captor said as he cut the thick ropes securing Franks to the bed. He recognized the voice as the leader.

"Yes, I think so."

"Very well my brother. You must leave quickly. As you leave this house follow the road for about two miles. You will eventually find American soldiers. It is dark outside and there is little lighting. Avoid everyone until you find other Americans. They patrol the streets."

"I don't understand. What is going on here?" Franks asked in utter disbelief.

"Silence my brother! There is no time to explain my actions. Right now your name is David, but you are Daniel. God is keeping the others sleeping as he did with the lions." He was referring to the Biblical story of Daniel and the lions.

"By the time they wake, you and I will be gone."

"Are you coming with me?" Franks asked as he rose from the bed.

"No. Before we part I must ask your forgiveness."

"Are you serious? I should thank you for sparing my life."

"No my brother; please, I beg of you. Forgive me of my sins against you."

"Very well."

The two snuck through the house and into the street. Franks' former captors were asleep. It was completely dark except for the moonlight. The two men turned to each other and the leader gave Franks a huge hug. Franks was still in a state of disbelief.

"Follow this road. Avoid everyone until you find your people," uttered the leader as he pointed.

"Why are you doing this?"

"There is no time to explain David Franks but I must ask one more favor from you."

"Are you kidding? Name it."

"Please tell everyone that you escaped, not released."

"Okay."

The leader started to leave and Franks grabbed his arm and asked "What is your name?"

"Mohammad Baghai. Your government has been looking for me."

"Thank you Mohammad Baghai" uttered Franks as he gave him a hug.

"Walk with Christ David Franks," Franks heard Mohammad exclaim as he disappeared into the darkness.

Franks thought that was a peculiar thing for him to say. Wouldn't something like "walk with Allah" be more appropriate? At any rate, he was not going to debate the issue.

Franks followed his instructions. Though he was severely weakened from his ordeal he managed to walk at a moderate, yet stealthy pace. Only once did he pass anyone on the street and easily avoided the two pedestrians by hiding in a darkened alley until they passed. Shortly afterwards, he was challenged by an American soldier.

"Halt!" An M-16 rifle was pointed at Franks' chest.

"I'm David Franks, the kidnapped reporter! Please don't shoot!" He stopped dead in his tracks and raised his hands.

"On your knees, hands on your head" was the instantaneous command of the soldier.

Out of nowhere two more of the soldier's comrades appeared. Franks felt two rifle barrels press against his back.

"Lay face down on the ground," was the next command, which Franks obeyed without any other prompting. With the rifle barrels still jabbing into his back, the first soldier frisked him, finding nothing.

"He's clean."

Franks felt the barrels withdraw from his back and immediately felt hands grasp each of his shoulders, lift him up and spin him 180 degrees.

Franks barely had time to say "thank you" to his rescuers before his lack of strength caused him to faint, collapsing into the arms of one of the soldiers.

THE Reverend Casey Edgars sat at his office on the grounds of the Christ Ministry Church, in Maryland, preparing a sermon for his weekly, televised Sunday service. He also had a weekly current affairs show. The unofficial advisor to numerous Presidents, Edgars had led a remarkable life—predicting major world events, economic ebbs and flows and the foibles of many world figures, with remarkable accuracy. At an age when many men of his generation had been collecting their social security checks for years, Edgars carried on a whirlwind schedule, habitually flying back and forth across the country, and across oceans, preaching the message of the CMC, with no signs of fatigue. Edgars had never married and, as a small child, had been kidnapped and later released. He allowed himself only one hobby—chess—when he had time to break from God's work. He was very good at chess. Once in A simultaneous exhibition against the world champion he dismantled the man, forcing his resignation in just twenty-nine moves with the black pieces. Edgars knew that he was a lightning rod, drawing the most vocal of supporters and detractors. But he was not concerned. His cause would not allow anyone or anything to distract him.

Now President Hays had notified him that, for his decades of religious, spiritual and public service, she wanted to present him with the Presidential Medal of Freedom. Though flattered he was not impressed, although he'd reluctantly agreed to accept the award at the White House, with the date and details to be worked out between his and the White House staff.

Edgars had other things on his mind. He had a sense of what and when important events were going to happen. It was a God-given sense; nothing that he could adequately explain, and he didn't have a desire to try, even though he had been asked to do so. It was his brilliance and analytical ability that allowed him to sort through clutter and invariably suggest a solution. He was getting his sense again. Something, some world event, was about to happen. He did not know yet what it was but Edgars was sure that he soon would.

"SHARP-SHOOTER is on the move," uttered a Secret Service agent into his lapel microphone as President Jennifer Hays strode past him.

"Good morning Ron. I thought you were going on vacation?"

"Good morning Mrs. President. I had to postpone it for a few weeks, but I am still going to the beach and go diving" remarked the agent as he fell in behind the Commander in Chief.

"Be sure to bring plenty of sun block."

"Yes ma'am, I will."

Ron Thomas was going to spend his vacation in Pensacola, Florida, Hays' adopted hometown.

Together they entered the elevator and descended to the ground floor. Exiting, they were greeted by another agent who opened the breezeway door to the Oval Office, or the "O" as Hays had nick-named it. Yet another agent opened the door to the outer office, next to the O. Hays entered her domain and started the coffee machine— she still insisted on making and pouring her own coffee. It was still dark outside as she gazed for a moment into the infinite peaceful blackness of the pre-dawn and allowed herself a moment to reflect on her life.

Originally from Wisconsin, Hays was a history professor by trade, teaching at the University of West Florida before her leap into politics. After her opposition to an on-campus political protest, one at which an American flag was burned, and an opposition for which she was reprimanded by the University administration, Hays was asked to consider running for Congress, replacing a retired Congressman representing the people of Florida's First District. Initially reluctant, she was persuaded and decided to run. The First District, heavily populated with retired military, responded favorably to her anti flag-burning stance and a ground swell carried her to a surprisingly easy victory. Three congressional terms and an international incident later, Hays ran against, and unseated, a three-term Senator from Miami. A year into her second term as Senator, Hays announced, from the very spot on the UWF campus where the flag was burned, that she would run for President.

The presidential election, against Senator Tim Dunston from South Dakota, was a bitter contest; the outcome in doubt until the last week before the Election Day. Hays had always had strong support from the conservative faction, and she managed to attract sufficient numbers of various minority factions to tip the balance in her favor in several "swing" states. Her campaign manager Andrew Shephard ran her campaign as a conductor would manage an orchestra. He adroitly and successfully managed to change the mindset of a majority of the voting public by portraying conservatives as "Main Stream Americans," and the opposition's liberal leadership as well-intentioned, but incompetent. The effect of the ad campaign allowed Hays to remain above the fray and, while not directly naming Dunston, forced him to defend his party and its hierarchy rather than attack Hays' platform.

A door opened and Shephard walked in, interrupting Hays' daydreams. Six feet tall, impeccably dressed, with Michael Douglas' good looks, he strode towards the President, carrying a briefcase in his left hand. Now the White House Chief of Staff, Shephard had personally called and woken Hays with the news of David Franks' escape from his captors in Iraq. She found it incredible that he could shower, shave, dress and travel across town while arriving only minutes behind her at the Oval Office.

"Good morning Andy, coffee?"

"Yes please. I could use some."

Shephard sat down on the sofa and spread out his materials on the coffee table.

Hays walked over with a cup in each hand and gave one to her Chief of Staff as she sat down opposite him in a Queen Anne chair.

"Okay, what have you got for me?"

"Yes Mrs. President. As you know several hours ago David Franks, the New York Sun-Times reporter in Iraq was rescued, or "found" would probably be a more accurate term, by American Army personnel. He's been severely beaten and tortured but somehow managed to escape from his captors. Presently he's being treated in a local MASH hospital and, as soon as he's able, Franks will be transported to Baghdad Airport and flown to Ramstein Air Force Base in Germany for further treatment and recovery."

"And debriefing, correct?"

"Yes, of course. The CIA wants to begin ASAP."

"That's fine as long as he's recovered sufficiently. He's not to be badgered or otherwise pressured into disclosing data until he's medically cleared to do so. We've made arrangements to fly his family to Germany to meet him, correct Andy?"

"That is correct Mrs. President."

"I also want someone from the FBI to escort Franks' wife and daughter until further notice. I'm sure the press will make a circus out of the rescue of one of their own."

"I'll call the Director at his home immediately after I leave here."

"Fine, now tell me about Franks," Hays said as she sipped her coffee.

"He's 32, married, with a three-year-old daughter. Franks was educated at NYU School of Journalism and went to work with the New York Sun-Times after college. He was on assignment in Iraq when he was abducted. The CIA believes that he was kidnapped because of his Jewish name, although he's Christian; Catholic actually. He was forced to make a video 'confessing' to his, and America's, 'crimes' which was posted on several web-sites."

"Is that what's on that DVD in your brief case Andy?"

"Yes it is Mrs. President."

"Let's take a look at it."

Shephard walked over to armoire and opened the doors, revealing a large flat-screen monitor and a DVD player. He inserted the disc into the player, used the remote to start it and took his seat again. The screen lit up and revealed David Franks sitting at a table in front of a curtain backdrop. Franks was wearing a simple, white robe, which covered all of his body save his head.

"I am David Franks," he began, speaking in monotone and not looking directly at the camera, as if he was reading a cue card. "I am an American CIA spy. I was captured while on a mission for the American Army. I am here, in Iraq, under the pretext of being a reporter for the New York Sun-Times but I was, in actuality, spying for the American Army, looking for targets to be attacked. As an American spy I have located numerous targets, which have been attacked, though all of these were non-military. The Americans, because of my actions, have killed many innocent Iraqi civilians. I have been tried, convicted and sentenced to death for my crimes. America has a long history of international aggression and imperialism. Most recently, the war criminal Bush, his son, the second Bush, and now President Hays have initiated wars against the peaceful nations of Iraq, Afghanistan and against Islam. Hays has continued to occupy Iraq, though it is clear to all that Americans are neither welcome, nor needed. Western decadence cannot, and will not, be tolerated in Muslim states."

"I have been advised that, because Islam is a peaceful religion and that the court which tried me is merciful, I may be pardoned. To spare my life President Hays must speak before the General Assembly of the United Nations and admit to, then apologize for, the United States' crimes against all Arab nations and Islam. She must immediately begin to withdraw all military forces from every Arab nation and release every person being held in this false war. In addition, the United States must pay ONE BILLION U.S. dollars each to Iraq and Afghanistan as war reparations. After these terms have been met this court will reconvene and consider a pardon for my war crimes. America has five days to meet these terms otherwise I am to be beheaded. Afterwards, I am told, my head will be mailed to The White House." The screen turned to snow and Shephard pressed the remote to turn the player and the monitor off.

"That was short and sweet," remarked Hays.

"Yes Mrs. President. The terms, as you and they both know would never be considered and are being used just as a pretext to execute an American. Franks, unfortunately, was just the unlucky victim, being in the wrong place at the wrong time."

"Do we know anything about the kidnappers?"

"We don't have any intelligence from the video. Franks' abductors were careful not to speak or be seen and the room where it was made was, apparently, well insulated, since we couldn't detect any ambient noise. These people did a good job at disguising their identities. We're assuming that the operation was at least approved, if not orchestrated, by Mohammad Baghai, the head of al-Qaeda in Iraq. He is Persian, rather than Arab, but a fanatical Muslim all the same. He was born in Kerman, a province in Iran, about the size of France, to well-to-do parents. His mother, an Iraqi, was a homemaker and his father was the bureau chief of SAVAK, in the United States—the Shah Mohammad Pahlavi's secret police and intelligence organization. Baghai, the younger, was educated at Harvard and later earned a law degree at the University of Tehran, after his father was recalled. Shortly before the Shah's overthrow, his family managed to escape Iran and return to the U.S. It looks like Baghai had a considerable amount of money stashed in a personal account at a Swiss bank. The father died three years ago; the mother lives quietly in upstate New York with another identity."

"During his time in America, Baghai became fervent about his religion, migrated to Afghanistan and fought the Soviets after they invaded. He became one of Bin Laden's lieutenants there. In between the Gulf Wars he popped up in Iraq and, after the death of al Zarqawi, took charge of al-Qaeda."

"Though we don't have any hard evidence, the fact that Franks' abduction was coordinated and executed perfectly, that the video has zero intelligence value, and considering Baghai's father was in Iran's secret police, lends support to the assumption that Baghai was behind this."

"I assume that Baghai saw all of Franks' personal effects—drivers' license, press credentials, lap top computer and the like; do we have any reason to believe that his family is in danger from other Muslims here?"

"Franks was just a pawn in this affair and Baghai knows that. He has bigger fish to fry. The local Muslim population generally keeps a low profile. Virtually all Muslims are good, upstanding people, earning a living, minding their own business and hoping others will not meddle into theirs. Those that are more vocal are being observed, in various degrees, in relation to just how vocal they are. No, the FBI doesn't believe that there's any danger to his family," replied Shephard.

"Very well Andy," said Hays as she poured another cup of coffee. "What else do we need to cover before the sun rises?"

"There are a couple of domestic issues that we need to discuss Mrs. President. Number one, is the opening ceremony of the Olympic Games in Chicago…"

CHARLIE Michaels fired off about a dozen rounds from his Tipman 7000 paint ball gun, "killing" the last member of the opposing team—a rival fraternity brother of Delta Kappa Alpha at UWF—winning the campus paintball competition and an invitation to the national collegiate paintball club championships. He trotted over to the opposing team's flag, captured it and ended the competition. At that point all his "brothers" mobbed him with congratulations. After the handshakes, hugs, hoots and howls, the brothers of DKA migrated back to their fraternity house, where at least one keg of beer was always on tap, and celebrated the victory.

Michaels was nicknamed "slayer" because he had a knack for making seemingly impossible shots with his paint ball gun, while rarely being hit himself. Michaels was relatively average in height at 5'11", but light and nimble. Sandy blond hair, with a wicked smile that appealed to the sorority sisters on campus, Michaels' "bad boy" image was a hit on the local social scene; he never seemed to have problems with his social life. It was after several dates that his flawed character began to show itself. He viewed himself as a sexual hunter and women as targets, or game, to be conquered. After he'd charmed a prospect out of her clothes, and bedded her several times, he usually lost interest, found some pretext or other to not to see her anymore and begin the search for another conquest.

Though intelligent and articulate, Michaels found his classes boring. Still, he managed to make the dean's list without much effort, attended classes sporadically and rarely studied until the night before a test. Besides his social life, all that he was really interested in was the local campus chapter of a political organization — Americans Against Military Occupation or AAMO. This typical radical college group piqued his interest because, as a small boy, he'd lost an older brother in the second Gulf War. AAMO also piqued the interest of the Justice Department. Attorney General James Scarboro, also of Northwest Florida had had the organization and its members investigated, which was a point of pride to all the members.

Though he had few memories of his slain brother John, the ones Charlie Michaels could remember were all fond. He had a framed picture of himself standing at attention, dressed in an army soldier's costume standing next to his brother in his uniform. Perhaps his most memorable experience was when, as a five-year-old, John took him to an isolated patch of woods and taught him to shoot a .22 rifle.

"Charlie, this is not a toy. It can hurt and even kill you. I lost the tip of my pinkie finger, when I was just cleaning the rifle, because I didn't follow the safety rules. Do you understand what I'm saying?"

"Yes John, I'll follow all the rules and pay attention," Charlie had replied.

The shooting lessons made Charlie feel proud, since he knew that no boys his age got to go shooting, and the experience bonded him to his brother eternally.

Charlie failed to comprehend the significance of the soldiers coming to visit Mom and Dad, and why others came to visit with food and seemed so sad. John's funeral was closed casket and Charlie didn't believe his brother was really dead. Months later, after asking "When is John coming home?" and getting the answer, "he's not Charlie. John died and is in heaven now," that he finally realized he'd lost his best friend as well as a brother. That traumatic experience was compounded exponentially when, several years later, both his parents were killed in a head-on car crash. To cover up his emotional scars, he developed his current persona. He was determined not only to be the best, but to crush any competitors. A 3.95 GPA was not good enough — only a 4.0 was satisfactory. Possessing a better than average knowledge on a subject would not do, Michaels had to be THE authority on it. If an hour was required to master a skill, he would spend at least six on it. If it took a week then he would spend a month.

As Charlie was celebrating his win by consuming mass quantities of cold beer at the Delta House, fellow fraternity brother and team-mate, Chris O'Callahan, nick-named "Hit Man," sauntered up with a beer in each hand and gave one to Michaels.

"Man I thought we were cooked when they were up two to one. How did you do it?" He was referring to Michaels being out-numbered yet managing to "kill" the last two enemy players without getting shot himself.

"Very simple Chris," remarked Michaels in a semi-condescending, yet friendly tone, "One, I have no peers in paint ball; I'm too quick and agile. Two, I imagined each of those last two as that bitch Hays."

"In fact I've thought of a new variation of capture the flag, which I call 'Assassination.' Instead of killing other shooters and capturing the flag, each team tries to shoot a life-like figure of a world leader. Put Hays with a bull's eye on her chest on the field and our team will NEVER lose!"

"Anyway it is off to bum-fuck Georgia for the championships."

"Yeah, what is the name of the college?" asked O'Callahan.

"North Georgia, but I don't know where it's at. Somewhere in North Georgia would be my guess," replied Michaels as his words began to slur.

"We'll need to find it on the Net."

"Not right now! It's time to get shit-faced!"

Both fraternity brothers, equally drunk, made their way to the keg to refill their cups.

AFTER releasing Franks and watching him disappear into the night, Mohammad knew that he would have to escape Tikrit, avoiding both the Americans and his former comrades. As the son of a Persian father and an Arab mother, he was comfortable interacting in either culture. "Fitting in" was not an issue. He had no trouble blending in with the population when he needed to; his father taught him covert techniques. The issue was that he'd always been a wanted man for al-Qaeda's terrorist activities in Iraq. He had personally killed five Americans, beheading one U.S. soldier several years ago, and had intended to do the same to Franks. Now he was a man pursued by two different hunters; he was more concerned about the sleeping cadre that he left than the Americans.

Mohammad had always believed that he was doing God's work and following God's grand design. Osama bin Laden had recognized his devotion to Islam. And, though Mohammad was Persian, he'd overcome that racial prejudice and earned the respect of all of those who came to know him. He was given the "honor" of beheading a captured American—a task that he took immense pleasure and pride in performing. The execution was recorded and Mohammad did not attempt to sever the man's head with a clean cut; rather, he drew the blade of the sword across the man's throat numerous times, taking several minutes to complete the bloody affair. Now he knew that his actions were wrong and that God had another plan for him, although he did not know what it was. He only knew that Franks had to be spared and that he, Mohammad, had to travel to Baghdad, then escape to Iraq.

Mohammad walked toward the Tigris River. He had always been a careful planner, both in Afghanistan and now in Iraq. Careful planning and God's will kept him alive. Now he had no plan, only his faith in the Almighty. He knew that God would provide. Tikrit was quiet and he passed no one. The Tigris was a slow, shallow, muddy river that originated in Turkey, passed through several major Iraqi cities, including Baghdad, before it joined the Euphrates River and exited to the Persian Gulf. As he approached the riverbank Mohammad spied a small rowboat with oars. Alas! God did provide for his needs. He would only be able to travel at night and would have to avoid the major cities of Mosul and Samara during the day. If he could reach Baghdad, the rest would be relatively simple. He had a safe house that no one knew about, except himself, several false identifications, food and money. He was confident in his abilities. His abilities had kept him alive in these dangerous times. The journey would not be easy, probably three nights to Baghdad. He would have to find a place to hide the boat during the day and sleep, finding whatever he could to eat. God would provide. Also, an undetermined amount of time would be necessary in his safe house, until he could slip away from the city and leave the country. Mohammad stepped into the boat and began to row. He did not know what lay in store for him, only that he knew that he was truly doing God's will.

# Chapter 2

Mohammad stood in front of a mirror shaving his beard and mustache. As he had predicted, it had taken him three days to travel from Tikrit to Baghdad via the Tigris. Traveling at night was very easy. Hiding his small rowboat and sleeping was a task he had accomplished with God's help.

After leaving Tikrit, Mohammad easily rowed down the Tigris, passing the lights of Samara. He could begin to see the sunrise in the East. At precisely the same time he also saw a small, but thick, cluster of bushes near the bank of the river. It would be perfect for his purposes. It would provide concealment for him, and his boat, and shade from the desert sun.

During his daytime slumber Mohammad dreamed. He dreamed of the Persian legend Hassan ibn al-Sabah, the Islamic world's first assassin. Hassan, also known as the "Old Man of the Mountains," was a Persian Fatimid missionary who had founded a secret order of religious fanatics in the eleventh century. He set up his headquarters, a mountain fortress called Alamut, in the hills of northern Iran. His followers became know as Hashashin; many were nothing more than desperados, smoking hashish before committing atrocities against the citizens of Persia.

Mohammad understood that he was the envoy in his dream and could see the obvious symbolism between Hassan's terrorists and the al-Qaeda network—though he believed that he was much more like Hassan than the envoy. His immediate plan was to make it to Baghdad, avoiding Americans and Arabs alike, then travel to Switzerland when he was able.

When Mohammad awoke it was dusk. There was no one in sight so he drank from the muddy waters of the Tigris, using his cupped hands. He didn't realize how thirsty he was. The water, gritty as it was, seemed to be absorbed by his mouth and throat before it reached his stomach. As soon as it was completely dark Mohammad began to row again. He knew that the Tigris widened the closer he came to Baghdad, which caused the current to slow and thus slow his pace also. Again, he saw no one the second night and, as sunrise approached, he found a suitable patch of bushes to hide the boat and himself. Again he dreamed as he slept during the day. This time he dreamed of the Ayatollah Khomeini.

In 1963 Khomeini, an Islamic clergyman living in the Iranian city of Qom, was sent a message by Shah Pahlavi to cease his seditionist activities against the government. Khomeini refused, was jailed, and later exiled to Turkey. From 1963 to 1979 he was forced to live in Turkey, Iraq and finally Paris, refusing to return to Iran until the shah left the country. Upon his return to Tehran, Khomeini used his charisma and oration skills to sway the population to his bidding.

Khomeini was not above deceit however. During the bloody Iran-Iraq war, when thousands of adolescent boys were killed and maimed, and before a major battle, Khomeini would have his minions deliver plastic keys to the young boy soldiers. These keys were called Keys to Heaven and supposedly blessed by Khomeini. Anyone who died wearing a key while fighting for Iran was guaranteed a place in heaven. The young boys, already driven to fanaticism, willingly and eagerly sacrificed themselves, drawing fire to themselves, away from the regular army. After the battles, more trickery was used. A helicopter would land near the scene of a battle, just out of sight. A man would get out dressed in long, flowing white robes, wearing an elaborate string of lights sewn into the garment, giving him the appearance of an angel. Dubbed the "Angel of the Battlefield," this Angel would move from victim to victim, blessing the boys, steeling the courage of the survivors for the next battle.

The final night of travel was a short one. Mohammad found the landmarks and rowed towards the bank. A block away was a typical apartment in the area. Mohammad removed a small cord from around his neck with a key attached. He unlocked the door and, without turning on a light, found the bedroom, collapsed on the bed and slept.

After awaking and shaving, Mohammad looked upon himself in the mirror. He was completely clean-shaven. His hair, however, looked as if he had spent three days in the desert without bathing and a month without any grooming. He was being hunted by the Americans, and his former comrades, and he needed to radically change his appearance. Without a second thought he took the shears, with which he had cut his beard and mustache, and began to cut his black matted locks until his head was nearly bald. The razor finished the job. Mohammad's beard, mustache and hair hid a striking face. With it all removed, the mirror revealed a ruggedly handsome man with an athletically trim torso. Although he had much more to do before he was ready to leave Baghdad, Mohammad felt relatively safe. Tomorrow he would make a false passport and contact the appropriate people to handle his business in Switzerland; then he'd travel to Zurich. For the next several days he would rest and remain in hiding until it was safer for him to leave the city.

FRANKS woke up to the stained ceiling tiles, and drone of an air conditioner, in what could only be a military hospital. He was no longer secured to a bed, though he still had an IV stuck in his left arm. Franks sat up a bit. It was then that that he noticed a middle-aged civilian wearing a blue suit that screamed FBI.

"Good morning Mr. Franks. I am FBI agent Rick Harris, assigned to you and your family while you're in Germany."

"Good morning to you. Where am I? What time is it? Are my wife and family here? If so, where are they? Are they safe?"

"Relax sir; you're in a military hospital in Ramstein Airforce Base in Germany. It is 0732 military time, which is 7:32 AM in civilian terms. Your wife and daughter are getting some breakfast down the hall and have an escort wherever they go. There's a guard outside your door. You and your family are quite safe. Let me page a nurse."

"How long have I been asleep?"

"You arrived here yesterday afternoon and have been under sedation since then."

The nurse arrived at that moment; a lady in her late twenties with brown hair and a peaches and cream complexion.

"Good morning Mr. Franks, I am Lieutenant Baker, the nurse on duty; how are you feeling?"

"Reasonably well thank you. Is that the door to the bathroom?"

"Let me get you a bed pan…" Baker replied as she began to turn away.

Franks cut her off in mid sentence. "You can get me a bathrobe unless you want to be embarrassed." Franks was wearing only a hospital gown underneath the covers.

"Mr. Franks I don't think it would be wise for you to exert yourself at this time," replied the lieutenant, obviously not comfortable with the unique situation of having her authority challenged.

Franks smiled as began to move his feet to the floor.

"Thank you Lieutenant. I appreciate your concern, but in less than ten seconds I'm going to the head. I really would like to have a robe please."

"I think your wife brought one over and it's in the closet," Harris interjected as he opened the door and tossed the robe over to the bed.

"Thanks."

After he finished nature's business, Franks looked in the mirror and was startled at what he saw. His face was gaunt, probably because he hadn't eaten any real food for several days, and he needed a shave and hair cut. His beard would require scissors before a razor could finish the job. Perhaps a barber on base could take care of that. He could see gray stubble in his week-old beard, and he longed for an hour-long hot shower. Leaving the bathroom, Franks was immediately tackled by his daughter, Tori.

"DADDY," was the scream as she began to climb his leg.

"Tori let me help your father back into bed," Isabelle said, a half step behind, hugging her husband with the same voraciousness as their daughter.

"Hi baby," Franks managed to utter while kissing his wife. He still had trouble believing that an up and coming New York City attorney would even give him a second look, much less become his wife.

"David Franks, do you have any idea what Tori and I have been through these last few days?" Isabelle was not doing a very good job of holding back her tears.

"I know babe. You'll never know how sorry I am about that. It's over now. I'm here and I'm not going back. How'd you know I was awake? I was going to walk to the cafeteria and surprise you"

"Agent Harris told us you were awake while you and Lieutenant Baker were testing each other's will. I hope you weren't mean to her. She's a nice lady. I think both of them are outside."

"When can we go home daddy?"

Breaking his wife's embrace Franks stooped down, picked up his daughter, walked over to his bed and sat down.

"I don't know darling. Let's see what the doctor's say. Okay?"

"Okay."

"Are you having fun here Tori-girl?"

Tori was named for Isabelle's younger sister, "Mary Victoria" who had died at the age of two. Franks agreed to name his daughter after her aunt for two reasons: First, because of the remarkable resemblance between Tori and her aunt's baby pictures (Franks insisted on calling her Tori, instead of Mary or Vicki as a stipulation); Second, was simply to placate his mother-in-law, who Franks considered overbearing and obnoxious at times. He had, on more than one occasion, curtly told her to mind her own business when he'd perceived her as interfering with his and Isabelle's personal affairs. The name was an inexpensive olive branch. "Tori-girl" and "darling" were Franks' two nicknames for his daughter. The other, Mary Victoria, was used when she'd been misbehaving.

"Yes Daddy! I liked the plane ride and I like all the big trucks! I got to ride in one!"

"Have you been good for mommy?"

Tori, always a daddy's girl, gave her father a look through her blonde bangs that could melt the coldest heart in seconds.

"I have most of the time."

"She wants to see everything and asks twenty questions of everyone. But, other than not being able to control a child's curiosity in a new environment, Tori's fine. She's been 'adopted' by every person on base, I think," remarked Isabelle.

At that moment Agent Harris, Lieutenant Baker and a man, obviously a doctor, walked back into the room.

"Good morning Mr. Franks I'm Colonel Moore, your doctor while you're visiting us. How are you feeling?"

"Actually, doctor, I feel reasonably well; a lot better than I look. I am hungry though. I wanted to have some breakfast with my wife and daughter."

Franks and the doctor shook hands.

"We can arrange to have some breakfast brought in for you sir. Why don't you lie back down? Lieutenant, would you have some breakfast brought in for our guests?"

The remark to Franks was a request, while the second was an order.

"Yes sir, doctor."

"Mr. Franks you seem to be doing well. It appears that you won't have any permanent injuries from your ordeal. All that I'd like to see you do is gain a little weight, and then we can release you. Your appetite is a good sign. Officially, you're in need of rest for an 'undetermined' period of time. The media, as you can guess, wants to interview you, as do representatives of our intelligence community. As long as you're in my care, and until you and I agree that you're strong enough, I'm not going to allow the media to intrude. I understand that the President is sending over a plane to transport you to New York, when you are fit to travel, and the CIA wants to interview you."

"That sounds reasonable to me doctor; although I get the impression that you have a distaste for the media. I assume you know that I'm a member of that media and I have no problems speaking to my colleagues."

Franks was again displaying one of the traits his wife found so attractive.

"David you WILL follow your doctor's instructions. Understand?" Isabelle interjected, displaying the demeanor of someone of her profession in a courtroom.

"Understood, dear."

There was no use objecting. He would be overruled.

DAHLONEGA, Georgia is located in the mountains of North Georgia. A beautiful town, it's an 1834 footnote in history as the site of the first gold rush in America. Along the square in Dahlonega, where a century and a half earlier, North Georgia's young men were mustered to fight their northern counterparts in the Civil War, a tourist will find numerous souvenir shops selling anything, from candy, to antiques to baseball caps. Approximately a mile from the square the campus of North Georgia College and State University is located. Founded in 1873, as Georgia's military college, it has since become co-educational; it still commissions officers for each branch of the service.

The UWF paintball team arrived at the local Days Inn and checked in to their rooms. Charlie and Chris shared a room. After everyone unpacked, the team gathered in the lobby. There was a banquet planned that evening for the teams; a get-to-know-you affair for the players and coaches of each team. Before the banquet, non-alcoholic cocktails were to be served while everyone mingled.

"Come on Chris. Let's go for a run down to the campus and check out the scenery."

"Sure Charlie. We need to be back and dressed in three hours for the banquet though."

"No problem. We have plenty of time. The campus is only about a mile away."

The two friends and teammates easily covered the short distance in a few minutes and continued past the campus towards the downtown Square. Along the way they came across a middle-aged lady sitting in a blue Lincoln Town Car with a flat tire. The vehicle was parked in front of a strip of souvenir shops along the Square; several shops had "Help Wanted" signs in their windows. The sidewalk had a few pedestrians but, because of the relatively early hour, was not particularly crowded.

After seeing some of Dahlonega's local flavor, the jog back to the hotel, a shower and a change of clothes into a coat and tie, the UWF team congregated in the lobby before boarding the two UWF vans for the short ride to the North Georgia Banquet Room. In the lobby, a beautiful, uniformed, female cadet was standing at parade rest, waiting as their escort. She was about three inches shorter than Charlie's height with dishwater blonde hair; one could tell it was her natural color. Her chest filled out her uniform nicely. Charlie zeroed in on her immediately.

"Excuse me."

"Yes?"

"Do you know how much a polar bear weighs?"

The cadet knew that she was being set up.

"I give up. How much does a polar bear weigh?"

A big infectious grin grew on Charlie's face as he delivered the punch line.

"Heavy enough to break the ice; hi I'm Charlie Michaels."

Charlie stuck out his hand.

The cadet, taken by surprise with Charlie's forward, somewhat aggressive approach, couldn't hold back a chuckle or conceal a smile.

"Hello Mr. Michaels I'm Cadet Second Class Heather Twig. I am your team's escort while you're here."

She shook Charlie's hand.

"Call me Charlie."

"I think we should keep everything on a professional basis Mr. Michaels."

Charlie leaned close to his next conquest and whispered "I know you have to quote the party line Heather, but your chuckle and your smile gave away your feelings. Don't be a spy, okay? I don't think you'd be a good one."

He walked away before she could utter a syllable.

Over three hundred guests representing the thirty-two teams, participating in the first National Collegiate Paint Ball Championships, met in the dining facilities of the University of North Georgia. Each teams' players and coaches mingled with others, consuming light refreshments for an hour before everyone was to sit down for the customary congratulatory speeches and, finally, the meal. While almost everyone else was socializing, Charlie had put Cadet Heather Twig in his cross-hairs and made preparations for his next conquest. Though she was not the most beautiful young lady he had plied his hobby upon; she was in the top ten. There was an innate quality about her that Charlie found enticing. Perhaps it was the fact that she was planning a military career, which was something that he detested, and made her something of a "forbidden fruit" to him; he didn't know for sure and it didn't really matter. All he knew was that he had his sights set upon her. Charlie could tell that she was interested in him as well after he'd set his tried and true plan of conquest in motion earlier that afternoon, in the motel lobby.

He had socialized for about three-quarters of the hour before returning to his assigned dining table. It was a coat and tie affair and Charlie looked very dapper in beige khakis, a yellow shirt and navy blue sport jacket. Charlie found that dressing sharply, always keeping his hair slightly in need of a trim, combined with his quick wit, made him irresistible to the ladies.

Walking up to her, Charlie again began to initiate small talk.

"Hello again Heather, are you enjoying yourself?"

"Mr. Michaels…"

"I've already told you to call me Charlie."

"Mr. Michaels," the cadet did not normally feel awkward in social settings but was feeling slightly uncomfortable and she could sense that Charlie knew this. "I didn't know that you were my CO and could give me orders."

"CO? Is that a military term? In case you haven't guessed, I'm not in the Army."

Charlie was being slightly condescending, which was a tactic he used to get a "lady of interest" peeved at him, afterwards he would charm her into bed.

"Yes it is. It means Commanding Officer. Someone who gives subordinates orders."

The cadet was trying hard not to show her interest in him and was doing badly.

"Oh, I see. In any case you are impressed by me," Charlie uttered with a cool confidence.

"No, I'm not."

"No?"

"No."

"Yes, you are."

Giving her a semi-wicked grin Charlie walked about ten paces away from her and turned his back.

It was about ten seconds after he walked away that Cadet Heather Twig approached Charlie. "All right I was; I am.

"You are?"

"Don't be so smug. Yes, you're an intelligent, attractive young man and you know it. Your self-confidence borders on arrogance and, though I can't explain why, I find you interesting. Of course you know that already don't you?"

Charlie was the one caught off guard this time. Usually women he engaged with melted like butter by this time. This was not the case with this young lady.

"Look I don't mean to be condescending, and if I came across that way I'm sorry."

He couldn't remember the last time that he'd apologized to anyone, much less a woman.

"I really can't say why but I find you just as interesting. That's very peculiar for me, considering my background. If we got off on the wrong foot, can we start over? Are you familiar with paint ball? I understand that your school has a team in the tournament also."

"No, I haven't really paid much attention to paint ball. Can you describe how the game is played to me Charlie?"

He was touched that Heather addressed him by his name.

"Sure Heather. I can call you Heather?" Charlie got a nod.

"There are six players to a team. The object of the game is to 'kill' the opposing team, capture their 'flag' and take it back to your base. There are numerous obstacles on the field of play, which provides cover for each side. Each time you're able to capture the flag, your team scores a point. There are two halves. The team with the most points wins."

"What happens if there's a tie?"

"Overtime, that's when things really get exciting."

Charlie was showing his enthusiasm and he could tell that Heather was truly interested in him and his passion for the game.

"The first team to capture the flag wins. If time expires, then the game is a draw. Some really crazy things can happen as the clock ticks down in the overtime period; people get desperate and take chances that normally aren't taken. It depends on how bad the team needs to secure a victory."

Everyone was beginning to be seated for, what Charlie was sure would be, a few boring speeches and an ordinary meal.

"Look Heather I'm sure that you're busy with school and I have things to do here as you know. I brought my laptop with me; would you care to exchange email addresses?"

"Sure."

She pulled out a pen and paper from inside her uniform pocket, scribbled on her pad and tore off the paper.

"Here is mine. It's a university address. Write yours down for me."

Charlie followed orders.

PETTY Officer Second Class Khalid Intavan was in the galley of the USS Gaffney, a guided missile frigate, supervising the preparation of the evening meal. The Gaffney was two days out of its port of Newport News, Virginia on a scheduled four-month cruise, along with the rest of the Third Fleet, to the Persian Gulf.

Intavan was originally from Morocco and had moved to the United States with his family when he was a child. Though he was a devout Muslim, he fit in well with his shipmates and always introduced himself as Cal Intavan.

During high school, Cal played soccer, ran track and was well-liked by his classmates. As a Muslim, Cal believed that Allah was the one and only God but respected everyone's belief in a supreme deity.

After graduating high school, with his family lacking the resources for him to attend college, Cal joined the Navy as a means to accumulate the funds necessary for higher education.

Cal excelled in the Navy but, at the end of the cruise and shortly before his enlistment ended, he'd have to make a decision: re-enlist or leave the Navy and begin college. His superiors had already begun subtly cajoling him, hoping to get him to "re-up." As his enlistment date approached, more "persuasion" would be applied by higher members of the ship's hierarchy. That decision would have to be contemplated another time. Right now Cal had to feed about 300 hungry sailors.

AFTER spending time in his Baghdad safe house Mohammad was anxious to depart the city. Making an authentic looking passport was relatively easy, requiring a picture of him, clean shaven, and the appropriate stamps from various countries, which "validated" him as Boris Mospaniouk, a Ukrainian national on business. Mohammad expected little or no scrutiny over his passport. His dark complexion was similar to Ukrainians and Russian was one of several languages that he had learned. Though he didn't consider himself completely fluent, he was not concerned; he was sure that he would not be quizzed in Russian at the Baghdad Airport.

After creating an AOL account, Mohammad contacted a Mr. Richard Federer of the Credit Suisse Bank via email, announcing his intentions of visiting the bank on business. Since Mohammad held a considerable amount of money in that bank—exactly how many millions he did not know; all of it had been transferred there, unlawfully, he was sure, by his father during the Shah's rule—Mr. Federer was very accommodating to Mohammad's request. He also sent David Franks an email, hoping that David would check his New York Sun-Times email account.

As he prepared to leave for the airport, Mohammad dressed in a dark blue business suit with subtle pinstripes. A white shirt, red "power" tie and black shoes gave him the corporate IBM look. Only a carry-on was packed. Mohammad intended to travel lightly and did not expect to return to the Middle East ever again. Mr. Federer would make arrangements for him to purchase any clothing or other necessities. Swiss bankers, he was told, in addition to normal financial responsibilities, expedited their clients' requests—especially clients with millions of dollars in their banks.

The ticket to Zurich was purchased via the Internet, paid for by an American Express account set up by Federer. Clearing customs at the airport was a perfunctory exercise, as he knew it would be.

As Mohammad boarded the plane, he did not know what travails awaited him, but he did know that his life was about to change forever and he suspected millions of other lives, Jew, Christian and Muslim, would be changed also.

# Chapter 3

Mohammad slept nearly the entire flight to Zurich. Unlike his sojourn to Baghdad, he did not dream. He had taken off his suit coat and had a flight attendant hang it in a closet, so that it wouldn't wrinkle. After all, image was important in the world of finance. Shortly before the pilot announced over the plane's intercom that the flight was going to descend, he awoke and had the same attendant retrieve his coat. Mohammad mentally surveyed his personal affairs. He had his alias, Boris Mospaniouk, a forged passport and an American Express credit card, with which he could obtain a small cash advance.

After the plane landed and taxied to the dock Mohammad retrieved his carry-on bag. Clearing customs was an inconsequential affair. He found an ATM machine and used his new American Express card to withdraw some pocket cash for his stay. As to exactly how long his stay would be, he was not sure. The length would not be long; others would determine the duration.

Leaving the airport, Mohammad boarded an electric streetcar headed for the Credit Suisse Bank and one Mr. Richard Federer. While riding he noticed that the passengers and pedestrians were dressed in similar attire to the occupants of the plane. This was the first time that he had been to Zurich and it struck him as an unpretentious city. There was not a lot of motor traffic and many people were walking, carrying expensive leather briefcases, with laptops stored inside undoubtedly. Everyone seemed to have a purpose, a single purpose—to create, preserve and grow money.

As the streetcar neared the Credit Suisse Bank, Mohammad stepped off. Entering the building, he approached a pretty middle-aged lady at the information desk.

"I have an appointment to see Mr. Richard Federer."

"Of course, what is your name sir?"

"Boris Mospaniouk."

"I will call him." She keyed a few strokes on her keyboard.

"Mr. Federer is expecting you. He will be down to meet you momentarily. Would you care to have a seat?"

"Surely."

Mohammad was seated no more than two minutes before two men walked up to him. One, from his uniform and the gun holster on his waist, was obviously a security guard. The other looked like a banking executive—stocky, probably 20 to 30 pounds overweight with thinning, graying hair—Mr. Federer, he assumed.

"Mr. Mospaniouk, I am Richard Federer," he said as he shook hands with Mohammad. "Would you follow me?"

The group walked to an elevator, Federer pushed the up button, and they rode in silence to the thirteenth floor. As soon as the doors opened, Federer dismissed the security guard and the two men walked to the end of the hall. Federer's corner office "oozed" with power. From the large mahogany desk and plush carpet to the paneling on the wall, the office told visitors that the occupant was a man of importance. Federer invited his guest to sit down in an expensive, overstuffed brown leather sofa as he took a seat in a matching chair.

"Mr. Baghai, may I offer you some coffee or a pastry?"

"No, thank you, and I do appreciate you not using my real name in the lobby."

"What can I do for you?"

"I have several requests. First, I need to know the exact amount, in U.S. dollars, of my account with Credit Suisse. Second, I want to transfer a portion of it to a bank of your recommendation, in the New York City. Third, I will be staying here for several days —exactly how long, I can't say— and I need accommodations at a nice hotel, using my alias, charging that bill to my account here. Fourth, since I don't know the duration of my stay here, and I brought only the suit that I am wearing, I'll need a tailor to fit me for seven days of business and casual clothing. Again, I want the bill deducted from my account."

Federer made decisive notes on a tablet.

"I can have the arrangements made within thirty minutes Mr. Baghai. Will there be anything else?"

"Is there a secure place where I can connect to the Internet and send emails?"

"Yes, of course. We have an unoccupied office that you may use. Fully secure, if you choose to use our Intranet, or you may connect with your laptop. It is two doors down. After you are finished you may return to my office and I will have your account balance and the arrangements you've requested."

Federer escorted Mohammad to the office and closed the door as he left. After connecting his laptop to the network, he began surfing the major media web sites. He did not have to look long to find what he was searching for. Each site reported that David Franks had escaped from captivity; exactly as Franks had promised. This would make Mohammad's mission much easier.

After logging off, Mohammad re-entered Federer's office. Federer stood up from his desk and motioned Mohammad to again sit in the leather sofa. Taking a seat beside him in the chair Federer reviewed his notes.

"Mr. Baghai, I have the information that you requested. Here is a printout of your account's activity and balance. As you know, there has been no activity and the balance is just over $53 million U.S. dollars. There are numerous banks in New York City that we do business with and can electronically transfer funds to."

"What is the first on the list?"

"American Bank and Trust."

"Transfer one half of my balance to that bank and see that an account is opened under the name of David Franks. I have his social security number, if you need it, to expedite the transfer."

Federer looked up, eyebrows furrowed quizzically.

"You do not want your name on the account?"

"No, that is not necessary, but you may open a second account using my alias with a balance of one million dollars."

"I have a taxi downstairs waiting to take you to a hotel I trust will meet your needs. You are registered as Boris Mospaniouk and an excellent clothier will contact you at your room for your fitting. Will there be anything else?"

"No that will be all. You have been very helpful."

The two men rose, shook hands and Mohammad departed.

THE tournament to determine the first Inter-collegiate National Paintball Champion began on Wednesday. There were thirty-two teams representing their respective universities, and they all had high hopes and expectations. Paintball had been invented in the eighties, club-level competitions began in the nineties and a professional paintball league formed after the turn of the century. "Ballers," as they liked to be called, were typically free spirits, very much like surfers and skateboarders. During competition, players would wear a long-sleeved jersey, knee and elbow pads, and protective eye and headgear resembling that of a hockey goal-keeper. The jerseys were invariably dark in color to contrast the light color of the gelatin paintball, making it easier for referees to determine if a player had been hit. Though the players wore the jerseys as a uniform, each player decorated his headgear as an expression of his individualism and unique personality. Skull and crossbones, "grim reaper" themes and "demon" faces, such as the design of the aging KISS rock legend Gene Simmons, were not uncommon.

Because paintball had only recently gained enough national interest, it had remained an intramural sport until this year. Invitations to the tournament were sent to the paintball clubs of various universities. Though not truly a national event, the ballers didn't hesitate to call it The National Championship. Lots were drawn to determine who the opponent of the each team would be. The Tournament would be played on three different fields, with games going on at the same time, in a single elimination format. The winning team advanced to play the next round on the following day. The UWF team drew the University of North Texas team. The game proved to be a mismatch. Immediately after the team congratulated each other with high fives and slaps on the back, they showered and the coach instructed his team to get a quick lunch before returning to the playing fields to scout the other teams. The team piled into the University van and went to a local restaurant near the Town Square. Charlie and Heather sat together and it was obvious to his teammates that they both felt a mutual attraction to each other.

"That match seemed relatively easy," remarked Heather as she poked at her food. She was more interested in conversation than her entrée.

"Was that a typical game?"

"No, that team wasn't particularly talented or organized. There are sure to be some teams here that are more talented and better organized. That's why we're doing some scouting after we eat."

"Reconnaissance!"

Heather's enthusiasm was elevated to a higher level now that she was able to make associations that related to her chosen profession.

"Yes, I suppose so." Charlie chuckled.

"Don't laugh at me." Heather's ego was visibly deflated by the perceived rebuke.

"I wasn't laughing at you Heather." Charlie took her hand and squeezed slightly.

"I just think it's amusing that I find myself attracted to a woman who is beautiful, intelligent but supports positions that I not only oppose, but find morally reprehensible."

Heather blushed at the compliment but challenged Charlie's verbal joust as she pulled her hand away from his.

"What do you mean by that Charlie? How do you know what positions I support?"

She was not one to back away from a challenge.

Charlie flashed his smile.

"Heather, I'm making some assumptions about you and I know what happens when one assumes."

He was referring to the cliché, "Never assume. It makes an ass out of you and me."

"We haven't known each other for very long. I know that I want to get to know you better. I didn't mean anything derogatory towards you by it."

He took Heather's hand again and flashed his smile. "Can we talk about this another time?"

Heather was immediately "outflanked," as one would say in military jargon. She was prepared for an argument and Charlie had deftly sidestepped the issue. She was touched by the manner in which he did so and it made her infatuation for him grow all the more. She squeezed Charlie's hand.

"Oh you are so suave and you know it don't you? Don't answer. You and I both know what you'd say."

Charlie paused for a moment, letting the electricity in the air linger. He'd never before thought of a woman as his equal. Though it was painfully obvious that they were as different as night and day, he knew that he'd never met a woman like her before and was not likely to do so in the future.

"It's time for us to leave Heather."

Standing up he did something that he'd never done before in his life. He grabbed the chair that she was sitting in and slid it backward to help her move away from the table. As the team left for the van Charlie put fifty cents into a newspaper vending rack and bought a local paper.

THE going-away party for Franks was as much for Tori as it was for him. She had charmed virtually every member of the hospital staff. A conference room was decorated with balloons, party streamers and Bozo, who was Tori's favorite clown, was present. Everyone was treated to yellow cake with chocolate frosting, also Tori's favorite, along with punch.

After the party, Franks and his family finished saying their goodbyes to everyone and were driven to the Boeing 767 which would be designated "Air Force One" when the President was aboard. Today it was "Air Force Two" since President Hays had sent the Vice President as her representative to greet the Franks family.

Thomas Norish Taylor, a retired Marine Brigadier General, and Vice President of the United States, walked down the stairs of the plane to greet the Franks. At six foot four and two hundred forty pounds of muscle, Taylor could have chosen to be a NFL linebacker instead of a professional soldier. Nicknamed "TNT," for his initials, his "explosive" temper and candid, untactful opinions, he was decorated with a Navy Cross in both Iraqi wars, and was awarded a third, along with a Purple Heart, in the occupation immediately after Sadam's government was toppled. He was promoted for his talent and ability, despite some powerful enemies he'd made over the years. A bullet in the hip, shattering his hip and upper left thigh, had dictated hip-replacement surgery and had effectively ended his military career. Before his retirement, Taylor was promoted to Brigadier General. Like Marine Corps legend Lieutenant General Lewis "Chesty" Puller, Taylor chose to have a senior Marine Non-Commissioned Officer pin the Brigadier stars on each shoulder; as much a token of respect to the enlisted men that served under him as it was a snub to officers who traditionally performed such duties.

Taylor, encouraged by his sudden popularity, was persuaded to run for the United States Senate, replacing retiring Senator. Taylor's blunt, shoot-from-the-hip personality made an instant connection with the Texas constituency; he won the election by ten points. Jennifer Hays' choice of him as her running mate was a matter of political necessity. Having no military background herself, her election committee felt that she needed a running mate who was a retired career military figure to "legitimize" the ticket. The fact that Taylor represented the state with the third most electoral votes made him the obvious choice. The partnership made sense from a political viewpoint, but the relationship was not a "match made in heaven." In simple terms, Taylor saw international issues in "black and white" terms, ignoring "shades of gray," not afraid to state his views, whether they were in, or out of step with the Hays administration. Though, like a good soldier, in the end he always followed orders and supported the President.

The Vice President was cordial in greeting the Franks family and even gave Tori a giant teddy bear wearing a Marine drill instructor's hat. He picked the child up and carried her up the aircraft's stairs, setting her down once inside the plane. All this was done for publicity Franks was sure.

"Mr. Franks, I'm so glad that you're well. It'll be a few minutes before we take off. Would you and your family care for a tour of the plane? And I'm sure your press associates would like to ask you a few questions."

"We'd be delighted sir," Franks replied.

"Let's dispense with the formalities shall we? Call me Tom."

The Vice President stuck out his hand to shake a second time, speaking with a Texas drawl and exhibiting an "aw shucks" demeanor.

"Call me David. This is my wife, Isabelle, and you've already gotten to know my daughter, Tori."

"Can I call you Tom too?" Tori asked.

"Of course you can dear," Taylor said raising his hand to silence her parent's objections.

"Tell me, Tori, have you ever seen how a great, big, jet airplane takes off?"

"No sir."

Franks was pleased that Tori remembered her manners.

"Well you and I are going to sit in the cockpit and watch the pilots take off, if it's all right with your parents."

"Is it okay mom and dad?"

"Is it permitted?" Isabelle asked, slightly concerned.

"It is, if I say it is. After we take off, if both of you are up for it, I'd love to have you up to the second level conference room for some conversation and refreshments. There's a bed for you if you need the rest. It's the same bed that several Presidents have slept in."

"That'd be great." Isabelle interjected. "Tori didn't have a good night last night. She had a nightmare about being attacked by giant monsters, and being saved by a 'bad guy'."

Both Franks and the Vice President raised their eyebrows at the contradiction.

"I know," Isabelle continued "It doesn't make any sense, but that's what she claims."

"Let's start our tour," Taylor tactfully interrupted.

"Afterwards Tori and I will get the pilot to show us how he flies this plane. Hopefully, she'll be ready for a nap by then. If you choose, you can speak to the press and afterwards I'd love to pop open a beer and just talk. I don't get much of an opportunity to chat with every everyday people much these days. Oh, the President has invited your family to visit her in the White House at a convenient time for everyone concerned. Have you been to the White House Tori?"

"Which one? I've seen lots of white houses."

The Vice President laughed.

"My wife doesn't drink, but I'd love to have an adult beverage Tom."

"I'd also love to get acquainted better Tom," Isabelle replied.

"Great! Let's go explore this big ole plane," bellowed the Vice President as he took Tori's hand and began the tour.

The Vice President and Franks were sitting in plush leather chairs, drinking a couple of bottles of Sam Adams beer in a conference room above and behind the cockpit of Air Force Two. Isabelle and Tori decided to take the VP's invitation and sleep in the bedroom next door.

"David, I'm glad that you're alive and well. I feel terrible even thinking about your adorable daughter being without a father."

"That's kind of you to say Tom."

"I don't need to tell you that you were damned lucky to get out of there alive, though I don't understand, for the life of me, why those Muslim terrorists would want to kill Western journalists."

"What exactly do you mean Tom?" Franks had the sense that he was going to get an "official, unofficial" lecture and he wasn't sure that he was in the mood for it.

"David, how long were you in Iraq?"

"I was there a couple of months."

"I was there a little longer under Bush 43. Before that, I was in Kuwait and parts of Southern Iraq under Bush 41. I can tell you with a hundred percent certainty that the Western media has not, in the past or presently, portrayed an accurate picture of events. Yes, any death of an American serviceman is a dagger in my heart and CNN is 'Johnny on the spot' to report it. But I have yet to see one report on the goodwill created by the United States in Iraq; not one interview of one Iraqi citizen who was oppressed and is happy at Sadam's overthrow and execution. They aren't hard to find. Someone killed the citizens in the mass graves. Who? The media neglects to answer that question. Did you know that thousands of canisters of poisonous gas were found in Iraq; and a mobile manufacturing facility? It was never reported by any of the media outlets. Why? Not good copy, that's why."

"Are you saying that the media has an agenda?" Franks quizzed the Vice President.

"Do you mean the media as an institution? No, I'm just referring to the people, probably only a few influential people, who seem to filter a certain view of the war to the public. It's been going on for years."

"So you concede that there's still a war going on?"

"Of course there is. When people die in combat situations, whether it's been declared or not, there is most definitely a war."

Franks knew he was being baited but asked anyway.

"All right Tom I'll bite. Tell me."

"Do you know your American history? Have you heard of General Pershing?"

"The name is vaguely familiar, though I can't recall him."

"Not many people, in this day and age, would. John 'Black Jack' Pershing graduated from West Point in 1884, fought in the Spanish American War and was Commander of the American Expeditionary Force in World War One. He was also in the Philippines and had some trouble with insurrectionists; Muslim insurrectionists. They were nothing more than your common, everyday terrorists, similar to those in the Middle East now; with a narrow view of world affairs and a fanatical belief that the entire world should conform to their values. Anyway, these terrorists had no qualms about killing Americans, or their own people for that matter, and made a real nuisance of themselves. Blackjack decided to put an end to their tactics once and for all. Care to guess what he did?"

"I have no idea."

"A group of these Muslim terrorists were captured and ole Blackjack lined all but one up in front of a firing squad."

"He let one terrorist live?" Franks asked; his interest piqued.

"He needed a witness. Just before he had the terrorists killed, Blackjack slaughtered a pig, a filthy beast in Islamic culture, and smeared the blood all over the bullets. After the terrorists were killed he buried them in swine-skin body bags, making the witness help with the burial. Then he released the witness, knowing that the man would tell his people. Blackjack Pershing didn't have any more trouble after that. "

"That's barbaric."

"Absolutely," remarked the Vice President in a matter of fact way. "But is it anymore barbaric than what happened on September 11th?" As a military commander, one has to be prepared to use whatever tactics are required to complete the mission. Vietnam should have taught us not to fight a war while attempting to placate public opinion. Bush 43 and the subsequent administrations, this one included, forgot that lesson."

Franks finished his beer and got up to get another.

"Do you want another one?"

"Sure David."

After removing the bottle caps and returning to his seat, Franks couldn't subdue his inquisitive nature as a journalist and began to quiz the Vice President.

"I don't agree with your beliefs Tom, but I do understand where you're coming from. Tell me, do you have a soft spot for all children or just my daughter?"

"I love kids of all ages David. Why do you ask?"

"I was curious as to how you reconcile your Gibraltar-like position against terrorists and terrorism with your teddy bear persona with small children? I guess what I'm asking is how you can advocate killing a Muslim, defiling the corpse in the most hideous way possible to that particular culture, and yet be so gentle to small child?"

The Vice President paused for a moment, giving Franks a piercing look before answering his question.

"You think there's a paradox David?"

"Yes, I do."

"I don't. I've already told you that I've spent a considerable amount of time in Iraq. I've seen the mass graves, the prisons, the torture devices and the tortured, the rape rooms and the raped. I have intimate knowledge of the evil that men do. Muslim terrorists are the worst. It has made me appreciate the innocence, the goodness, if you will, of our uncorrupted youth. Children are not born evil; they're made that way. There would be no such thing as a suicide bomber or a jihadist if someone had loved them in their youth instead of teaching them to hate. Besides, I have always been a sucker for kids. Am I making any sense David?"

"You sound somewhat like a pacifist Tom."

Gimlet-eyed, the Vice President glared at Franks.

"No, I'm not one at all. People who hate have to be dealt with—using the harshest means possible."

"Do you mind if I ask how you were wounded Tom? I understand you became somewhat of a legend because of it."

Taylor chuckled, breaking the tension that had suddenly developed. "I don't mind at all David. I got, what is called a 'million dollar wound,' a type of wound that allows a soldier to be medically discharged. I got shot in the ass and it shattered my hip, which necessitated a hip replacement. The rub was that I didn't want to be a millionaire. I thought I could rehabilitate after the surgery, but the Marine Corp retired me instead."

"How did it happen?"

"I tagged along with a platoon as they patrolled through a small village. Now in the desert there is no landscape. A convoy is seen miles away; it creates quite a dust cloud. Though it rarely happens, the men in a patrol always know whether or not there's going to be trouble as soon as they arrive at any village. Do you know how?"

"How?"

"Children. They line each side of the road as we arrive. As I said, the Iraqi people are almost always happy to see us. The United States' Armed Forces have created a lot of goodwill that rarely gets reported."

Franks did not miss the Vice President's jab at the media.

"If there aren't any small children around, we know to be on our toes. On this particular patrol the terrorists were especially sneaky. We saw a handful of women and small children as we entered the village, but none as we continued through. We didn't catch on until they opened up on us. To make a long story short, a girl, about your daughter's age, was caught in the crossfire and was scared stiff. She was going to get hit if she didn't move. One of the men, Sergeant Jewel O'Kelly recognized that, dismounted his Hummer and attempted to grab her, but he was hit. I was closest to the two and, without thinking, ordered the others to provide suppressing fire as I jumped out. I threw the girl over my shoulder and dragged the wounded Marine back to the Hummer. I was hit as I was jumping on. The girl was scared, but otherwise unharmed. Sergeant O'Kelly also recovered and is currently stationed at Quantico."

"That's an incredible story, but why do you find it funny?"

"I've never been politically correct and never afraid to speak my mind. I've stepped on a few toes in my day David, ruffled more than a few feathers. That didn't make me friends with everybody, if you get my drift. My enemies in the Corps gave me a third Navy Cross and made sure the promotion board gave me a Brigadier's star but they also made sure that I was medically retired."

"Is that funny?"

"No, but after I was elected Vice President most of my military enemies started to retire also. You see I have the President's ear on military affairs and I have a long memory. You could say that they could see the writing on the wall."

"Are all of them retired?"

"No, there are still a few that are still around but, as I said, I have a long memory. Anyway, I've said plenty. What kind of movies do you like? Behind you is a cabinet with a great selection of DVDs."

Franks selected Constantine, a Keanu Reeves movie.

THE story was intriguing. John Constantine just returned from hell. Having the ability to recognize biblical demons on earth, and to travel back and forth between earth and hell, he was attempting to save a lost soul. John Constantine had been born with a God-given blessing, or curse, depending upon the perspective, to recognize beings on earth, not of this earth. As a small child, these abominations caused him indescribable torment. His parents, believing his plight to be just a case of too many horror movies and an active childhood imagination, took him to numerous psychiatrists. But, since Constantine's problems were neither medical nor emotional, but rather spiritual, the visits were not helpful. As a child Constantine was an introverted boy, rarely socializing with his peers; the abominations causing him withdraw within himself. As a teenager these same abominations caused him to take an overdose of sleeping pills and kill himself—at least temporarily. Though clinically dead for approximately two minutes, emergency room doctors were able to resuscitate him. Suicide, in the Christian faith is the one unforgivable act—the cardinal sin. Because Constantine had committed the unforgivable sin, he spent those two minutes in hell. It was dark and foreboding. Screams of hopeless agony could be heard in the background. Burning embers everywhere, yet there was no fire. Lost souls were visible everywhere, yet every soul was totally and completely alone. Demons roamed, randomly attacking damned souls, as if for entertainment.

# Chapter 4

As Charlie had predicted, UWF and North Georgia were headed for a collision in the final game of the first National Collegiate Paintball Championships. Though each team appeared to be equally talented, their chemistry was as different as night and day. UWF used personal initiative and the natural athletic ability of its players to defeat their opponents. North Georgia counted on military discipline and tactics to achieve the same result.

The paintball Championship media coverage could have been better. Each team provided plenty of contrasting styles and personalities. UWF was the flashy team, wearing their collective emotions on their sleeves, while North Georgia was the stoic, disciplined unit. While the UWF team customized their jerseys and headgear, reflecting each player's personality, the North Georgia team wore camouflaged jerseys, head gear resembling Kevlar helmets and marched in formation, as they sang cadence, to and from each destination.

The contest proved to be as interesting as the contrasting teams. UWF, relying on instinctive creativity and personal initiative seemed to give North Georgia problems initially, with the Floridians quickly capturing their opponent's flag and winning the first point. UWF, through their aggressive, risky play continued to score points and built a respectable lead of 6-1 as the first half neared its end. It was at that point that the cadets began to adjust their tactics and counter the style of their freewheeling opponents and managed to score the last point of the first half.

It was in the second half that North Georgia began to assert itself. Throughout the tournament the North Georgia team used various combinations of fire and maneuver tactics against the opposition. Two and sometimes three man teams would assault a sector of the playing field. One man would lay down suppressing fire against the enemy, while the other members of the assault unit would reposition for an advantage in space and eventually a "kill" of the enemy in the sector. The elimination of an opponent would result in two tangible advantages, as well as one psychological plus. First, and most obvious, was the numerical superiority of having six against five. Second was the advantage of space, which allowed greater freedom for further maneuvering. The third advantage, though very real, was almost impossible to quantify. Fighting from a position of inferiority, when one was equal or superior, almost always requires an adjustment of mentality, be it in paintball or armed combat. The adjustment from an attack mode to a defensive one is often difficult. Positions in which a unit is spread out usually cannot be defended because they are easy to cut off and destroy. This requires the defender to pull back his lines and consolidate, thus surrendering more ground and allowing the attacker more room to maneuver.

It was during the second half that the North Georgia team employed a brand new fire and maneuver tactic that UWF hadn't seen and didn't have an adequate answer to. Previously, North Georgia had used either a two or three-man assault team to attack a flank. In the second half the cadets used a four-man assault team and attacked in the heart of the UWF position. Keeping a man in reserve and providing suppressing fire as needed, four men rushed the center of the field. One man on each end would cover the flanks, while the two center men penetrate as far as feasible. Once the position was secured, the flanker who had the least opposition would re-deploy and penetrate further up the center, while the reserve man covered the vacated sector with suppressing fire. When executed properly, the effect of this tactic would force the opposition to re-deploy in defensive positions, crossing predetermined fields of fire, where there was a greater chance of being killed, allowing the tangible and psychological advantages to be brought to bear. It was obviously a tactic that had been practiced countless times and saved for an occasion. The cadets of North Georgia dominated UWF in the second half and won the match 10-8.

As the clock struck zero, Charlie collapsed in the middle of the field and began to cry. Having captured six of the eight enemy flags, he'd single-handedly carried his team to near victory. He'd given every iota of ability, desire and effort in his team's endeavor and had no energy left. Chris walked up to his teammate.

"Hey buddy let me help you up."

"Leave me alone," Charlie managed to utter, as he wiped the sweat and tears from his eyes.

Chris got down on one knee and consoled his friend and teammate. "Charlie, you left everything you had on the field today. You know that you're the best player on the field. Hell, if hadn't been for you single-handedly eliminating those last two players back in Pensacola, we wouldn't even be here. Our team just wasn't as good as those jarheads today. Are you going sit out here all day and cry like a child, where your girlfriend can see you, or act like a man and congratulate the other team?"

Chris had an uncanny knack of being able to push Charlie's buttons.

Charlie slowly got up stood erect and squared his shoulders.

"Eat shit. O'Callahan."

He broke out his infectious smile and gave Chris a hug. Together they trotted over to the rest of their team and shook the hand of each of the victors.

Heather was waiting for Charlie and the team. It was no secret among the team of the affection between the two, though Heather had to maintain the appearance of professionalism. Charlie's teammates were all surprised that he took such an un-Machiavellian attitude towards her. In fact, one might mistakenly assume that Charlie had been a gentleman all his life.

"Are you feeling better Charlie? You certainly look and smell better than you did 45 minutes ago."

Heather was happy to see that her new male interest seemed to be taking his team's loss well, though she was slightly dejected that he'd be heading back to Pensacola in less than an hour. Both of them agreed to continue to correspond and Heather had invited Charlie to her home for a visit after he finished his term at UWF. Charlie readily agreed and was eager to work out the details.

"Losing sucks, but I was lucky," Charlie said, giving Heather a hug; taking her hand they began to walk towards the team bus, which would take them to the hotel for check out and then to UWF.

"Oh, how so Charlie, tell me please?"

"I met you Heather."

Charlie seemed surprised that Heather had asked such a silly question.

Heather, realizing Charlie's background, his attitude towards women and the fact that he was naturally irresistible towards the opposite sex, was touched and flattered by the sincere compliment which came completely out of the blue. She was simultaneously flushed and speechless.

"Heather, I want to tell you something."

The couple walked a few paces away from the rest of the team.

"What is that Charlie?"

Suddenly the always-poised and unflappable cadet had a lump in her throat.

What Charlie told her made her squeal in delight, jump into his arms and give him a hug that was much more than affectionate.

DAVID Franks and his wife, Isabelle, waited in a concourse of New York International Airport for the arrival of Swiss Air Flight 837. Sitting beside his wife, Franks opened his laptop and reviewed the series of incredible e-mails that he'd received from his former captor,

Mohammad Baghai.

My brother, I am pleased to learn that you are well. I hope that your family is well also. I must ask a favor of you. I will be coming to America. It would please me to see you when I do. Could I impose upon you to meet me at the airport

Franks replied:
Mohammad, I am fully recovered and my wife and daughter are fine. Now I must ask you a question. ARE YOU CRAZY? You're still a wanted man by the United States. The fact that you spared my life will not absolve you of the other crimes that you're accused of. If you come to America and if you're apprehended, as you likely will be, you'll stand trial for your crimes.

Mohammad:
My brother, yes, I understand completely. In fact, I am counting on the truth of your prediction. Now, when I arrive in New York, will you meet me at the airport? I know that this sounds incredibly strange and does not make any sense to you, but if you agree to meet me you will find that it all makes perfect sense. Now, I ask you again. Will you meet me at the airport?

Franks:
Very well, I agree.

Mohammad:
Thank you my brother. I will turn myself in, but I do not intend to do so without legal representation. Would you please hire an attorney to represent me? I have opened an account in your name at American Bank and Trust, with sufficient funds to cover the costs.

Franks:
My wife is an excellent attorney. Contact me with the date, time and flight number.

Franks and his wife, Isabelle, stood up to await the arrival of Mohammad when the flight landed. The passengers would have to clear customs before claiming their bags and meeting with their friends, family or business associates. Franks remembered Mohammad as a bearded Arab terrorist, dressed as any typical Arab. He did not recognize the bald and clean-shaven man dressed in an IBM like blue suit, white shirt, red "power" tie and black wing tip shoes, carrying a leather brief case.

"David, my brother, I am glad to see that you are well," Mohammad exclaimed as he grabbed each of Franks' shoulders, gave him a hug and kissed him on each cheek.

"Yes, I am; in no small part because of you. Mohammad let me introduce my wife, Isabelle. She is a criminal defense attorney and is willing to represent you as soon as you explain your motivation for your strange behavior."

"Mr. Baghai, it is a pleasure to meet you."

Isabelle offered her hand to Mohammed.

Mohammad took her hand, but instead of shaking, he kissed it.

"Mrs. Franks, my sister, I asked your husband for his forgiveness for my sins against him, now I beg your forgiveness. I can only imagine the anguish that I put you through."

"I was in anguish and I forgive you for your crimes against my husband, if you'll accept my thanks for sparing his life. Mohammad, as your attorney, we must be on a first name basis. Call me Isabelle. My husband tells me that you insist on turning yourself in. As your attorney, we need to discuss your situation. I've rented a hotel room at the Hilton where the three of us can speak privately."

"That is an excellent idea Isabelle, though there is something more that I require before we discuss my circumstances." Mohammad replied.

"What's that Mohammad?" Isabelle asked.

"I should have thought of this before now. Can one of you call a priest? I assume that you know one. I really cannot discuss anything about me, or my circumstances, without one present. My explanation will be perfectly clear to everyone concerned."

"Let me call Father Paul," Franks said as he pulled out his cell phone and began to dial.

Franks, the journalist, Franks, the attorney, Father Paul Stewart and Mohammad sat a small conference table in the room. Paul Stewart was an average man—about five foot ten, about 160 pounds, blonde hair, thick, full of body and was Franks' boyhood friend. In fact, he had married Isabelle and David. Originally from Illinois, as an adolescent he'd moved to New York with his family and left behind scores of cousins.

"Father, I want to thank you so very much for meeting me and my friends. I am Mohammad Baghai. You may have heard of me. Nothing favorable, I am sure. Indeed, I have done some very evil things in my life and I intend to turn myself into the U.S. authorities before the day is out, but it was important to me to speak with you first. Isabelle is my attorney and is completely at a loss for my motivation. I will explain myself shortly and I assure all of you that not only does the course which I have chosen make complete sense, but it is the only direction that I may go. Let me say further that, I have studied American law and I am fully aware of my plight and the consequences of my actions. I will be tried and likely convicted; in which case I will likely be sentenced to die."

"Mohammad, why in God's name, would you pursue such a suicidal course of action? The absolute best case scenario is that you get life imprisonment. In a federal case, 'life' means life. There is no opportunity for parole after 25 years," Isabelle asked her new client incredulously.

"Because I expect your President to pardon me," Mohammad replied as he stared at Isabelle.

"Why would she do that? That makes no sense at all."

Again, Isabelle was stunned and incredulous.

"Actually it makes perfect sense Isabelle. I will explain myself momentarily. But first, as I had discussed, I need to have a conversation with Father Paul. Both of you are welcome to listen."

"Very well Mohammad, we're all listening. What can I do for you?"

Turning to Franks, Mohammad spoke.

"David, my brother, the night that I released you, I was no longer a Muslim." Turning to Father Paul, Mohammad spoke again.

"Today, I wish to be baptized a Christian. You can do that now can't you Father?"

"Of course I can but, to be perfectly frank, I have concerns about your sincerity."

Mohammad spoke in a manner, which left no doubt about sincerity.

"Father, are the actions of someone who releases a man, whom he has sworn to kill, insincere? Is this same man insincere by turning himself in to a country where he will face the death penalty? My brother David knows, but I doubt you or Isabelle do, that when I was in Switzerland I transferred a large fortune into an account here in New York, in his name. Does that strike you as insincere? I am speaking in terms of millions of dollars and I still have an equal amount still in Switzerland, which I intend to transfer the majority of to the Church. Does that strike you as insincere?"

"You did what?" Isabelle screamed.

"I will explain later Isabelle. Father, I beg of you, please baptize me a Christian. If your conscience will not permit you, I will have to contact another priest to accommodate my wishes."

His expression softened.

"Father, please do this great favor for me. I promise you, that before you leave this room, all of you will understand."

There was a pensive moment of silence before Father Paul spoke.

"David would you get a cup of water and bring it to me so I can bless it. Mohammad, we will do this again in a church, in a more formal manner at a later time, if you wish. But in the eyes of Almighty God, you will become a Christian shortly."

"Certainly, Father."

Father Paul prayed silently for a moment and then he took the glass of water from Franks and made the sign of the cross over the cup.

"Mohammad, kneel and pray."

Mohammad followed instructions.

Father Paul poured the cup of water over Mohammad's head. The water rolled down the front of his forehead; down over his closed eyes and down his chin.

"In the name of the Father, the Son and the Holy Spirit, I baptize you. Rise up my son."

Mohammad stood up, his eyes moist with tears rather than water, and gave the priest an embrace that seemed to last for an eternity.

"Thank you Father. Now let us sit again at the conference table. I have an incredible story to tell, one that is stranger than fiction; yet every word of it is true. Afterwards, all of my actions will make perfect sense to you."

Each member of the group took a seat at the table. David turned on a recorder and Isabelle took notes on a pad.

Mohammad began his tale.

"David, my brother, on the night that I released you, you were mere minutes away from your death."

"Yes I know that. What changed your mind Mohammad?"

"The proper question is who changed my mind and the answer is Jesus Christ," Mohammad replied.

"Are you saying that you had an epiphany?" Father Paul inquired.

"Much more than that; let me continue. You must understand that in Islam, Jesus is considered a Prophet of Allah, like Moses or Abraham; but a mere man, not the son of God. That night, I realized that Jesus is in fact Lord. Actually, 'realized' is not the correct word, maybe 'revealed' is better, but I am digressing. It was 3 a.m. I awoke and checked my wristwatch with the intention of waking my comrades and executing David. The next twenty-three minutes changed my life utterly and completely."

Mohammad paused for a moment.

"For the next twenty-three minutes I found myself in hell."

"You are speaking in a figurative sense." Isabelle remarked.

"Absolutely not Isabelle, for twenty-three minutes I was literally in biblical hell!" Again Mohammad paused.

The tension in the air was so thick that it could be felt and tasted.

"Do continue Mohammad," Father Paul finally said.

"After I woke I suddenly found myself flying through the air, out of control. I landed, flat on my back in, what appeared to be, a kind of dungeon. The cell was about fifteen by ten feet and had large stone walls and a door with steel bars. I was naked with, what I can only describe as, a spotlight shining on me and, though I wanted to get up, I was unable to move. Though I didn't know at the time where I was, I thought to myself that this had to be a bad dream. But instinctively I knew, what I was experiencing was real."

"The first thing that I really became cognizant of was the incredibly hot temperature. It was hotter than any human being should be able to survive. Though my flesh didn't burst into flames, as I felt it should, the heat did seem to draw every measurable quantity of strength and energy that I possessed. It took, what seemed to me, a super-human effort just to lift my head and look from side to side. It was then that I noticed that I was not alone in the cell. Standing near one wall, I saw two abominations."

"I call them abominations because it was apparent to me that they were not of this earth. Both of these beasts were over ten feet tall. Though they were not, by any means, human they were not animals either. The best way that I can describe them, and my words do not do justice, is that they resembled a reptile; sort of a cross between an alligator and a lizard, though they stood upright and their heads could swivel and look in any direction. Their skin was rough, scaly and had sharp fins protruding from their bodies. Each abomination had several arms and legs, all stout and unequal in length, with long, sharp claws, as well as vicious-looking sharp, reptile-like, teeth. They each reeked of a most horrible stench that I had ever smelled in my life."

"The abominations spoke to each other. I had never heard their language, yet I understood their conversation. It was a blasphemous, awful conversation, the theme of which was their hatred of God almighty."

"After a few moments, they turned their attention towards me. It was obvious that these abominations were not pleased at my presence, but they did not approach me. These abominations had a hatred of me that was nearly equal to their hatred for our Lord. I was terrified. I wanted to get up and run, though I hadn't any strength to move. I cannot say whether or not I was 'paralyzed with fear.' All I can say is that, in addition of being unable to move, I had a complete and utter feeling of despair; of hopelessness. I was emotionally empty."

"After a few more moments, the light that was shining on me went out and the abominations attacked me. It was completely dark, but I could still see the abominations. One picked me up with one hand. It was if this creature had the strength of a thousand men. It shook me violently, threw me against the stone wall of the cell and I fell to the floor. I felt that every bone in my body was broken. Again, I wanted to try to leave but I could not move. The second abomination picked me up and squeezed me as it began to rub my back against the sharp fins and rough scales of its body. I could feel my flesh being ripped from my bones. He took his claws, plunged them into my chest ripped them outwards, shredding bones and flesh. The wounds should have been immediately mortal, yet not one drop of blood flowed from my body. The second abomination threw me, like a rag doll, to the floor near the door. I pleaded for mercy, but the abominations had none; they seemed to mock me."

"I managed to gather enough energy to crawl out of the dungeon, but only because the abominations allowed me to do so. After a period of time I was able to stand. My only thought was to try distance myself from the cell as quickly as I could. I wanted to run yet, because of my physical exhaustion and mental torment, I could only take small steps."

"As terrible as my ordeal was, I became even more horrified. I heard the deafening din of countless people screaming; in physical torment. It occurred to me at that time that I was in hell. I thought to myself, *why am I here? I have been doing the work of Allah.* I had no answer."

"Looking off to my left I could see the glow of flames along a barely visible skyline. In the distance I could see a mammoth pit, from whence flames were emerging. I began walking towards it. The ground all around was barren rock. Nowhere was there a sign of green life, no humidity at all. Several days ago I was reading in the Book of Luke in the Bible about the man who lived a wicked life, was condemned and longed for just one drop of water. I longed for a drop of water. As I got closer, the screams of the tormented souls grew louder. As I approached the edge I saw all the evil souls of humanity, throughout the ages, being consumed by fire. Yet, as they suffered the agony of being burned alive, their flesh did not burn. I could tell that their torment was immeasurable and infinite."

"Smoke and fire rained down upon each of the lost souls inside the pit. Each of them was trying to climb out, though none was able. Then, without notice, I found myself in a cave. Hundreds of smaller abominations lined the walls of the cave. Some were the size of bears, others the size of gorillas. All of them were grossly disfigured, with elongated, twisted limbs and rotting flesh. In addition, I saw strange-looking rats, spiders, lizards and worms moving in all directions along the cave's walls. Looking upwards, I could see an opening in the cave and I began ascending. How I was being lifted out of the cave I could not say, but once I was out I could see the entire inferno of hell and the lost souls in it. Inside the mammoth pit I could see each soul inside an individual pit; each one suffering the torment that I have described. Each soul suffered individually, without human contact, without hope."

"As I continued upwards, I again found myself in the center of the spotlight. It was a brilliant and pure white light, which blinded me. At center of the light were three beings. I recognized two of them instantly. One, I did not. The first was our Lord, Jesus Christ! Though I could not see his face and he did not utter a word, I knew that he was not God's prophet but, indeed, he was the Son of God.

"I fell to my knees at his feet and uttered the only thought in my mind at the time."

"What was that?" Father Paul inquired.

"Jesus. He replied 'I AM.' I can't describe the spectrum of emotions that I experienced. Utter shame and humiliation, fear, terror and indescribable joy. Inner peace replaced the void in my soul. I actually saw and touched his wounds."

"He reached down and touched my shoulder. My strength, which had vanished from me when I entered hell, returned. I was able to stand. My thought was Lord I know that I my sins were so terrible that I deserved to be in hell, but why did you rescue me when I was suffering the fate that I deserved? He answered before I could utter my question: 'Many people do not believe that hell truly exists; even some of my own people do not believe that hell is real'."

"Jesus said to me, 'Go and tell them about this place. It is not my desire that any should go there. Hell was made for the devil and his angels. It is not your job to convince their hearts. That responsibility belongs to the Holy Spirit. It is your part to go and tell them'."

"I had dozens of questions that I wanted to ask our Lord. One was concerning the demons. Again he answered each question before the words passed through my lips. Why do they hate me so much?' Jesus said, 'Because you are made in my image and they hate me.' They are so powerful. Jesus replied, 'All you have to do is cast them out in my name.' Instantly, the demons that tormented me were dwarfed a hundred times in size."

Mohammad paused from his tale, "I need a drink of water."

David retrieved bottled water from the refrigerator. Mohammad took two or three swallows and continued.

"Jesus revealed to me that He was saddened by all the souls on the path to Hell. Several verses in the Book of Luke discuss this. He showed me a continuous stream of lost souls. He allowed me to feel a portion of the sorrow that he feels for each soul. I could not stand the sorrow for more than a few seconds and begged him to stop."

"I did not understand why I felt so hopeless, so helpless when I was a believer. Once again Jesus answered. 'I am not Allah, I am Lord. I kept your knowledge of my existence away from you so that you could experience exactly how a lost soul feels. Mohammad, my son, I have chosen you to tell my people the truth, to tell my people that hell does exist, to tell my people to stop killing their brothers and sisters. TELL THEM THAT I AM COMING VERY, VERY SOON'."

Franks interjected.

"You said that there were two more beings, Mohammad."

Pausing for a moment, Mohammad took a deep breath and continued.

"Yes, I did my brother. I mentioned this because it puts this in a very human context for me."

Mohammad paused for a few moments as if he was ill at ease with the thought of continuing.

"There were two other entities with Jesus; a man and a young girl. I recognized the man instantly. He is the reason that I am here instead of in another part of the world. Unlike being in our Lord's presence, where my fears and anguishes vanished, looking at the second presence made me feel afraid and ashamed. Not in the sense that I have just described, but he contrasted how perfect and sin-free our Lord is against the terrible sins that I was responsible for. I did not want to look at the man's face, but I could not avert his gaze. I wanted to move away from him, but I could not lift my feet. After a moment, the man moved to me and placed both his hands on my shoulders. 'I, too, forgive you Mohammad. Go to America and begin your mission as our Lord instructed. Mary will give you guidance.' I assume that he is referring to The Virgin Mary."

Mohammad paused again as if unwilling to continue.

Franks instinctively prompted him. "Who was he?"

After a pregnant pause Mohammad replied. "His name was Christian J. Welter."

"Where have I heard that name?" The reporter asked.

"He was the first American soldier that I executed. I beheaded him, as I intended to do to you my brother. It was a hideous sight. I saw every feature of the man. From his missing digit on his hand to the bloody wound I made when I sliced through his neck. I saw his swollen eyes and the burns and bruises which I inflicted on his body. His head appeared not to be attached correctly, as if it was unnaturally twisted."

"And who was the third?" Franks asked.

"A little girl; about 3 years old, I do not know her. She did not speak to me."

"Why did you wait so long before coming here and why didn't you announce your arrival?" Isabelle queried.

"I wanted to use the media to announce God's message. Since I already have a 'relationship' with David, my brother, it made sense to me to wait until he had recovered from his injuries and was back in the United States. I also thought it would be wise to hire an attorney to represent my interests. You both know why I requested Father Paul to be here."

Mohammad turned to the priest. "Thank you again Father."

"You are very welcome Mohammad," Father Paul replied.

Isabelle took control of the discussion. "Mohammad, you understand that you'll be facing the death penalty for your crimes?"

"Yes, I know that Isabelle, but that is not a concern. After Jesus retrieved me from hell and before he placed me back in Tikrit, he allowed me a small glimpse of Heaven. There are no words that can be uttered by any man, in any language, that can describe how wonderful Heaven is. If my crimes require my life, then I will meet all of you in paradise at a later time. However, when I was in our Lord's presence, I did not get the sense that this will be my fate. I intend to plead guilty to the crimes that I will be charged with. I will need you to apply for a presidential pardon. David, I am sure you, with your resources, can tell the world my message. That is what is most important. Believe me, after my message is announced, I will be denounced as a heretic and become a marked man in the Muslim world. Prison will probably be the safest place for me."

Mohammad let out a sigh and had the look of a man who'd had a terrible burden lifted off his shoulders.

"My brothers and sister, you have heard my story and my intentions. Isabelle what do you suggest?"

"Mohammad, are you willing to trust my judgment, as long as I follow the spirit of your desires?"

Isabelle was now in professional mode and ready to issue instructions as a general directs units in a battle.

"Certainly."

"Good, tonight you and my husband will spend the night here. Don't leave this room. Don't make any phone calls. David will get anything that you may need for tonight. Order room service for your meals. David, I'll come back here in the morning with a change of clothes for you and we'll discuss the arrangements that I will make. Do you have any questions Mohammad?"

"I have no questions Isabelle."

"Father, I assume that you can rearrange your schedule to be here tomorrow?"

"Of course Isabelle," Paul replied.

Isabelle stood up and gave her husband a kiss. "I'll call you later on your cell. I love you."

"I love you too dear."

"Father would you care to escort a lady home?"

"I'd be delighted."

"I have to make a call and tell my boss I won't be in tomorrow," Franks told his wife. "I won't discuss why, only that I have the exclusive on the biggest story of the century."

"I understand dear. Just don't discuss any details."

"I understand."

Franks picked up his cell and dialed a number. "Roger, this is David. I won't be coming in tomorrow. I got an exclusive on the biggest story in the history of print journalism."

Franks paused. The others in the room could tell from the muffled voice that he was getting the third degree from his editor, Roger Thomas.

"Roger, I'm not at liberty to discuss it now. I'll email you the story by the deadline this afternoon. You can either run it or not, but you will. I am not exaggerating when I say that this is the biggest story of the 21$^{st}$ century. After you read it, it'll become clear why I can't make it in."

Franks was getting another earful from his boss.

"Good bye Roger." Franks hung up and turned his ring tone off.

Isabelle and Father Paul departed, leaving Franks and Baghai to contemplate, among other things, the meaning of life and religion.

Isabelle and Father Paul now both shared a confidentiality privilege with Mohammad: Isabelle, serving as his legal counsel and advisor; Father Paul serving as Mohammad's spiritual advisor.

"Father, tell me your impressions of Mohammad and his story, please?"

"What do you mean?"

"Well, now that I'm Mohammad's attorney, I can advise and represent him on the legal aspects of his dilemma, if that is the right word. But I can tell you his explanation for coming to the U.S. won't hold water in court or in the public's opinion. I'm not convinced that he has any legitimate defense. That leaves two courses of action. One, plead guilty and rely on the mercy of the court, or two, flee the country. The first course of action equates to life imprisonment as the best-case scenario; a presidential pardon is a pipe dream. I didn't get the sense that Mohammad would consider the second option. I suppose I'm asking for your opinion of Mohammad's story from a religious perspective."

"Do I believe him Isabelle? Do I believe that he actually visited hell? I don't have a definitive yes or no answer. His actions speak to his sincerity. His description matches Biblical and other accounts of hell."

"Other accounts, Father?"

"Yes Isabelle. Do you remember the three prophecies of Fatima?"

"Could you refresh my memory Father?"

"Certainly, on May 13th, 1917 the Virgin Mary appeared to three children in Fatima, Portugal and made monthly appearances on the 13th of each month until October. She made three predictions. The first dealt with the end of the First World War. The second dealt with the start of the Second World War and the third, the Vatican announced in 2000, was the assassination attempt of Pope John-Paul II on May 13th, 1981."

"I don't see your point Father."

"I'm sorry Isabelle, I'm digressing. The Virgin Mary showed these three children a glimpse of hell. I will have to review but, as I remember, Mohammad's description of hell matches the description of the children of Fatima."

Father Paul parked the car in front of the Franks' apartment building. "Thank you for the ride Father. I'll call you this evening."

MOHAMMAD was taking a shower when Isabelle and Father Paul arrived. She brought coffee and doughnuts and a change of clothes for her husband.

"Hi dear." Franks said as he gave Isabelle a hug and a kiss.

"Good morning. How did the two of you sleep?"

"Good morning Isabelle, my sister. I slept very well. Father Paul, it is good to see you my brother." Mohammad said as he walked out of the bathroom. He was wearing slacks, a dress shirt and shoes.

"I'm glad to see you also Mohammad. Are you hungry? We brought coffee and doughnuts."

"I don't know about Mohammad, but I'm hungry," Franks replied.

"Good. Now before we eat, I suggest that I hear your confession Mohammad. As a Catholic Priest and God's representative, I am empowered to absolve you of your sins. This is usually done in private, or we can do it here in front of David and Isabelle."

"I would rather do this in private for the first time father."

Mohammad faced David and Isabelle. "I mean no disrespect to you, my brother and sister."

"No offense is taken Mohammad." Isabelle replied.

"Very well then, Mohammad, let's you and I adjourn to the next room for a few moments."

"Certainly Father."

The priest and the terrorist stepped into the next room so that the murderer could be spiritually cleansed.

# Chapter 5

Mohammad kneeled in front of Father Paul and began to confess his sins.

"Bless me Father for I have sinned. This is my first confession. As you know, I became a Christian yesterday. Before that, I committed many sins, most I cannot remember. Though I thought I was doing God's work, I realize now that I was wrong."

"Mohammad, confess the sins that you do remember," Father Paul replied.

"I have killed dozens, if not hundreds of soldiers in Afghanistan and in Iraq. I am only referring to those who I faced in combat. Perhaps my most abominable sins are the seven executions that I personally performed. These men were defenseless and did not deserve to die. There are many more sins that I cannot remember Father. I am sorry for all of them."

"Very well Mohammad, on behalf of our Lord, Jesus, I absolve you of your sins. Now for your penance, I want you to recite the Lord's Prayer. You have it in front of you."

Mohammad picked up a sheet of paper and read it aloud. Afterwards he rose and walked out of the bedroom to the conference table, where Franks and his wife were waiting. A copy of the New York Sun-Times lay in front of them with the following headline in three-inch high print: "Terrorist sneaks into U.S. He will surrender today." The story began: "al-Qaeda terrorist and suspected murderer, Mohammad Baghai, furtively entered the United States yesterday and is planning to surrender to the FBI today…"

Isabelle initiated the discussion.

"You've become quite a celebrity Mohammad. I have made arrangements for you to turn yourself in, keeping within the spirit of your wishes. I left a voice mail for Agent Rick Harris at the local branch office of the FBI and informed him that I represent a client who is wanted by the United States government. I didn't use your name. Although if they've seen today's front page, I have no doubt they know it's you. I identified myself and I've gotten several call backs; I've yet to respond to any of them. Shortly, I intend to return Mr. Harris's calls and inform him of the situation. Undoubtedly, the authorities will arrive promptly and take you into custody. I will travel with you to the holding facility, probably Riker's Island. You're to say nothing to anyone, unless I am present and have advised you to do so. Is that clear?"

"Certainly."

"The government may attempt to move you to an undisclosed location and hold you indefinitely. To pre-empt them, I've prepared a motion to require them to keep you within the State of New York. That will be the minor skirmish. The war will be in obtaining a pardon from the President. I've done some preliminary research on the procedure. Basically, an application has to be filed with the 'pardon attorney' at the Justice Department. He reviews it and makes a recommendation to the President. There's a suggested twelve-step application and I'll work on it with you at a convenient time. Now, I can't stress this enough, you are not to discuss your legal issues with anyone except me, or a member of my law firm. You deposited an incredible amount of money into a bank account. Believe me; it's going to take a good chunk of it to accomplish what you desire."

"It is what God desires Isabelle," Mohammad interrupted.

"What God desires," Isabelle corrected herself.

Turning to her husband and Father Paul, Isabelle addressed her male associates.

"For the time being, I want both of you to promise not to discuss this affair with anyone. There may come a time when publicity will be useful and I want to keep all my cards close to the vest and use our 'Aces' when they will provide the most impact. Is that understood?"

Franks nodded. Father Paul objected.

"Isabelle, I would suggest that I consult with my superiors. Anything I discuss with them is protected by the same privilege that Mohammad enjoys with you and your law firm. They may very well be able offer insight and some expertise in this matter."

"Yes, you're correct Father. That'll be fine as long as Mohammad doesn't have any objections."

Mohammad interjected again.

"My brothers and my sister, you all have my permission to exercise your judgment, as it concerns my case, with my blessing. I want you to remember that you are God's instrument and ultimately my fate rests in his hands."

"Very well then," Isabelle said as she pulled out her cell phone and began to dial.

"Agent Harris? This is Isabelle Franks. I'm sitting next to my client, Mohammad Baghai, and he wishes to turn himself in…"

JENNIFER Hays' election to her nation's highest office was a miracle in American politics. A political neophyte who, in a few years, rose from obscurity, she'd gone from rookie Congressperson to Florida

Senator and then to the Presidency. It was enough to cause the best Las Vegas bookmaker, giving odds, to cringe in dismay.

Hays waited until everyone was seated in the "O" before beginning. Coffee and tea had been served, now it was time to discuss the latest issue that had fallen in her lap, Mohammad Baghai. Mohammad had mysteriously sneaked into the country and turned himself in. Seated with her was Andrew Shephard, her Chief of Staff, Vice President Taylor and James Scarboro, her Attorney General. These three men Hayes trusted implicitly. Scarboro and Shephard, she had known for a number of years while Taylor had earned her respect and trust while they were in the Senate.

"Gentlemen, as all of you know, Mohammad Baghai, arrived in New York City yesterday, checked into a local hotel, contacted a prestigious law firm for representation and then contacted the FBI to surrender himself. Jim what more can you tell us about our Mr. Baghai?"

Scarboro, a lean six foot tall, blonde attorney from the most prestigious law firm in North West Florida, succeeded Hays as the Representative of Florida's first district after Hayes moved on to the Senate. He was as comfortable in an Armani suit as he was in denim jeans and a polo shirt. In fact, during the summer, he was known to invite clients to his yacht for week-long fishing cruises and wear nothing but swimming trunks, ball cap and deck shoes the whole time. Because of his close working relationship with Hays, many assumed that he would be a nominee for a federal district judge position, or at least a federal attorney; instead Hays offered him the Attorney General cabinet post.

"Yes Madam President, yesterday Isabelle Franks, a junior partner of the New York law firm O'Donnell Levin and Jones, contacted FBI agent Rick Harris and informed him that she had been retained by Mr. Baghai. She further stated that he was in a hotel room in New York with her and that he wished to surrender himself. Agent Harris, and his team, met and arrested Baghai. Present with Baghai were his lawyer, Isabelle Franks, her husband David Franks and Father Paul Stewart, a Catholic Priest. He was taken to Rikers Island, New York's municipal prison and placed in isolation. We intended to transfer him to a suitable federal prison, but the District Attorney's office received a motion to prevent his transfer outside the State of New York. It has been scheduled to be heard in District Court the day after tomorrow."

"Why did Baghai suddenly decide to turn himself in to American authorities?" Hays asked.

"Good question," Scarboro replied. "He lawyered up and hasn't said a word to anyone. Mrs. Franks instructed Agent Harris, as soon as he entered the room, not to interrogate Baghai. He hasn't uttered half dozen syllables in his cell."

"How do you know this? Has his cell been bugged?" Vice President Taylor queried.

"We have an agent posted outside his cell and, no, we don't have his cell bugged," Scarboro replied. "But, that's why we want him in a federal penitentiary so we can." Scarboro's dead pan expression cracked with a smile.

There was a pause just before the group broke into uproarious laughter. After a moment Hayes began again.

"Do we have any indication as to why Baghai suddenly decided to end his career as a terrorist and begin one as a guest of the federal penal system? He's been educated as an attorney, here in the U.S. He's got to know that he'll be strapped to a gurney and have a needle stuck in his arm. Does anyone know why a priest was present? None of this makes any sense."

"Maybe he found God," Remarked Taylor in a sardonic voice, created, molded and polished from seeing men die at the hands of armed Muslims.

Shephard chimed in, "Certainly possible, but I don't think it's likely. Baghai is a fanatic. As bin Laden's lieutenant he would have to be a devout Muslim, as well as a hater of America. Though Islam and Christianity believe in the same supreme deity, there are major distinctions. First and foremost is that in Islam, Jesus Christ is considered to be a Prophet of God, very much like Moses, and not the Son of God. In Islam, the Prophet, Muhammad, is considered to be Allah's last and greatest prophet. Christianity doesn't recognize Muhammad as a prophet. In other words, Christianity and Islam are incompatible in the same way that Christianity and Judaism are incompatible. The fact that a Catholic priest was present is puzzling; I don't think that it's particularly important."

"We need to know why he's here," Hays remarked to no one and everyone present. Her train of thought again was directed to the Attorney General.

"Jim you said that Baghai's attorney, Franks' wife, has filed a motion to prevent him from being moved outside the State of New York?"

"Yes ma'am."

"We have a federal facility in New York don't we?"

"Yes we do. Delmont is a medium-security facility in central New York."

"We can take measures to make it maximum security by assigning some FBI agents to guard him 24/7 in an isolation cell can't we?"

"Certainly."

"Then we don't need to oppose the motion to prevent him from being moved. Instruct the attorney not to oppose the motion and communicate this to Isabelle Franks."

"I will take care of that immediately after this meeting," Scarboro commented.

"Good, and Jim, this is the most infamous prisoner in U.S. history. The world will be watching how we handle the situation. He is not to be mistreated in anyway. I want daily reports on his situation. Make it known that I will deal brutally with anyone who mistreats, or allows mistreatment, of Baghai. This whole affair will be conducted by the numbers. Is that clear?"

"Yes it is Mrs. President."

"Very well this meeting is adjourned."

THE building housing the U.S. District Court House in Brooklyn was an imposing edifice. Built over one hundred years before, with generous quantities of marble, the eighty-seven steps led pedestrians to a massive stoop, supported by half a dozen fluted columns. Dozens of other tall building circled the courtroom building. Mohammad stepped out of the gray government van and began his climb. He wore a Kevlar vest and was handcuffed. Five FBI agents surrounded him. Positioned around the agents were numerous uniformed police officers; they screened the six men from the hostile crowd screaming their outrage at Mohammad. Clearly, the people wanted blood.

Mohammad was hustled up the steps and into a private holding cell where Isabelle was waiting for him.

"Good morning Mohammad."

"Isabelle, my sister, I am so happy to see you again!"

"How are you been treated Mohammad?"

"I have been treated very well actually. I have a private guard outside my isolation cell. I have plenty of time to read."

Mohammad smiled for a moment.

"In fact that is about all that I can do."

"I understand. Is there anything that you need?"

"Can you send me plenty of reading material?"

"Yes I can. Mohammad we need to review the proceedings."

"Certainly."

"Shortly, you will be taken upstairs and be formally charged with your crimes. We will waive the formal reading of the charges. The judge will ask you for your plea. You WILL plead not guilty."

Isabelle had changed modes and was giving orders, which were to be obeyed and not questioned. "This will give our team additional time for our public relations machine to work on public opinion. Following your wishes, we will change our plea to guilty at a time when I believe; it will be most beneficial. Is that clear?"

"Of course."

"Afterwards you will be transported to the Federal Penitentiary at Delmont. I have a meeting with the assistant district attorney immediately afterwards. You can expect to see me at least once a week for some time to come. Do you have any questions?"

"No."

"I'll meet you upstairs."

The courtroom was a stodgy, musty room, perhaps sixty feet wide and one hundred feet deep, divided in half, horizontally by an ornate railing. On one side were the judge's podium and witness chair, the jury box was to the right, the defense tables just in front of the railing. Mohammad was escorted to where Isabelle stood, by one of the two wooden tables.

The bailiff announced the next case on the docket, "The people versus Mohammad Baghai."

Isabelle stood and squared her shoulders. "I'm Isabelle Franks. I am representing Mr. Baghai your honor. We have a hard copy of the indictment and waive reading of the charges."

"How does the defendant plead?" the judge asked Mohammad.

"Not guilty, Your Honor," Mohammad replied.

"What is the peoples' position on bail?"

"Remand, Your Honor," replied John Gant.

"What is the defendant's position?"

The question was technically asked of Mohammad, but the judge was gazing at Isabelle.

"We do not oppose the government's position."

"Very well, the defendant is remanded. Counsel for both sides will contact this court for a trial date."

The Judge banged his gavel and Mohammad was led away.

Gant walked over to Isabelle as she was packing her briefcase.

"Do you still care to discuss the case? I have a conference room available."

"Of course Jack."

The two attorneys walked a short distance to small room with a conference table. They sat across from each other and sized each other up.

Gant initiated, what he assumed to be, negotiations on a plea arrangement.

"Isabelle, the government has a solid case against your client. You're an excellent attorney and of course, you know that. I don't know what your client's motivation for turning himself in is but the government is prepared to be lenient in sentencing, if your client is prepared to plead guilty for his crimes."

Isabelle allowed herself a faint smile.

"Define lenient Jack."

"We will do life in prison instead of the needle." The term "needle" was slang for death by lethal injection.

"Jack, my client came to America with the intention of pleading guilty. He understands the magnitude of his crimes and hired me to negotiate his best sentence. He appreciates the government's offer and we will get back to you shortly. However, I want to inform you that I will be petitioning the President for a pardon."

Gant smirked.

"That's not likely to happen. Why would the President grant a pardon?"

"Actually Jack, my client and I think it's very likely to happen. I want to thank you for your plea offer. I will communicate it to my client."

Isabelle stood up and walked out the door. Gant was flabbergasted.

DAVID Franks and Father Paul sat in a local television studio; they were having microphones attached. It had been two weeks since Mohammad made his first appearance in District Court. They were about to be interviewed by Ken Shugart, the host of "America Today." The duo had become overnight celebrities since Franks' exclusive story of Mohammad's surreptitious arrival in the United States and his surrender to the authorities. He'd received dozens of interview requests and had purposely waited several days before agreeing to any of them. This was the first part of a two-pronged strategy to gain maximum publicity for Mohammad.

"Good morning. Today we have New York Sun-Times journalist David Franks and Father Paul Stewart. Both were in the hotel room when al-Qaeda terrorist Mohammad Baghai surrendered to the FBI. In fact David Franks' wife Isabelle is representing Baghai. Gentlemen, good morning."

"Good morning and good morning Ken," was the reply from the guests.

"David, last week you, Father Paul, and your wife arranged for Mohammad Baghai to secretly arrive in New York and surrender himself. Your wife represents Mr. Baghai. My question to you is why did he decide upon this erratic course of action?"

Franks' pet peeve was accuracy and it was obvious that the host had not done his homework. He was slightly annoyed.

"Actually Mohammad arranged his own arrival. He advised me of his intent via email. During our correspondence he made it clear that he intended to surrender with or without my help. Once we met at the airport, he requested that I contact a priest. Paul, my childhood friend, was my immediate choice."

"I stand corrected. Your wife represents his legal interests."

"Correct. During our correspondence Mohammad requested an attorney for obvious reasons and I naturally suggested my wife."

"Father, will you tell us how and why you were involved in this scenario?"

"Surely Ken. The short and simple answer to your question is that Mohammad realized he was a sinner and that his actions were wrong. The more complicated answer is that he realized that Jesus Christ is our Lord, our God and our Savior."

"What are you saying Father?"

Shugart was astonished by the priest's reply.

"I am saying that before Mohammad surrendered I baptized him, heard his confession and absolved him of his sins."

"He converted to Christianity? Why did he do that? What was his motivation?"

Shugart was astonished at the direction that the interview had taken and sensed that this was an explosive topic, which was about to blow up.

Franks interjected "Ken, before Paul answers, let me say that when Mohammad was holding me hostage he told me himself that I would be executed. He graciously allowed me a meal and time to make peace with God. Resigned to my fate I prayed and fell asleep. When he woke me up, initially, I thought it was his intention to kill me, but it soon became apparent to me that Mohammad had a life-altering experience. He released me and instructed me to be silent, not to wake up his associates, and gave me directions to reach safety. His actions didn't make any sense to me at the time, but made perfect sense when he explained himself to my wife, Paul and me. I actually made a cassette recording of his explanation and if you believe him, as Paul and I do, his motivation makes perfect sense."

"Would either of you care to elaborate?"

Father Paul began. "Mohammad was a devout Muslim. He, or anyone who knows him, will tell you that. He is now a baptized Christian. Why did he change his core beliefs so abruptly? Why did he voluntarily come to America to surrender himself, knowing that he would face the death penalty for his crimes? The answer is very simple. Shortly before the appointed time of Franks' execution, Mohammad was plucked from his bed and shown the pits of hell by our Lord Jesus Christ."

"WHAT?"

Shugart was becoming unhinged.

"For twenty three minutes Mohammad Baghai experienced the hell that lost souls experience for eternity. Afterwards he was pulled from hell and briefly spoke to Jesus. At that time, if one is to believe his tale as we both do, Mohammad realized that Jesus is indeed the Son of God, not a Prophet of God as Islam claims, and that's why he requested that I baptize him."

"Father, do you really expect the American public to believe such an incredible tale?"

Shugart managed to dial down his emotions a couple of notches.

"We recorded our conversations and, specifically, Mohammad's explanation during our time in the hotel room. At a future point in time we'll release it and I believe anyone who listens to it will concede his sincerity."

"When will we be able to hear the recording?"

Franks answered the question. "Ken, my wife and her legal team will determine when, and under what circumstances, the recording will be released. I'm handling Mohammad's public relations, not his legal plight."

"So you're acting as Baghai's agent?"

"Yes I am Ken and I don't make any apologies for doing so. Mohammad spared my life and, as I've said, I believe his explanation."

Father Paul interjected "Ken to pre-empt your next question let me add that the Catholic Church also supports Mohammad. If one believes him then Mohammad is a prophet."

Shugart turned towards the camera. "That's all the time we have; incredible revelations. Thank you, David Franks and Father Paul Stewart for being our guests today. This is Ken Shugart for America Today."

# Chapter 6

## *Delmont Correctional Fac*

Mohammad woke up in his isolation cell, from a nightmare. He was sweating profusely. Though it was only in his imagination, Mohammad had just spent another ordeal in hell. It was every bit as real as his original experience, only Jesus and the murdered soldier were not present. However, the small child that he had seen before was.

*Lord Jesus! I do not know why you have brought me back to this place of eternal damnation. I certainly deserve punishment for my sins in the ever after, and on Earth. Lord Jesus, this child could not have done anything to deserve to be here! Hear my plea! Do with me as you choose, but take her away!*

Mohammad recalled his nightmare.

*Silence Baghai.*

The child spoke in as if she was giving orders.

*Jesus is protecting me from the fire. I am not suffering. Baghai, why have you not preached the message that you were told to? Jesus will come for you soon. There are souls being lost every day and it saddens Him. Spread the divine message. Do so today. The people will listen.*

Mohammad sat up on his bed, a four-inch-thick foam-rubber mattress on a cement slab, and wiped the sweat from his brow with a small washcloth.

APPROXIMATELY twenty five miles south of the North Georgia campus, following Georgia State Road 400, is the City of Cumming, the county seat of Forsyth County, Georgia. Heather was taking Charlie to meet her parents for the first time. Charlie had found room to rent near the campus. During the time that Charlie had been living in Dahlonega the two had spent virtually every spare minute they had together. Charlie had invited her back to his rented room on several occasions, but she had refused his invitations. Instead the two would act like typical college students, going to parties on the weekends, attending baseball games and going to movies. Heather had wanted to introduce him to her mother and father for several

ut this was the first time Charlie had been able to get a full
end off from his job at Paintball Atlanta.

The couple pulled up into the driveway of a palatial lakeside
house. Charlie was on his best behavior. He opened the passenger
door and, holding hands, they entered the house. Waiting in the parlor was a couple in their late fifties or early sixties, both with gray
hair. Mr. Twig's hair was thinning and he had a bit of a beer belly.
Mrs. Twig was a gracious southern belle, a perfect complement to
the "rough and tumble" appearance of her husband.

"Mom, Dad, this is Charlie Michaels, the boy that I've been telling
you about. Charlie, these are my parents, Ralph and Jo Ann Twig,"

Ralph extended his hand and shook Charlie's.

"Good to meet you son."

"Likewise Mr. Twig."

Charlie took a firm grip of his hand and shook it vigorously.
Then Charlie, in his most elegant style, took Mrs. Twig's hand and
gently squeezed it.

"Mrs. Twig, now I know where Heather got her good looks, it's a
pleasure to meet you ma'am."

"Thank you Charlie. You're a charmer, aren't you? You may call
me Jo Ann and my husband Ralph. Heather has had nothing but
good things to say about you."

"Yes ma'am, thank you."

"Charlie, we're going to grill out back on the deck in a little while.
Why don't you and I get your suitcase while Heather and my wife
get some refreshments together? You do drink beer don't you?"

"Sure."

"Good. Honey, I'll have my usual. Heather, you will be in your
room. We're going to put Charlie in the guest room."

Drinks were served on a huge deck attached to the rear of the
house, allowing a magnificent view of Lake Lanier. Ralph was drinking, what appeared to be, an expensive bourbon whiskey, while
Heather and her mother were having iced tea. The group exchanged
small talk.

"Charlie, Heather tells us that you're from Florida. Why don't
you tell my wife and me about yourself?"

"Yes sir, I am from…"

"Call me Ralph son."

"Ralph, I'm a senior at the University of West Florida, in Pensacola, Florida."

"Hold it son, how is it that you're up here in Georgia and still
going to school?"

"I only lack two classes to graduate and I'm taking them on-line.

All I need is a computer and an Internet connection. Anyway, I met Heather when our college paintball team came to Dahlonega to participate in the National Championships at North Georgia. Heather was our team's escort and liaison. As you know, she and I hit it off, so I decided to move up here. While my team was here, I found a room to rent and a job."

"What do you want to do when you finish your studies Charlie?" Ralph continued the game of twenty questions.

"I will have a degree in business administration and my GPA is nearly 4.0, but to tell you the truth, I haven't found anything that excites me, other than paintball."

"Have you thought about being an insurance agent Charlie? Ralph owns an agency," Jo Ann asked.

"I haven't thought about it ma'am," Charlie replied.

"Charlie you'll have to forgive my wife. She'll say just about anything that comes to mind. Jo Ann, an agent has to be licensed by the state of Georgia, in both life/health and property/casualty. To pass the test requires intense study and preparation."

"You did it dear."

"Yes I did, because I was bored out of my mind after I retired from the airlines and I could study eight hours a day. Charlie may not want to take the equivalent of two college courses to prepare for the certification exam after graduating from college. Anyway, why don't you and Heather bring out the steaks while I fire up the grill and explain the finer points of grilling to Charlie?"

Charlie and Ralph walked over to the propane grill and lit it, as Heather and her mother went to the kitchen.

"You mentioned that you were retired from the airlines Ralph. Were you a pilot?"

"Yes, I retired from Delta. Before that I spent six years in the Air Force, flying F-15s."

"Heather didn't mention that you were in the military. Is that why she decided to attend a military college?"

"No, she was only three when I got out. I guess she had a patriotic urge after 9/11, like almost everyone. Unlike most, she never lost the desire to serve. Her mother was against the idea, she wanted Heather to attend the University of Georgia, earn a degree, meet a young man, get married and start having grandchildren. Though Heather looks just like Jo Ann, she's more like me in disposition and once she has a goal, she'll do whatever it takes to reach it. Jo Ann, as you will learn, is set in her ways and on occasion she and Heather have tested each other's will. It was sort like the 'irresistible force meeting the immovable object.' They had several disagreements about some of her old boyfriends for instance. Anyway, she didn't want Heather to get involved in this business in the Middle East and, though I share Jo Ann's concerns, I reluctantly support Heather's decision. Heather applied to all the service academies, but couldn't secure an appointment. Instead she applied for a ROTC scholarship here, at North Georgia. That appeased her mother, being so close to home, at least temporarily."

"Has Heather told you of my anti-war convictions?"

"Yes, she has."

"How do you feel about this mess that we're in Ralph?"

"The wars in Afghanistan and Iraq were completely justified and necessary for our national security and, despite what the left wing continues to whine about, it was never about oil or imperialism. However, the United States has become an occupation force, in a country that clearly does not want us there. What Bush and the subsequent administrations should have done is make the Iraqis pay for their liberation, construction, repair of their infrastructure and training of their civil defense. Believe me, if we had forced them to open up their pockets and pay for our services, which we did not, the Iraqis would have been a lot more motivated to stand on their own feet and we would have been in and out in no time."

"Anyway, enough of geo-politics, I hear my wife and my daughter coming with the steaks. How do you like your rib-eye?"

"Medium-rare Ralph."

Ralph grimaced in mock agony. "Oh, you're a cannibal also I see."

"We are not cannibals dad," Heather warned her father emphatically as she walked up with a plate of thick rib-eye steaks.

"Anyone who eats meat that is still bleeding is a cannibal. Ooga booga." Ralph was doing an impersonation of a cannibal.

"Charlie, please ignore my husband. Ralph is very opinionated and normally doesn't listen to contrary points of view once he's made up his mind. We call him Mr. Spock."

"That's because all my opinions are based upon facts, sound reasoning and logic" Ralph retorted.

"See what I mean Charlie."

"Enough! I give up! Heather would you fix me another drink and Charlie looks like he's ready for another beer."

"Sure Dad."

The grill sizzled as the rib eyes were placed over the flames.

TORI Franks woke her mother and father up. Isabelle looked at the alarm clock. It was just after three in the morning. Tori had been crying.

"What is it dear?"

"Mommy, I saw the bad guy again. I got scared."

"Would you like to sleep with Mommy and Daddy?" Isabelle asked her daughter.

"Yes" Tori replied in between sniffles.

"Tell you what darling, I'll go check your room to make sure he's not there and then we can all go back to sleep. Okay?"

"Okay Daddy."

Tori and Isabelle were both asleep by the time he came back to bed.

THE President convened her circle of advisors for a Saturday meeting. The usual suspects were present: Scarboro, Shephard and Taylor. Dress was casual, since it was the weekend. The topic of the meeting was Mohammad Baghai.

"Gentlemen, Mohammad Baghai was arraigned on several murder charges and he pled not guilty. I understand that he intends, or at least is agreeable, to changing his plea. Now I hear that he wants a pardon; no, expects a pardon. Jim what can you tell us about this?"

"As you mentioned Madam President, Mohammad Baghai pled not guilty to all charges. Immediately after the arraignment, assistant district attorney John Gant met with Baghai's attorney, Isabelle Franks to discuss a recommended life sentence in return for a guilty plea. The details, as to what specific charges, were to be determined at a later time. At that time Franks informed Gant that her client intended to plead guilty in the near future. She also informed Mr. Gant that she intended to petition the President for a pardon, though she did not elaborate further."

"Does he want a pardon before, or after, we string him up and thin-slice his gonads?" Taylor said. He was visibly surprised and upset.

"Did she give any indication as to what basis that I should grant a pardon?"

"No ma'am she did not. In fact Mr. Gant asked her that very question, after he was able to stop laughing. It sounds to me to be a negotiating tactic; you ask for the sky and settle for less."

"What about his claims of having an epiphany?" Hays asked.

"Probably another tactic Mrs. President," Scarboro replied.

"However, by turning himself in, Baghai has nothing to negotiate with," Shephard remarked.

"These are definitely not the actions of a sane man. Can we have a psychiatrist examine him?"

"No, Madam President, unless he invokes an insanity defense we cannot have a conversation with him. At this point they don't intend to present any defense," Scarboro replied.

"We haven't considered one very significant aspect to this matter," Taylor chimed in.

"What is that?" Shephard asked.

"The press; I don't need to tell anyone that they'll be all over this in no time. Why don't we use it to pre-empt this situation?" It was a rhetorical question, though Taylor continued. "Instead of the press asking 'why isn't the President pardoning Mohammad Baghai,' why don't we float a trial balloon that the President is willing to consider commuting Baghai's sentence to life?"

"Not a pardon Tom?"

"Hell no, there is a too much blood on that man's hands." Taylor adamantly exclaimed.

"Tom, take a breath. I haven't said that I was going to pardon anyone. Furthermore, I am not so inclined. On the other hand, I haven't said that I wouldn't pardon anyone. Your idea about the press is excellent but I'm not going to rule out any course of action. Am I making myself clear?"

The question was directed to everyone and everyone nodded in agreement.

"Good, gentlemen thank you for your time on a Saturday. I will let you all go now."

The meeting was adjourned.

MOHAMMAD woke up at exactly at 6:00 am. He knew the time because that was the regular time for the inmates to arise for a head count and march to the dining hall for breakfast. Since he was in isolation, Mohammad received his meals in his four by eight foot cell. After eating his meal, Mohammad placed his metal tray on the ledge, welded next to a small rectangular opening in the solid steel door. It was 7:00 a.m. and the prisoners were returning to their cells after eating breakfast. Mohammad turned off the water intake to his stainless steel toilet and flushed twice, emptying the water in the bowl.

Though he'd been in this prison for less than a week, Mohammad had received a unique education. By emptying the water from the toilet bowl and the plumbing, Mohammad could speak into the bowl and his words would echo through the pipes to any and all other toilets with clear pipes.

"Hello? Is anyone listening?" Mohammad asked after he knelt down near the bowl.

"Yeah, whadaya want?" A sinister voice echoed out of the bowl.

"What is your name my brother?"

"First off cocksucker, I aint your brother, second, who wants know?"

"My name is Mohammad Baghai. May I ask yours?"

"You can call me Slash. Is Mohammad an Arab name? Are you one of these terrorists?"

"I am Iranian actually. And, yes, in my previous life I was a terrorist."

"What do you mean 'in your previous life?' You call this a life? Whadaya in for?"

"Murder, Slash, why are you here?"

"Drug running across interstate lines; I was muling between Miami and New York when I got caught."

"Muling, I am not familiar with that term. What does it mean Slash?"

"You're kidding right? "

"No Slash."

"Muling means that you're carrying drugs from one place to another for someone else. For a murderer you don't know shit. How'd you get caught?"

"I turned myself in."

"WHAT THE FUCK? Why did you do something stupid like that?"

"I had to Slash."

"What do you mean?"

"Slash, let me ask you a question. Is muling drugs the worst thing that you have done in your life?"

"I've had a few minor scrapes before but this is the most serious thing that I've been caught at. Why do you ask?"

"I told you that I was here for murder, but not for one murder. I have been charged with seven murders and I have actually committed many more. I will almost certainly be sentenced to death. I was what you might call a real bad guy."

"You mean a real bad dude."

"Do you believe in God Slash?"

"I dunno, why?"

"I do. Do you have any idea why?"

"Look asshole, do you have a point to any of this?"

"Yes, Slash, my brother…"

"I told you that I am not your brother."

"I know Slash. Please hear me out. Many people believe in the one God, and that Jesus Christ is His son. That Jesus died on the cross to ensure that we could be saved. Do you know this Slash?"

"Whatever, look, I thought you Muslims believed in Allah."

"Muslims do believe in Allah, but I am not Muslim. I am a Christian."

"Even though we are speaking through a toilet I can smell bullshit a mile away. You are full of it man."

"Slash, up until a recently, I was a Muslim. I was baptized a Christian because I now believe in Jesus Christ, the Son of God, our savior. I now believe in Heaven and hell, which before were imaginary concepts to me, but now are very real. I now believe in the Holy Bible as the true word of God. Before I only accepted the Koran as the word of Allah."

"There is a reason why I believe all of this, but I can tell that you doubt me. I have worn out my welcome. Can we talk again? I am supposed to meet the prison chaplain."

"Whatever man, I got plenty of time on my hands."

Mohammad had tried to preach God's message, but felt like Moses did the first time he met the Pharaoh Ramses. Slash, like Ramses, was unconvinced. Mohammad hoped that he would do better the next time.

IT was 0300 and Cal was standing watch amidships, on the starboard, or right side of the Gaffney. The fact that he was standing watch at 3:00 in the morning wasn't unusual; it was his turn in the rotation. What was unusual, and dangerous, was that there was a tempest of immense severity. Thirty-foot waves were crashing over the port, or left, bow. Men on watch had the responsibility of being the eyes of the ship, notifying the bridge of any potential threat to the ship, though Cal didn't understand why there had to be a manned watch, especially on a night like this one. There was a new piece of technology called radar. Cal was one of three men in the middle of a six-hour watch—one man on the bow and another on the port amidships. He was "fortunate" in that the superstructure of the ship protected him from the wind and waves. The other two men weren't as lucky. The three men were secured to the ship by a harness and cables, which prevented them from being washed overboard.

As storms went this one was, on a scale of one to ten, probably an eight or nine. Cal was marking the time when he would be relieved. His slicker was keeping him dry but the salt water, which sprayed over the railing, burned his eyes. Without warning, the klaxon alarm sounded.

"Man overboard! Man overboard! Man hanging over the bow!" the speaker roared.

Cal knew immediately what had happened. Bill Carson, the man on the bow, had undoubtedly been washed over the steel cable railing by a wave, breaking over the bow, as the Gaffney's bow was plowing through the wave. Carson was probably still secured to the ship by his harness, but if he was still alive, he wouldn't be for long. A human body, battered by the sea against a steel ship, in the middle of a storm, didn't promise a man a long life. A rescue party was always on standby for such situations but it usually took several minutes for the team to reach the downed man. Carson might not have that long.

Cal didn't wait for orders but acted upon his own initiative. Using each of the two snap hook cables attached to his harness, Cal intended to move to the bow of the Gaffney by clipping the hooks to the cable railings of the ship. By alternating the snap hooks to a different section of the railing, he would be able to move to Carson and pull him back on board, without endangering himself.

Cal steadily progressed toward the bow, pausing and bracing himself when the Gaffney's bow pitched downward from a wave. A spotlight above the bridge was pointed on the snap cables, holding Carson to the ship. Cal made it to his shipmate in about a minute. Carson was still alive, though he was in bad shape. His left arm appeared to be broken by the odd angle it was in. Undoubtedly, he had swallowed plenty of salt water.

After securing himself to the railing Cal began pulling Carson up. The spotlight lit the bow up almost like it was three p.m., instead of three a.m., and Cal could see the terror, hope and relief in his shipmate's eyes. Carson grabbed the railing with his good left arm as Cal pulled him back on board by his harness. It was a Herculean effort. Cal had to reel Carson in as a fisherman would a large fish. Each time the bow plowed into a wave Carson would rise relative to the railing and Cal would pull in the slack. After two such motions of the ship, Carson was on the deck. The two sailors collapsed on the deck and held on as they awaited the rescue party, about thirty feet away.

"Are you hurt?" Cal yelled over roar of the storm.

"Thank you, thank you, thank you!" Carson also yelled to be heard.

"Are you hurt?!"

"My arm is broken but I can't feel it. Thanks again!"

The rescue team arrived before Cal could reply.

IT was a beautiful Saturday on Lake Lanier. The temperature was in the mid-70's, the water was still reasonably calm and the lake was quiet; the majority of the lake's boaters were just getting out of bed and wouldn't be on the water for at least another hour. Charlie and Heather had been riding her parents' Jet Ski for about an hour. Though the Twigs had two, Heather and Charlie rode one together. They had beached the Jet Ski on the bank of a secluded cove. Both were still wearing their life jackets and were just floating in the dead calm water, allowing the flotation devices to support them. They were enjoying each other's company. Charlie was wearing black and yellow nylon swimming trunks that came down to just above his knees. Heather was wearing a red one-piece swimsuit, which would turn any male head in her direction. In fact with her blonde hair wet, she looked like an Olympic swimmer, which was something that Charlie had not fully appreciated until now.

In the time that they had known each other, Charlie's hormones had been steadily flowing. Though he'd been a gentleman thus far, Heather knew of Charlie's lady-killer reputation and what motivated him. She'd made a point of not going to his room and Charlie didn't press the issue when she refused his invitations. Heather knew that Charlie was the one she wanted to marry, but she wasn't sure Charlie felt the same towards her, at least not yet. Though she wasn't a virgin, Heather didn't want to give in to her desires, at least not until she could be sure of Charlie's feelings.

"Heather, I hope you know where we are because these small islands and coves all look the same to me."

Heather held back a chuckle. "Yes, you ding-dong. We're about a mile from home. I'll be happy to show you on a map when we get home."

"What? You had me motor all around this lake to get me confused and lost and we're a mile away from home? You did this on purpose didn't you; just to take advantage of me?"

Charlie broke out one of his infectious grins as he pulled Heather towards him. He didn't exert any effort since they were both floating.

"Charlie Michaels you had better behave!"

She thought that she was going to have to refuse one of his advances.

"I am behaving and I think that I've made a favorable impression on your mother and father but I want to talk to you about something."

Charlie's tone took a serious note.

Heather saw that she had misjudged Charlie's intentions. Suddenly, her heart started to beat faster and she could feel a lump developing in her throat.

"What?"

"Heather, I didn't move up to Georgia on a whim. I've never made ANY significant changes in my lifestyle for anyone before. I know you have a year to go after this semester before you finish school and you have a service obligation afterwards. Do you plan to make a career of the military?"

"I really hadn't thought about it Charlie. Why do you ask?"

"I'm not anti-military but I have no desire to be a part of it permanently, either directly or indirectly."

"Charlie what are you trying to say?"

"Heather I'll be graduating shortly and I need to find a real job to support myself and a family someday. Paintball Atlanta is not going to fit the bill. Was your mother just making small talk or does your Dad need someone at his agency?"

"Do I fit into your plans Charlie?" Heather's throat was suddenly dry.

Charlie drew Heather closer and positioned her so she was directly facing him.

"You ask a lot of questions; especially questions that you should already know the answers to Heather. Look, an insurance agent can get a job anywhere right? I don't plan on following you across the country, or around the world, for twenty or thirty years while you're 'being all that you can be.' However, I'd consider being an insurance agent anywhere you are until you get out of the service."

Heather wasn't sure she heard Charlie correctly.

"Are you saying what I think you're saying Charlie?"

"I just said you ask too many questions. I moved to Georgia to be close to you Heather. Yes, I want to be with you. I am not going to ask you for your hand now, but I intend to, if you'll have me. Yes, you are part of my plans."

Heather literally lunged out of the water, wrapped her arms around Charlie's neck, her legs around his waist and gave him a kiss that lasted for what seemed like eternity.

"You can speak to my father later today or tomorrow about a job, but let me talk to Mom first. Okay?"

"Sure. Now that I've expressed my honorable intentions towards you, does that mean that I get to kiss you more often?" Charlie asked his question with a wicked grin as he leaned forward to kiss her again.

"As often as you like."

Heather closed her eyes as their lips touched.

# Chapter 7

Reverend Edgars stood before his congregation and via television cameras, his national audience. He was impeccably dressed in a slate-gray suit, powder-blue shirt and red tie, which complemented nicely his graying hair and six-foot frame. Taking the microphone and walking around and in front of the podium, he began his sermon.

"My brothers and sisters in Christ, today I am going to discuss a very important topic, without a doubt the most important topic which I have discussed to date, and perhaps the most important topic that I will ever address, especially in light of current circumstances."

The entire congregation was on the edge of their seats.

"The Bible tells us in its numerous books and chapters that God, at various times, uses men to deliver a message to mankind. I believe Mohammad Baghai is such a messenger. I believe that Mohammad Baghai is God's Prophet."

The congregation was stunned into silence.

"Jesus Christ has sent a message about hell and is using Mohammad Baghai as his instrument."

"There is irrefutable evidence, but in order to understand it, one must understand Islam, the religion of Muslims. I want to take a few minutes to explain Islam to laypersons. Mohammad Baghai, as many of you already know, has rejected Islam and is now a baptized Christian. Why did he convert? The answer has at least two parts, which are intermeshed. The second part I will address later in the sermon, but the first is that the Christian God and Allah are two separate entities and that Islam is, in fact, an anti-Christ religion."

"The Muslim religion called Islam, which means submission, was created by a man called Muhammad. He was born in 570 AD, in Mecca, in present day Saudi Arabia. During the course of his early life Muhammed traveled to different lands throughout the Middle East, meeting different cultures and observing different peoples who worshipped various pagan idols, in addition to Christians and Jews who worshipped our Lord."

"Muhammad often went to the mountains outside Mecca to meditate. Once, in 610 AD, he was in a cave on Mount Hira, Muhammad had a life-changing, indeed a world-changing experience. While meditating, he heard a voice that ordered him to "Recite." Alarmed and confused Muhammad replied 'I am not a reciter.' Muhammad feared that an evil spirit was in his presence and that it had mistaken him for an ecstatic prophet (sometimes called a kahin or a reciter). Muhammad felt a powerful pressure, as if a huge hand had gripped his torso and was squeezing him. Again the command came. 'Recite!' The grip was released and for a moment. Muhammad was breathless. Afterwards, he again said aloud the words. 'I am not a reciter!' A second time the huge grip squeezed him and again a command came. 'Recite!' The grip was released. Again Muhammad cried in agony. 'I am not a reciter!' The grip squeezed again for several moments and then released again. This time the spirit said 'Read in the name of your Lord and Cherisher! Who created man out of a clot of blood? It was He who taught the use of the pen; taught man that which he did not know?'"

"Muhammad was now certain that it was a demon that was tormenting him, and it had mistaken him for another; Muhammad was illiterate and could learn nothing from the pen. He ran from the cave prepared to jump from the mountain to end his life. The voice resonated again. 'Oh Muhammad! Thou art the apostle of God and I am Gabriel.' Initially, Muhammad was reluctant to accept what Gabriel had revealed to him. It was Muhammad's wife, fifteen years older and wiser, who persuaded him to return to the cave again. After several more visits to the cave and the subsequent revelations, Muhammad was reduced to a pathetic state. He was often found in a fetal position, crying like a baby. Ladies and gentleman this is a very important point which I will come back to later. Finally, Muhammad began to believe that he had been chosen as God's messenger. Gabriel revealed to him that Allah was more than a pagan deity; he was the creator and God of all man. Allah must be given reverence and obedience. Non-believers must be converted and submit to his will. 'There is no god but Allah and I, Muhammad am his Prophet!' became the mantra for the remainder of his life."

"This is the genesis of Islam. Let me inform you what exactly Islam teaches before we can reach any conclusions. Every devout Muslim subscribes to what is called the 'Five Articles of Faith,' also known as the 'Five Pillars of Islam, or 'Arkan al-Islam,' in Arabic. They are belief in God, belief in angels, belief in scriptures, belief in prophets and the doctrine of the last day. They are simple and easy to understand. I will now discuss each one."

"First, Muslims believe in one god, whom they call Allah. I have said earlier that Islam is an Anti-Christ religion. It is actually a religion begun by a demon via deception of an illiterate man. It encompasses many elements of Christianity and Judaism, including the Old Testament prophets. Let me ask each and every one of you in the audience and those viewing from their living rooms: Is there anywhere in the Bible where God used an angel to frighten someone, on his behalf, to become a prophet? Did God use an angel to communicate to Moses, Abraham, Noah or Daniel? No! He spoke to them directly. Have any of the prophets ever been left in a whimpering state after communicating with God? No, never! Would God allow any of his angels to scare and intimidate a prophet, as Muhammad was after communicating with Gabriel? Each and every one of you already knows the answer."

"Second is belief in angels. Gabriel, or Jibril, as Muslims call him, is indispensable in the Islamic faith; it is not a stretch of the imagination that angels figure prominently here. Islam teaches that there are two angels assigned to each person on earth, with one recording his good deeds and one recording his evil deeds. One can easily see the image that has developed over the years in Hollywood of an angel standing on one shoulder of a man and a devil standing on the other, each urging him to do good or evil. The fallen angel in Islam is called 'Shaitan,' clearly derived from 'Satan.' This 'Shaitan' has his subordinates as 'Satan' does."

"Islam also teaches that there are creatures called 'jinnis.' A jinni is neither an angel nor a fallen angel, though they can commit either evil or good deeds. Hollywood has derived the word 'genie' from 'jinni.' It should not surprise anyone that a religion originating from a demon spirit should be pre-occupied with the spirit world."

"The third article is belief is scripture. The Koran is the Islamic equivalent to the Bible. It contains 114 chapters, called 'surahs.' Any Muslim will tell you that it is a compendium of revelations from Muhammad. Again, I am speaking of Muslim Prophet, Muhammad, not the Christian Mohammad Baghai. However there is a little known fact that I want to bring to light. Muhammad did not write one word of the Koran—he was illiterate! Depending on which scholars you believe, it was not written until forty to fifty years after his death, by men who had to remember the words of his sermons."

"Reading the Koran is a challenge indeed! The book is twisted in literary convolutions and contradictions. In one part it says to kill Jews and Christians, yet in another it says to let them live in peace because they are people of the book, meaning believers in God. Furthermore, the Koran is only considered authoritative in Arabic. Now ladies and gentlemen, how many of you know that only 30percent of Muslims are literate and fewer still can read Arabic. This means that over 70 percent of the world's Muslim population can't read their holiest scripture. As I just said, reading the Koran is a challenge—for most Muslims that is. Can the same be said for Christians and the Bible? It's no wonder that there is no consensus as to what Islamic doctrine is. In fact, Islam is what Islamic leaders say it is."

"Muslims also revere a book called the 'Hadith,' which is a collection of sayings of Muhammad. Again, Muhammad wrote none of these quotations; rather they were written by his follower's years after his death. Islam also reveres the Torah, Psalms and the Gospels, because they are messages of God delivered to mankind before Muhammad. This is important because converts can still believe in portions of their former religion while, in clear conscience, convert to a new religion."

"This leads me directly to the fourth article, belief in the prophets. Islam teaches that Muhammad is Allah's, God's, last prophet. Before him were all the prophets in the Old Testament: Adam, Noah, Abraham, Moses and Jesus!"

Reverend Edgars had rattling off his sermon in machine-gun fashion, but now he paused.

"Ladies and gentlemen, let me be crystal clear here. Jesus, in Islam, is not considered the Son of God, but only a prophet! He is not even Allah's greatest prophet; Muhammad is! In fact, Jesus, according to the teachings of Islam, did not die on the cross; an imposter did, while Jesus was assumed into heaven. The absurdity of my last statement needs no further comment."

"Finally, the fifth article is the doctrine of the last day. This is a twisted and perverse concept, which graphically shows Islam in its true light. Paradise, as described in the Koran is a place where Allah's faithful are rewarded. They lie on posh couches and drink wine from goblets. May I remind all of you that alcohol is forbidden in Islam? The rewarded souls are served by 'maidens of paradise' or 'houris' or virgins, whom they may fornicate with freely and as often as they choose. Again let me remind you that such behavior on earth is forbidden in Islam. The fate of Islamic women in Islam is not clarified in the Koran. They may become houris and serve the men or receive some other unstated reward. Their place in the afterlife is not clear."

"Islamic paradise is described in the Koran, but the greatest indictment against this myth is that forbidden behavior on earth is rewarded in Islamic paradise!"

"Furthermore, a Muslim has no guarantee that he will enter paradise. He must continually do good deeds and hope that his actions outweigh his sins. Christians, on the other hand, as you know, only have to ask God's forgiveness and accept Jesus as their Lord and Savior."

"How does a Muslim ensure that his good deeds outweigh his sins? Islam is a religion of action. Let's go back to those Five Pillars of Islam."

"The first pillar, the 'shahadah,' is the Islamic creed and a Muslim's declaration of his allegiance to Allah. All Muslims are required to proclaim seventeen times a day this simple phrase: 'There is no God but Allah and Muhammad is his Prophet.' This testament is whispered into an infant's ear at birth and a corpse's ear upon his death. The genius of this is in its simplicity, especially in light of the fact that a majority of Muslims are illiterate. The message is repeated over and over again. No deviations are allowed. Eventually, after enough repetitions, the uninformed masses believe the message. I would like to remind everyone that the Nazi party used this technique on the German population against the Jews in Europe before the outbreak of World War Two."

"Daily ritual prayer is the second pillar, called the salat. The salat is not a request or a wants list to Allah. It is a devotion of one's heart and mind instead. Islam requires that it be done five times daily. The times are at sunrise, shortly after noon, late in the afternoon, shortly after sunset and at night. Again no exceptions are allowed, except in time of jihad. Seven preconditions must be met. First, it must be prayer time; second, the body must be washed for the sake of ritual purity; third, clean clothes must be worn; fourth, the location must be clean; fifth, the body must be covered and a woman must wear a scarf over her hair. The concept is that Allah does not judge anyone upon their sex, rather upon their sincerity. Sixth, everyone must face Mecca, the Saudi Arabian city, while praying and finally, anyone performing the salat must be sincere."

"Charity, or the 'zakat,' is the third pillar. Usually, Muslims freely give 2.5 percent of their income to charity. However, in some Muslim countries, the zakat is legally demanded. This causes an unusual situation in these countries. Beggars, knowing that charity is required, often show no gratitude for other's generosity and are not motivated to improve their lot in life. Now let me ask you ladies and gentlemen, do you see any parallels between the described scenario and young teenaged girls getting pregnant, becoming welfare mothers and expecting government support? It seems Islam has started a trend here in the United States."

"Every year Muslims, during the Islamic month of Ramadan, are required to fast during daylight hours and read the Koran. This fast is called the 'sawm' and is the fourth pillar. It is intended as a spiritual cure for the foibles of human nature. Muslims believe that by fasting, they cleanse their bodies, minds and spirits to gain enlightenment from Allah."

"As commendable as this appears, the reality of the situation is that many Muslims change their sleeping patterns so that they are awake at night and sleep much of the day! This allows them to follow the letter of the law, though it clearly violates the spirit."

"The fifth and final pillar is a pilgrimage to Mecca, called 'hajj.' Every able Muslim is expected to travel to Mecca once in his or her lifetime. I have little to offer on this subject. Muslims perform rituals which are sacred to them but have little or no relevance in the modern world. Visitors to Mecca on a hajj shed their clothing and put on a seamless garment, and for the next seven days are not allowed to shave, cut their nails and are required to walk barefoot. Ultimately, every Muslim kisses a black stone, located in a cube-shaped building called the 'Ka'bah,' completing the hajj. Anyone completing a hajj has their sins are erased. Now, let's think about this for a minute. According to the teachings of Islam, a Muslim can kill a fellow human being, not feel any remorse or contrition and be forgiven for his crime by completing the hajj."

"Enough on the five pillars of Islam. There is another, more controversial doctrine, which was taught by Muhammad. I am speaking of 'jihad.' Jihad translated from Arabic means 'struggle,' though it is often interpreted to mean 'holy war.' In Islam there are four jihads, a struggle of the tongue, a struggle of heart, a struggle of the hand and a struggle of the sword. It is the struggle of the sword that frightens most non-Muslims. Now I have already told you that Islam means submission. The purpose of the jihad of the sword is to forcibly imprint the will of Allah on non-Muslims; 'infidels' is the term. Muhammad, again I am speaking of the Muslim, not Mohammad Baghai, the Christian, taught that the only stern measures had to be used in dealing with people who defy Allah's will. Ladies and gentlemen, there are no shades of gray here. The Koran is clear on this topic. I can quote numerous surahs in support of this position and I don't need to remind any of you of the events of recent history either."

"Why is jihad so prevalent? Specifically, why do young Muslims willingly kill themselves in the name of jihad? I want to remind all of you again that Islam doesn't guarantee that anyone will go to heaven. A Muslim's sins are weighed against his good deeds and Allah makes the decision. There is only one exception to this. Muhammad taught that anyone who died while in a state of jihad of the sword would reserve a place in paradise. There is recent history that supports this belief. During the 1980's Iran sent waves of willing adolescent boys in waves of attacks in their war with Iraq. Thousands were slaughtered and thousands more were maimed. Can any of you think of anything more evil than purposely sending to their death, regardless of the reason?"

"I have spoken at length about the religion that is called Islam. I hope that I have convinced you with the examples that I have cited that it Islam is a twisted evil religion. I stated at the beginning of the sermon that Islam is anti-Christ. Let's discuss that as it relates to Mohammad Baghai. Mohammad Baghai was as a devout Muslim as there is on Earth. He is also an intelligent man—educated here in the United States. I want to bring to your attention to the fact that he was Persian, Iranian and that he was Osama bin Laden's lieutenant in Afghanistan. Now bin Laden is Arab, a Saudi Arabian. Arabs and Persians traditionally do not like each other. Now how did Baghai win bin Laden's trust? Baghai did so only by being a devout Muslim."

"Ladies and gentlemen I have already explained that Jesus Christ is recognized, only as a prophet in Islam, not our Lord. Now after our Lord retrieved Mohammad Baghai from hell, he recognized that Jesus was God and not a Prophet of Allah. Now after having to concede that one of the most sacred tenants of Islam is wrong, he was forced to the realization that the whole premise on which Islam is based is bogus. This is the second part of my explanation as to why he converted to Christianity."

"Mohammad's epiphany motivated him to perform some extraordinary actions. First, he released David Franks, the man that he intended to kill. Second, he came to the United States to answer for his crimes. These crimes are terrible, ghoulish crimes against Americans, which carry the death penalty. Crimes that Mohammad Baghai freely admits he committed and for which he has not offered any defense. Thirdly, he has renounced Islam, been baptized and accepted Jesus as his Lord and savior."

"Ladies and gentlemen, Mohammad Baghai will plead guilty to his crimes and will be sentenced in six weeks. At best he will receive life in prison without parole, though he is likely to be sentenced to death by lethal injection."

"Now, I am here to tell you that Jesus did not empower Mohammad Baghai with His message only to have him die by the needle, or to have him spend the rest of his life in prison. There is no parole for a federal life sentence. Life in prison does mean life." Reverend Edgars again paused for dramatic effect.

"The President has the power to pardon anyone for his crimes. This is prescribed in the Constitution. With a stroke of a pen, Mohammad Baghai's crimes will be erased as Jesus washed away our sins with his blood. I urge everyone to contact the White House by telephone, letter or the Internet. Anyone using the Internet may communicate via my web site, where there is a special link to the White House site. I understand that there may be Americans who may have reservations about pardoning a murderer; that doing so goes against the grain of those that believe that we are a nation of laws. I would answer those people by saying that saying that a Presidential Pardon is lawful and that pardons have been issued for less honorable reasons. Furthermore, this is what God has planned. He has forgiven Mohammad and wants him to be His messenger. Who are we to question Him?"

"Ladies and gentlemen, we are at a critical time in our history. It is time for the Christians of America to make politicians heed the will of their constituents. Contact the President. Contact your Senators. Contact your Representative. Demand that they urge the President to pardon God's prophet. Circumstances demand immediate action and God is watching. Before we conclude let us pray…"

ABU Sabaya turned off the television in his Chicago safe house and cursed. He could not believe what he had heard. This "Reverend Edgars" was a pig. It was obvious to all true believers that Mohammad Baghai was a traitor to Islam, corrupted by the United States and this televangelist was just an instrument of the decadent American culture.

It would not be long before a blow would be struck against the Americans, a blow, years in the planning, which would bring the American government to its knees. A blow that, when struck, would call all Muslims to rise against, and fight, Americans everywhere. All the necessary assets were in place. All that was required now was Allah's blessing and for the appointed date and time to arrive. The international media would be present to broadcast the event as the sword was dropped.

# Chapter 8

Andrew Shephard sat across from the Reverend Casey Edgars, drinking coffee and exchanging pleasantries. Shephard, sent by President Hays, was visiting in an "unofficial" capacity. The White House had been besieged with emails, phone calls and "snail mail" since Edgars' televised sermon on Mohammad Baghai. Edgars had continued to "ratchet up" the pressure by replaying the sermon and holding press conferences. A ground swell of public opinion was developing in Baghai's favor.

Officially the White House's position on the matter was that President Hays had not made any decision on a pardon since an application had not been submitted. Unofficially, Hays was inclined to commute a death sentence to life in prison, should that particular scenario become the case.

Since he had known the Reverend for over twenty years, Shephard had been given the responsibility of communicating the White House's position to Edgars. In fact, Edgars had baptized Shephard as a child and had become a mentor figure to him. As a teenager Shephard had considered pursuing a life in the ministry and following in the footsteps of his mentor. The two had discussed the topic on several different occasions. The "soothsayer," as Edgars was known, advised Shephard against such a decision, but instead suggested public service.

Shephard had taken the advice and spent four years in the Marine Corps as an infantryman. He had also taken courses at a local college. After he served his enlistment, Shephard began his college career in earnest, realizing that his interests were in government—a more secular career path.

His higher education did broaden his horizons. Shephard realized that he could serve God by serving humanity via politics.

"So Andy, I'm guessing that you're not here to discuss the Medal of Freedom that the President plans to award me."

"To tell you the truth that isn't a concern of the President though I can schedule the appointment. Reverend, the President is concerned that your rhetoric concerning Mohammad Baghai is having an adverse affect on the judicial process and may be dividing the country."

"How is that Andy?"

"The President prefers to let the legal process run its course."

"Andy, the course of action that I've proposed is completely legal. It's prescribed in the Constitution. Both you and the President know that."

"Yes it is Reverend, but the President is not prepared to pardon Mr. Baghai. This issue is political dynamite and she does not intend to inflame the passions of American, or World, opinion."

"Andy, I'm concerned with neither public opinion, nor politics. I am concerned, however, with God's opinion. Believe me when I tell you that though He will not interfere with the American judicial process, God wants Mohammad Baghai pardoned. I believe, no, I know, that he is a chosen spokesman for our Lord."

"A prophet. Are you certain?"

"I am one hundred percent certain Andy. Believe me when I say that, though I'm not a politician, I have commented on plenty of political affairs. Andy, you're correct that this is political dynamite and you also know that I've been remarkably accurate in my predictions. I'll tell you next time we meet how and why that's been so. Right now I want you to do me two favors."

"What's that?"

"I want the administration to do a background check on me, the kind of background check done for a top-secret clearance. I'll be happy to sign any authorization that may be required."

"You said two favors?"

"I want you to use the resources of the government to find someone for me."

Edgars wrote a name on a piece of stationery put it in a sealed envelope and gave it to Shephard.

"Here is his name, or was his name, at the time I knew him. He is an Israeli National living in the United States. His name has, almost certainly, been changed and he's probably in some sort of witness protection program. Ask your friend Mr. Scarboro to help you. It shouldn't be too difficult."

"How do you know him?" Shephard had a quizzical look on his face.

"He and I have mutual acquaintances. Andy, do me this favor; I know this doesn't make sense. Most of this will be clear afterwards. I will remain silent on the Baghai issue for few days, to give you enough time to complete this task. Then I'll come to your office to discuss this affair further. By all means share what you find with the President and I will be at your disposal to clarify anything else that is still not clear."

Shephard rose and shook hands with the soothsayer; not knowing where he was being led but knowing that it was exactly the direction his mentor had planned.

MOHAMMAD was kneeling in front of the toilet again. The water had been drained from the bowl and the pipes as before. Slash, along with several others, was listening.

"I thought that I'd invite a few of my friends to listen to you man." Slash bellowed as he tried to hold back a laugh. He thought that the previous conversation was amusing.

"Thank you Slash. I know that you are not ready to accept what I told you as the truth, but I am glad that you and your friends are at least willing to listen to me again."

"Sure man. Not like we got something better to do."

"My brothers…"

"This guy calls everyone his brother," Slash interrupted.

"Yes, thank you Slash. To me all of you are my brother. I am a murderer. Soon I will plead guilty for murdering American Soldiers though I have killed many others. I do not know what my fate will be, though I am not worried."

"I have seen what happens after someone dies, Slash. There is a Heaven and hell. God gave me the privilege of seeing both just before I was about to murder someone. I know everyone here is aware that there is a God, or at least knows someone who believes in God. Believe me, my brothers, as bad as this prison may be, hell is a thousand times, no, a million times worse. None of you want to go there. I do not know what any of you have done and some of you may believe that your lives are beyond redemption. You are wrong. God will forgive you. All you have to do is ask Him. God wants you to respect life. You do not know how? All you have to do is ask Him. He will show you how. God wants you to respect yourself and your fellow man. You are not sure how? All you have to do is ask Him."

"Hold on man!" Another voice echoed from the toilet.

"Are you saying that all I gotta do is ask God a question and He will answer me?"

"What is your name my brother?"

"Draino, man."

"That is an unusual name. Does it have a meaning?"

"Yeah man. I'm Draino because I make things happen."

Laughter from several voices echoed through the pipes.

"Draino, God may not speak to you as He spoke to Moses or any of the other prophets, but if you have a question or need guidance, He will show you the answer."

"Oh yeah? How?" Another voice spoke.

"He will show you a sign that you will easily recognize. Something will happen that resolves the conflict. I cannot say what. But I can say with certainty that if you believe in God, and ask for His help, He will give it. It may not be in the way that you expect, but He will help you."

"This guy is whacked." Laughter rose to a crescendo.

"My brothers, I do not know any of you, but I know that God will show one of you, in His own way. The truth is what I am telling you."

Laughter roared through the toilet bowl. Mohammad felt crushed. He had been given divine instructions and had failed miserably. He was ready to cry.

"Take heart Mohammad. Your audience will come to embrace your message. Just keep preaching it." A voice spoke from behind the steel door.

"Who are you my brother?"

"My name is Agent Scott Ramsey. I'm one of your FBI guards. I am also a Christian. I'm aware of your life's recent events and actually I do believe all of your claims. Look Mohammad, I'm not supposed to be speaking with you so don't expect regular conversation, but keep up your work. Your message is true and the truth can't be denied. I pray for you and I believe that God will deliver you from your plight."

"Scott, do you know what happened to me?"

"Yes, I've read your accounts and yes I believe your claims, in fact I know that they are true."

"Thank you for expressing your confidence Scott, my brother."

"You have a Bible don't you Mohammad?"

"Yes of course."

"Continue reading it. God will show you, through it, what he wants you to preach."

"Thank you Scott. I am so tired and need to lie down to rest. God bless you, my brother." Mohammad was exhausted, lay down and closed his eyes.

JIM Scarboro scanned the background check of Casey Edgars as he waited outside the Oval Office. He was to meet with President Hays in about five minutes. In the day and age of $100 government screwdrivers and $800 toilet seats, the time and money spent to compile this report was an even greater waste of public tax dollars. A normal background check involved a thorough review of one's finances, tax returns, criminal background, politics, club memberships, religious affiliation and the like. Personal interviews of friends, family and associates were conducted. The normal time frame for such a background review was between 90 and 120 days. An accelerated review could be done in 60. This one was done in two weeks—and it revealed nothing that was not already common knowledge. Reverend Edgars was a public figure and had been one for virtually all of his life. The only instances of anything out of the norm was that he had the uncanny ability to predict future world events and that he had been kidnapped and released, for no reason, when he was a small boy.

The "soothsayer" had also asked to find a man in witness protection. This was proving to be much more difficult, though it shouldn't have been. That was peculiar. The Justice Department had records on all government witnesses and this man, according to his own people, was not under government protection and surveillance. Undoubtedly some entry-level employee deleted a record in a database by mistake. The error would be found and this man would be located. The President would not be happy, though the error appeared to have occurred at least three administrations before this one.

"The President is ready for you now." A voice resonated from the other end of the room.

Scarboro opened the door and was immediately greeted by President Hays. She was on the phone and smiled as she motioned the Attorney General to sit down on one of the two sofas that faced each other, perpendicular to her desk, and sandwiched an ornate coffee table.

Hanging up the phone and walking to the opposite sofa Hays say down.

"What have we got Jim?"

Scarboro handed over a folder with the report.

"Nothing unusual or unexpected other than he was kidnapped and released when he was fourteen. The police reports on the incident are missing, but more than likely they've been misplaced after all this time. A few years later, he became ordained and founded the Christ Ministries Church. He has a weekly religious television show. From time to time he has used his position and notoriety to comment on society and take on national and international affairs. What is unusual is that he is ALWAYS correct in his assertions."

"Oh come on Jim." President Hays was obviously not buying that claim from Scarboro.

"Madam President. Inside your folder you'll find documentation of the predictions Reverend Edgars has made, the dates that he made them and the dates that he was proved correct. In EVERY case that Edgars has made a prediction, what he said would happen, happened."

Hays reviewed the list for a moment.

"He also asked us to locate am man. What was his name?"

"Jacob Rabin. We haven't been able to locate him. Reverend Edgars indicated that he was an Israeli citizen in federal witness protection. The Justice Department doesn't have a record of any 'Rabin' in protective custody, of any kind. Either Reverend Edgars is mistaken or the records have been lost or misplaced."

"Judging from his track record, I don't think Reverend Edgars is mistaken and Justice Department records concerning witnesses under federal protection are not lost and are not misplaced! Jim, I'm going to schedule a meeting with Reverend Edgars next week. Officially, it will be to present him with the Medal of Freedom. However, we will discuss his background check and Mr. Jacob Rabin in private. I want that file on my desk at least 24 hours before I meet with him. I understand that this happened long before you took this job, but it is your problem. Do what ever you have to and find that file. Understand Jim?"

"Yes Mrs. President."

Hays got up and went to her desk and buzzed the intercom. "What is my next appointment?"

Scarboro knew he was dismissed.

CHARLIE logged on to the State of Georgia Insurance Commissioner's Web site. He was looking for the results of his test scores on his life/health and property/casuality insurance exams. A typical person would normally take a month to prepare for each of the two exams, usually taking preparation courses for each examination. Charlie took two weeks to prepare, studying the state manual and notes that Heather's father had provided. He'd driven down to Atlanta and took both exams on a Saturday.

Charlie hadn't the slightest doubt that he had passed both of the exams; 70 percent was the minimum passing score, his question was if he'd scored 100 on each exam. Charlie input his exam control number and social security number. A minute later he found out the results. One hundred on life/health and 96 on property/casualty—not perfect but definitely good enough. He called Heather on his cell phone.

"Hello Charlie," Heather answered recognizing the number on caller ID.

"Hi. I wanted to give you a call. Something's happened. I'm going to have to quit my job at Paintball Atlanta and go back down to Pensacola," Charlie said in a somber voice.

Heather was in a state of stunned silence. "Charlie what happened?"

Charlie was having a quiet chuckle at Heather's expense.

"I just got my scores from the insurance exams and I thought I'd go down to Pensacola and sell some of my fraternity brothers some life insurance. Oh, by the way, do you think your father would hire me?"

Charlie couldn't hold back his laughter any longer.

"Oh you jerk," Heather said realizing that she had been duped.

"Charlie, I'm so proud of you. Of course Dad will hire you. I'm going to call him right after I hang up. Mom will make him take all of us out to dinner. Will you be free this weekend?"

"I should be Heather."

"Great! I'm going to call mom right now. Can we see each other tonight?"

"Well let me check my schedule." Charlie was not through yanking his girl friend's chain.

"Did I just say that you were a jerk? You can pick me up after class."

"Okay, see you then. Love you."

"I love you too Charlie."

CAL and his fellow sailor, Bill Carson, both lay in beds next to each other in the Gaffney's sick bay. The term sick bay implied a hospital which, in the Gaffney's case, was a misrepresentation. The "hospital" consisted of six beds and was staffed by a Navy Corpsman; not a doctor. The Corpsman had x-rayed Carson's arm, revealing a compound fracture of the ulna, and then splinted it. Surgery and several pieces of stainless steel hardware were going to be required to repair Carson's arm. He would be transported off the Gaffney as soon as possible since the frigate didn't have the medical facilities required.

Cal, on the other hand, was ordered to sick bay only as a precaution. He wasn't hurt, but he was ordered to sick bay for bed rest only. The corpsman had given him a vitamin shot and advised him to get some rest. Getting rest was going to be a problem since the Gaffney was still in the middle of the storm and pitched and rolled with every wave.

It was a few minutes later that the Gaffney's skipper, Commander Hampton, walked in to the sick bay.

"Ten-hut! Skipper on deck." The corpsman bellowed as he stood attention. Cal and Bill Carson were the only others present. Protocol did not require them to stand at attention; only make eye contact with the skipper.

"As you were," Hampton ordered.

The corpsman left the room. It was apparent that the skipper wanted to speak to Cal and Carson.

"How are you feeling seaman?"

"Like A-Rod took batting practice and used me as the ball skipper."

"The corpsman tells me that you'll need a few screws inserted in your arm to put you back together."

"That's what he tells me also."

"Carson, it's still too nasty to transport you now, but as soon as it calms down I'm going to have you flown to the Bush to have your surgery and then you'll probably be ordered state-side for recuperation."

The Skipper was referring to the aircraft carrier George H. W. Bush, the flagship of Task Force 3, which was cruising to the Gulf of Oman, code-named camel station. The Gaffney, though part of the task force, would show the American Flag in the Persian Gulf.

"Yes sir."

The skipper paused for a moment, turned his attention towards Cal and almost instantly changed from Dr. Jekyll to Mr. Hyde.

"Intavan, I've been in the Navy for over 20 years and I have never seen such a stupid act. We had a trained team prepared for just that contingency."

Cal was prepared for a "dress-down" from the skipper. He knew what he'd done was technically against regulations but he didn't expect this. He'd considered Commander Hampton a fair and even-handed skipper.

"In my 20 years in the Navy, I haven't seen a comparable act of bravery either. Congratulations. I wish I commanded a hundred men like you."

Hampton changed back to Dr. Jekyll again; his somber expression transformed to a grin and he stuck out his hand for Cal to shake.

Cal was caught off guard by his skipper and after a moment shook Hampton's hand.

"Thank you skipper."

"You are due to re-up soon aren't you? Have you made a decision?"

"No sir, I haven't."

"Good. After you get out of sick bay I want you to come see me about that. Understand?"

"Yes sir, but I'm confused," Cal replied.

"Oh, what are you confused about Intavan?"

"Skippers don't normally get involved with the re-enlistment of the crew. Why am I getting your attention?"

"I told you that I wish that I had a hundred men just like you, didn't I?

"Yes sir."

"That's your reason. We'll discuss that more when we sit down face-to-face. Both you men get well quick."

"Yes sir" Cal and Carson uttered in unison.

The skipper left sick bay.

"Cal, I want to thank you again for saving my life, but I have a question," Carson said as he sat up in his bunk and turned to face Cal.

"What's that Bill?"

"Why?" Cal had a pensive expression on his face.

"Bill, are you asking me why I risked my life to save yours? Or are you asking why a devout Muslim, in light of current history, would risk his life to save a Jew; or a Christian for that matter?"

"Yes."

"First of all, I assume you or anyone else would do the same for me. I realize that's a superficial answer that just scratches the surface of your question. The real answer is that, in actuality, Islam is a peaceful religion. These terrorists that you see on TV kidnapping and killing innocent people, justifying their actions by issuing bogus fatwas…"

"Hold it Cal, what's a fatwa?"

"I'm sorry Bill. A fatwa is a legal/religious ruling by a universally-recognized Islamic scholar or an Islamic body. Bin Laden and al-Qaeda have issued dozens of them to justify their actions, and none are legitimate."

"Why is that?"

"Bin Laden is by no means a scholar and al-Qaeda is not a recognized Islamic body, they're a bunch of terrorists."

"I see."

"The Prophet, Muhammad, in Chapter two of the Koran, I can't remember the exact verse, praised all Jews and Christians who live virtuous lives. Muslims believe that Muslims, Jews and Christians worship the same God. So, to answer your question, why did I, a Muslim save you, a Jew? I did it because a Muslim, a true Muslim, one who reads the Koran, believes and attempts to follow the teachings of the Prophet, Muhammad, would do so without hesitation. It is part of my fitrah."

"Fit what?"

Cal laughed.

"Fitrah. It's Arabic and translates, literally, to moral compass, but I suppose infidels like you can think of it as a conscience. Now, if you'll shut up, I want to get some rack time. Oh, Bill?"

"Yes, Cal?"

"I promise that I won't slit your throat in your sleep."

Carson laughed.

"Thanks, I appreciate that."

# Chapter 9

President Hays and Jim Scarboro were in the midst of a tense discussion in the O. Reverend Edgars, and the press, were waiting outside. Edgars was to receive the Medal of Freedom, the highest honor that the United States awarded a civilian. Hays had given Scarboro instruction to find one Mr. Jacob Rabin, an Israeli national living under federal witness protection, but who had mysteriously disappeared. There were no records of such a man in any federal protection.

"What do you mean, this man doesn't exist?"

Hays was visibly upset. She expected results from the people who worked for her. Scarboro had always produced for her in the past.

"Madam President there are plenty of men with the name of Jacob Rabin. None are, or were, ever in witness protection. None are Israeli Nationals either."

"So you're telling me that Reverend Edgars is mistaken?"

"Not necessarily, but we need more data."

Hays was not happy, but she could see that she wasn't going to achieve anything by belittling the Attorney General.

"Very well Jim. I'm going to invite Reverend Edgars in and, later, the press for a photo-op. After the ceremony I want you and Andy to come back in and the four of us are going to have a 'come to Jesus' meeting. Excuse the pun. Now will you excuse yourself while I meet the good Reverend?"

"Certainly," Scarboro got up and walked to a side door.

The President pushed a button on the intercom. "Would you invite Reverend Edgars in please?"

"Right away, Mrs. President."

A moment later the soothsayer walked into the O. He was dressed impeccably in a navy-blue pinstripe suit, white oxford shirt and a red power tie.

"Reverend Edgars, thank you for coming; please sit down," Hays graciously said as she rose from behind her desk and met him half way.

"Thank you Mrs. President." Edgars said as he sat down in one of the twin ornate sofas.

"What would you care for, coffee or tea?"

"Tea would be fine Mrs. President."

Hays poured two cups of hot tea. "Reverend, in just a minute the press will be invited to take pictures of us as I present you with the Medal of Freedom. After they leave, I have invited some of my staff to discuss the Mohammad Baghai situation with you. I hope that is all right with you."

"Certainly, Mrs. President, in fact I assumed that would be a topic of conversation when I came here."

As if on cue, the press photographers marched into the Oval Office and began to set up. Everyone in the group had photographed a dignitary or other distinguished person in the Oval Office at least a dozen times and the setup was completed quickly.

Pictures were taken of Hays and Edgars exchanging pleasantries. Afterwards, Hays stood up and retrieved a mahogany box from her desk.

"Let's begin shall we? Reverend Edgars, will you please stand?"

Edgars stood up.

"Reverend Edgars, for your years of service, as an advisor to dozens of public servants, at both federal and state levels, in both a spiritual and political context, for years of service to our Lord, God, for years of service as the social conscience of our nation, on behalf of the citizens of the United States of America, it is my privilege to present you with the Medal of Freedom."

Hays walked around to Edgars' back and attached the ribbon, holding the medal around his neck.

"Thank you Mrs. President. It is a privilege and an honor to accept this award. I must thank the staff and congregation of the Christ Ministries Church, and most importantly I must thank our Lord; without him none of my achievements would have been possible."

Just as quickly as the ceremony began, it ended. The photographers filed out and a moment later the White House Chief of Staff and the Attorney General came into the O and sat down.

Hays took a seat also and began. "Gentlemen you all know each other. Reverend I usually include the Vice President in meetings such as this, however, as Vice President he is President of the Senate and there is an important vote that will need his vote to break a deadlock."

There was an appropriation bill being voted upon that was going to require Taylor's tie-breaking vote to for passage.

"I certainly understand Mrs. President."

"Reverend Edgars, I wanted to speak to you personally and express my position on the Mohammad Baghai issue. You also made a very unusual request to my chief of staff when you and he spoke last. The request in itself, a background check of yourself and the location of a person are not that unusual. What was unusual was that this person, Mr. Jacob Rabin, does not appear to exist. At least not an Israeli citizen named Jacob Rabin, under witness protection."

"Mrs. President, I can assure you that he does, or did, exist. He may have died," Edgars replied to the President.

"We will come back to Mr. Rabin. However, I want to discuss Mr. Baghai with you. Reverend Edgars, the President of the United States is the chief law enforcement official in America. I would consider it presumptuous of me to interfere with the laws of the land only because a vocal segment of the American population desires it. Though I am not philosophically opposed to a pardon it is, and will remain, my position to let the legal issues run their course before a petition to pardon Mr. Baghai is considered."

"Mrs. President, what I have suggested is completely legal, as prescribed by the Constitution, so by definition it is not 'interfering' with the laws of the land. Furthermore, there is precedent for I suggest. President Ford pardoned President Nixon before Nixon was even charged with a crime."

"Reverend Edgars we can debate the technical aspects of my job, but that is not my intent. I am not prepared to pardon Mohammad Baghai at this time. I did not say that I would not but that is a discussion for another time. What I would like to know from you is your interest in Baghai and your interest in Jacob Rabin.

"My interest in Mohammad Baghai and Jacob Rabin are interwoven."

"How is that?" Scarboro spoke for the first time.

Edgars turned to the Attorney General. "I assume that all of you have read my background check and that it included a biography of me?"

Every one nodded in agreement.

"Andy would you give us a thirty-second summary of it?"

"At an early age you showed the ability to predict future national and international events with remarkable accuracy. This included the Yom-Kippur Wars in Israel, the Tet Offensive in Vietnam, the Iranian Hostage Crisis in 1979, and the assassination attempt of Pope John-Paul II in 1983. Sadam Hussein's invasion of Kuwait in 1989 and the World Trade Center attacks on September 11. The list goes on. The only other unusual aspect of your life is that you were kidnapped and later released under mysterious circumstances in 1974. You became an ordained Methodist Minister and started the non-denominational Christ Ministries Church."

"Yes, that is correct but in addition to that, and I realize that you had no way of knowing, I also predicted the Kennedy assassination and the Arab-Israeli Six-Day War in 1967. I was a toddler and a small boy at the time and my parents didn't report it to the authorities. Furthermore it was my prediction of the Yom-Kippur War that caused me to be kidnapped."

"I'm not following you Reverend" Hays commented with a perplexed look on her face.

"Mrs. President my ability is a God-given gift. I have tried to use it, as I believe that He would want me too. Believe me, I have been offered much to use it in less than scrupulous ways. I have never mentioned to anyone how it works and I trust that the present company will keep my confidence. The best way that I can describe my ability and it's not a complete or accurate description by any means, is the opposite of a memory."

Edgars saw three confused faces.

"Let me explain. All of you grasp the concept of an elderly man who has vivid memories in some cases, while in other cases the memories are 'fuzzy'?"

Edgars got nods in agreement.

"I see the future the same way, only in reverse. Some of the future events which I 'see' are crystal clear, while others are fuzzy. Some of the fuzzy events become clear as the important date approaches, sometimes they don't. Some significant events I don't see at all and come as a complete surprise to me as it does to everyone else. I don't have an explanation as to why that is the case, but it is what it is."

"Please continue Reverend. Explain how your gift caused your kidnapping," Hays prompted Edgars.

"My parents were good Methodists and in September of 1973 I told them what I foresaw the following month. They tried to ignore me until I reminded them what I said about Kennedy's assassination and the Six Day War in 1967. They called our pastor. After several discussions, I convinced him of the truth of what I claimed. He contacted a local rabbi, a rabbi who had emigrated from Israel by the way, who I reiterated my claims to. Now I want you all to understand that some things I see are fuzzy, while others are crystal clear and this impending war was one of them. I recited dates, locations and battle plans for both sides. I was able to discuss concepts and tactics that a typical twelve year old would have no notion of."

"After several more 'conferences' my pastor and the rabbi agreed to take a 'wait and see' approach and dropped the matter. At least that was what my parents and I were led to believe."

"History proved me correct. Egypt and Syria attacked in 1973 when I said they would, where I said they would and as I had predicted Israel prevailed, but only after the issue was in doubt for several days."

"Reverend I am still not following how your revelation caused your kidnapping or how Jacob Rabin ties into this," Scarboro interjected.

"I am tying up all the loose ends now sir. Apparently the rabbi had connections with important Israeli government officials and reported our conversations to them. On June 6, 1974 an Israeli team, probably from the Mossad, kidnapped me with the intent of taking me to Israel and holding me prisoner, permanently. Jacob Rabin was a member of that team and was the one who later released me."

"What?" Hays screamed so loud that a secret service agent opened the door and stuck his head in to make sure the President was not in danger.

"Everything is fine Ron," Hays reported to her guard.

"Reverend, you must not have your facts straight. Israel is an ally and would not commit an act of war, such as that, based upon one isolated incident," Hays said.

"Mrs. President I do have my facts straight and I wasn't kidnapped based upon one isolated incident." Edgars' cool and calm demeanor starkly contrasted the President's flustered personality.

"Please continue Reverend," Shephard interjected.

"I have already told you that some events I am able to see clearly and others are not so clear. The Black September attack on the Israeli Olympic team in Munich in 1972 was an event that I foresaw, only in vaguest way. I wrote a letter to the Israeli Olympic Committee and to the Israeli Embassy in Washington to express my fears. Understandably they were ignored. It was based upon these two predictions, I assume, that the Israeli Government made the decision that I was vital to their national security and kidnapped me."

"In the early morning hours of June 9, Jacob Rabin released me while his associates slept. Several weeks later my family and I met Mr. Rabin for the first and only time. He apologized to my family and me and explained the events from his perspective. While he was guarding me he had an epiphany. He told us that Jesus Christ appeared before him. Jacob, a Jew, instantly realized that Jesus was the Son of God. He told me that Jesus asked him why he was persecuting one of His children. He helped me escape and turned himself into the CIA."

"Not the FBI?" Scarboro asked.

"He was clear about that. He made his way to Langley, Virginia and surrendered himself. I understand that he was debriefed. He was an intelligence asset. He also told us that he was baptized a Christian. I have no idea what happened to him afterwards, though

I understand the CIA told Israeli officials that they knew what they had attempted and to keep their 'hands off' of me in the future. The rabbi in question was quietly deported back to Israel."

"Mrs. President, even a blind man can see that Mohammad Baghai has had the same kind of epiphany. Jesus Christ does not make appearances to every Tom, Dick and Harry. Furthermore, anyone with a double digit IQ can deduce that Jesus has a purpose for this man and it is not to be strapped to a gurney to die, or to spend the rest of his life in prison. The sooner he is pardoned the sooner he can perform the work that God wants him to do."

"I want you to know that I will use any and all means available to me, to not only spare this man's life but to see that he fulfills God's plan for him. Furthermore, should you oppose His plan for Mohammad Baghai, our Lord will create the circumstances required to see that His plan is carried out. I can't say how. This is something that is fuzzy to me right now, but please believe me when I say it will happen and, when it does, you will know it."

"Casey you have gone way too far. No one insults and threatens the President of the United States, especially in the Oval Office." Shephard's face was red with anger at his mentor.

"Andy no threat or insult was intended."

Turning towards the President Edgars continued. "Mrs. President please accept my apologies if I offended you in any way."

"No offense was taken Reverend. I appreciate your candor I will thoughtfully consider your perspective in dealing with the matter."

Edgars took his cue and stood up. "Thank you for your valuable time Mrs. President, but there is one more issue of the utmost importance that I must mention."

"What is that Reverend?"

"Mrs. President, it concerns one of my 'fuzzy' visions. I get the sense that your life may be in danger; perhaps there will be an attempt on it. I can't see anything specific now, but if it becomes clear I will certainly notify Andy or the Secret Service if you prefer. In any case, please be careful."

"I will Reverend. Thank you for the information."

Edgars exited the Oval Office, leaving the three to contemplate the conversation.

"Andy, you know Reverend Edgars better than the rest of us. What do you think?"

"Do I believe his incredible story Mrs. President? Yes I do. Do I believe that he will go to war on Mohammad Baghai's pardon? Absolutely, he is a man of principle and he believes he is in the right. It is hard to defeat anyone with convictions."

"Jim, tell me what you know about the CIA protecting people inside the United States?"

"It's outside the CIA's charter Mrs. President. Such issues are under the domain of the FBI and the Justice Department. I will dig up what I can as soon as I leave here."

"Do that Jim; I want a call from you by 5 PM today with whatever you have. I am going to invite the CIA Director for a chat tomorrow. Something is not kosher here and I want to get to the bottom of this. Good day everyone."

Scarboro and Shephard left President Hays to her thoughts.

JIM Scarboro sat at his desk and dialed the direct number to the oval office. After two rings President Hays answered.

"Jim what did you find out?"

"Mrs. President, not a lot. I don't have access to any CIA databases to verify Reverend Edgars' story. I was, however, able to determine that what he said may be true."

"What do you mean?"

"Mrs. President, as you know witness protection is the responsibility of the Justice Department and the Attorney General. The CIA does not have that responsibility or authority, or at least it didn't."

"I'm listening"

"It seems that in 1972 President Nixon signed an executive order that allowed the CIA to provide witness protection in the way Reverend Edgars described. The executive order didn't raise much fan-fare but it may have allowed Jacob Rabin to live in this country on the tax payers' dime."

"So Mr. Jacob Rabin, in all likelihood, is living somewhere here and Reverend Edgars is telling us the truth?"

"It is a definite possibility Mrs. President."

"Okay, thanks Jim. You will call me when, and if, you uncover anything else that relates to this issue?"

"I certainly will Mrs. President."

Hays hung up the phone. It was obvious that there was more to this affair than she knew. She didn't like what she knew of it so far and her intuition and political instincts told her that she wouldn't like what she was about to find out.

THE Smith House, Dahlonega's and North Georgia's finest restaurant was located one block off of the Square in Dahlonega. Ralph and Jo Ann Twig, Heather and Charlie were dressed in coat and tie and evening gowns and enjoying a fine meal at Ralph's expense. Ralph, aided by a couple of stiff drinks, was in an expansive mood. Jo Ann and Heather, both non-drinkers, were intoxicated by the ambience of the dining room and by the company; Charlie was nursing a beer so Ralph wouldn't be the only adult consuming an adult beverage.

"So Charlie, I understand that you're looking for a job?" Ralph inquired.

"Actually, I already have a job Ralph. I'm looking for career."

"Good point." Ralph chuckled a little louder than decorum would dictate due to his inebriation.

"Since you're licensed to sell insurance I just happen to have a position available if you're interested?"

"Of course I'm interested Ralph. Did you think that I wasn't?"

"No, but I don't want you to have any false allusions about the job. We've discussed the matter before, but I want you to be certain of what you're getting into," Ralph continued.

"Ralph dear, you and Charlie can have that conversation tomorrow. Tonight we're here to enjoy each other's company and enjoy a good meal," Jo Ann interrupted. Though she was soft-spoken, it was obvious that her words carried plenty of weight in the Twig family.

"Of course, dear," Ralph knew that he'd already lost a battle that hadn't even been fought.

"Charlie, Heather tells me that you have to drive back down to Florida."

Jo Ann deftly changed direction of the conversation.

"Yes Ma'am." Charlie was still not comfortable addressing Heather's mother by her first name.

"I left Pensacola in a hurry and there are some loose threads that I need to tie up. Say good bye to some friends, close out bank accounts, collect old mail and that sort of thing. Oh, I also need to file an application to graduate, though that's a formality. I haven't decided if I want to participate in the graduation ceremony or not."

"How long will you be gone?"

"I'll probably be gone for four or five days. I don't have any family. I should be able to get everything wrapped up in a couple of days. I might spend a day or so selling life insurance to some friends of mine, that is, if I have a job."

Charlie flashed a smile at Ralph.

"Charlie, of course you will, won't he Dad?" Heather spoke for the first time as she squeezed Charlie's hand.

"I suppose I could find something for Charlie to do."

"Don't be a stick-in-the-mud Dad. You've said several times that a good insurance agent is worth his weight in gold."

"Heather I told your father that we are not going to discuss business while we're having dinner. That goes for you also," Jo Ann reminded her daughter.

"You're right Mom. Hey Dad, you mentioned before that you wanted to learn how to scuba dive. Charlie dives."

Yes, I have been kicking around the idea. Charlie is that true?"

"Yes Ralph, I learned how to dive a couple of years ago. I took a class as an elective in school. I haven't been to any of the exotic places that you may have read about though. The most interesting place that I've dived is the aircraft carrier USS Oriskany, which is sunk in the Gulf of Mexico outside of Pensacola Pass."

"Well maybe, for a graduation present, we can all take a vacation where you can do some diving Charlie," Jo Ann added.

"Mrs. Twig, I appreciate your offer, I really do, but that is not necessary," Charlie remarked.

"Nonsense young man, we haven't taken a real vacation with the whole family in several years. We certainly can afford to take one and you're welcome to come with us. You are the first boyfriend of Heather's that both Ralph and I approve of. That is just the reason Ralph needs to take lessons and I have no doubt that Heather will want to learn also."

Jo Ann leaned toward Charlie and pseudo-whispered, "in case you don't know she is a bit of a tom-boy."

"Mother," Heather said, pretending to be shocked and offended at her mother's comment, though she was not fooling anyone and she knew it.

"You don't want to learn Mrs. Twig?"

"Heavens no Charlie, I'll be perfectly happy to work on my tan, pool side."

"Great, that's more money that I am going to spend," Ralph added.

"Dad, you and I both know that you and Mom had saved the money for me to go to college and you and I both know that my scholarship hasn't forced you to spend any of it."

"Ralph, that will be enough from you," Jo Ann instructed her husband.

The server brought the meals to the table and that brought the discussion to an end.

PRESIDENT Hays was sitting at her desk when the CIA Director entered, with folders in hand.

"Sit down Al; I hope you have plenty to tell me."

Alan Reynolds, Hays' appointee to head the CIA, had the persona and physical appearance of a used car salesman: slicked-back hair, shifty eyes and an expanding midriff. His physical appearance was contrasted by his impeccable dress, an Armani suit and Bruno Magli shoes. Reynolds handed two identical folders to the President. He also had a third one, with material that was important but not urgent at present. It was going to require the President's attention at some point in time and Reynolds hoped to have a few minutes to discuss it with her after the examination and discussion of Mr. Jacob Rabin. Reynolds handed one of the files to Hays, containing the Rabin's dossier. Hays briefly scanned the document. A picture was attached. It showed a swarthy man with black wavy hair, but otherwise no other remarkable features. The document listed a chronology of significant dates in beginning with the time Rabin presented himself at CIA Headquarters to the day he died, four years ago.

"So this man was under government protection at one time?"

"That's correct Madam President. Jacob Rabin, on June 11, 1975, walked up to the guards at CIA Headquarters and turned himself in. Originally he requested political asylum but it was decided that by providing witness protection he could keep a much lower profile."

"He was debriefed for several weeks while arrangements were made for him to assume his new identity. It was a relatively easy task since he was single. We changed his name to 'Jake Robbins' and moved him to Texas. He provided a wealth of information about Israel's national security and intelligence. We consulted with him, off and on, through the years."

"How did he support himself?"

"We set him up as a postal carrier, and he was paid handsomely for his consulting. He died of natural causes four years ago."

"Did he marry or have children? This report doesn't indicate it."

"Never got married and he didn't have any children. Madam President, I realize that this is a sketchy report but I only had 24 hours to compile it. There may be more, and if there is, I'll report it to you, but for now this is all I have."

"Very well. Mohammad Baghai will appear in District Court in two days and enter a plea for his crimes. My sources tell me that he'll plead guilty. Undoubtedly the pressure to grant a pardon will begin to increase exponentially and I want all the data that relates to this matter before I publicly defend my position on the matter. Get back to me, one way or the other, in a week, will you?"

"I will Madam President. Now there's some business that needs to be discussed concerning Iran."

"You've got five more minutes Alan."

"Thank you for the time ma'am."

Reynolds handed the third file to Hays. In it were several satellite photographs and several pages of intelligence summary. It showed two semi-tractor-trailers on a desert highway.

"Madam President, these pictures were taken by satellite, over Iran, of what we believe to be truckloads of radioactive waste material. It is enough to make several hundred dirty bombs."

"We know this how Al?"

"We have assets on the ground confirming this."

"How reliable are these assets?"

"Nothing is one hundred percent certain in the intelligence business, as you know, but the data that they've supplied in the past has proved to be reliable."

"How were we able to get satellite photographs of mobile targets?" Hays asked.

Satellite photography was excellent for viewing permanent landmarks such as cities, mountain ranges, rivers and other geography. However, because the locations of geo-synchronous satellites, relative to fixed points on earth, were known to all in the intelligence community, mobile targets could easily be disguised, or moved to different locations, without being photographed from above.

"We know these trailers are capable of holding radioactive material by the design and measurements of the trailers. You'll notice how the construction of the trailer is significantly different from a typical trailer. Our assets told us what was being transported and the timetable for the move. We just happened to have a satellite passing by at the time."

"Is Nassiri behind this?" Hays was referring to Iranian Prime Minister Hassan Nassiri, a former Iranian general, who was well-connected to the religious community.

"Undoubtedly he is Madam President."

"Do we know his intentions?"

"We don't have any data but radioactive waste material is only good for one purpose, the construction of a dirty bomb."

"Is this all the intelligence we have Al?"

"Yes it is."

"How did they obtain this material? They don't have the reactor plants to make it themselves."

"Our best evidence is that it was purchased and transported from the former Soviet Union. I've included a summary of how we believe it was moved to Iran."

"Very well Al I'll read it tonight and get back with you on it."

"Thank you for your time Madam President."

MOHAMMAD sat beside Isabelle in the U.S. District Court Room. In a moment the judge would enter and he would plead to the charges against him. As he wished, Mohammad intended to plead guilty and accept his sentence. A sentencing date would then be set. Isabelle had briefed him on the public relations campaign for a pardon. It was quite extensive. An incredible amount of publicity had been generated between Isabelle's husband, David, Father Paul and the Reverend Casey Edgars, but he didn't care. Mohammad knew that, whatever God's plan was and however he fit into it, the plan would be fulfilled; no efforts by any man, whether in support or opposition, would change it.

"Mohammad you're only going to be charged with one crime. This is a tactic. The government is assuming that you'll plead innocent, even though I informed them that you would not. They're also assuming that if you're found not guilty, or if Mr. Gant doesn't like the sentence imposed, you can always be charged with the other murders."

"Very well, I understand Isabelle, my sister."

"All rise! This court is now in session. The honorable judge Stephen Cobb is presiding," the bailiff cried.

"Please be seated," Cobb said as he sat down.

"What do we have today?" Cobb asked rhetorically. Mohammad's case was the only one on the docket and the gallery was filled with the press.

"The United States Government versus Mohammad Baghai, one count of murder in the first degree," an echo came from one end of the bench.

"Are the parties ready to proceed?" The judge asked.

"John Gant for the United States your honor. We are ready."

"Isabelle Franks for Mr. Baghai your honor. We are ready. We will waive formal reading of the charge and are ready to enter a plea."

"Mr. Baghai, how do you plead?"

"I plead guilty your honor."

The five words created a deafening commotion in the court. The press had heard of the rumors that he intended to plead guilty, but no one really believed them. They'd assumed it was just some sort of legal maneuver.

"Order in the court; I want order in this court! If there is another outburst like that I'll have the bailiffs clear the court room."

Cobb pounded his gavel and the occupants quickly silenced themselves.

"Mr. Baghai, I assume your counsel has advised you, but I am required to ask. Do you understand that by pleading guilty, you are admitting to the crime of murder?"

"I do your honor."

Mohammad began to feel dizzy.

"You also understand that I can sentence you from twenty-five years in prison, at a minimum, to death by lethal injection?"

"I do your honor."

Mohammad had to steady himself by placing one hand on the table in front of him.

"Your counsel has advised you that once your plea of guilty is entered, you forfeit your right to appeal?"

Mohammad never got a chance to reply. He collapsed on the table in front of him.

"We need a doctor here NOW," Isabelle screamed as she grabbed her client by the back of his prison jump suit, preventing him from tumbling forward over the table.

An even greater chaos invaded the courtroom and the bailiffs, instead of clearing the chambers, attempted to aid the newly convicted murderer, Mohammad Baghai.

# Chapter 10

Isabelle, her husband and Father Paul were sitting in an uncomfortable, poorly-lit hospital waiting room, which smelled of disinfectant. Year-old magazines with tattered pages were littered the end tables. A custodian was vacuuming the worn carpet. There was miscellaneous chatter in the halls, the admitting office and in the triage area.

Isabelle had ridden in the ambulance with Mohammad, along with a FBI agent she hadn't met, and had called her husband and Father Paul on the way. Upon arrival, Mohammad was immediately rolled away, with the FBI agent a step behind. Isabelle was directed to the waiting room. The three had been waiting for almost an hour when the emergency room doctor came to see them.

"I'm Dr. Barry Shapiro, the ER doctor."

"What happened to him doctor?" Franks asked the question that the other two were going to ask.

"I was going to ask your wife the same question. He appears to be in a coma, but there's no reason for him to be in one. We did a CAT scan and can't find any injury to the brain. I asked his FBI guard if he had fallen, gotten sick or had anything else unusual happen to him while he was in prison, but he wasn't any help. So, Mrs. Franks, is there anything you can tell me about what happened earlier this morning?"

"No Doctor, he just keeled over the table in front of us, with no notice."

"There are two small wounds on each of his hands. I suppose he got those somehow when he collapsed, but they're nothing serious." Shapiro remarked to no one in particular.

"At any rate, a specialist is on the way in. Hopefully, he'll have answers to your questions."

Father Paul spoke for the first time. "Doctor, I'm a priest and Mohammad is Catholic. Do I need to administer the last rites to him?"

"No Father, Mohammad's condition is not life threatening."

"When can we see him? Isabelle asked."

"Not until he's examined by Dr. Wyngate, our expert on neurology. As I said, he's on the way in now."

"Thank you doctor," Franks remarked as Shapiro turned and left.

"We need to make a statement to the press. I have no doubt that the networks are broadcasting as we speak," Franks remarked to his wife.

"Good, I'm going to give them something to broadcast. Gentlemen, let's give an impromptu press conference, shall we?"

A few steps later, in front of the main entrance, Isabelle Franks began the press conference.

"Good afternoon ladies and gentlemen. I'm Isabelle Franks. I represent Mohammad Baghai. Most of you may already know my husband David."

Her last remark drew a few chuckles because David was one of their colleagues.

"To my left is Father Paul Stewart. We have a few comments to make."

"Earlier today, Mohammad Baghai pled guilty to one count of murder. Immediately after his plea, he collapsed on the table in front of me. He was rushed to this hospital and was examined by the emergency room doctor. He reported to us that Mohammad is in a coma; the cause and severity of which has not been determined. We understand that an expert will be examining him shortly. At this time, his condition is serious but not life threatening. Information will be made available, as it becomes available. We will now be happy to answer questions."

The questions came from all directions in rapid-fire fashion, but were the type to be expected and were easily answered.

After the press conference the group walked back to the waiting room, a nurse behind the counter waved to the three and motioned them to her.

"Dr. Wyngate just finished examining your client and was looking for you. Let me page him."

"Thank you very much," Franks replied.

A moment later, a man who could easily be mistaken for a NFL linebacker, appeared in a white, lightweight medical coat with "Dr. Wyngate" embroidered on it.

"Hello, I'm Glenn Wyngate."

"Hello Doctor, I'm David Franks, this is my wife Isabelle, Mohammad's attorney, and this is Father Paul Stewart."

"I have examined your client and the emergency room doctor was correct. He is in a coma; we're going to run some more tests to determine the severity. I'm going to make a statement to the press to that effect but I wanted to inform you first."

"Doctor, how did this happen?"

"Mrs. Franks, people suffer a coma for a number of reasons, the most common of which is head trauma; sometimes it's caused by severe alcohol intoxication."

"That's not the case here Doctor. My client has been incarcerated" Isabelle remarked.

"Yes, I'm familiar with your client's notoriety. We test for that to eliminate all possibilities. In this case diabetes appears to be the cause. We tested his blood sugar and it was off the scale."

"So how is Mohammad being treated?"

"Father, the diabetes is being treated with Lantis, a type of insulin. We'll have to tweak the amounts until we get the glucose levels under control, but that shouldn't be much of a problem. When and if he regains consciousness we may be able to treat him with oral medication instead of insulin. We'll have to see how that plays out. Unfortunately, there's not a lot that we can do about the coma. He could recover tomorrow, two weeks from tomorrow, two months from tomorrow or never. We'll just have to wait and see."

"When can we see him?"

"Father, he's being moved to intensive care. We'll keep him there for a few days and see if he recovers soon. If he doesn't then he'll need to be moved to a facility that can accommodate his needs. I don't think prison will be suitable. You can see him as soon as he's moved. Now if you'll excuse me, I must attend to my patients.

"Thank you Doctor," Isabelle replied.


CHARLIE and Heather were walking around the Square in Dahlonega, window shopping and killing time. It was a Friday afternoon and most of the student body was leaving campus for the weekend. Charlie was going to leave for Pensacola the next morning. Heather was beginning to miss him already, even though he hadn't left yet and he'd only be gone for a week.

"Charlie, what time are you leaving tomorrow?"

"I thought I'd get up at five and be on the road by six Heather."

"Have you packed?"

"No, but I don't have much to pack. I thought I'd do it in the morning."

Heather rolled her eyes.

"Mom and Dad want to say goodbye to you. If you leave from their house, you can save almost an hour drive time. If you're going to stay a week you can't just throw seven days of clothes in a suitcase in an hour. Come on, I'll help you. Besides I've never seen your room. You don't live far away."

As Charlie was driving with one hand, the other was draped around Heather's shoulder and holding her right hand. Heather squeezed it and made a decision.

"Charlie, where will you be staying?"

"I'll be at my fraternity house."

"Your fraternity house where all those sorority girls are running in and out?" Heather was speaking her to her boyfriend in a semi-serious vein.

Charlie pulled up to the house, opened the passenger door and flashed his lady-killer smile. He recognized that he was being tested and reacted instinctively.

"Heather, you ought to know I'm not interested in 'those sorority girls.' I'm interested in you and only you. Let's have this discussion inside." "All right Charlie."

Charlie unlocked the ornate mahogany door, which opened to a private entrance to Charlie's bedroom.

"Here we are. As you can see I don't have an elaborate ward-robe," Charlie said as he turned and opened his closet. He didn't notice that Heather was unbuttoning her sweater until he turned around.

"Don't look so surprised. My parents want to say good-bye to you and we can't do this at their house."

Heather finished unbuttoning her sweater and took it off. She was wearing a red Victoria Secret lace bra, which presented her bust in an appealing fashion. Charlie did a double take.

"Like what you see?"

"Heather, I didn't bring you here to get you into bed." Charlie was having difficulty choosing his words—a rare occurrence for him.

"I want you to have a vivid memory of me while you are in Pen-sacola, an incentive to hurry back. Now are you going to undress me or am I going have to do it myself?"

Charlie didn't need any further prompting.

DRIVING down Georgia 400, Heather was cuddling next to Charlie. His right arm was around Heather's shoulder. Charlie was correct in his assertion that he didn't have much to pack and, after he and Heather took a shower together, they packed his clothes in fifteen minutes. Both were lost in thought.

Charlie couldn't believe his good fortune. He knew that Heather would not have slept with him unless she was ready to do so—on her own terms and no one else's. She was as intelligent as he was, good looking, great personality and was truly interested in his inter-ests and desires. He couldn't believe his own thoughts, but Charlie thought he had found his life partner.

Heather broke the silence. "So you will call me when you get there?"

"Of course I will Heather."

"Will you still have you old room?"

Charlie laughed.

"My rent is paid until the end of the term, but knowing the lousy snakes I have for fraternity brothers, my room was probably taken over the day I left. It's not a problem though; I'll sleep in Chris's room."

"Who is he?"

"You remember him. Chris O'Callahan. He was on our paintball team."

"Yes, I do. He was the 'Hit Man'?"

"That's his nick-name. He might as well be my real brother, in addition to my fraternity brother. We are that close. He does have mean streak though."

"How is that Charlie?"

"We pledged at the same time and one night our pledge master took us out to a bar that served quarter beer. Needless to say we consumed several. We ran into some members of a rival fraternity and had some words. Chris got real pissed and later that night he shot marine type rescue flares at their fraternity house. He can be your best friend or your worst enemy. He and I hit it off, in part because he was adopted and I had an adopted brother."

"I didn't know that you were adopted, only that your mother and father are deceased."

Charlie's parents had died in a car crash after his brother died.

"I wasn't. My older brother was adopted before I was born. My family's a sensitive subject for me Heather, so can we talk about it another time? There's still plenty that you don't know about me, but you'll know everything before long. My brother John died while he was in the army. That's why I joined AAMO and I'm against the war."

"AAMO? What's that?" Heather wasn't aware of the anti-war organization.

"Americans Against Military Occupation. It was organized at UWF and has been investigated by the Department of Justice," Charlie said with pride in his voice.

"Let's not go there Charlie. That's something you and I will just have to agree to disagree on."

Heather, as one might expect, was as adamant in her beliefs on the war as Charlie was with his.

"You're right Heather I don't want to pick a fight. We're here."

Charlie pulled up into the Twig's driveway.

PULLING into the fraternity house Charlie saw several pledges, supervised by Chris, cleaning up the yard. A "pledge" to a fraternity is a probationary member who is considered for full membership by the regular fraternity brothers.

"What's up man? It's good to see you again Charlie!"

Chris gave his fraternity brother a bear hug.

"I had to come back to Pensacola to take care of some loose ends."

"Well, you came at the right time. We're having a mixer with the tri-alphs. I got the pledges cleaning up the yard. Hey, we got a keg already tapped. Let's go in and have a beer Charlie."

"Cool. I need to get my clothes." Charlie turned towards his car.

"Hold it! Charlie you have forgotten your place."

Chris turned to the closest pledge and motioned him over.

"Roy! This is Brother Charlie Michaels. Get his bag and put it in my room."

"Yes pledge master!"

"You're right Chris; I have forgotten how things are run around here."

"I think your room is occupied so you can crash in my room Charlie."

"Appreciate that Chris. Let's go have a beer."

Walking into the foyer, he spied a keg of beer on ice inside a 55-gallon drum cut in half, handles welded on either side. A sleeve full of plastic party cups was on a nearby table. Charlie grabbed two while Chris filled them.

"So why did you really come back Charlie?"

"I have to tie up some loose ends and, believe it or not, I'm now a licensed insurance agent in Georgia. I thought I'd announce it to the brothers at the next meeting and maybe sell a life insurance policy to the some of the seniors. If they don't have jobs yet they will soon and you're number one on my list O'Callahan." Charlie broke out one of his infectious grins.

"No shit! Actually Charlie, I may be interested. I've come into some money and might consider a life insurance policy."

"Really Chris, I didn't think anyone would leave you anything!"

"Ever hear of lostmoney.com?"

"No."

"It's a web-site that connects people who are benefactors of unclaimed cash, from wills, insurance policies, etcetera, to the companies or attorneys for a finder's fee. I stumbled on it by accident and it turns out that I have a long lost uncle who left me some money. I'm going to claim it next week."

"How much money are you talking about Chris?"

"Six figures man!"

"Kiss my ass! Are you shittin' me?"

"I'm for real Charlie."

"Damn! Well, Mr. Millionaire you can buy me a beer now and some insurance before I leave."

O'Callahan, a member of the nouveau riche, poured another beer for his friend. "Hey let's walk down to the dungeon. I got something to show you."

"Sure."

The dungeon was a huge basement that ran the whole length and width of the fraternity house. In it was assorted junk collected over the years, filing cabinets, holding records of the brotherhood, some video games and, at one end, a makeshift shooting range. A three-foot diameter bulls-eye, pocked-marked with small holes, was painted on three-quarter-inch plywood placed in front of a trap, much like what was used at shooting range. Chris picked up a modified paintball gun. It had a gun sight welded to the barrel. He handed it to his friend.

"Take a few shots. It has a rifled barrel."

Charlie squeezed off a few rounds, hitting the center of the bulls-eye each time.

"You didn't have any lead pellets Chris?"

"Sure but they'll tear up that plywood. You can see what a .22 rifle did." Chris was referring to the chips in the plywood.

"I'm going to have my gun modified like this one Chris. I want to try some shots in here also."

"We can go out any time. But tonight we have other, more important matters on the agenda!"

"You're right about that Chris. Let's go get another beer!"

IT was the middle of the night. Mohammad lay in his hospital bed in a state of limbo. In-between life and death, Mohammad's body suddenly shook violently. Alarms sounded as his body continued to shake, throwing the cover off his body. The ICU nurse and Ramsey held Mohammad down until the shaking ceased. After several more nurses and a doctor arrived, Ramsey took his cell phone out of his pocket and dialed Paul Stewart.

"Father Paul?"

"Yes?" Father Paul had obviously been asleep.

"This is Scott Ramsey, Mohammad's guard. I'm sorry to wake you but you need to come to the hospital right now. Mohammad just had a seizure."

"Is he all right?"

"I believe so, but that's not why I'm calling. I believe that I've just seen a miracle."

"I'll there in thirty minutes Scott."

# Chapter 11

The mixer between the Alpha Alpha Alpha sorority and the Delta Kappa Alpha fraternity was a wild party, even by DKA standards. Beer flowed freely. Virtually all the brotherhood, as well as most of the tri-alph sisterhood welcomed Charlie as if he was a long lost brother. Charlie was reveling in his newly-discovered celebrity status; he had more than one co-ed suggest that the two of them make an early departure from the party and adjourn to a near-by apartment.

Though Charlie was tempted he begged off. Charlie was nursing his second beer of the evening, while virtually everyone else was on their sixth or seventh. He always remained sober at fraternity parties, allowing his whit, charm and acumen to remain sharp while others' dulled as the evening's festivities wore on.

As the mixer was starting to shift into overdrive, Chris and four other brothers approached Charlie with menacing looks on their faces. Had it been anyone but Chris with that look Charlie would expect trouble, serious trouble. However, this was Chris, and he knew that everything would be all right.

"You need to come with us bro," Chris instructed his friend as the four other brothers surrounded Charlie.

"Sure. What's going on?"

The group walked upstairs to the chapter meeting room and the door was locked and bolted. The furniture in the room was arranged in a manner similar to that of a television courtroom, complete with a judge's podium and jury box, with a six-man jury already seated. Charlie immediately knew what was to happen. He was about to be to put on trial, a P. W. Trial. The initials P. W. stood for "pussy whipped." He had participated in over a half a dozen or so in his time as a Delta Kappa Alpha brother, as a juror and a prosecutor. The defendant was ALWAYS found guilty in a P. W. Trial.

Charlie was forcibly seated in the defendant's chair and he was and hand-cuffed, as a defendant in a real criminal case would be.

Chris assuming the role of the prosecutor, the most honored role of such a trial, began.

"Your Honor, members of the jury, Charlie Michaels, a beloved brother of the Delta Kappa Alpha Fraternity is accused of the high crime of allowing himself to be addicted to pussy. He is addicted to just one twat, a cunt belonging to one G. I. Jane of North Georgia

College."

"Charlie met her while he was participating in the paintball championships and less than a week later he moved up North Georgia because of his addiction. The prosecution will present evidence, in the form of bra and panties found in the defendant's suitcase, belonging to G. I. Jane. We will also present testimony from several tri-Alph sisters who propositioned, and were rebuffed, by Mr. Michaels, which is further evidence of his crime…"

Charlie began to crack a smile. The bra and panties were kept in the meeting room and were at least 10 years old. The sorority sisters' propositions were a new twist. The brothers would be shocked to know that if this trial had been held two days earlier that an innocent man would be convicted the crime. Though he would never admit to it, since he had to maintain his reputation! Following the script, Charlie would be shown the bra and panties and asked how he pled. The reply would be guilty and he would have to ask the court for mercy. The only real question would be his sentence. Though the judge would announce the sentence after "careful consideration," it had already been decided.

The judge, Kevin Black, sitting in his chair above the court, addressed Charlie.

"These are serious charges Mr. Michaels. Do you wish to see the evidence against you?"

"Yes, I would, your Honor" Charlie replied, following the script.

"Will the prosecution present the evidence?" Kevin asked Chris.

"Here it is your Honor."

Chris gave a cigar box to Kevin, who promptly opened it and examined the contents.

"Very convincing, show it to the defendant."

Chris took the box from Judge Kevin and handed it to Charlie, who promptly opened and took out a brand new matching set of ladies' undergarments.

"As you can see your Honor this is irrefutable proof that Mr. Michaels is pussy whipped by G. I. Jane."

Holding the set above his head and facing the jury, Chris shouted, "camouflaged underwear!"

The jury gasped then began a chant, "guilty, guilty, guilty!"

Kevin pounded his gavel. "Order in the court! Order in the court! Mr. Michaels, the evidence is overwhelming. How do you plead?"

Charlie stood up and spoke, "I plead guilty your Honor."

"Mr. Michaels, are you ready to be sentenced?"

"I am your Honor and I ask the court for mercy."

"What is the prosecution's position on sentencing?"

"The prosecution requests, no, I am sorry, DEMANDS the maximum sentence your Honor."

"I agree," Kevin replied.

"Charlie Michaels I sentence you to serve the rest of the evening at SAMMY'S, under the supervision of the brotherhood present. The sentence is to begin immediately. Court is adjourned."

Judge Kevin Black pounded the gavel and the participants filed out of the chapter room.

FATHER Paul met Agent Ramsey at the ICU ward and they exchanged handshakes. Ramsey had introduced himself to Paul and the Franks on a previous occaision. Paul looked like he'd just been awakened to call upon someone in need. Hair uncombed, in need of a shave and eyes bloodshot; he'd taken only enough time to get dressed and drive to the hospital. Ramsey gave Paul a cup of coffee.

"Here Father. It looks like you could use a cup. I didn't know how you like your coffee. Cream and sugar are over there."

Ramsey pointed to a table.

"Thanks. Black is fine," Paul said as he took a sip.

"So, Scott, what happened?"

"Mohammad had a severe seizure almost an hour ago. I'll call Isabelle and David Franks later this morning, when the sun comes up. There's no reason they need to be here right now."

"Is Mohammad all right now? And why did you call me, not Franks?"

"The doctors have him stabilized, but that's not why I called Father. While he was in the middle of his seizure, I helped the nurses keep him from falling off his bed; his bed sheet fell off, exposing his body. I saw something miraculous."

"I'm not following you Scott."

"Father let me show you."

The two walked to Mohammad's bed and Ramsey removed his cover. Mohammad appeared peaceful. He had bandages on each of his hands and feet. Paul lifted Mohammad's hands and carefully examined them. There was a trace of blood on each side of the bandage on each hand. He then looked at both of Mohammad's feet. Both were bandaged and both extremities had blood beginning to show through the gauze on the top and bottom of the feet.

Father Paul looked at the FBI agent, recognizing the sign from God.

"Mohammad will need a lot more security."

SAMMY'S GO GO was a typical stripper bar. It had three stages with a naked, buxom female dancer on each stage. The dancers wore a decorative elastic band around their upper thigh, which held that dancer's tip money. When the dancers weren't on stage, each would put on flimsy clothing and hustle more tips by having customers buy them over-priced drinks.

Most of the dancers were crowded around the DKA group. With his substantial financial windfall, Chris was buying his fraternity brothers drinks, and made sure Charlie was getting special attention in the form of table dances. At ten dollars per three-minute dance, each of the dancers was happy to oblige. At 1:30 in the morning, Chris pulled one of the prettiest aside, spoke to her for a minute and tipped her $20. About ten minutes before closing time, a group of dancers "kidnapped" Charlie, put him on the main stage and sat him down on a chair. The entire troop of dancers paraded in front of Charlie until closing, with everyone giving Charlie a lap dance and intimate hugs. After the conclusion of the set Charlie walked off the stage and gave Chris a hug.

"Thanks man! You and the guys are great," Charlie told his best friend.

"We're not done yet bud! I got two strippers accompanying us back to the house for a private show!"

"Which ones?"

"The one I was speaking to earlier and her roommate. Here they come now. Charlie this is Devine and Jasmine. Ladies, this is my best friend, Charlie. I know both of you are going to take special care of him." Chris said as he put an arm around the waist of dancers.

"Bro, you don't believe in sharing?"

Charlie grabbed the hand of a strawberry blonde dancer called Jasmine and looked straight into her eyes and flashed his lady-killer smile.

"Jasmine, I'm Charlie. Has anyone sober in here ever told you that you're beautiful?"

Jasmine averted her gaze. Charlie, even in the dim lighting, could tell that she was blushing.

"Ladies, shall we adjourn to the fraternity house?"

Chris, hand still around Devine's waist, began walking to the exit. Charlie, still holding hands with Jasmine, was right behind.

The party reassembled at the chapter meeting room. Chairs were arranged in a circle. Devine and Jasmine plied their craft to loud music and the raucous howls of the brotherhood. Several brothers actually got up and danced with the two naked dancers. As the man of the hour Charlie was required to dance several sets with Jasmine and Devine. After a set was finished, Charlie returned to his seat and Chris offered him a hand-rolled cigarette. After he'd taken a huge toke, Charlie knew that it wasn't made of tobacco or marijuana, but rather some "designer drug," undoubtedly paid with some of Chris's new money.

"What is this Chris?"

"It's hash man. I scored some Friday. Try it."

Charlie was in a delicate situation. He didn't want to offend his best friend but he had a firm, personal conviction not to do drugs. Chris knew this but assumed that the special occasion warranted an exception. Charlie immediately wondered if Chris had hired the dancers to more than just dance. Charlie was not going to have anything to do with that under ANY circumstances. Despite a night on the town, Charlie was committed to Heather. Charlie decided to side step the dilemma and passed the hash down to the next brother.

"Next time maybe, Chris. I got to take a leak." Charlie said as he got up and to go to the bathroom.

As dawn approached, the party wound down. A taxi was called for the dancers. Charlie and Chris crashed in Chris's bedroom. In addition to his regular bed, Chris had a love seat that folded out into a twin-sized bed, in which Charlie would sleep in during his stay.

"Thanks for everything Chris. You're great!"

"No problem bro. You want to take a couple of hits of hash before we crash?"

"I can't Chris. I have to take a drug screen test for my new job, when I get back and a negative result would really fuck things up for me. You understand." Charlie told the white lie to his best friend.

"Yeah, it sucks doesn't it?"

"Chris, I'm wiped out. I am going to bed and sleep for a week!"

"That's a great idea, good night Charlie." Chris said, though it was morning.


AT about the same time President Hays was meeting with her chief of staff, Isabelle and David Franks met Scott Ramsey.

"Thank you for calling us Scott." David said as he shook the FBI agent's hand.

"You are certainly welcome David."

"Can you tell us what happened?"

"Isabelle, about three this morning Mohammad started having seizures. I helped the nurse keep him from falling off the bed and that's when I noticed wounds on his hands and feet. In light of Mohammad's circumstances, I suspected that they were the mark of the stigmata and called Father Paul Stewart."

"Stigmata? I'm sorry; I never paid much attention in my catechism class."

"David, do you know who Padre Pio was dear?" Isabelle asked her husband.

"Padre Pio was a stigmatic," Ramsey interrupted.

"Anyway, a stigmatic bears the wounds of Jesus Christ. Mohammad has wounds on each of his hands and feet. Paul agreed that the wounds could be the stigmata and left to speak to the Cardinal. A stigmatic is a pious individual who, Catholic doctrine teaches, is marked with bloody wounds in the same areas of the body as Jesus Christ."

"Mohammad Baghai is not exactly what one would call a pious individual Scott." Franks remarked.

"Not when he was a Muslim, but he's a Christian now. I assume that his religious conversion is a reflection of a change in his moral compass. Besides, God makes such a decision. Who are we, mere mortals, to determine what is in a man's heart?"

"Scott, you seem extremely well-versed in this area?" Isabelle asked the FBI agent.

"My father was as devout as anyone I have known. He made me serve as an altar boy, catechism, Mass every Sunday, eat fish on Friday, you name it. He wasn't one to discuss his instructions either. Yes, I am knowledgeable, but it's because I had to be."

"Scott, thank you for calling us, I think my wife and I are going to have some breakfast, and then I have some research to do on stigmata. Would you care to join us?"

"Thank you David but I'm still on duty."

"Another time, then."

David and Isabelle Franks left the ICU, while Scott Ramsey said a silent prayer.

DAVID Franks was sitting in front of his computer, researching stigmata on the Internet. He was a little ashamed that he wasn't particularly knowledgeable on the subject of stigmata, though he was getting a quick education. He had copied and pasted numerous notes for his article: "Stigmata are bodily marks, sores, or sensations of pain in locations corresponding to the wounds of Jesus Christ. An individual bearing stigmata is referred to as a stigmatic…"

Most of the data was not going to be useful in the column Franks intended to write on Mohammad's condition; it was too technical. But, it was better to have too much data and pare it down, than not to have enough.

The doorbell rang. Franks was glad. Gathering information via the Internet was easy; deciphering it into usable data was something else entirely. He needed a break before he continued. Franks got up to answer the door.

"Hi Paul, I was just doing some research relating to our friend Mohammad's condition. You want to help?"

"No David, I have a favor to ask"

"Okay what is it?"

"After I baptized Mohammad, I spoke to the Cardinal about Mohammad's claims. He was interested, though non-committal. Today, after I saw Mohammad, I took pictures of his wounds and showed them to the Cardinal. He believes, as I do, that Mohammad may indeed have stigmatic wounds. The Cardinal also requested a recorded copy of Mohammad's story. I believe that the Catholic Church will back Mohammad's cause, but the Cardinal made it clear that the Church needs a copy."

"Paul the original recording is at Isabelle's office. I can have a duplicate made and delivered to you later today, or you can pick it up, if you prefer, provided that you can assure me it'll not be released without our approval. Can you give me that assurance Paul?"

"I can David and I'll personally pick it up if that is all right with you."

Franks picked up the phone and spoke to Isabelle.

"Okay, Paul, let's go pick up Mohammad's recording."

C.C. Frost, the White House Press Secretary, stood at a podium, in front of the White House Press Corps. "C.C." was her nickname, short for Cecilia; she was a native of Youngstown, Ohio and a graduate of Ohio State University. A brunette, standing only 5'2", she had an affable personality and, despite her diminutive stature, had an intimidating demeanor that could be turned on and off like a light switch.

An hour before she'd had a "face-to-face" with President Hays. The topic of the meeting was Mohammad Baghai. A one-on-one meeting between a President and press secretary was not uncommon; several topics were always covered. Today the first, last and only topic was the White House position, as it related to Mohammad Baghai's condition and legal status.

"I have a statement before I take questions," Frost began.

"Several days ago, al-Qaeda terrorist Mohammad Baghai pled guilty to murder in U.S. District Court. He collapsed from a diabetic coma immediately after doing so. This morning Mr. Baghai suffered a series of seizures; a complication from his coma."

"Mr. Baghai is scheduled to be sentenced in five weeks. There have been numerous communications from various sources concerning a pardon for him in light of his religious epiphany and the fact that he freely submitted himself to U.S. authorities."

"It is the White House's position not to interfere in the legal process as it runs its course. There is a procedure and application for a Presidential Pardon. An application has not been received, so it would be premature to comment on a pardon at this time. I am ready to answer any questions.

The questions were perfunctory and address with dispatch until the last one.

"So religious and political factions will not influence the President's decision?"

"As I said earlier, any pardon application, on behalf of anyone, would be considered solely upon its merits."

"Even in light of the fact that he has developed stigmatic wounds since his seizures this morning?"

Frost had been prepared for all the previous questions, but this one came out of the blue and she was not prepared to answer it. She gave an inadequate reply.

"No, not at all, The White House does not speculate on such matters. That will be all for today. Thank you very much."

Frost exited the press conference as dozens of questions bombarded her.

# Chapter 12

Reverend Edgars was standing in front of the podium, about to give his weekly sermon. He had learned of Mohammad Baghai's seizure late last night and immediately comprehended its significance. Today's sermon would be brief, impromptu and to the point. His prepared sermon would be tabled for another time.

"My brothers and sisters in Christ, I had a prepared sermon today but I'm not going to use it. I am going to speak to you extemporaneously. I have asked each and every one of you to pray for Mohammad Baghai. I have asked each and every one of you to pray to our Lord to grant President Hays the wisdom to pardon Mohammad Baghai. I have asked each and every one of you to contact the White House, to contact your Senators and Congressmen and express your desire for a pardon. I have said that God does not want Mohammad Baghai to spend his life in jail. I have said that God does not want Mohammad Baghai to die for his crimes. Despite the hundreds of thousands of letters, emails and phone calls President Hays has remained silent on the issue. Ladies and gentleman, my brothers and sisters in Christ, I am here to tell you today that God has not remained silent in regards to Mohammad Baghai's welfare. Last night God sent a message loud and clear to the world; that Mohammad is indeed his messenger."

Edgars paused for effect.

"Last night I got a phone call from my friend Cardinal Michael Mahoney. He told me that God had sent a sign expressing His desire for Mohammad to deliver His message. Let me say this in another way. God has said that He wants President Hays to use her power to pardon Mohammad, so Mohammad can do God's work."

"Some you may be aware that last night Mohammad Baghai, who was already in a diabetic coma, suffered a seizure. This was reported in the early morning news. I am told that he is all right, though his condition is unchanged. What was not reported is that God has made his prophet a stigmatic."

"A stigmatic is someone who possesses the sign of the stigmata. Many of you may not be familiar with the term so let me explain what the stigmata is."

"Stigmata is a holy phenomenon, usually associated with Catholics, but not always so, in which a pious individual is marked on his body with the crucifixion wounds of Jesus Christ. Mohammad has such bloody wounds on each of his hands and each of his feet. Priests under Cardinal Mahoney have confirmed this. These wounds are always generated spontaneously and never heal; though they never become infected. It has been reported in some cases that the wounds emit a sweet, perfume type of aroma."

"Skeptics will undoubtedly claim that someone inflicted these wounds on Mohammad. This is most definitely not the case! Mohammad was under the 24-hour supervision of an intensive care nurse and guarded by an FBI agent. Both were in the room the entire time. No one harmed God's Prophet. Time will also prove me correct when his wounds neither heal, nor become infected.

"Others may claim that Mohammad is not pious, so that he cannot be a stigmatic. I would like to remind you that Paul of the New Testament was not pious and, in fact, persecuted Christians before God called him to do his work. My point is that Paul and Mohammad were both sinners and God, in His infinite wisdom, called both to do His work and deliver His message."

"The first stigmatic known, in 1222, was the Catholic Saint Francis of Assisi in Great Britain and there have been hundreds since. One of the most famous and one of the most recent was Padre Pio."

"Padre Pio was born in Italy in 1887 and died in 1968. He bore the stigmatic wounds for over fifty years. On October 22, 1918 he wrote a letter to his spiritual advisor describing his stigmata. I would like to read this letter to you now. The letter was written to Padre Benedetto. I got this letter from the Internet. It is short but poignant."

Edgars took a letter from his coat.

"On the morning of the 20th of last month, in the choir, after I had celebrated Mass, I yielded to drowsiness similar to a sweet sleep. All the internal and external senses and even the very faculties of my soul were immersed in indescribable stillness. Absolute silence surrounded and invaded me. I was suddenly filled with great peace and abandonment, which effaced everything else and caused a lull in the turmoil. All this happened in a flash."

"While this was taking place, I saw before me a mysterious person similar to the one I had seen on the evening of August 5th. The only difference was that his hands and feet and side were dripping blood. The sight terrified me and what I felt at that moment is indescribable. I thought I should die and really should have died if the Lord had not intervened and strengthened my heart which was about to burst out of my chest."

"The vision disappeared and I became aware that my hands, feet and side were dripping blood. Imagine the agony I experienced and continue to experience almost every day. The heart wound bleeds continually, especially from Thursday evening until Saturday. Dear Father, I am dying of pain because of the wounds and the resulting embarrassment I feel in my soul. I am afraid I shall bleed to death if the Lord does not hear my heartfelt supplication to relieve me of this condition. Will Jesus, who is so good, grant me this grace? Will He at least free me from the embarrassment caused by these outward signs? I will raise my voice and will not stop imploring Him until in His mercy He takes away, not the wound or the pain, which is impossible since I wish to be inebriated with pain, but these outward signs which cause me such embarrassment and unbearable humiliation."

Edgars put the letter back in his coat. "Ladies and gentleman, do you see any parallels? Mohammad Baghai is in a 'sweet sleep'. He hasn't woken up yet but believe me, he will. I pray that he will be allowed to do God's work. I implore you pray. President Hays must pardon him. I encourage all of you to continue to contact all your elected officials. Demand that they communicate to the President your desires to have Mohammad pardoned. Continue to pray to our Lord to soften the President's heart. Let us all offer a prayer now..."

CHARLIE spent most of Sunday recovering from the festivities of Saturday night. It was after two in the afternoon before he rose from bed. After taking a shower and getting something to eat, he checked his cell phone and saw that he'd missed a call from Heather. She'd left a voice mail that she was upset he didn't call her when he got to Pensacola yesterday.

Charlie called and apologized explaining that he really hadn't had a chance to call her since the DKA brothers had a big party that night, that he'd behaved himself, and that he'd been up most of the night. It was a white lie but though Charlie may not have "followed the letter of the law," he did follow the spirit of it. Today he was going to take it easy, hang out at the fraternity house, watch sports on TV and he told Heather that he'd call her again later that evening.

After appeasing Heather, he made a phone call to a local scuba diving shop and made a reservation on a dive boat. Charlie intended to dive the aircraft carrier Oriskany, the world's largest artificial reef, at least once more before he moved permanently to Georgia. Though there were other locations to dive in the Pensacola area, the "Mighty O," was the most famous and attracted divers from around the world.

Charlie was lucky. There happened to be a trip scheduled the next morning. Charlie had a complete set of diving gear in storage he'd get later that day. All he needed was two scuba tanks, which the dive shop would provide. Divers, even with complete sets of gear, generally chose not to purchase tanks; they were easy enough to rent from any local dive shop.

Monday morning, Charlie got up at 5:00 a.m. in order to be at the Scuba Shack, Pensacola's best dive shop, by six. Gene Fredrickson, a scuba diving instructor, had owned the Scuba Shack since the early 1980's, after he left another dive shop. Fredrickson no longer instructed classes, he now hired others to do that, but he still personally took out virtually every dive charter on his boat the WET DREAM, which was docked directly behind his place of business on South Palafox Street.

After parking his car, Charlie grabbed his cooler and dive bag, an extra large, heavy-duty, nylon bag, containing all his equipment and walked to the counter to pay for his trip. After signing his credit card receipt he rolled his gear bag to the dock, boarded the boat and assembled his gear and after finishing his task Charlie looked at his watch and saw that it was only 6:15; the charter wasn't scheduled to leave until 7:00. At that same moment a linebacker-sized black man, obviously going diving also, made eye contact with Charlie.

"Excuse me. Are you from around here? Is there a McDonald's or someplace around here to pick up some breakfast? My name is Ron Thomas by the way."

He offered his hand to Charlie to shake.

Charlie took his hand, shook furiously and flashed his smile.

"Hi, I'm Charlie Michaels. I don't live here now, but I used to. Yeah, there is a McDonald's close. I was just thinking about some food also."

"Great! I'll drive if you navigate Charlie"

"Deal."

Ron drove a late model Ford Mustang Cobra with an automatic transmission, though he didn't drive it as if it was a muscle car. He opened up the console and took a CD and put it in the player. Charlie noticed what looked a like a badge before he closed the lid and assumed that he was a cop.

"So Charlie, you said you used to live here? Where are you living now?" Ron asked Charlie, just to make conversation.

"I live in Dahlonega, Georgia."

"Where's that?"

"It's about 60 miles north of Atlanta. I went to school here in Pensacola at UWF. I have a job that I'm starting, in Dahlonega, and I'm down here to move my things."

Ron pulled up to the drive-thru.

"What are you having Charlie? I'm buying."

"Thanks, I'll have an Egg McMuffin."

"Two Egg McMuffin combos," Ron spoke into the speaker.

Charlie and Ron both ate their sandwiches on the drive back and didn't converse much. After Ron parked his car at The Shack he bought a USA Today newspaper. It had the following headline: TER-RORIST STILL IN COMA BLESSED OR CURSED BY GOD? Charlie glanced at the headline for a moment, but didn't give it a second notice.

"Something to read during the trip," Ron remarked to Charlie.

"Okay Ron, I'll see you on the boat. Hey look, you want to buddy up when it's time to get wet?"

Charlie was using scuba diving slang. Translated, Charlie asked his acquaintance if he wanted to dive together when the time to came to enter the water.

"Sure."

The WET DREAM left the South Palafox Street dock promptly at 7 a.m. The charter boat would have to navigate southwest through Pensacola Bay to the Pensacola Pass, then turn southeast to the air-craft carrier/artificial reef. The trip normally took just over two hours. Once at the correct spot, a deck hand would dive down to the super structure of the Oriskany, which was 70 feet deep, and chain the an-chor line to a secure anchoring point. During this time the divers would don their wet suits and gear for the first of two dives. Some-times the water in the Gulf of Mexico was choppy and some days, like this one, the Gulf was smooth. Charlie struck up a conversation with Ron who was glancing at the morning's sports section.

"So Ron, I noticed the badge in your console, but I didn't get a chance to ask you what you did for a living."

"I'm in the Secret Service."

"Oh really, you look like you should be playing football to me."

"I did play linebacker for Florida, but I tore up my knee my se-nior year. After my surgery and rehabilitation, I went to the NFL combine and worked out, but my speed wasn't what it needed to be and I wasn't drafted. Anyway, I was a criminal justice major so I ap-plied to the Secret Service and here I am."

"What do you do for the Secret Service?"

"I'm assigned to the White House detail. I guard the President."

"No shit! How long have you been doing that Ron?"

"It's been a little over a year now."

"So you've been in the Oval Office, aboard Air Force One and so forth?"

"Yep."

"Do you listen to her conversations with others? Get inside her head, know what she is thinking?"

"Sometimes, I do but not nearly as often as you might think. It's not my job to express my personal views to her. It's my job to protect her; jump in-between her and a bullet, if necessary."

"What's her plan for exiting the Iraq?"

Ron chuckled.

"If I told you, I'd have to kill you."

"Ah come on."

Charlie could tell that his new friend was only kidding.

"Actually, she wants to withdraw from Iraq quicker than you might think but she's not prepared to leave Iraq in chaos and probable civil war, which would happen if our forces were withdrawn now."

Ron flipped the paper to the front page and pointed to the headline.

"Actually Charlie, this Mohammad Baghai business has required most of her attention lately. There's tremendous pressure from the religious right to pardon Baghai, while the Iranians, hell all Muslims, want him dead. President Hays, as the head of the government, wants to enforce and follow the laws of the country. That's her constitutional duty. Have you paid any attention to this issue at all Charlie?"

"Not really."

Charlie didn't like having his opinions on the Iraqi situation challenged. Even though some of what Ron said made sense, he still didn't agree with him, and his ego had been deflated slightly.

"Anyway the captain just announced to start getting ready. Are you ready to get wet?"

"You bet. Ron, the flight deck here is at 120 feet. That gives us fifteen minutes no decomp bottom time with a two hour and twenty-nine minute surface interval. If we go 80 feet on the second dive we'll have 22 minutes bottom time. Now, those figures are from the charts; I have a computer so the times will vary a little. Are you okay with that plan?"

Ron, seeing that Charlie clearly knew his business, was happy to follow lead.

"Sure."

The diving conditions were nearly perfect. Charlie and Ron jumped into the dead calm waters of the Gulf of Mexico. Visibility was at least 60 feet, and Charlie could see the outlines of the super structure when he and Ron entered the water.

Descending down the anchor line, Charlie and Ron stopped

their descent at 75 feet by releasing just enough air, from their tanks to their BC's, to keep from sinking or rising. The effect was that they were both suspended as if floating in space. They marveled at the immensity of the super structure. Barnacles encrusted the entire surface of the aircraft carrier. Schools of fish swam all around its 60-foot height. Barracuda, nature's equivalent to a torpedo, could be seen in the distance patrolling for a meal. Someone could spend 10 dives exploring all the hatches and compartments of the steel tower alone.

The 900-foot flight deck, also covered with barnacles, was clearly visible about 50 feet below. Charlie motioned Ron to follow him down. There were numerous compartments to explore though it was not likely that they ever would. 120 feet was about the maximum safe depth for a recreational dive and 15 minutes was not enough time to explore anything. Charlie took a small waterproof dive light and shined it in the nearest hatch. He motioned Ron over. Inside was a large grouper. Charlie estimated it was at least 200 pounds. Grouper was an excellent fish to eat, but this one didn't show the slightest concern with Charlie and Ron's intrusion.

Looking at the timer on his computer, Charlie saw that it was time return to the surface and gave Ron a "thumbs up" sign. The two slowly rose along the super structure to the anchor line and then to the surface, pausing at 60 feet for one minute, to allow some of the nitrogen gas to purge. The two divers, after that aquatic pit stop, ascended the last 60 feet following the anchor line to the boat and were helped aboard by a deckhand.

Divers confined on a boat will eat; drink plenty of fluids, read, nap or chat with other to pass the time. Charlie, as a result of his trip, the all-night party Saturday and his early rise this morning, decided to take a nap.

After the required time in between dives Captain Gene announced to everyone that it was time to go diving. Charlie, up from a good hour and a half nap felt revitalized, exchanged his empty tank with a full one and put on his gear. He and Ron stepped off the charter boat, feet first, and descended down the anchor line. As planned, the two stayed at the eighty-foot depth and explored the super structure, as did most of the other divers.

There were compartments, hatches, nooks and crannies all around. Divers did not penetrate any rooms beyond; specialized training for diving shipwrecks was required for that, but Charlie did have a waterproof, pressurized flashlight and he and Ron could use it to explore the darker areas of interest.

The bridge of the ship had the window panels removed, leaving several large openings for the divers to maneuver through. Charlie and Ron did so, entering a compartment measuring approximately 15 by 50 feet. Though all the hardware and instrumentation had been removed, Charlie imagined the ship's captain, sitting in his captain's chair, giving orders to the men on the bridge. The Oriskany was obsolete years before it had been decommissioned. It was retired from the fleet and sunk at its present location, and Charlie was amazed at what an incredible piece of machinery an aircraft carrier truly was.

Charlie was brought back to reality by a tap on his shoulder. Turning around he saw Ron give him the most serious sign a diver can give to another. Drawing a flat hand across one's throat, while underwater was a universal sign that you could not breathe.

Charlie's regulator, like most, had two second stages and he gave this second, "octopus," stage to Ron and firmly grabbed him by the arm.

After Ron drew a couple of breaths, Charlie motioned for the two to ascend. Both squeezed through the window panel of the bridge, found the anchor line and ascended. Several minutes later they were on the surface and the danger averted.

"Thanks man, you saved my ass down there," Ron exclaimed.

"What happened Ron?"

"I don't know. One minute everything was fine and the next I couldn't breathe."

"We'll take a look at your equipment when we get on board."

"Okay."

After the two climbed aboard and removed their equipment, Charlie examined Ron's tank and regulator. His pressure gauge showed that he had plenty of air in the tank. That meant that the regulator was the problem.

"Ron, let me take a wild guess. You bought most of your gear used?"

"Yes."

"You bought your regulator on eBay, or some other website, right?"

"Uh-huh. eBay, I got a great deal on all of my stuff."

"But you didn't have your regulator serviced when you got it though."

Charlie didn't ask a question, but made a statement of fact.

"I didn't think about it Charlie."

"There's no telling how long it's been since your regulator has been serviced. It has got o-rings, silicone diaphragms and various stainless steel parts that wear out. That's your problem."

Charlie was pleased and felt vindicated, from earlier in the day, that his knowledge of scuba diving trumped Ron's.

"In any case, thanks a lot. I owe you one."

Ron shook Charlie's hand with his right hand and gave him a bear hug with his left at the same time.

"No problem man. You would have done the same for me, I'm sure."

Ron had a twelve pack on ice as well as sub-sandwich. After dismantling his equipment and storing it into his bag, Ron walked over to Charlie, with a beer in each hand.

"Want a beer Charlie?"

"Sure. Thanks."

Ron handed him a can of Budweiser.

"Tell me something, you just out of college right?"

Charlie popped the can and took a swig.

"Actually, I graduate this term and the only classes that I have left I'm taking online. I have a job in Georgia and I'm down here to move my things up to my new home."

"It may not be any of my business, but all of your equipment appears to be brand new. How does a poor college student afford all this?"

Charlie laughed laughter of anguish. His eyes began well with tears. Ron could see that he had just struck a sensitive area.

"I'm sorry if that subject is off limits Charlie. I didn't know."

Charlie wiped away the moisture from his eyes.

"No, it's not a problem Ron. It's a subject that I rarely discuss. Growing up, I had a brother who died in Iraq in combat. Several years later both my parents died in a car accident. A truck driver fell asleep at the wheel and hit them head on. I don't have any other family. Between the life insurance and the court settlement, I did well financially. I also have my parents' house that I am going to put on the market. Anyway, scuba diving was an elective in college. I took it and liked it and I had a few dollars to buy new gear."

"I am sorry to hear about your family Charlie."

"Hey, you didn't know." Charlie regained his composure quickly.

"You can understand my interest in America's presence in Iraq. I truly believe that we really don't have any business there and I know that my brother would be alive now if America's military was never there to begin with."

"Yes I do Charlie, but you're simplifying a complex issue. America has been in Iraq, and other parts of the Middle East, for legitimate reasons. You're an intelligent man and I'm not going to rehash them. If the voting population doesn't like the policies of the government, then it elects representatives to change that policy. Your generation has traditionally bitched about issues, but historically they never show up to vote each election. Get political if you want to change things."

"I have Ron. Have you heard of AAMO?"

"Yes I have, Americans Against Military Occupation. They have a web site and have popped up on our radar screen. Are you a member?"

"Yes I am. Not only do we have a web site; we've been investigated by the Attorney General. Why is the Secret Service concerned with a college organization?"

"You are being disingenuous Charlie. AAMO is a multi-campus college organization that has suggested acts of civil disobedience to publicize its cause. The Secret Service evaluates all possible threats against the President and takes all legitimate ones very seriously. Even to the point of detaining anyone perceived as a threat to the President, while she is in the area."

"Do you perceive me as a presidential threat Ron?"

Charlie wasn't sure of the direction the conversation was taking.

"Are you?" Ron asked in a serious tone before his face broke into a broad smile.

"No, Charlie, AAMO is really small potatoes compared to, say protecting President Hays at the opening ceremonies at the Chicago Olympics. You can't imagine having to plan to safeguard someone against 80,000 potential killers in the stadium. That's going to be a huge nightmare."

"You're going to be there Ron?"

"That's what I'm paid to do."

"Maybe I'll see you on TV. Hey, can I have your email address? I'd really like to stay in touch with you, if you don't mind."

"Sure, it's on my business card." Ron took a card from his wallet.

"Thanks Ron. It's been great meeting you but right now I am going to take another nap."

Charlie found a spot to lie down and closed his eyes.

CASEY Edgars opened his eyes. Before going to sleep he had been contemplating his sermon from this morning. He knew that his position concerning Mohammad Baghai was correct but his message was not being communicated effectively enough. How could anyone dispute God's will? The facts were obvious. He also knew that the measures that he had taken thus far had not been effective. What else could be done to make the President see the error in her ways?

Before retiring he prayed for God's guidance. His sleep was not a restful sleep. In his dreams, Edgars continued to go over the issue over and over again. What more could he done to aid Mohammad Baghai? Finally it came to him! It was so simple. The simplest plans were always the best. Tomorrow he would contact the appropriate people and God's will would be done.

# Chapter 13

Iranian Prime Minister Hassan Nassiri sat in a studio, about to make an address to the citizens on the Iranian National Radio Network, in the government offices, in Tehran. A former Iranian Army General, Nassiri still held virtually all the power of his former position and frequently exercised it. Though his title was prime minister and he, in theory, was accountable to the voting population, in practice his position was much more like that of Hitler; firmly embedded in power and unlikely to be removed, except by a coup. Hassan had no intention of letting a coup happen.

Though he had no compunction about achieving his goals through intimidation and brute force, Nassiri would first try persuasion, reason, salesmanship or cajoling. In American vernacular, he would use the carrot and stick approach to achieve his political goals. The carrots were usually tasty and he made sure that everyone knew how big a stick he carried.

Nassiri was well connected to the Islamic religious community, having married the daughter of a prominent and respected ayatollah. As a junior officer in the Iranian army he was able to survive the purges, shortly after the downfall of the Shah and the ascension of Ayatollah Khomeini in 1979, by having his father-in-law vouch for him.

With most of the senior officers deposed, Nassiri rose quickly in rank, using his religious connections to allow him to pick the most prestigious assignments. Through these assignments he was able to establish a network of military and political contacts for future reference, while still remaining in the good graces of the religious faction of the Iranian population, thanks to his father-in-law.

His religious fervor was an act, of course; just a means to an end. When he felt that his wife had accelerated his career as far as possible, Nassiri had her murdered. He arranged to have her assassinated by poison that didn't leave a trace. A willing subordinate accidentally tripped in front of the two, while they were purchasing groceries from a vendor, and brushed against her injecting her with a lethal dose. After apologizing profusely, and begging forgiveness for the affront, the assassin was forgiven and went on his way. Two hours later his wife was dead. Nassiri gained immeasurable popularity in the news by accepting Allah's will, while grieving for the viewing Iranian public.

Nassiri didn't care about Islam or the 23 or 72 virgins, he couldn't remember how many, that awaited him in Paradise. He did care about power and the perks that went with it. On the numerous occasions when his assignment required him to fly out of the country, Nassiri exercised his power, always making sure there were plenty of young virgins for him to deflower, in various sadistic ways, during the flight. Afterwards, the young women were sold into slavery. Wealthy Japanese businessmen were always eager clients.

Nassiri made periodic speeches on the radio, as often as his political sense told him it was necessary. This time his political sense rang alarm bells in his head. Every politician, as a matter of necessity, had to make alliances with different factions. New alliances often alienated older ones. A recently alienated alliance was with the religious faction. Mohammad Baghai was a stroke of luck that would happen once in a lifetime. By rejecting Islam, Baghai had made himself an object of scorn for every Muslim in the world. Nassiri would use his bully pulpit to denounce him, claiming Allah was exacting his revenge on Baghai. The religious zealots would be appeased and brought back into his camp. Chuckling to himself, he realized that zealots of any type were easy to manipulate, if you knew which buttons to push. Nassiri enjoyed pushing psychological buttons almost as much as exercising his power.

"My brothers and sisters, in service to Allah, I speak to you today, not as your Prime Minister, but as a fellow believer in Allah and the Prophet Muhammad. I am speaking of the Persian Traitor of Islam, Mohammad Baghai. Some of you may know him as an Iranian from Kerman, who was fighting with our fellow Muslim brothers of al-Qaeda, but rejected his faith and now lies near death, struck down by Allah."

"For my brothers and sisters who are not familiar with him, or his dastardly deeds, let me discuss the subject for a moment. Mohammad Baghai is the only son of Mansur Baghai, a prominent member of Shah Pahlavi's secret police SAVAK He served as SAVAK's chief in the decadent United States of America. America was where he received his education at an American University. An education intertwined with drugs. An education fused with pornography, an education ignoring Allah. It is an education ignoring the teachings of Allah's Prophet Muhammad." Nassiri was embellishing but no one would know otherwise.

"Later Baghai returned to Iran and learned the error of his evil ways. He became devout in his faith and even joined his Muslim brothers in Afghanistan; later fighting the American devils in Iraq. I say devils because America and its evil, imperialistic Presidents have had a long history of war with Muslims. Reagan invaded Libyan air space with naval airplanes and shot down planes of the Libyan Air Force, defending their country. The first Bush, without just cause and under false pretext, invaded Iraq. Under Clinton, the United States Air Force attacked numerous civilian targets in Serbia, killing hundreds of people. The second Bush attacked Iraq again with even fewer pretexts than his father. Carter and the American Marines were defeated by Allah's power before they attacked, here in our beloved country. Now Hays, perhaps Islam's greatest enemy has maintained the American Army in Iraq, when it is clear that it is neither wanted nor needed."

"America has a long history of imperialism against infidel countries also. After a war with Spain, the United States assumed control of Cuba and the Philippines. After World War II, America occupied Germany and they still haven't left! A student of history can discuss American imperialism in Korea and Vietnam. Do I need to continue?" Nassiri continued to play fast and loose with the truth but the majority of the population didn't know and those who did dared not challenge him on the facts."

"Brave Muslims have stood against evil America. They have been in our prayers each and every day. Now Allah has answered our prayers! Mohammad Baghai had denounced Allah and Islam and Allah has struck him down! Hays, the she-devil who has waged an imperialistic war against Muslims around the world, will also be struck down! Allah will strike a blow against evil Americans, a blow greater than any in history is coming. America will be brought to her knees; the American Army will be ousted from, not only Iraq, but the entire Middle East…"

"I'VE heard enough Tom."

Vice President turned off the digital recorder. President Hays' gang of three, Taylor, Shephard and Scarboro were in the O.

"This minor domestic law enforcement issue has taken international implications and is rapidly spinning out of control. Our allies are beginning to suggest that I pardon this man."

"This idiot wants to speak at the United Nations General Assembly. What in the hell is going on? And why haven't we found out more about this Jacob Rabin? I know he fits into this puzzle somehow. And what is this stigmata business?"

Shephard passed a manila file folder to each member of the group.

"Madam President, I have the latest from the CIA. The majority is just a rehash of what we already know. The short version of the additional data is that Rabin did not have a wife or family in Israel, nor did he get married here in the States. He did, however, have a long-term relationship with a woman, a Kathleen Mueller, and she had a son, Jacob Mueller."

"Is Rabin the father?" Hays asked.

"The birth certificate, a copy is in each of the files, doesn't list a father, though we assume that he is."

"Why is that?" Scarboro asked.

"Common sense would dictate that he is considering the circumstances."

Taylor groaned and rolled his eyes.

"I know. I know," Shephard said defensively.

"There's more. The CIA has not found a single photograph of the boy. The CIA is walking on thin ice because the FBI normally does domestic investigations. Something may very well turn up, but we have not found one high school year book photo, not one newspaper clipping. Nothing at all, we don't know what he looks like. Rabin was Mossad, and knew a little about making someone disappear; after college at the University of Texas, he did just that. Do the math and it adds up."

"Do we know this lady's address Andy?"

"Yes, we do, Mrs. President."

"Jim, I want the FBI to interview her tomorrow. I want to know what the story is on this Jacob Rabin. Brief the agents personally via telephone and instruct them that they are to use the soft touch on this woman. Take care of it."

"Yes Mrs. President."

"Now Andy, can you tell me about stigmata and how it relates to Mohammad Baghai?"

"Mohammad, after a seizure, spontaneously developed bloody wounds on his hands and feet, similar to the Biblical wounds of Jesus Christ. The Catholic faith calls these wounds stigmata and someone possessing the wounds, a stigmatic. The wounds are considered holy and are permanent, inflicted upon a pious individual by God. They do not heal but never get infected. Some stigmatics have been known to have extraordinary abilities, such as the ability to cure diseases, some even have the ability to predict the future."

"So our friend in a coma can heal the sick but he can't cure himself?" Taylor asked rhetorically.

"Still dead set against Baghai Tom?"

"Damn straight I am Jim. That man has too much American blood on his hands. Put him in front of a firing squad for his crimes and I want to be the one with a rifle." Taylor replied.

"You're not seriously considering a pardon for him, Mrs. President, are you?"

Sensing that the Vice President was letting his emotions get the better of him, Hays interjected.

"Tom, it has always been my position that I will not consider a pardon for Mohammad Baghai unless, and until, the legal process is completed. A good politician will never, say never, but I'm not inclined to pardon him. C.C. has stated my position on the issue. Should he get the death sentence I may be agreeable to commuting it to life. Tom, you may not like my position but I expect you to support it. Understand?"

"Yes, I do, Mrs. President." Taylor, the soldier, always obeyed a direct order.

"Tom, I've decided that I am not going to Chicago for the Opening Ceremony of the Olympics. I want you to substitute for me. I have a feeling that this situation is going to get worse and I want to stay here. Andy has the tentative agenda and will give it to your staff to finalize the arrangements."

"Very well Mrs. President."

"Jim, I want Mrs. Mueller interviewed tomorrow morning, and want a report tomorrow afternoon, and Jacob Mueller located the next day. Clear?"

"Yes Mrs. President."

"Good. Now if you all will excuse me I have another meeting in less than five minutes."

The meeting was adjourned.

PRESENTLY, Mohammad, in his heightened state, was reviewing one of his earliest major sins. His seven murders of American soldiers were well known and documented, though he had committed one other murder much earlier in Iran, which was unknown.

As a law student in Iran, Mohammad was visiting his father's hometown in Kerman City. He had no real reason for being there except to see the city and province of his family. He stayed at a local inn, a modest motel by western standards but very lavish compared to the area. Mohammad was from a family of means and stood out in a poor province of Iran. Also, because of his family's means, Mohammad was allowed, and could afford, to carry a small pistol. After praying at the Mosque he went to a local coffee shop and sat down to sample a cup of the local flavor and have a small afternoon meal. Mohammad knew that he was being spied on by all of the locals but he didn't care. After his meal it was time for the Zuhr, the afternoon prayer. Walking back to his room Mohammad found an employee, an old man, in his room stealing Mohammad's money that he left in there. Taking his sidearm Mohammad held the man at bay until the authorities arrived.

Mohammad enraged that such a crime was perpetrated upon him, insisted on immediate justice and because his family still had quite a bit of clout, he got it. The old man was taken to the town square for a show trial and punishment. He freely admitted his crime saying that he was taking money to buy food to feed his large family and begged forgiveness. Mohammad did not accept the man's explanation and ordered the "four spikes" as punishment. The old man was stripped to the waist and tied face-down, spread-eagle to four stakes or spikes. The punishment was to be 100 blows from a bundle of pomegranate branches, soaked in water. The branches were pliant and administered pain similar to a cat-o-nine tails.

The old man was slight in build and begged forgiveness after every blow. After awhile the man's wife rushed out of the crowd and tried to cover her husband. After she was restrained, the beating continued. The wife freed herself from her captors and knelt before Mohammad, kissing his feet, begging for mercy.

"Please sir! My family is starving. My husband was only taking money to feed us! Have mercy on him!"

"Away from me woman or I will have you tied to the stakes and punished also!"

At first the man shrieked after each blow, blood began to ooze from the wounds, then the shrieks became moans and finally only the sound of silence could be heard between each blow. After the 100 blows were completed, Mohammad ordered the man untied. He was dead.

Mohammad did not understand why God was making him remember his sins. He had confessed them and knew that he was forgiven. Perhaps it was because Mohammad knew that others wanted him dead as he had wanted the old man dead. It didn't matter though. Mohammad wanted to spread God's message, but he would gladly submit to whatever God's plan was. God's will would eventually be done!

KATHLEEN Mueller was sipping her morning coffee in her kitchen of her suburban Houston home, when the doorbell rang. An elegant woman, about 5'6" tall, with more gray hair than brown, she lived comfortably from Jacob Rabin's estate. She was a religious woman, and attended mass regularly. Quite a contradiction, considering that she'd never married the man whose son she'd had. It did not matter though. Jacob explained why he could not marry her. After many hours of prayer, she accepted the reality that she was just a small part in God's plan.

Getting up, she answered her door. A man and a woman, appearing to be in their late thirties and late twenties respectively, were holding badges for viewing.

"Kathleen Mueller?" The man asked the question, obviously knowing the answer.

"Yes, I am."

"I'm Agent Larry Giles. This is Agent Dana Fox. We're from the FBI. Can we ask you some questions?"

"Of course, I was just having a cup of coffee. Would the two of you come in and join me?"

"Yes, thank you ma'am," Fox replied.

Mueller escorted the two FBI agents to her parlor, invited them to sit and came back with a serving tray, holding a ceramic pot, three cups and cream and sugar. She poured coffee for her guests and, after a sip, initiated the discussion.

"So Mr. Giles, what can I do for you?"

"Agent Fox and I are here to ask you a few questions about your husband and your son."

"I was never married to Jacob, Mr. Giles."

"I misspoke ma'am." Giles apologized.

"What do you care to know? Since you're here, I'm guessing that you're interested in my son?"

"Yes ma'am, you're correct, we are trying to locate your son. Is that a picture of him?" Fox interjected.

"I appreciated your candor Miss Fox. Yes it is."

Mueller reached over to an end table, picked up a picture of her son and gave it to Dana Fox. The picture showed a dark-haired, swarthy young man with a pearl-white smile.

"It was taken a couple of years ago. He is about your age Miss Fox. What do you want to know about my family?"

"Initially we were attempting to locate your husband before we found out that he passed away. Now we're interested in speaking with you and your son."

"Well, I'm here and happy to answer your questions Mr. Giles."

"Thank you for your cooperation Miss Mueller. Will you tell us about how you met Jacob?"

"You know, of course that he was an Israeli National, a member of Mossad, and that he converted to Catholicism?"

"Yes ma'am."

"I met him at Church actually. He was several years older than I was. I consider myself devout in my faith and I was equally devout at the time. I think he could sense that. I was impressed that he took his faith as seriously. We started dating. At first, he didn't talk much about himself. He was just a government employee, but I could tell that he had plenty to say, though he wasn't prepared to discuss it. It didn't matter to me though he and I had the same interests and I began to fall in love with him. Eventually, he told me his incredible story in bits and pieces. Are you familiar with it?"

"I am, but only partially, ma'am." Fox answered the question. She was lying. Both she and Giles had been briefed last night.

"He told me of his background, that he was a member of a military squad sent here to kidnap the Reverend Casey Edgars when he was a child, and that he had an epiphany."

"Yes, he said that Jesus Christ appeared to him and that because of that epiphany, he released young Casey Edgars and turned himself in to the authorities. But both of you already knew that."

Mueller knew the two agents were fully briefed and were just attempting to pump her for as much information as possible. Up to this point, she had only told them what she knew that they already knew. There was a pause for a moment.

"Would you care to continue Ms. Mueller?"

"Agent Giles, let's stop playing games with each other, shall we? I asked you a question. If you want me to continue you will answer my question."

Mueller left no doubt that she was in control of the conversation.

"Yes ma'am, you are correct. We already knew what you have told us."

"What do you want to know about my family?"

"Both you and Jacob were devout. Why didn't you get married and why did you give your son your surname instead of his?"

Fox asked attempting to defuse a potentially confrontational situation before it got to that point.

"The answer is very simple young lady. It was a matter of faith and trust. I didn't believe his story originally, but after I fell in love with him, I came to believe him because of my faith in God. He said that he would love me as his wife but we could not marry. I was willing to share my life with him, under his terms."

"And why did you name your son Mueller instead of Rabin?" Fox continued.

"Jacob said that it would be better if he took my name and not his. I trusted him and that is what happened."

"Why did your son change his name? What's his new name and why can't we locate him?"

"Agent Giles we raised little Jacob as a Catholic; baptism, first communion and confirmation. When he was old enough to appreciate it, Jacob told Jake, which is what we call him, of his epiphany. Jacob advised him one day it might be important to change his name. I really don't have an explanation as to why, but that is the reason. You might want to ask him, except he doesn't want to be found right now."

"Why is that Ms. Mueller?"

"Agent Giles, Jake contacted me several days ago and said that I might be getting a visit like this. It has to do with this Mohammad Baghai business, though he didn't elaborate. He told me that he would contact you when circumstances were appropriate. Do you have a card so I can have him call you?"

Mueller was clearly enjoying her fifteen minutes of fame at the expense of her guests.

Giles was becoming perturbed. Fox could sense that and continued the discussion.

"Why doesn't he want to be found Ms. Mueller?"

"You'd have to ask him dear."

"And he's confident that he can hide from the resources of the United States Government?"

"Child, you wouldn't be here if you knew where he was and you seem to have forgotten that my 'husband' was Mossad. He knew something about counter-intelligence, disappearing and creating new identities. I was never interested in such things but Jacob instructed little Jake on the subject. Of course I know you're going to try, but I don't think you'll have much success."

"So you don't intend to cooperate with us?"

"Not anymore than I have already Agent Fox."

"Ms. Mueller you realize that it's within our discretion to take you into custody?"

"Mr. Giles, if you were seriously considering doing so, which you are not, you will not."

"You know this how Ms. Mueller?"

"I have my sources Agent Giles and even if your instructions were to arrest me you would not."

Mueller was enjoying the verbal jousting more than she thought she would.

"Oh?"

"In my kitchen, you'll find a laptop computer. On the screen you'll see a picture of this room. This entire conversation has been digitally recorded and linked to my secure web site. My son can access the web site and release this conversation to the World Wide

Web. I don't think the FBI wants to have to answer questions why an old lady was arrested because a FBI agent's ego was bruised. Do you? Now unless you intend to arrest me, our conversation is over."

"Ms. Mueller, is there a reason why you are taking a confrontational attitude with us?"

"Agent Giles, Agent Fox, it's not my intention to be hostile to either of you, though it may seem that way. This Mohammad Baghai business is bigger than you are, bigger than I am and bigger than the President. Either by coincidence, or by design, my son and, by extension, myself are involved in it, though I believe it's providence, and not coincidence. Secular threats don't impress me. I'm too old to care. I hope you can appreciate my position."

"Thank you for your time Ms. Mueller," Fox spoke to her host.

As the agents left Mueller's home and drove away they discussed their interview.

"I have to report to the Director and the Attorney General as soon as we get back to the office. He's undoubtedly going to ask me my impressions of her, and if I think she's involved in her son's disappearance. I don't think she is actively participating, but I certainly believe that she knows where and why her son is hiding, if that is the correct term. Do you concur with me Dana?"

"Absolutely, I'd go so far as to say that I don't believe she has any compunction about getting directly involved in this business should she feel the necessity."

"I concur. My only real question is how soon the President, or another power to be, wants this man found." Giles remarked. People could hide their identities but if enough resources were brought to bear anyone could be found. Both he and Fox knew that.

"I suspect that we'll know within an hour after we make our report Larry. Do you want to bet?"

"Not really. I think the more the heat is turned up on the President the quicker a resolution will be, whatever it may be. I am going suggest that Ms. Mueller be watched for a while. I don't think she'd make a stupid mistake, like contacting her son, but something could happen. It'll take a judge to sign a warrant if they want to go that route. But, that'll be for the Justice Department Attorneys to prepare."

# Chapter 14

Abu Sabaya was reviewing his preparations for the assassination of the Vice President of the United States of America, Thomas Taylor. Originally, the plan was to kill the President, the she-devil, Jennifer Hays, who was scheduled to appear in the Opening Ceremony of the Summer Olympic Games, in Chicago; however, she'd changed her plans. Now Taylor would be present instead.

Sabaya, a Filipino, whose real name was Benino Marcos, was raised as a Catholic on the island of Luzon. Sabaya's parents were well-to-do and Marcos had been educated in Manila's finest private schools; he'd wanted for nothing. For whatever reason though, Marcos found such a lifestyle offensive. He renounced his previous life and worldly possessions, converted to Islam, and moved to the Southern Philippine Island of Basilan, taking the name of his mentor, Aldam Tilao, a.k.a. Abu Sabaya, or "bearer of hostages" in Arabic.

Marcos' conversion was a matter of faith and moral principle. His conversion to jihadist was a trade that he learned from Tilao. It was at a local mosque in Basilan that Marcos first met Tilao, the head of Abu Sayef. Marcos did not know Tilao personally but was aware of Abu Sayef and its political goal of independence for the predominately Muslim islands of the Southern Philippines.

"Do you believe in our cause, young Marcos?"

"I do."

"Are you willing to fight our enemies on behalf of our cause?"

"I am."

"Can you kidnap, and even murder for our cause, in the name of jihad, if the need should arise, young Marcos?"

"I can."

Marcos knew that while in a state of jihad, a man's sins, regardless of the severity were automatically forgiven by Allah.

"Are you sure?"

"I believe so."

"You believe so?! Can you rape a married woman in front of her husband, if our cause required it? The question caught Marcos off guard and he responded spontaneously, yet honestly.

"I cannot do that."

"Ah, but Allah believes that you can. I present you with your sword."

Tilao presented every new member with a sword and Marcos did not have to wait long before he used it. In May of 2001 Marcos, Tilao, and the entire cadre of Abu Sayef kidnapped about 20 people, including three Americans, two of whom were a missionary husband and wife, from a resort on the island of Mindanao, returning by motor boat to Basilan.

The group remained on the run from Philippine authorities for over a year, fighting periodic ambushes from the Philippine Marines. It was during one of these ambushes that the third American was wounded and eventually unable to keep up with the group. Tilao/ Sabaya ordered his execution.

"Please don't kill me! I want to see my children again."

The American begged for his life.Tilao/Sabaya had no pity. One mighty swing lopped off the third American's head.

The terrorists and their hostages continued their deadly game of cat and mouse with the Philippine military for over a year, fleeing to the larger island of Mindanao, again by motor boat. Marcos and his comrades showed no compunction about raping the female hostages, when the urge arose.

"Why do you do this to women? Doesn't Islam respect women? Didn't the Prophet Muhammad say that 'women are the twin half of men'?" The missionary wife, having a rudimentary knowledge of Islam, asked Marcos.

"Woman, who are you to speak to me?"

Marcos launched himself into a diatribe.

"Yes Muhammad did say that, but in your ignorance, you have quoted him out of context. Muhammad, in the text that you refer to, was speaking in reference to a husband and his wife. Islam respects the sanctity of marriage and that is why you have not been taken and will not be taken. I insisted that you be spared and you will not be defiled. These women on the other hand, do not respect themselves. Why should we respect them? They do not cover their bodies; in fact they show their bodies off like a whore would. Can you tell me that you have not seen them on the beach, nearly naked, in their bikinis, sun-bathing topless? Men lust over them. Does your husband allow you to dress in such a way that men lust over you? No, he doesn't. Women who act like whores can, and should, be treated like whores."

"My brothers and I are on jihad. Do you know when Islamic law allows jihad?"

Marcos did not allow his hostage to answer.

"Jihad is allowed when it is necessary to defend your community from aggressors, to liberate people from aggressive regimes and to remove any government that will not allow the free practice of Islam. The Philippine government, and indirectly, the U.S. government, is guilty of all three crimes. A Muslim is automatically forgiven of all of his sins while he is on jihad so none of us are concerned about your 'so called' crimes. I expect to die as a martyr, a shaheed. All shaheeds are not only forgiven of their sins but are guaranteed paradise as a reward for their supreme sacrifice. Don't speak to me about my sins. Allah has forgiven them and I am not concerned."

The hostages' hell on earth finally ended in June of 2002 when Philippine Marines attacked and killed many Abu Sayef on Mindanao. The missionary husband was also killed. Abu Sabaya/Tilao and Marcos managed to escape, but were separated during the process. The Marines killed Sabaya/Tilao, along with most of his surviving group, in June of 2002 while the group was attempting to relocate from Mindanao to Basilan. Marcos did not suffer the fate of his comrades because he was unable to join Sabaya/ Tilao for the journey and remained on Mindanao.

Tilao's death gutted the leadership of Abu Sayef and Marcos was forced to go into hiding, leaving Basilan. Marcos, eventually migrated to the northern island of Luzon and the capital city of Manila, where the majority of the Filipino population was Christian. Marcos' decision to immigrate to America was an easy one. The Philippine Marines, who murdered Tilao, were given intelligence by the CIA and rather than fight Americans in his native land, Marcos decided to conduct jihad on American soil, but only after training with his Islamic brothers in Iran. It was in a training camp in Iran that he polished his small arms skills. He also learned to build an almost undetectable car bomb that could level half a city block and he perfected the craft of dirty bomb construction. Radioactive materials from the former Soviet Union had been paid for and would be used some time in the future. Alas, that was destined to be another martyr's jihad and place in paradise. Tilao was now in paradise, having died while conducting jihad and Marcos had little doubt that he would face the same fate when he killed Taylor.

The plan was simple. The simplest plans were always the best. There were a number of Muslims on the Philippine Olympic Team and one had already agreed, through back channels, to "disappear", at the appropriate time. This would allow Sabaya to substitute himself, march with the team during the opening ceremonies, and dash to the Vice President as the team marched by the reviewing stand, killing him with a concealed handgun before anyone could react. Sabaya expected to be killed, of course, securing his place in paradise. But his death and his Internet manifesto would illustrate the righteousness of Abu Sayef's cause and the evil corruption of the United States.

PRESIDENT Hays picked up the phone at her desk. Jim Scarboro was on the other end of the line.

"Yes Jim?"

"Mrs. President I have the field report of the interview of Kathleen Mueller, the common-law wife of Jacob Rabin and mother of Rabin's son."

"We are sure that Rabin is the father?"

"Yes, she admitted that Rabin was the father of her son."

"Do we know his name and where he is Jim?"

"She refused to identify him or his location and we have not discovered his new name or address."

Scarboro braced for a rebuke.

"What are we doing to locate him Jim?"

"I have already briefed you on our normal procedures in such cases and that is how we are handling this matter now, Mrs. President. However the field agent in charge, Larry Giles, suggested that we secure a search warrant so we can listen to her phone calls, intercept her mail and such."

"Do you think that surveillance would do any good Jim?"

"I think her, or probably her son would already have anticipated such a move and taken the necessary precautions, but I still recommend doing it. Sometimes you get lucky."

"Why is she being uncooperative? Did the agent attempt to use the weight of the government to coerce her cooperation?"

"Agent Giles did and she was totally unfazed. In fact she had set up a digital recording of their conversation and threatened to put it on the Internet as proof of the FBI's heavy-handed tactics."

"How soon before we find this man?"

"Assuming that he's here in the United States, it shouldn't take any more than a week or two. Only the U.S. Government can make someone disappear completely and we know that wasn't the case here. He is buried deep, no doubt about it, but he doesn't have the resources. We will find him. It's only a matter of time. Time is actually on our side. Baghai is still in a coma. If he dies then all of this is moot; if he lives then we can, and should in my opinion, continue to adhere current position and let the legal issues wend its way through the process."

"Now assuming that we do find him, we don't know if, or how much he can help us with the Mohammad Baghai affair."

"No, Mrs. President, we don't. That remains to be seen."

"Okay, Jim, get a search warrant. Have one of your attorneys tell a judge whatever he needs to get one and see if anything shakes loose. Keep me advised."

"Yes Mrs. President."

The President of the United States, the most powerful person in the world, hung up the phone feeling utterly helpless.

CHARLIE had exited Georgia State Road 400 in a rented U-Haul truck, carrying most of his worldly possessions, and was a few minutes from the Twig's house. It was Friday afternoon and Charlie had finished all his business in Pensacola and even managed to get in a second dive trip, during his weeklong stay.

It had also been a productive trip from a business perspective as well. Charlie had sold three life insurance policies, one to Chris and two others. His banking accounts were closed and the funds were electronically transferred to his Georgia Bank. Charlie had contacted a real estate agent and had his parent's house listed for sale. The agent expected the house to sell within four or five weeks. He had also sold his car, so purchasing another vehicle would be the first order of business tomorrow. All in all Charlie would miss his home of 23 years, especially the fresh seafood, Pensacola was famous for Red Snapper, but was happy to start his new life in Georgia.

Charlie pulled into the Twig's driveway. Heather saw Charlie pull up and was outside to greet him immediately with a huge hug and kiss. She looked gorgeous in her jeans, a simple white blouse and high heels.

"You have no idea how much I missed you," Heather told her boyfriend in between hugs and kisses.

"I missed you too Heather."

"Don't you ever leave anywhere else again without me, understand Charlie?"

"Oh? I hope you're prepared to go to Pensacola in a few weeks. I've decided to participate in my graduation ceremonies."

"Do you mind if my mother and father come down?"

"Not at all."

"I'll ask them, but I'm sure that they'll want to. Where's your car Charlie?"

"I didn't want to tow it behind this truck so I sold it. I'm going to need a ride to a car dealer tomorrow. Do you know a taxi driver?"

Charlie flashed one on his wicked evil grins.

"The best driver and the cheapest fares in the City of Cumming," Heather said as she kissed him again.

"Why don't the both of you come inside? I have some refreshments and your father will be home shortly. I know he'll want to grill out." Jo Ann called from the porch.

Charlie and Heather broke their embrace, Charlie grabbed his briefcase, and the couple walked to the house. Charlie gave Jo Ann a hug, which she returned. Charlie appreciated her warmth and hospitality. He felt that he'd been accepted as a member of the Twig family.

"It's good to see you again Jo Ann." Charlie had finally gotten comfortable with addressing her by her first name, instead of Mrs. Twig.

"Charlie, I'm happy to see you. Did you have a good time in Florida?"

"I did, but I'm happy to be home."

It immediately dawned on both Charlie and Jo Ann at exactly the same time that "home" was in Georgia and not Pensacola. Both recognized the significance of Charlie's last remark and recognized that Charlie was now a member of the Twig family.

"Well we're happy to have you back. Come inside now, we'll get your bags later. I know that truck wasn't very comfortable. Would you like a beer?"

"Maybe later Jo Ann, right now some ice tea would be just great."

"Go grab a chair on the deck, Heather and I will get a pitcher of tea and join you. Ralph should be home shortly and we can catch up with each other until then."

"Yes ma'am."

Charlie put his briefcase on the deck near his chair and sat on the deck gazing at Lake Lanier. The sun was setting low on the horizon. He enjoyed the water and being near the lake. He'd be able to go boating and jet skiing. Maybe he wouldn't miss Florida so much. Charlie's daydream was broken when Jo Ann, Heather and Ralph walked out onto the deck and took seats at the patio table. Ralph had loosened his tie and had a drink in his hand.

"Glad to see you made it back all right Charlie. How was your trip?" Ralph said as he stuck out his hand.

"It was long and uncomfortable in that U-Haul truck. Glad I'm back." Charlie shook Ralph's hand vigorously.

"So, Heather tells me that you have to take another trip down to Pensacola?"

"Yeah, I decided to take the walk and get my diploma."

"Heather said it would be all right with you if the three of us accompany you and watch you graduate."

"I'd be happy to have you all come down and watch me."

"I think we can make room in our schedules," Ralph replied.

"I sold two fifty thousand and one hundred thousand dollar policy. I sold them to three of my fraternity brothers. I have them in my brief case."

"That's a good start. I'll look at the applications after we eat and get them turned in on Monday."

"Sounds great, oh, you won't be able to guess who I met while I was on the dive charter."

"I have no idea, but I'm sure you'll tell us," Ralph said.

"I met a member of the Secret Service, who is assigned to protect the President. He was on vacation and wanted to dive the carrier also."

"You met one of the President's bodyguards? That's fascinating." Jo Ann replied.

"He's an interesting guy, played football at the University of Florida and travels with the President. He's been on Air Force One and in the Oval Office. He and I were dive partners and we had an interesting conversation while we were on the boat."

"What's his name Charlie?"

"Ron Thomas, Ralph. He played linebacker at Florida eight years ago."

"I remember him. Heather, you remember the Georgia-Florida game that I took you and your mother to. He sacked our quarterback on a blitz that killed our drive and they won the game. I think he got hurt in the bowl game later that year." The Twigs were Georgia Bulldog Fans.

"Yes Dad. You were down in the dumps for a week after the game."

"He did say that he got hurt and couldn't play in the NFL." Charlie said.

"Sounds like you had an interesting week Charlie." Ralph said as he finished of his drink. "I'm going to change. Jo Ann, will you get the steaks ready so I can throw them on the grill when I come back?"

"Of course, dear."

Ralph and Jo Ann left Charlie and Heather together,

"Heather, I need to find a self-storage unit tomorrow, so I can unload my stuff. I also need to turn in the truck and look for a car."

"Do you have a lot of things?"

"My truck is pretty full. I also want to look at apartments; you know where the nicer ones are, don't you?"

"Yes, in Cumming or Dahlonega?"

"I was thinking about Dawsonville actually, so I can be in between my new job and you. We can certainly look at ones in Dahlonega also."

Dawsonville, Georgia was just off of Georgia State Road 400 in between Cumming and Dahlonega, an easy drive North or South.

"I know two or three places. How soon do you want to move Charlie?"

"There's no rush Heather, but I don't want to live in the Hitt's spare room forever. There's not enough privacy." Charlie flashed one of his smiles.

Heather knew exactly what Charlie meant by "privacy."

"Charlie Michaels we need to walk down to the dock, away from my parents' ears."

Charlie and Heather walked hand in hand to the edge of the lake and on to the dock, where the Twigs kept a 20' fiberglass pleasure craft and their two jet skis. There was a wooden bench built into the dock.

"Charlie, I know what you meant by privacy and I know that you know that I wasn't a virgin, the first time we were together, but…"

Heather was having difficulty saying what she wanted to say.

"Heather…"

"Let me finish Charlie. I, I don't sleep; I haven't slept with many men. I don't know why I slept with you when I did, except that I was feeling insecure, which is unusual for me. You've made more than one advance before and, to your credit, you were a gentleman when I refused."

Heather was on the verge of tears now.

"Charlie you told me once that you've never made any significant changes in your life for anyone before. The truth is that I haven't made any changes for someone before either, but I would for you, in a heartbeat."

"Charlie, I don't think you know just how hard I've fallen for you. Mom knows. Dad may have a clue, I don't know for sure. I was so afraid that you might have rekindled a romance with an old girlfriend and I'd get a phone call saying that 'it's been fun Heather.' Can you understand what I am feeling?"

Charlie took Heather's hand, pulled her close and looked deep into her eyes.

"Heather, my feelings towards you is what's bothering you?"

Heather nodded.

"Tell you what. I've just changed my plans for tomorrow. We're going to skip looking for a car. I can borrow yours for a few days can't I?" Heather nodded yes. "Good. Tomorrow I'm buying you an engagement ring and, afterwards, I'm asking your father for your hand. Think he'll say yes?" Charlie smiled a wicked, yet innocent smile.

The air seemed to leave Heather's lungs; all she could do was hug her fiancée.

"Can you keep this secret until tomorrow afternoon?"

Heather still could barely speak. "Yes. Yes. Yes," Heather managed to whisper.

"Good. Now, you're a mess. I have a handkerchief, but your eyes are red. You need some Visine."

"Mother will notice and ask."

"Not a word until tomorrow Heather," Charlie said sternly.

"What will I tell her Charlie?"

"Heather, you would know much better than I what she'll believe. Now I haven't actually asked you to marry me but I will tomorrow after I speak with your Father. You are going to say yes aren't you?"

Charlie was looking into her eyes again.

"You're asking stupid questions now," Heather said as she closed her eyes and kissed him.

AFTER Charlie and the Twigs had breakfast Saturday morning, Charlie and Heather took Heather's car and went shopping. Three hours and seven stores later it was time for lunch. Sitting down and gazing at a menu, Heather was literally walking on air for the entire day.

"So Heather, do you think you want to look at the other stores or did you see something that you would be happy wearing on your finger for the rest of your life?"

"Charlie, I have a confession to make."

"Let's see. You told your mother some time after breakfast?"

"How did you know?"

"I saw her looking at us through the curtains as we were pulling out of the driveway. Her smile was as big as yours is now. It wasn't hard to figure it out. Now is your mother going to tell your father?"

"I swore her to secrecy Charlie."

Charlie laughed uproariously.

"Just like I swore you to secrecy Heather?"

Heather blushed.

"I can see why people use the cliché 'loose lips sink ships'," Charlie said in mock disgust. "Since the cat is out of the bag, I need you to do something for me."

"What's that Charlie?"

"Call your mother. Tell her that when we get back to let me speak to your dad privately for a few minutes."

"Charlie, how are you affording this? We haven't looked at a ring for less than $2500."

"Heather, I never claimed to be a poor college student and I'm not. We never discussed everything about me; we can do that some other time all right? Right now I'm starving."

After lunch Charlie and Heather agreed on a ring and diamond. Charlie paid for it with a debit card. Fifteen minutes later the stone was mounted on the ring and Charlie placed the ring on Heather's finger. Heather gave Charlie a bear hug.

"You know you still haven't asked me the question that usually goes along with this type of jewelry."

"Nor will I, until I speak with your father. That's the one part of my plan that I can still control at this point."

Pulling into the Twig's, Charlie opened the passenger door and held Heather's left hand as the two walked up to the front door.

"I want you to find your mother and leave me and your father alone to discuss personal matters. Any questions?"

"No Charlie."

Heather was too proud and happy to argue.

Walking inside, Charlie and Heather found Jo Ann in the kitchen. Heather showed her mother her left hand and got a smile and a hug in return. Charlie paused for a moment and Jo Ann pointed to the deck. Charlie, understanding Jo Ann's sign language, waved and walked outside. Ralph was sitting at the patio table with a drink. Charlie took a seat next to him.

"Son, if you haven't learned this lesson already, you will learn that Twig women don't keep secrets worth a damn," Ralph said as he took a sip from his drink.

Charlie immediately knew that the cat was out of the bag, but he couldn't get a read on Ralph's feeling on the matter. Ralph could sense what Charlie was thinking.

"Relax son, if you came to ask for my permission to marry Heather you needn't worry, you have it. I appreciate your desire to adhere to traditions."

"Ralph, I wanted to explain how all this happened. It all transpired pretty fast."

"You haven't gotten my daughter pregnant have you?" Ralph whispered

"No sir! I haven't," Charlie shocked by the question, exclaimed.

Ralph broke into laughter. "I got you on that one son. That last question we'll keep between ourselves. And if I know my wife and daughter they're eavesdropping somewhere just out of sight. You two can come out of hiding now."

Heather and Jo Ann walked onto the deck. Jo Ann wanted to give Charlie a hug.

"Hold it! There is something that was forgotten!"

"What's that Charlie?" Heather asked.

Charlie took a knee in front of Heater. "Heather Twig, will you do me the honor of being my wife for the next forty or fifty years?"

"Oh Charlie, of course I will."

Charlie got up and together he and Heather accepted Ralph and Jo Ann's congratulations.

KEN Shugart and Casey Edgars sat facing each other in a television studio. Edgars was Shugart's guest on the weekly show America Today. Shugart had the exclusive interview of Edgars' crusade to have Mohammad Baghai pardoned. Shugart had previously had David Franks and Father Paul Stewart on the show several weeks before. The subject had taken on a life of its own. Baghai had pleaded guilty to murder but had fallen into a coma immediately after doing so. While in a coma, his supporters claimed, he'd received the mark of the stigmata. His detractors claimed that the marks were a fraud.

"Good morning America. I am Ken Shugart and our guest today is the Reverend Casey Edgars, founder of the Christ Ministries Church. Reverend Edgars has been, perhaps, the most vocal proponent for a Presidential Pardon of the former terrorist, Mohammad Baghai, who is now in federal custody and in a diabetic coma. Reverend, I want to thank you for being with us today."

"Ken it's a pleasure; thank you very much for having me."

"Reverend, you, almost from the beginning, called for Mohammad Baghai to be pardoned, claiming that he is a prophet sent to deliver God's message."

"Yes Ken, I have. My position is clear and my reasons are on the record. For anyone who is not familiar with Mohammad Baghai and why he should be pardoned, I invite you to visit my new web site, ."

"Why are you here today, Reverend?"

"Ken I could certainly rehash why I believe, no, excuse me, why I know that Mohammad Baghai is God's messenger, but today I thought Mohammad's cause needed to take another tack."

"Please continue Reverend."

"Clearly God has a purpose for his prophet. President Hays has been reluctant to expedite God's plan for Mohammad. Let me make this perfectly clear. By refusing to pardon Mohammad Baghai, the President is defying God's will. This is completely unacceptable! He will not remain in a coma for very much longer, believe me. God will restore him to the living world before long and it will be up to the President to pardon him of his crimes. Ladies and gentlemen, my brothers and sisters in Christ, we are all servants of God. President Hays seems to have forgotten that she is a servant, not only of the American people, but also of God."

"My brothers and sisters in Christ, as one of God's servants, I am willing and hopefully able to do God's will. Earlier, I invited you to visit my new web site, www.pardonGodsprophet.com. When I say it is new, I mean it is brand new. The web site was just launched yesterday. I purposely waited to announce its creation for a specific reason. In addition to presenting the facts of the Mohammad Baghai matter, there is a button on the web site that is inactive now but will become functional in 48 hours. The name of the label on the button is blank now, but will read 'Impeach the President,' if President Hays has not pardoned Mohammad Baghai, God's Prophet, in 48 hours."

Shugart found it impossible to keep hide his stunned expression. Edgars was correct. This revelation was a blockbuster.

"Reverend surely you're not suggesting that President Hays should be impeached for choosing not to pardon a self-confessed murder?"

"Ken it's time that our representatives in government realize that they serve the God-fearing citizens of the country. No, I don't want the President impeached, but if that's what it takes to get God's Prophet out from under a death sentence and out of jail so he can deliver the message, then I will utilize every fiber of my being to do so."

"Reverend do you really believe that the act of not pardoning a self-professed terrorist rises to the level of a level of a 'high crimes and misdemeanors,' as the Constitution says requires impeachment?"

"Ken it was Gerald Ford, Congressman at the time and later President, who said that Congress decides what is a 'high crime and misdemeanor.' What I'm saying is that it's time that our government officials start to work for the will of their citizens. If they cannot, or will not, then I say it's time to get new representatives in government. This issue is clear-cut. There are not any shades of gray here."

"In 48 hours I will activate the page on my web site that will allow any God-fearing man or woman to input their name and address showing support of God's cause. These names will be compiled in a database and forwarded to their respective Congressman and Senators. Hopefully, the President will realize the error of her ways and this will become a non-issue. If not, I am prepared to follow this to its resolution."

"Incredible revelations today, Reverend Edgars, thank you for your time with us today. I am Ken Shugart and this is <u>America Today</u>."

# Chapter 15

It was Sunday morning and Andrew Shephard barged into the O. Casey Edgars sent him an email Friday informing him that he would receive a DVD delivered via courier and that he should view it. Shephard already knew that it was the recording of the America Today show. Such revelations were never secret for very long and the White House had sources to give the administration a "heads up."

Walking into the Oval Office, Shephard could see that Hays was not happy, not that he expected her to be in a jovial mood.

"What is this lunatic think he's doing?"

"Madam President have you seen the show?"

"Yes, I've seen the DVD and I've visited his web site. Is this guy really serious? Andy, how does a man go from being a guest at the White House to demanding my impeachment on non-existent charges?"

"Reverend Edgars obviously believes in his cause and is committed to doing whatever it takes to achieve his goals."

"Andy, you spoke with him before; what does this man think I'm going to do? Did you communicate to Reverend Edgars that I'd consider a pardon after Baghai was tried and sentenced? I know I did when I presented him with the Medal of Freedom."

"I did. As I discussed with you then, and as Reverend Edgars reiterated to you after the ceremony, he considers Mohammad Baghai a prophet of God and mere mortals, even Presidents, do not question God's wisdom. In his eyes, by not granting a pardon immediately, you are presenting yourself as an obstacle to God's will."

"So I'm being judged by Edgars, a mere mortal, because I am interfering with a divine plan?"

"That is the gist of his position."

"Andy, you know me well enough to know that I'm not going to be intimidated, cajoled or blackmailed by some religious fanatic. It has been my position, and will continue to be my position, that, barring extraordinary circumstances, I will consider a pardon for Mohammad Baghai only after the legal process has concluded and a pardon application has been properly submitted. I am going to have C.C. Frost reiterate my position at tomorrow's press conference."

"I have a suggestion Madam President."

"What's that Andy?"

"Mohammad Baghai's attorney is Isabelle Franks. Perhaps it might be wise to invite the Franks here officially, as a social function but, unofficially, to discuss Mohammad Baghai's circumstances. Isabelle Franks could certainly bring the pardon application and advocate its merits to you. Perhaps that would appease Reverend Edgars? Mohammad Baghai's attorney gets a one-on-one sit down with the President and the situation is defused, while you haven't compromised your position on the issue."

"We would have to include Taylor," Hays said pensively.

"Not a problem. After the introductions and chitchat he can give David Franks and his daughter the tour, while you and Mrs. Franks discuss Baghai. Mrs. Franks stipulates that she will communicate to Reverend Edgars that you are impressed with the merits of the application and you will give it serious consideration. Reverend Edgars dials back his rhetoric and takes down his web site, after I contact him to communicate that 'unofficially' you will pardon Baghai, after he is sentenced and the commotion had died down. It's a win-win scenario and this gets nipped in the bud."

"I didn't say that I would pardon Baghai, Andy."

"No, I did. The decision to pardon will be made by you at the appropriate time. In fact, by having C.C. forcefully restate your position tomorrow, you can plausibly claim that you never intended to grant a pardon and point to the press conference as proof, if you decide upon that course of action."

Hays considered the situation. Though she didn't like to make back room deals, and this one involved a double cross, she realized, from her time in Congress and the Senate, that arrangements were made in similar fashion quite often and this one appeared to be a political necessity.

"You're fine with orchestrating this Andy?"

Hays was mindful that Edgars was a father-like figure to Shephard.

"Fine is probably not the correct term but I can live with it."

"Set it up personally Andy, and get back with me as soon as you've confirmed everything."

"I will Madam President."

DAVID Franks was working alone at home Monday morning. Tori was at a daycare center. It would be next year before she'd start school and, though he would have loved to have his daughter at home with him, with her natural curiosity and proclivity to play twenty questions, Franks would never get any work done.

With his recently acquired celebrity status, and the clout that went with it, Franks was able to convince his editor that he could do most of his job at home; the tasks that couldn't be completed at home could usually be done in one day at the office. Franks knew that Roger, his immediate boss, and the other powers that be at the Sun-Times really didn't have a choice in the matter. Franks was a hot commodity in journalistic circles and all parties knew it. Feelers had been sent out by several other media groups and though Franks was happy at his present position, he was not above using his leverage to his benefit. Undoubtedly, Franks would move on in the future, but presently he wasn't inclined to do so. He liked being a big fish in a small pond. Moving up would position Franks as a smaller fish in an ocean. Working at home was a perk, reserved for a select few at the paper, which he relished.

Franks was deep in thought when his landline rang. Franks had two cell phones but he had them turned off. Anyone who Franks wanted to speak with knew his home number. Others, who didn't have his home number, well, that's what voice mail was for.

"Hello."

"David Franks?"

"Yes, I'm David Franks. Who is this?"

"Mr. Franks, I'm Andrew Shephard, President Hays' chief of staff."

"What can I do for you Mr. Shephard? How did you get my number by the way? It's supposed to be unlisted."

"Good question. Someone on my staff gave your number to me. I believe that shortly after you were released from captivity and recovering from your injuries, the White House did a background investigation on you. I would assume that your home phone number was obtained at that time, probably from your employer. I attempted to call you at work, and on your cell, and left a voice mail."

Franks smiled. At least "big brother" was not completely omniscient. Shephard didn't seem to know that he had a second cell.

"Anyway, the purpose of my call is to invite you and your family to the White House to meet the President. I understand that Vice President Taylor invited your family to White House while you were flying back from Germany. He will be present as well. The Vice President has told me that he and your daughter hit it off on Air Force Two."

"Yes, they did. When is the invitation for?" Franks knew that the topic of Mohammad Baghai would be discussed and the timing with Casey Edgars' new web site wasn't a coincidence.

"The President would like to meet you at your family's earliest convenience, later this week if possible. Now Mr. Franks I know you're a journalist and what I'm about to say is off the record, agreed?"

"Very well."

"Officially, the visit is to honor the Vice President's invitation, to your family, to visit the White House. Unofficially, President Hays wants to discuss Mohammad Baghai's pardon application with your wife."

"I appreciate your candor."

Franks, despite his suspicions appreciated forthright communication, free of ambiguity.

"When do you think you and your family would be available?"

"I am fortunate enough that I can arrange my schedule to suit me, however, I can't speak for my wife. I'll be happy to call her after I hang up and discuss it with her."

"Can I call you back later this afternoon?"

"Tell you what, Mr. Shephard…"

"Call me Andy, the President does."

"Okay, please call me David. Andy, you have my company email address?"

"Yes, I do."

"Send me an email to confirm this conversation and I will reply later today with a date that is best for us and we can nail down the specifics over the phone."

"That sounds fine David. I look forward to speaking with you again."

Franks hung up the phone and immediately dialed his wife's private office number.

"Isabelle Franks."

"Hi honey."

"Hello dear. How are you?"

"Fine, hope you're the same. You won't guess who I just got a phone call from."

"Tell me."

"Andrew Shephard, the White House Chief of Staff just called me."

"Oh really, you're not pulling my leg?"

"I'm completely serious dear."

"Okay, what did he want?"

"We're invited to visit President Hays and Vice President Taylor at the White House. Taylor invited us to visit on our flight back from Germany when you and Tori were sleeping. The President wants to discuss Mohammad's pardon application with you, while Tori and I get a tour; she wants to keep that confidential. But anyway, I accepted the invitation for us, with the stipulation that it doesn't conflict with your schedule. Mine's pretty flexible.

"David, are you kidding? I can adjust my schedule as needed. How often does an attorney get to visit the White House, meet the President and get to bill the time to a client?"

"Okay then, I'll make arrangements and let you know tonight. Love you."

"I love you too."

## Mohammad Baghai, God's Prophet or Allah's Traitor?

Presently, confessed murderer Mohammad Baghai lies in a New York hospital's intensive care unit, in a coma, waiting to be sentenced. Baghai's care is overseen by a team of doctors and nurses while he is guarded around the clock by FBI agents. Right wing religious zealots claim he is a prophet sent from God and demand that President Hays pardon him of any and all crimes he has committed. At the same time Muslim leaders claim he is a traitor to Islam and deserves to die by beheading.

Who is this "paradox of personalities?" He has admitted to killing Americans in the name of Islamic Jihad, yet he is now a baptized Christian and has conducted sermons to some of his fellow inmates, while in prison. He fought alongside bin Laden in Afghanistan, yet he was educated in the United States. He is Iranian by birth yet he gained the trust and respect of prominent Arab members of al-Qaeda and fought the United States in the Arabic country of Iraq. Finally, he entered the United States, admitted guilt to his crimes yet he refuses to be debriefed by CIA and FBI officials, who hope his intelligence would save American lives.

There is no simple answer to any of these questions. Mohammad Baghai can certainly answer them and perhaps he will when, and if, he recovers from his coma and resolves his legal issues. In the meantime, answers to these and other questions scream to be answered immediately, which this multi-part series will attempt to do.

Mohammad Baghai was born in the province of Kerman, Iran, the only child of Mansur and Amina Baghai. Baghai's father was a member of Iran's secret police and intelligence organization, SAVAK—the equivalent of the CIA, FBI and Secret Service and for several years the bureau chief in the United States, stationed in New York, enjoying diplomatic status.

During Mansur's tour in America, Mohammad attended an exclusive private high school and, later, Harvard. Mohammad Baghai was a friendly and well-adjusted teenager and did well in school, graduating near the top of his high school class. He did equally well at Harvard, completing a degree in international studies.

No one, at that time, perhaps not Baghai himself, had any indication that he would become a terrorist with a reputation of savagery, equal to "Carlos the Jackal." Baghai's father, Mansur was recalled to Iran, leaving Mohammad to complete his last semester at Harvard. Afterwards, he returned to Iran and entered the University of Tehran to complete a law degree, finishing two years later. It is during this time, as a law student in Tehran, that Baghai, a non-practicing Muslim, indicated from his non-attendance of local mosques in America, became fervent in his faith, though it is not known why. Again, we have another question without a satisfactory answer.

Probably Baghai's first indication of his religious passion and his vicious nature can be first seen when he was still a student at Tehran University.

Mallekah Pakravan is an Iranian national living in New York City and is a registered nurse by trade. Her father, Mansur Pakravan, worked multiple jobs, scraping a meager existence to support his wife and daughter in Kerman City, Iran, the same Kerman City where Mohammad Baghai spent his childhood. Neither Baghai, nor Mallekah Pakravan had ever met before, until Baghai had her father murdered.

While on a break in-between terms at Tehran University, Baghai visited Kerman City. His mother and father were both living in Tehran at the time so Baghai rented a motel room, with the intention of visiting friends. One day after, taking a meal at a restaurant and praying at a local mosque, Baghai returned to his room to find Mansur Pakravan in it, apparently attempting to steal money from him.

Baghai, enraged at the crime, managed to hold Pakravan and had the local authorities summoned. Through the use of intimidation—Baghai's father was a powerful man in Iran—Mohammad was allowed, through local customs, to conduct a trial. He acted as prosecutor, judge and jury. The outcome was never in doubt. Mansur Pakravan was a frail man in his late fifties and he freely admitted his crime, claiming that his family was on the verge of starving and that he needed money to purchase food; he begged for Baghai's mercy.

Baghai was deaf to these pleadings for mercy and ordered the old man to suffer the "Four Spikes" as punishment. Pakravan was stripped from the waist up and tied face down, on the ground, spread eagle to four spikes. Baghai ordered one hundred lashes. Mallekah, barely an adolescent child, along with her mother both crawled and begged at the feet of Baghai as local constables were beating Pakravan, but Baghai kicked them both away.

Mallekah can't say for sure when her father gave up his life but it was well before the hundredth blow. Her father's mangled body was buried and she and her mother continued their frugal existence. The beating was so gruesome; the punishment was so over the top, that the Iranian Government actually paid a monthly stipend to Mallekah and her mother. Baghai was never punished for his actions.

Shortly after Baghai found his Muslim faith the former Soviet Union invaded Afghanistan. Osama bin Laden, the 911 master-mind and leader of al-Qaeda, created and led a resistance movement against the Soviets and called for all Muslims, around the world, to gather in Afghanistan and conduct jihad to repel the infidels. Mohammad Baghai answered bin Laden's call and fought alongside fellow Muslims to defeat the Soviets.

Baghai, either through demonstration of his bravery, his religious devotion, his organizational abilities or a combination of all, quickly rose to become one of bin Laden's lieutenants. He has been videotaped in the background of several bin Laden interviews, which is a privilege bin Laden reserves for his most respected subordinates.

After Desert Storm, Baghai traveled to Iraq to become al-Qaeda's leader there. Baghai's first murder has been described. In the subsequent parts of this story his activities, as al-Qaeda's number one man in Iraq, will be reported. Major terror attacks against coalition forces, as well as the capture and murder of American soldiers, will be documented. Whether Mohammad Baghai is a prophet, as some claim, is a matter of faith and a matter for debate. What is clear is that during his time in Iraq, Baghai was a very vicious and evil man.

# Chapter 16

Charlie and the Twigs found and rented a mini-warehouse Sunday afternoon and unloaded Charlie's belongings into it. Charlie had complete furnishings for an entire home so it took the four of them over two hours to empty the truck.

Monday morning Charlie drove Heather to Dahlonega, to the North Georgia campus, to attend class, with Charlie keeping Heather's car. After dropping her off, Charlie checked his mail. Satisfied that all his business was attended to, Charlie drove back to Cumming so he and Jo Ann could return his rented U-Haul truck.

"Thank you for being my taxi service this morning Jo Ann."

"I'm happy to do it Charlie. I was surprised that you had so much furniture though."

"It belonged to my mother and father. I got my fraternity brothers to help me pack the truck."

"Heather told me about your parents. I am sorry Charlie. I don't mean to pry but will you tell me about them?"

"Jo Ann since we'll be related shortly it's appropriate that you know about my family. I don't like talking about it. You can certainly understand why."

"Charlie if you'd prefer another time I understand."

"No Jo Ann, right now is fine. I had an older brother, named John, who was adopted. My mother and father weren't able to have children. Several years afterwards, for whatever reason, they conceived me. John enlisted in the army and was in Iraq, after the first Gulf War, when he was killed. I was only four at the time."

"Charlie, I am sorry." Jo Ann could tell that Charlie was emotionally distraught.

"My parents and I never really got over John's death. Oh, they coped; and I never saw either of them mourn him, though I know they did."

"Of course they did Charlie, as all parents would."

"I grew up as a normal child, I suppose; until college anyway. My father was an engineer at a local business and my mother was a homemaker. I found school ridiculously easy, played soccer in high school and paintball on the weekends. I enrolled at UWF, lived at home and joined my fraternity. It was during the summer of my freshman year that my parents died in a head-on car wreck. Between the life insurance, the estate and the wrongful death lawsuit, I was reasonably well off but I didn't have any family. Then, when I met Heather I decided to move here. It was an easy decision on many levels."

"We're thrilled that you did Charlie."

"After the funeral, I moved into the fraternity house. It may not make any sense but I couldn't live in my house, just too many memories; but I couldn't bring myself to sell it, until now. It was the only connection to my family."

"It makes perfect sense Charlie. I also understand you had some rather wild experiences living there. Not having any family support at such a crucial time in your life, I think it's remarkable that you've done as well in school as you have."

"You and Heather don't keep many secrets, but thank you for the compliment."

"Charlie, Ralph and I are both proud we have you as a member of our family. Heather has told me of your 'bad boy' reputation in college. She was concerned that Ralph and I wouldn't like you. I think I mentioned before, that Ralph and I didn't care for most of her previous boyfriends. Most of them were good boys but didn't have any plans or goals. They were just going to graduate high school and get a job making eight dollars an hour at Wal-Mart. Some didn't seem to have any manners at all. None of them were going anywhere with their lives. Heather saw something special in you Charlie; so do Ralph and I."

"What do you see in me Jo Ann?"

"Charlie, did you know Ralph and I were married for four months before my parents knew about it?"

"No I didn't. That is so unlike you Jo Ann. Ever since I've known you, you always seem to expect, no, demand that everything be done properly. How did Ralph convince you to get married under those circumstances and how did you hide that from your parents?"

"We eloped and didn't tell my mother and father. I finished the term while Ralph was doing his basic training. I was in college and Ralph had just joined the Air Force's officer training program. We had dated some but I saw something special in him, just the way Heather sees the same thing in you. I was willing to put my life on hold for a few years, while Ralph served, much like you are going to do when Heather graduates. I see a lot of myself in you Charlie, so how could I not love you?"

"Jo Ann I had no idea. Heather never told me any of this."

"Of course she didn't; I told her not to. She knew that she wanted to marry you not long after you two met."

"Before I first met you and Ralph?"

"Yes. She didn't tell me in those words but I knew. A mother knows these things."

"Jo Ann, I can't tell you how good you've made me feel, but you already knew that didn't you?"

"Charlie, a mother knows these things."

TORI Franks was playing twenty questions with Ron Thomas in the ante room outside the Oval Office. Tori wanted to know why it was called the O and Secret Service Agent Thomas was not having much success explaining the concept of a nickname. She was cute as a button, wearing a pink dress, and her innocent curiosity made her even more adorable.

Tori was in remarkably good spirits despite not sleeping well the night before. She had woken up in tears, in the middle of the night, and crawled into her parents' bed again. She'd had another nightmare about the bad guy again. Tori could never remember much of the details of any of the dreams but always insisted that the bad guy was a nice man. Isabelle and David were concerned about Tori's nightmares but assumed that they were a product of her vivid imagination and would pass in time.

Tori didn't show any ill effects from last night's drama and she was "entertaining" the White House staff.

"Tori-girl, you know your real name is Victoria, but we call you Tori?'

"Yes daddy."

"It's the same thing here. The real name is the 'Oval Office' but 'O' is what the President calls it. It is the nickname."

"Why doesn't the President call it the 'OO'? It's got two Os."

"Maybe I can ask the President, Tori. I have to have a special meeting with her okay?" Isabelle attempted to pacify her daughter.

"Okay mommy."

President Hays, at that moment, opened the door and greeted her guests.

"Good morning Mr. and Mrs. Franks. I'm Jennifer Hays. Would you please come in?"

David and Isabelle stood up.

"Mrs. President, I'm David Franks, this is my wife Isabelle and this is my daughter, Tori."

Franks and his wife exchanged handshakes with the President.

"That's my nickname. My real name is Victoria." Tori said as she walked up to the President.

"Tori, my nickname is Jenny. How are you young lady?"

"Fine ma'am."

"Why don't we all come inside my office?"

The group of four walked into the O. Inside was Vice President Taylor. Tori immediately recognized him and ran tried to give his leg a hug. Taylor scooped her up and she gave his neck a bear hug.

"Hello there Tori, how have you been?"

"I have been good Tom," Tori replied.

"Tori, you know better than that. Call him Mr. Taylor. Mr. Vice President, I apologize, my daughter seems to have forgotten her manners." Isabelle scolded her daughter.

"Mrs. Franks that's quite all right, I had given her permission to call me Tom on our trip back from Germany, if you recall," Taylor said, as he lowered Tori to the floor, still holding her by the hand.

"I do Mr. Vice President, but Tori knows to be on good behavior and manners are expected from her," Isabelle replied.

"Mr. and Mrs. Franks I have invited the Vice President to sit in on our discussion."

"Excuse me Mrs. President; I was under the impression that just you and my wife would be discussing the pardon issue. I am a journalist and my job is reporting the news."

"Mr. Franks I understand that your profession may be in conflict with the proceedings here. I do believe that you have some pertinent information that relates to the topic and as long as we understand that what is discussed here is off the record, I have no objections to your presence. I have a nursery for Tori and, after we are finished here, I would love for your family, the Vice President and myself to have lunch."

"That is very gracious of you Mrs. President. David will not publish anything discussed concerning Mohammad Baghai, isn't that correct?" Isabelle replied, shedding her mindset as a White House guest and assuming her attorney role; giving orders, as she thought appropriate in this case, to her husband.

"Everything is off the record Mrs. President," Franks said.

"Fine, I'll have my administrative assistant take Tori down the hall. We have some children's DVDs and she'll be supervised by one of the Secret Service Agents."

"Thank you Mrs. President, we brought some coloring books also," Isabelle said to the Commander in Chief and then she knelt down to Tori.

"I want you to go with the nice man and watch movies on TV. Mommy and Daddy have to have a talk with the President. I want you to be good and, after we are finished, we can have lunch."

"Okay Mommy." Tori hugged her mother, then her father, and then left with an agent who appeared on cue.

"Why don't we all sit down at the coffee table and keep things informal. Can I offer anyone some refreshments, coffee, juice or water?"

Franks gave his wife a glance.

"No, thank you, we're both fine."

The group sat facing each other. Isabelle assumed the initiative.

"Mrs. President I have two copies of the pardon application that I have prepared for Mohammad Baghai. Now if you will…"

"Isabelle. May I call you Isabelle?"

Hays got a nod from Isabelle.

"I appreciate your presenting this application to me. I have fifteen minutes allotted on my schedule for you to present your case. Of course I'll be happy to listen to you during lunch, if necessary. My pardon attorney will review it and advise me on the application's technical merits. What I'd like you to do is present your case for a pardon. Mind you, though I haven't made a decision, I am not inclined to consider granting a pardon, or even grant clemency for Mr. Baghai, until the legal process is completed. I also want to advise you that though the Vice President has remained publicly silent on the issue, he has confided to me on several occasions that he categorically opposes a pardon for Mr. Baghai under any circumstances. So impeaching me won't benefit your cause."

Isabelle was thrown off her game, but just momentarily. The President of the United States, sitting in the Oval Office of the White House was not your typical participant in any legal negotiation and this was essentially a negotiation with the President acting as a quasi-judge and quasi-jury.

"Mrs. President, neither me nor any member of my firm has contacted Reverend Edgars. His attempt to coerce you into pardoning my client is his doing and his alone and has nothing to do with me or my husband."

Hays seemed satisfied with Isabelle's explanation.

"Very well continue Isabelle."

"Mrs. President, in my application for my client, I have detailed my case. The short version is that there is no single case which directly points to the reasons why we believe Mohammad Baghai should be pardoned."

"I wouldn't think so," Hays replied.

"However, there are several instances that, while they don't hit the bulls-eye, they do hit the target so to speak. What I'd like to do is briefly discuss each one, then piece them together in a metaphorical mosaic, to make my argument for a pardon. Will that be satisfactory Mrs. President?"

"That will be fine Isabelle."

"Let me begin by saying that, except in cases of impeachment, the President of the United States can pardon, under Article Two, section two, any person he or she chooses, for any reason. In the next few minutes, I hope you'll find the reasons, which I'll present, carry enough weight to grant Mohammad Baghai a pardon."

"Continue Isabelle."

"There is precedent for a pardon of terrorists."

"I don't believe it." The Vice President spoke for the first time.

"Begging your pardon sir, but in 1999 President Bill Clinton pardoned thirty six FALN terrorists, Puerto Rican separatists with a history of bombing and kidnapping, as well as arson, prison escapes, intimidation and the like. In 1975, four members of this group bombed the Frances Tavern building in Lower Manhattan. Four people were killed and sixty were injured. The group had been tried and convicted of the bombing, but Clinton argued that their sentences were too severe for the crime."

"I remember that. Clinton tried to 'buy' Puerto Rican votes for his wife when she was running for the Senate," Taylor interjected.

"You are correct Mr. Vice President. That was the assumption, voiced by many," Isabelle replied.

"The point is that a President can pardon virtually anyone; in this case President Clinton used a flimsy, even transparent, excuse to grant a pardon in order to advance a political agenda."

"Go on Isabelle," Hays moved the discussion along.

"Thank you Mrs. President. In 1971 President Nixon pardoned former Teamsters boss Jimmy Hoffa while he was serving a 15-year sentence for jury tampering and fraud, with the stipulation that Hoffa would not, and I am quoting now, 'not engage in direct or indirect management of any labor organization' unquote, until 1980. Mrs. President, as a History teacher you probably recall that Hoffa disappeared in 1975, assumed to be murdered."

"Yes I do Isabelle."

"My point is that President put conditions on his pardon of Hoffa, and you could certainly do the same."

"What conditions are you suggesting?"

"That, of course, would be entirely up to you, though I do have some suggestions, which I will discuss after I have finished, if that is all right with you ma'am?"

"Okay, what else?"

"In 1983 financier Marc Rich was indicted for tax evasion; we are talking about millions of dollars, by the way, multiple counts of tax fraud providing money for illegal oil deals to Middle Eastern countries. Rather than face the charges against him, Rich fled to Switzerland and remained there until President Clinton pardoned him in the last week of his second term."

"I don't remember the details of that. Would you elaborate Isabelle?" Taylor asked. Isabelle sensed that his hard-line position might have softened a little. Perhaps he was connecting the dots and beginning to see the picture that she was creating.

"Certainly, Mr. Vice President, there were rumors that Rich 'bought' a pardon with enormous campaign contributions to the Clintons, by Rich's ex-wife, Denise, who was still living in the States. Investigations were launched but nothing was substantiated."

"Finally, President Andrew Johnson granted a blanket pardon to most Confederate citizens, in 1865, requiring only that they take an oath of loyalty to the United States. He also pardoned Dr. Samuel Mudd; the doctor who set John Wilkes Booth's broken leg, not knowing he was President Lincoln's assassin. Mudd was convicted as a conspirator in the Lincoln assassination and was sentenced to a term in the Dry Tortugas, in the Florida Keys. Dr. Mudd treated guards and inmates alike when a lethal flu infected the island. President Johnson pardoned him on humanitarian grounds," Isabelle continued.

"Mrs. President, summing things up and doing a little compare and contrast, my client, a self-confessed former terrorist who, rather than flee justice, voluntarily traveled to the United States to face justice. Rather than demanding a trial, a right he is certainly entitled to, he has pled guilty to the charges against him, and will plead guilty to any additional charges."

"I will not address the religious reasons for granting a pardon. Reverend Edgars has expressed them more eloquently than I could ever hope to and I do believe them to be legitimate. Also, as I mentioned earlier, a President doesn't need a legitimate reason to grant a pardon. Be that as it may, I have summarized what I consider legitimate reasons to justify a pardon. Furthermore, a pardon, issued by you, could and should stipulate that my client, Mohammad Baghai, would also swear an oath of loyalty and be available to the CIA, and any law enforcement organization that you deem appropriate, for intelligence debriefing. As you know, the FBI has already attempted a debriefing before he suffered his medical issues. My client was willing to discuss the matter then but I advised him to remain silent at the time."

"Let me add something if I may," Franks spoke up for the first time.

"Of course David," Hays relied.

"When I was kidnapped, I had a unique opportunity to observe Mohammad. I looked him eye to eye from six inches away. I saw the eyes of a killer, without emotion and without pity. I was nose to nose with death. On the night that he released me, I also saw him eyeball to eyeball, again, only I saw a human being, not a killer. For whatever reason, divine or secular, my friend Mohammad, and he is my friend, has changed and he deserves a chance for redemption."

"Mr. and Mrs. Franks, I am impressed by your arguments and I will give them careful consideration before I make a decision."

"Thank you Mrs. President, Mr. Vice President," Isabelle replied.

"Now I'm getting hungry. The Vice President and I had a disagreement on what should be served. He wanted Texas beef and I wanted fresh Florida Red Snapper. We compromised and we're having a surf and turf today. I instructed the White House Chef to prepare some hot dogs for Tori in case she would rather eat that."

"That's very thoughtful Mrs. President," Isabelle said.

Hays and her guests set politics aside and enjoyed a fine meal.

# Chapter 17

Jim Scarboro was sitting at his desk and had a headache. He had just received a report from the FBI, summarizing Kathleen Mueller's surveillance; it revealed nothing. President Hays would not be happy. Reverend Edgars had not released any of the data from his web site but rumors floating around were that the hits numbered in the hundreds of thousands. Scarboro suspected that the number was exaggerated, though there was no real way of knowing. The good Reverend was a smart man. He had adroitly maneuvered Hays into a box and was letting her stew in her own juices.

In addition to the Baghai business, the President had informed him that she was going to be the commencement speaker at the graduation ceremonies at the University of West Florida. Though the security was technically a Secret Service matter, the FBI had been given the task of screening the students participating in the ceremony.

There was an elaborate screening process designed to raise red flags on any likely threats based on felony criminal records, political affiliations, radical organization affiliations and the like. Of the 3,722-graduating students only thirty four were deemed to be possible threats to the President; less than one percent. However, everyone had to be investigated. Twenty-four lived in the Pensacola area, nine had families out of town and one student had two addresses. Charlie Michaels had an address in Pensacola and a background investigation showed that he'd been working in a small North Georgia town, Dahlonega, for several months but did not have a registered a address until he signed a lease on an apartment last week. This young man's record was clean but Scarboro remembered seeing his name before. AAMO, was a vocal college group that was anti-war and anti-Hays. Michaels was probably not a threat. College students, who knew "everything" as undergraduates, inevitably lost a significant portion of that knowledge, yet gained a proportional measure of wisdom once they entered the work force. In any case, Charlie Michaels would have to be investigated.

Scarboro reached into his desk drawer and swallowed two aspirin.

PRESIDENT Hays also had a headache and popped a couple of aspirin, followed by a mouthful of bottled water.

"Send them in," she said with a note of frustration. Hays had agreed to meet a bi-partisan congressional delegation to discuss "domestic affairs," though the only likely topic likely to be discussed was Mohammad Baghai. It was not a secret that since Reverend Edgars' web site launched, virtually every Senator and Congressman had received hundreds and, in some cases thousands, of pieces of correspondence from their constituents and Edgars had not released the data collected from the Save Baghai web site!

South Dakota Senator, Tim Dunston, who Hays had defeated for the Presidency, led the delegation. Undoubtedly his office had received emails and phones calls from the good people of South Dakota, demanding a pardon for Baghai, but Hays knew Dunston well enough to know that he was only here to extract whatever measure of political flesh that he could. Dunston, it was rumored, having lost the election by an eyelash, was contemplating another run at the nation's highest office. Hays, in her second term, didn't have a stake, but she did have a personal disdain for Dunston.

The delegation of four entered the "O." There were two Senators and two Congressmen, comprised of two Democrats and two Republicans. Dunston was keeping appearances unbiased, though Hays knew better. Dunston played politics from the Lyndon Johnson school; everything was fair and nothing was off-limits. Basically the ends justified the means as long as you didn't get caught.

Hays met the delegation at the door.

"Gentlemen, it's a pleasure to see you again. Please come in and sit down." Hays said as she shook the hands of each of the members.

"It's always a pleasure to speak with you Madam President," Dunston replied as the group got settled in the two facing sofas.

Accompanying Dunston was John Isacs, the Senior Senator from Georgia and a Republican. The two Congressmen were Cedric Wrangler, a Democrat, and the House Judiciary Committee Chairman from Harlem, and William "Billy the Kid" Johnson, a Native American and Republican from New Mexico, known for speaking exactly what was on his mind. Tact was not his strong suit. The delegation, in addition to being politically balanced, was geographically and ethnically balanced as well.

Wrangler was just window dressing for Dunston. The Congressman was elected by over eighty percent in his last election and was one of the few elected officials in Washington that was not concerned with the Baghai affair. He would back the Democratic Party line, so long as he was not perceived to buck the African-American agenda.

Isacs and Johnson were two relatively conservative politicians. Both represented conservative, God-fearing constituents. Georgia was the buckle of the Bible Belt. Isacs knew who buttered his bread; Johnson was a Roman Catholic and, though he'd not publicly commented on the issue, the fact that he was present at this meeting spoke volumes about his position. Dunston had indeed done his homework well.

Hays chose to sit in a Queen Anne chair, which placed her perpendicular to her guests. She had a specific reason for her choice of seating arrangements. Her norm, when entertaining dignitaries or conducting a business discussion in the "O," was to sit alongside her associates, removing the invisible barrier of the Presidency, which was a tactic which could cause the most confident man to become insecure. Today, by sitting higher than her guests, she wanted her guests to know that she was in command and that they were going to march to the beat of her drum and not vice-versa.

"Can I offer you some coffee or bottled water?" Hays asked her guests and received four heads shaken in the negative.

"Very well then, shall we get down to it?"

"Thank you Madam President. We're representing our colleagues in expressing the legislative branch's concerns about the domestic policy of your administration," Dunston began before Hays interrupted him.

"Senator, if I may. Excuse me for interrupting, but if we're here to discuss domestic affairs, I'll be happy to query you as to why the federal budget has yet to be balanced, even though I have proposed such every year that I have been in office. The controlling party in Congress has ridiculed my education reform proposals, yet they've never offered an alternative. If domestic affairs are really on the mind of my friends on Capital Hill, then I'm prepared to discuss that with you for the rest of the day. Somehow I don't believe that's the case, is it?"

Dunston was about to retort when Johnson replied.

"Madam President, you are quite correct in your assumptions. I personally agree with your domestic positions and my voting record supports my claims. I am speaking personally, and for a number of my colleagues in the House, when I say that we've received numerous contacts, through all sources of communication, regarding your intentions of a pardon for Mohammad Baghai."

"The people in Georgia, while they certainly don't condone his terrorist past, do respect that he's a changed man. And that prominent members of all denominations of the Christian faith believe that the Almighty has given Mohammed Baghai a message, a fact which deserves some consideration in the legal process," the Senator from Georgia interjected.

"You're talking about a pardon, Senator?"

"A pardon is certainly a possibility or you could commute his sentence, whatever it may be, to time served, assuming that he recovers from his medical issues. By commuting his sentence, he still has a criminal record but he's allowed to deliver God's message," Isacs continued.

"You're sounding very much like a televangelist that I know, Senator." Hays said, referring to Casey Edgars.

"I am echoing the feelings of my constituents Madam President."

"President Hays, my people are telling me that, though Baghai was a despicable person in his previous life, now he is a changed person. His actions demonstrate his sincerity and don't need comment. The public opinion in my district is trending two-thirds towards a pardon. I know this is a political hot potato for you and my people don't want to have articles of impeachment brought to the floor of the House, but you know better than I do that public opinion is fickle."

Wild Bill Johnson got his two cents into the discussion.

"Is that a veiled threat Congressman?"

Hays recognized the significance of a Congressman, from her own party, suggesting her removal from office.

"Not at all Madam President, I am just stating the obvious."

"Congressman, if such preposterous charge were brought against me, I would resign. Vice President Taylor is also opposed to a pardon for Mohammad Baghai; even more vehemently opposed than I am. So my removal from office would not accomplish your goal, whatever it is. Believe me gentlemen; this is not a fight that you want. There would not be any winners."

Hays was speaking to Johnson, but her comment was directed towards Dunston, and he knew it.

Dunston, as if on cue, chimed in for the first time.

"Madam President, we are a diverse country, with diverse opinions and diverse political agendas. However, a majority of the country appears to have rallied behind Mohammad Baghai and is demanding a pardon for him. As a politician, you know that public opinion can be shaped and molded, but sometimes it runs its own course and elected officials sometimes have to hold on for the ride. This is such a time."

"No, Senator, it is now and has always been time to stand up for principles. Mohammad Baghai has pled guilty to a murder. Not just any murder but the murder of an American soldier. He will likely be charged with others. I am not prepared to grant a pardon until the legal process is concluded. I will not be threatened, blackmailed or otherwise intimidated into granting a pardon to him until the process is completed. I will not compromise on this issue. I have been on record with my position and I will reiterate it again soon. Now if you gentlemen do not care to discuss any domestic issues of substance, this meeting is concluded."

"Thank you for your time Madam President."

Dunston, along with his associates said in unison as they left. Hays rose and sat behind her desk. Her headache had not subsided. Shephard walked in at that moment.

"You heard all of the conversation Andy?"

"Every word, were you serious about resigning?"

"If it came to that I would. I'm not going to embarrass myself, or the country, the way Clinton did."

"Madam President, if you don't mind me asking, why are you so vehemently opposed to granting a pardon? Reverend Edgars is correct; there's nothing illegal or unconstitutional about it. So, I'm assuming that you are morally opposed to granting a pardon in this case," Shephard asked her boss.

"Are you handling me, Andy?"

Hays smiled for a second then suddenly became pensive.

"Andy, you know that, before I met you, while I was a grad student in Wisconsin, I was married and Steve, my husband, a contractor, died in a car crash, in a head-on collision from a drunk driver. The driver only had a few scratches."

"Yes, I knew that. It's common knowledge."

"What isn't public record is that three weeks after I buried Steve, I found out that I was pregnant."

"I didn't know that. How did the press not discover that after you threw your hat into the ring?"

"After I the funeral, I decided to get into my car and drive. There were just too many memories in Madison for me to deal with at the time. I needed to get out of town. I wrapped up my affairs and found myself in Arizona. It was in Winslow, I was visiting the meteor crater, for no particular reason, other than it was there. That was when I miscarried. An ambulance took me to a hospital. I found out that I was pregnant and lost my baby at the same time. It was a girl."

Hays was tearing up. She was telling a tale that no one, or at least very few people, knew.

"Losing my husband and losing my unborn baby within a month gave me an appreciation of life that most men and women take for granted, I think. There was a priest, Father Frank Adams, who met me at the hospital while I was recovering. He helped me work through my mental agony those first few days. I asked him why God would take my husband and my baby. He didn't have an answer for me, but he did say that mankind worships a loving God and, because God loved both Steve and my baby, he took them and they were both in Heaven."

"I don't want to see Mohammad Baghai put to death, yet he has killed many and has to answer for his crimes. He is sincere. His actions speak volumes to that and, though I have ambivalent feelings about the issue, I haven't ruled out the possibility of pardoning him. Andy, I'm sure that you'll agree that this is an issue that should be considered carefully without emotion, based upon the merits and not on outside influences. Wouldn't you agree?"

"Certainly."

"That's why I've taken the position that I have."

Hays took a tissue and dried her eyes. Her catharsis to her chief of staff had visibly lifted an invisible weight off her shoulders.

"Will that be all Madam President?"

"Yes, Andy, that's all. Thank you."

"I'm always at your disposal," Shephard said as he left the Oval Office.

Hays' headache suddenly vanished.


FBI agent Martin Schrader, was sitting at his desk doing perfunctory telephone interviews for the investigation of Charlie Michaels, from the Gainesville, Georgia office. Schrader, an overweight, balding man in his fifties, once had a promising career but he never fulfilled his, or the agency's, expectations. Gainesville, Georgia was approximately 60 miles north-northeast of Atlanta, and on the other side of Lake Lanier from Cumming. The Gainesville field office, as opposed to the Atlanta office, was type of location where new FBI agents cut their teeth and veteran agents were sent to serve their remaining time in the agency until they retired. Schrader fell into the latter category. Work was mundane and, after nearly 30 years of service, Schrader was ready to retire.

He'd been given this assignment after the President decided to participate in the graduation ceremonies at the University of West Florida. This boy Michaels was graduating and had raised some sort of red flag. Michaels had moved to Georgia. Currently he was living in the city of Dawsonville. Gainesville, the closest location to Dawsonville, was conducting the investigation on Michaels, rather than the Mobile, Alabama office, which was the closest location to Pensacola.

Michaels was working for an insurance agency, Twig Insurance

Group in Cumming. Schrader dialed the number. A receptionist answered the phone.

"Twig Insurance Group. How may I direct your call?" The female voice on the other end answered in a perky voice.

"Good morning. This is Agent Martin Schrader of the FBI. May I speak to the owner or manager?"

"That would be Ralph Twig. Let me connect you."

Schrader waited a moment listening to elevator music before Ralph picked up the phone.

"Hello, this is Ralph Twig."

"Mr. Twig, I am Martin Schrader of the FBI, over across the lake in Gainesville. How are you sir?"

"Fine, why do I have the pleasure of conversing with the FBI?"

"I'm conducting a routine telephone interview in an investigation of Charles Michaels. I understand that he works for your agency?"

"Yes he just started working here a couple of weeks ago. Why is Charlie under investigation?"

"Mr. Michaels will be participating in the graduating ceremonies at the University of West Florida in Pensacola shortly, which President Hays will be speaking at, and his name came up as a possible threat to the President. I am interviewing various people to ascertain whether the threat is credible."

Ralph broke into uproarious laughter.

"Did I say something funny Mr. Twig?"

"I apologize Agent Schrader, please forgive me. Charlie Michaels is not a fan of the President, but he is not a threat to her."

"Why do you say that?"

"I've had conversations with him and I think I know him pretty well. He belonged to some sort of group protesting the occupation of Iraq while he was in school, but he lives here now. He's an excellent student and even better human being and oh, by the way, he's engaged to my daughter Heather. She is a ROTC student at North Georgia. Now does that sound to you like he's a threat to the President?"

"I don't make that decision sir. I only gather the data, but no, it doesn't. I want to thank you for your time and for your information, everything I have heard about the young man supports what you have just told me. Have a good day sir."

"You do the same also," Ralph hung up the phone and walked down the hall to Charlie's office.

"Did you know that you were on the FBI's ten most-wanted list?" Ralph asked in a semi-serious tone.

"Excuse me?" Charlie knew that Ralph was joking but didn't

comprehend his comment.

"I just got off the phone with the FBI. It seems that someone believes you're a threat to the President. You have the right to remain silent by the way."

Ralph let loose another burst of laughter.

"Are you serious Ralph?"

"Completely, since President Hays will be speaking at your graduation, and because you belonged to whatever anti-war group from college, you've been deemed a possible threat to her."

"Incredible, this is all because I actively voiced my opposition to our occupation forces in Iraq? Are they trying to muzzle me?"

"I don't think so Charlie. The agent I spoke to said it was a routine investigation and that nothing he'd discovered about you indicated that you were a threat."

"Oh? Who else have they been speaking to?" Charlie sounded irked.

"Relax son. He was just doing his job. If your job was to protect the President, or anyone important, you'd do exactly the same thing."

"Ralph, you're missing the point. I am minding my own business, participating in my graduation ceremonies and because the President decides she wants to participate, I get investigated? Do you see anything wrong with that picture?"

"Charlie if you were living in Red China, you'd be arrested and held without due process for this; in the grand scheme of things a small investigation is nothing. Come on; let's go to lunch, we can pick up my wife at the house. Jo Ann wants to see you; she hasn't seen you in just about a week."

Charlie and Ralph left the office to pick up Jo Anne, though Charlie continued to stew intenally over President Hays.

# Chapter 18

Hassan Nassiri was sitting in his office. He was reviewing a status report on a pet project of his, a radiological dispersal device or RDD, better known as a dirty bomb. A dirty bomb combines radioactive material with conventional explosives, spreading radioactive material over a large area. Nassiri had the materials to build it and the perfect man to manage the project, General Mansur Bakar, who was waiting outside his office, ready to advise him on the project's status.

Unlike him, Bakar was a fervent Muslim and possessed a nuclear engineering degree. Like Nassiri, he had risen through the ranks of the Iranian Army and because of his passionate religious devotion was respected by the Islamic powers in Iran, allowing him to survive the purges of the eighties.

Nassiri pushed a button on the intercom.

"Send General Bakar in."

A moment later a swarthy man in his early sixties, with a barrel chest and a back as straight as the starched creases of his uniform trousers, came in and stood at attention. A salute immediately followed; his right hand quivered slightly, as it snapped to the bill of his cover.

"General Bakar reporting as ordered sir."

"Sit down General."

"Thank you sir."

"General, I have read your report, but I had you come here to personally brief me. I do not want to have any misconceptions about what I read, comprehend and believe to be true versus what actually is the truth. Am I being clear?"

"Perfectly sir."

Bakar appreciated Nassiri's frankness. Other members of the Iranian Military feared the Prime Minister and Nassiri knew that, using that fear to help obtain his objectives. Bakar, on the other hand, made it his practice to be thoroughly prepared for whatever his assignment demanded and never attempted to be politically correct; always being truthful and cogent

"You may begin General."

"Mr. Prime Minister, from a technical standpoint, the project is completed. My primary concern is the quality of the radioactive material. In this case it is strontium 90, which is extremely suitable for our purposes. Strontium 90 is a nuclear-reactor-produced isotope but it is difficult to manufacture, and virtually impossible to do so undetected, because of the limited number of facilities capable of making it. There are other reactor-produced isotopes, which are also suitable, americium 241, californium 252, caseium 137, cobalt 60, iridium 192 and a few others. However all these isotopes are also reactor-produced and, since the facilities required to produce them are limited and can be monitored, it would be difficult to obtain them undetected."

"The strontium 90 is acceptable quality for our purposes General?"

"Yes sir, it is."

"General, I have a virtually, unlimited supply of strontium 90 inside Iran's borders."

"Mr. Prime Minister, that is impossible."

"General, I am not in the mood to mince words. Believe me when I say that Iran possesses sufficient quantities of strontium 90 for at least 100 weapons of mass destruction."

"Mr. Prime Minister, let me make a point and then ask you a question."

"Certainly, General."

"A RDD, or 'dirty bomb' is not a weapon of mass destruction, it is a weapon of terror and kills by dispersing radioactive material, via an explosion, into the atmosphere. The explosion of a nuclear device would normally kill tens of thousands of people, as opposed to a RDD explosion, which kills a few dozen. In theory, sir, it does not have to kill anyone. Furthermore, in addition to radiation sickness suffered by the population from a nuclear device, the infrastructure would become useless for years from the radioactivity of any metal material which the strontium 90 contacted."

Nassiri raised his eyebrows as if the light bulb of an idea suddenly turned on.

"You said that you had a question General?"

"Yes Mr. Prime Minster. If you say that Iran possesses plenty of strontium 90, of course, I believe you, but how was it obtained? Our country doesn't have the means to produce it."

Nassiri smiled.

"General, there is an amusing story concerning your question and I will relay it provided that it doesn't go beyond this room."

"It won't Mr. Prime Minister."

"It seems that in December of 2001, three loggers from the former Soviet Province of Georgia were in the middle of some forest, found a portable thermoelectric generator and used it as a heating source for several nights. General, what do you think was the power source for that generator?"

"Strontium 90, Mr. Prime Minister, but I don't understand how we possess enough material for one hundred RDDs."

"General, that generator was the power source for some type of location-directional beacon in a remote area of what was the Soviet Union.

Now, just how many remote areas do you think are there in the Soviet Union and how many of these remote areas have directional beacons?"

Bakar understood how such quantities of strontium 90 had become available without raising undue notice but didn't understand how such materials were moved to Iran.

"Mr. Prime Minister, how was the strontium 90 moved to Iran?"

"It was via the black market General. It seems that the sister to one of loggers was married to a member of the Russian Mafia. The loggers died, of course, but the Mafia realized what a windfall it had discovered and shopped the material around the black markets of the world. We had unlimited financial resources and you can guess the rest. The only real issue was moving the material to our country. It has taken all this time to get it here. And that idiot Bush invaded Iraq because he thought Saddam Hussein had weapons of mass destruction."

Nassiri broke into laughter for a moment then continued.

"The only real question now is how and when to use our weapons. Do you have any suggestions General?"

"That would depend on the objectives Mr. Prime Minister. I can speak for military objectives but, in the current climate, almost any military objective is interwoven with political objectives, which I have neither expertise nor experience in."

"You make an excellent point General. Are you suggesting that we should collaborate?"

"Mr. Prime Minister, I am a career military man. I take orders from the proper authority. As a former military officer, you know that. It is not the place for the military in this country, or any other for that matter, to collaborate. The military can advise, if so ordered, but then it is its duty to obey any and all lawful orders given by the proper civilian authorities."

"Again, General your point is well taken. You have reaffirmed to me that I chose the correct man to manage this project. I have some ideas that I am considering, but I am not ready to discuss them at this time. Thank you for coming."

General Mansur Bakar took his cue to exit. Standing up rigidly, he saluted smartly and departed. Nassiri was already lost in thought and barely acknowledged Bakar. He didn't mention that he had plans to assassinate Baghai and Hays.

CASEY Edgars stood at the podium, conducting a press conference in the CMC compound. It was time to turn up the heat on President Hays. She had neither pardoned the Prophet Mohammad Baghai, nor indicated that she intended to do so.

Edgars understood that Hays was stuck between the proverbial rock and a hard place, in the sense that she could not appear to bow to the "religious right" for political reasons, even though Edgars could sense that she knew that it was the correct course of action. Political obstacles be damned! God had chosen Mohammad Baghai as His spokesman! A blind man could see this clearly and God's will be done! The President would conform to God's will, and if it meant another person taking the oath of office as President, then so be it!

"Ladies and gentlemen, thank you for coming today. Ten days ago, I announced the launching of a new website, pardonGodsprophet.com. During the announcement I urged President Hays to pardon Mohammad Baghai for his crimes. I also announced that if she did not pardon God's Prophet within 48 hours, I would open a new page and database on the website, which would collect names and addresses of God-fearing American citizens, who, first, believe that Mohammad Baghai is God's Prophet, second, believe that he should be pardoned so he can spread God's message and third, believe that President Hays should be impeached for not granting God's Prophet a pardon."

"Sadly, President Hays has not granted God's Prophet a pardon. I would ask each and every American to pray for her to realize the error in her way."

Edgars paused for a moment and bowed his head.

"Ladies and gentlemen, as I promised, I have sent the names of God-fearing Americans who have visited our website to the appropriate members of the Senate and House of Representatives. In the seven days that the pages demanding either the pardon of God's Prophet or the impeachment of the President have been active, over a quarter of a million Americans have visited the website and plainly understand that God has plan for His Prophet. I will now entertain questions."

The press initiated a feeding frenzy of questions. Edgars fully expected it and was prepared to answer each and every one.

"Reverend, exactly how many hits has your website had?"

"As I said, over a quarter of a million, I can't say exactly but I will have the webmaster post the total on the website."

"How often, and how long, will you continue to release the number of hits to the site?"

"Every week sounds reasonable to me and for as long as it takes to force the President to pardon God's Prophet."

"Reverend, it's apparent that you're making a concerted effort to identify Mohammad Baghai as a holy man with a message; the most obvious of which is identifying him, not by his name, but as God's Prophet, why?"

"Because, Mohammad Baghai is God's Prophet."

The press corps broke out into laughter.

"Reverend, as a man of the cloth, you seem to have a God-given talent; would you care to explain how you and Mohammad Baghai are similar?"

"There is no similarity between God's Prophet and myself."

The room was utterly silent as Edgars paused a moment for effect.

"I have been blessed with certain God-given insights, if that is the correct term. God gave me the wisdom to recognize my abilities and I have tried to use them as I thought He would want me to. Now I want to be completely clear, I have never once had a conversation with our Lord, other than in prayer. Mohammad Baghai, God's Prophet, on the other hand, was scooped up, tossed into the flaming pits of hell, picked up by our Lord Jesus Christ and personally given instructions. All of you, I am sure can distinguish the difference."

"Reverend, you play chess as a hobby; let me ask you a question in chess terms. What do you envision as the end game to your campaign? What happens to Mohammad Baghai when, and if, he is pardoned?"

Edgars got a laugh from the reference to the game of chess.

"To draw an analogy to chess, we are at a critical point in the game, which could go in two opposite directions. On the one hand, if President Hays refuses to grant the pardon to God's prophet, that she knows is God's desire, then ultimately, I foresee that she will be impeached and removed from office. On the other hand, if she does pardon God's Prophet, then I do not know what the ending is. Only our Lord can say. This is the middle game and it could go in different directions, depending on several variables."

"So you're saying that President Hays will be impeached for not pardoning Mohammad Baghai?"

"Yes, that is what I said."

"Is that what you believe, or a prediction?"

"That is what I foresee, but I can't guarantee it."

# Chapter 19

It was about 5:00 a.m. in the foyer of the Al-Farooq Mosque in Chicago. Abu Sabaya was preparing for Fajr or the Morning Prayer ritual. Iside the mosque was a 20-foot by 2-foot trough filled with water. Sabaya and dozens of others were performing wudu, a symbolic cleaning of their hands, face and feet, with the water in the in the trough, for the Fajr. Like many of his male worshipers, Sabaya was wearing a white tunic and white slacks and white ball cap with the bill removed. After taking off his shoes Sabaya completed his cleaning process, he turned to walk into the mosque as another worshiper bumped into him. He was an Arab, in his mid-fifties, Sabaya judged, also wearing similar slacks and tunic.

"Excuse me, my brother," The worshiper said.

"No, excuse me. Allahu Akbar!"

"God is greater" was the translation, an incomplete sentence, with the connotation that God was greater than anyone or anything.

"Allahu Akbar, my brother," Sabaya said. He continued inside, didn't pay any more attention to the man, took a three-by-five foot carpet remnant and placed it on the floor to pray upon. Some worshipers brought their own prayer mat, but most of the worshipers borrowed one.

Sabaya was not concerned with being discovered. He had been careful not to be conspicuous, renting a nearby extended-stay motel and using a false identification obtained from al-Qaeda contacts in Manila. During the evening, Sabaya read the Koran or watched television.

The group, mostly of men, with a few women, entered the main hall, or musalla, divided into two groups by gender and faced the Holy City of Mecca.

Led by the Iman, a stately man in his sixties, the two groups folded their arms over their chests, bowed and knelt, following a procedure all Muslims around the world followed, to begin the prayer or "salat."

The worshipers, as if on cue, began the salat ritual again. Upon kneeling facing Mecca, each worshiper began to silently recite another few verses, of their choice, of the Holy Koran.

"Let those who fight in the cause of God, who sell the life of this world for the next life. To the one who fights in the cause of God, whether he is killed or achieves victory, we shall soon give him a great reward. And why shouldn't you fight in the cause of God and of those who, being weak, are being mistreated; the men, women and children whose only cry is, 'Oh Lord! Save us from this land whose people are oppressors, and bring to us from You someone who will protect us, and bring to us from You someone who will help.' Those who believe, fight in the cause of God, and those who reject faith fight in the cause of evil. So fight against the friends of Shaitan."

Sabaya had chosen and memorized those particular verses for a reason. In them, the Prophet Muhammad discussed jihad. Sabaya's original jihad was against the Philippines, he was now in a struggle against the "Great Shaitan" or "Great Satan," America.

It was clear to Sabaya that Allah had saved him from death to continue the jihad. He did not expect to live after he killed the Vice President, but he had no doubt that he would achieve victory by killing him and gaining his "reward." The Prophet Muhammad promised any "shaheed," or martyr, Paradise for his or her supreme sacrifice.

His morning prayers completed, Sabaya rose from the floor and walked to the shelf where his shoes were placed and put them back on his feet. The man who had bumped into him was retrieving his shoes well.

"Hello again, my brother," the stranger said.

Sabaya became suspicious, but ignored him. Sabaya had been careful not to stick out in a crowd; Allah's mission was too important.

"I know Allah has forgiven your sins, but will He forgive the sins that that you will commit?"

Sabaya knew he had been discovered and reached under his tunic to withdraw a pistol from his waistband, keeping it under his tunic. At the same moment he grabbed the man's tunic and drew him close as he pressed the pistol into the man's ribs and whispered into the man's ear.

"I don't know who you are, though it is obvious that you know who I am. We are going to walk outside and find a place where you will tell me who you are and what you want. Then I will decide whether to let you live or not."

The stranger was not intimidated and didn't budge.

"I would have believed that the bearer of the sword would use a knife, not a gun."

The stranger was referring to Sabaya's participation and membership in Abu-Sayef, the decimated Philippine separatist organization.

Sabaya relaxed ever so slightly, but still kept the pistol in the man's ribs.

"How do you know about me or Abu-Sayef?"

"Relax my brother, if I was not on your side, on Allah's side, you would either be captured, or more likely, if you are as courageous as I believe you are, dead already. Yes, let us walk outside to a place of your choosing and discuss your purpose here. Keep your gun pointed at me if you feel it necessary, though I can see in your eyes that you already know that no harm will come to you by my hand."

Sabaya had remained alive by being careful. How he had been discovered was a mystery that this man would soon reveal or he would be dead.

"We are going to walk out of the mosque and around the corner, where we can speak above whispers. If you scream, I will kill you. If you run, I will kill you. When we are alone I will ask you questions and you will answer them. If I don't believe your answers, I will kill you. If you hesitate or I believe you are withholding information, I will kill you. After you answer all of my questions I will decide if I will kill you."

Sabaya spoke to his acquaintance in a whisper.

"I would expect nothing less from you, my brother," the stranger retorted in a calm tone.

The two men walked out of the mosque, with Sabaya walking a half a step behind and to the left of the stranger, with the pistol still jabbed into the stranger's ribs. Exiting, the two walked down the block and turned into an alley. The first rays of dawn appeared and an occasional passerby could be seen as the pair walked away from the mosque. Sabaya grabbed the man's left shoulder, spun him around, took the pistol from under his tunic and backed the stranger against a brick wall.

"Now, you seem to know everything about me, 'my brother.' Now it is your turn to tell me about yourself," Sabaya said to the stranger in a mocking tone of voice.

"Benino Marcos," the stranger addressed him, using Sabaya's Christian birth name, "My original name is not important. Like you, I have changed it. I am now Malikul Mawt."

Sabaya forced a thin smile. "And what does the 'Angel of Death' want with me?"

Malikul Mawt was Arabic for 'Angel of Death'. Sabaya was not fluent in Arabic but he knew enough of it to recognize words and phrases, from studying, after his conversion.

"Your hatred of America is at least equal of that to mine. American interference has prevented Basilan, and other southern islands of the Philippine group, from becoming independent; American interference, by supporting their puppet Israel, has also prevented my fellow Palestinian brothers and sisters from claiming their rightful homeland."

"You still have not told me anything about yourself, and I am growing impatient." Sabaya emphasized his point by boring the barrel of the pistol into the Angel's chest.

"No my brother, it is time for you to make a choice. I, too, am on jihad and if you choose to kill me, then I will greet you in Paradise. You have a mission, to kill the Vice President and die a shaheed. Now, do you want to just kill one man or bring the Great Satan to its knees and, perhaps, see Basilan gain its independence in your lifetime?"

Sabaya looked into the Angel's eyes. He did not see fear, only resolve. It was that resolve that tipped the scales for Sabaya to spare the Angel's life.

As if on cue, the Angel sensed what Sabaya was thinking.

"Put your weapon back under your tunic my brother, you have no need of it."

Sabaya put his gun underneath his tunic.

"Come my brother; let me show you what I am referring to. We have much to discuss."

The two men walked back to the Angel's car and, in less than five minutes, were outside what appeared to be a small abandoned warehouse. It was a cinder block building, two stories high; the windows on the second story were all broken; the windows on the first floor were boarded up. Graffiti decorated the walls. A roll-up door was at one end of the building, a regular commercial steel door at the other. The Angel pulled up by the roll-up door and got out of the car, leaving the motor running. He unlocked the door, pushed it up and got back into a car, driving it into the warehouse. Once inside, he closed the roll-up door.

Sabaya got out of the car, with his gun drawn. He still didn't trust the Malikul Mawt.

"My brother, you and I are the only ones here. There is no need for your weapon, but I see you do not yet trust me. Go check for yourself so that you are satisfied I am telling you the truth."

"My brother, you know all about me and I don't even know your real name. We will walk every inch of the building, you in front of me. After I am convinced we are alone, I will put away my weapon," Sabaya said in a mocking tone.

"You are wise to be cautious."

The two men walked the entire length of the warehouse. Sabaya didn't see anything that appeared unusual, just pallets, empty boxes, crates, scattered newspapers and two cube steel boxes, about two feet square in dimension. There was a motorcycle parked in the corner, with a tarpaulin draped over it. The warehouse appeared as if it hadn't been occupied in months, or years, and it was in a deserted area of the city.

"I rented the warehouse, and a house to live in, over a year ago using a false identity, long before security safeguards were initiated. The landlords have yet to contact me, since I signed the leases, and I don't expect them to as long as I continue to pay the rent on time. There is little chance that I will be discovered."

Sabaya still held the pistol level at the Angel's chest.

"You and I are the only two people who know about my intentions and the contents in this warehouse."

"What is in this warehouse that anyone needs to be concerned about?"

"Inside one steel box is a lead cylinder which contains radioactive material. Inside the second box is sufficient dynamite to destroy the radioactive material and spread it all over the place. I believe the Americans call it a 'dirty bomb.' I am sure you can understand the significance."

"How did you find me?" Sabaya asked.

"After Abu Sayef was destroyed, you went to Manila where you accessed your family's money. Al-Qaeda knew who you were, and I understand that a believer works for that particular bank. You had money transferred to a Chicago bank into an account under your Christian name. Your devout faith was known, so I began to pray at all the mosques. There weren't too many Filipinos. It wasn't hard to figure out what your destination was, and your probable target."

"How are you so certain that the Americans aren't following us now?"

"I have been living in Chicago for over a year, minding my own business and staying out of the spotlight. If the Americans knew who, and where I was, this close to the Olympics, I would have been arrested already. In fact, I am risking compromising this mission by contacting you."

"And why did you decide to pick me?"

"You spent time in Iran, and received training in the use of dirty bombs, did you not?"

Sabaya finally understood and lowered his gun.

AT about the same time Sabaya was performing Fajr, half a world away, Cal was performing isha'a, the evening prayer ritual. After performing wudu in a sink, he spread a piece of carpet on the deck of a nearby storage locker; the Prophet Muhammad stated that not only must the body be clean to perform salat, the ground must be clean also. After facing in the direction of where he thought Mecca lay, he began isha'a. After it was completed, Cal rolled up his carpet and was returning to his bunk when Pat Thomas saw him.

"Cal, the skipper wants to see you in his quarters ASAP!"

"I'm on the way thanks."

Cal walked briskly to the skipper's cabin, directly behind the bridge. An order "on the double" would mean run but since the order was only "as soon as possible," it meant a fast walk, though you never kept the skipper waiting. Three minutes later, he knocked on Commander Hampton's quarters. Cal didn't expect the meeting to last long either. The skipper was a no-nonsense man who didn't beat around the bush.

"Enter," Hampton said in a conversational tone. "Intavan, close the hatch behind you. Sit down."

Cal entered and then closed the hatch behind him. Hampton was sitting at a small metal government desk. On it was a manila folder with a paper clipped picture of Cal.

"Yes sir."

"I've been reviewing your file. Your record is outstanding. What is it going to take to keep you in the Navy?"

"Skipper, it's not quite that simple. I couldn't afford to go to college and the Navy is a means to an end. I like the Navy; military life requires discipline, which meshes well with my faith, but I don't see myself as a cook for the next twenty years."

"Neither do I; you're much too talented."

"What are you saying skipper? I'm not following you."

"I told you in sick bay the other day, that I wish I commanded 100 men just like you. Intavan, I'm nominating you for the Navy Cross." The Navy Cross was an award for valor, second in prestige only to the Medal of Honor.

"There will be a camera crew from CNN coming onboard to interview and profile you. Apparently someone thinks your rescue of Carson is a great human-interest story, considering your heritage. The Navy decided it wants some good public relations. I'm not sure that you'll get the award but the paper work and the PR will nicely complement an application to OCS."

"OCS?"

"Officer Candidate School. How do you feel about becoming an officer?"

"Skipper, you've knocked me for a loop. I don't know how I feel.

I haven't thought about it at all."

"It's a 16-week program, at the end of which you'll receive a commission in the Navy Reserve as an Ensign. You'll be expected to attend college and earn a degree, at night, when you have shore duty. The Navy will reimburse you for your tuition, provided you make satisfactory grades. You have to apply for a slot. Here's an application. I expect it returned to me at 1800 hours tomorrow, either completed or blank. If it's completed, I'll forward it, along with my recommendation. If it's blank, I'll muster you out of the Navy as expeditiously as possible."

Hampton paused for a moment.

"Intavan you're right. Cooking, in the Navy, or as a civilian is a complete and utter waste of your talents."

The skipper handed Cal the application.

"Dismissed."

"Aye, aye sir."


SENATOR Tim Dunston was playing his favorite game, politics. It was a little past ten o'clock, and Dunston had been exchanging chit-chat and a drink with Jim Richt, the aging Speaker of the House of Representatives, in Richt's office. The time was chosen so nearly everyone would have already gone home, yet not so late as to cause undue notice to the pair by anyone who may still have been present at the Capitol—politicians still worked late on occasion. Richt was 79 years old, from West Texas. He had announced that his next campaign would be his last, "win, lose or draw," though there was little chance of the latter two contingencies. Richt had never received less than 60 percent of the popular vote in any of his elections. As the Speaker, and with his political acumen, Richt was easily the second most powerful man in government. He used his position to block or expedite legislation, depending on his agenda, acquiring the nickname of "the hammer" for "knocking legislative bills around." No major piece of legislation left a committee without Richt's knowledge and approval. Members of the Senate, staff of the Executive branch, and even foreign dignitaries, paid homage to the hammer. Dunston was paying homage. He was about to propose a political deal, never proffered before and not likely to be proffered again.

"Mr. Speaker, thank you for seeing me on such short notice. I know you have plenty on your plate and your time is precious."

"Senator, I'm always happy to make time for a fellow colleague. Can I offer you another drink?"

"Thank you."

The Speaker took both glasses, refilled them with ice and Jack

Daniels and returned to his desk, handing one glass to Dunston, who was sitting opposite to him.

"What can I do for you?"

Richt knew this had to do with Mohammad Baghai, Reverend Casey Edgars and impeachment, but he wanted to hear what Dunston had to say. Dunston's attempt to bully President Hays with his "Gang of Four" meeting had not yielded results. Dunston, like any good politician, always had a backup plan and Richt assumed that this was the purpose of the meeting.

"Mr. Speaker, you've had a long and distinguished political career and you have gone on record saying that you intend to retire after serving one more term in the House."

"Yes, politics is like an addiction and I need another two-year fix," Richt commented with a chuckle.

"Tell me Mr. Speaker, in all your years of public service, have you ever encountered circumstances such as these? I'm referring to this groundswell of public support for a particular cause."

"You're referring to the pardon issue?"

"I am, Mr. Speaker."

"Senator, I'm assuming that you're here to 'feel me out' to determine my position on a possible impeachment of the President?"

"Mr. Speaker, let me be completely frank; as long as it's with the understanding that what you and I discuss doesn't leave this room."

"Of course."

"You are, arguably, the most powerful Speaker of the House in the last fifty years. You've become so powerful because you're an excellent politician."

Richt smiled. "I won't disagree with you Senator."

"An excellent politician recognizes, and takes advantage, of opportunities when they present themselves, wouldn't you agree?"

Richt knew he was being set up but, since this conversation was off the record, he followed along.

"Yes, Senator, I agree, and that's why you're here and we're having this conversation. You want to know if I'll allow the House Judiciary Committee to hold hearings on impeachment proceedings, provided, of course, it's determined she has committed a 'high crime and misdemeanor'."

Richt had hit the target, but not the bull's eye. Dunston would mention his proposal in its entirety shortly.

"Wouldn't the Judiciary Committee determine that Mr. Speaker?"

"Yes, that is correct."

"Mr. Speaker, I know that you're not a fan of the President's policies and since you've announced that you are only going to serve one more term, you're politically invulnerable, that is, if you were ever vulnerable at all. I on the other hand still have political ambitions and, by definition, have to watch my back."

"What are your political ambitions, Senator?"

"Just over six years ago, I lost an election I should have won. Mr. Speaker, you should be addressing me as 'Mr. President'."

"And you want to run for the Presidency again in a year and a half? But how does the impeachment of President Hays enhance your chances against Tom Taylor?"

Though Taylor hadn't announced his intentions to run for the nation's highest office, it was not a secret that he intended to.

"Mr. Speaker, you know, as well as anyone, that the President and Vice President are 'married' for the time they're in office together. The political sins of one are the sins of the other. The same is true for the praises. But let's discuss the sins of the Hays administration, shall we?"

Dunston chose the word "sins" to emphasize his point.

"You're referring to the pardon issue?"

"I am. Mr. Speaker, no one scratches their ass in the House without your knowledge and consent. Any Articles of Impeachment against the President whether real or imaginary would have to have your stamp of approval to proceed. Again, hypothetically, if Articles of Impeachment were sent to the Senate for a trial, I, as Senate Majority Leader would have quite a bit of influence on the outcome."

"Senator, you still haven't answered my question. How does Impeachment of the President further your agenda of attaining the Presidency?"

"Mr. Speaker, yes, I want to be addressed 'Mr. President' in less than two years time and I believe the simplest way to that end is for me to address you as 'Mr. President' for the remainder of the current Presidential term."

Richt was speechless for a moment. Did he hear Dunston correctly? Was Dunston suggesting that he take the oath of office? How? If Hays was impeached and removed from office, assuming that legitimate charges were found, what about the Vice President?

"I'm not sure I heard you correctly," Richt finally muttered. He couldn't remember the last time when he was caught completely off guard.

"Yes you did Mr. Speaker. I'm suggesting that you raise your right hand, while you place left hand on a Bible and take the oath."

Dunston paused and for ten seconds or so neither politician said a word. Both men stared into each other's eyes.

"Please continue Senator."

"There's nothing in the Constitution that says both the President and the Vice President cannot be impeached and tried for the same crimes, at the same time. As you know Mr. Speaker, the line of succession, prescribed in Constitution, after the Vice President, is the Speaker of the House."

Richt immediately understood what Dunston was aiming for but wanted Dunston to say it.

"How do you fit into this Senator?"

"After you take the oath of office, there will be a vacancy in the Vice President's office. You will be required by the Constitution to nominate someone to fill it. I will be your choice. At the end of the term you retire, as you have stated that you would, on a President's pension, in addition to your Congressional pension, and I run for the Presidency again. As the Vice President I, have an inherent advantage of being the Vice President during the campaign."

"Two questions Senator."

"Yes Mr. Speaker?"

"First, what if I decide to run for a term after I serve the remainder of the current term?"

"That is, of course, your choice, but I'm 25 years younger than you. I expect that I'll be around after you've retired or died."

Dunston didn't mince words. Politicians were brutally blunt when speaking to each other privately. He knew Richt wouldn't be offended.

"And what is your second question. Mr. Speaker?"

"What if I didn't pick you to be my Vice President?"

"Mr. Speaker, there is honor among thieves," Dunston said, though he had a contingency plan for that as well.

Both men broke into laughter.

"Senator, let's discuss Articles of Impeachment, shall we?"

A dark political deal had been struck.

# Chapter 20

Abu Sabaya and Malikul Mawt had just finished the zuhr, the noontime prayer ritual. They had eaten a "brunch" meal about 30 minutes earlier. Each of them rolled up their mats and put them into a closet.

"Malikul, we must discuss important matters. You know what I mean."

"But of course, my brother."

The Angel turned on a stereo, tuned in a FM station and turned the volume slightly above what would be considered normal.

"As I told you yesterday, I have been here for a year and I don't have a reason to be suspicious, but I still remain cautious. If anyone is eavesdropping they will not be able to understand our conversation."

"I understand."

Malikul Mawt was born Yasser Saleem. Though he was a Palestinian Arab, he easily passed for an Italian to anyone who was not of that bloodline. He spoke the language as fluently as he did Arabic. Only his accent betrayed him. During his time in Chicago he used fake identification with an Italian name.

His eyes were jet black, eyes devoid of compassion, devoid of pity and devoid of remorse. His hair was salt and pepper and his limbs were short, stout and muscular.

In the inner circles of al-Qaeda, the Angel had developed a reputation of steel will, no fear of death or pain, by proving himself over the years, surviving interrogations, torture and imprisonment. In times of duress, the Angel could take his consciousness to a different dimension.

During his time in Chicago the Angel lived well but not ostentatiously, though he did partake in occidental female flesh. Keeping "under the radar" was necessary and everything else was secondary. Though Islam forbade alcohol and gambling, it was allowed while on jihad, which was fortunate for the Angel. As an "Italian" the Angel had developed a taste for Italian wine and finer foods. He developed an affinity and became proficient at black jack. He also developed an even greater affinity for the women who hung around the successful black jack players. These women were easy to seduce, in fact they wanted to be taken, and the Angel, regarding them as nothing more than whores, had no reservations about using their bodies for his personal pleasure and entertainment.

On more than one occasion, while playing black jack at a private party, where the buy-in for the game was for several thousand dollars, he would zero in on a woman of interest, buy her a drink and, at the end of the game, would invite her to ride home with him in a limousine. The women unfortunate enough to accept would be offered a drugged glass of wine from the limousine's bar leaving them incapable of resisting the humiliations that the Angel would subject them to.

"If I may guess, you want to know how I discovered you, my plan and why I decided to contact you. Am I correct?"

"Continue, Mawt."

Sabaya still didn't completely trust his host.

"Abu, you, like I, come from a land where the population is Muslim, but is ruled by infidels."

Palestine was controlled by Israel, and Basilan, like many of the Southern Philippine islands, was predominately Muslim, but controlled by a Christian government in Manila, a city in the Northern Philippine island of Luzon.

"The Israeli Army killed my parents when I was just a toddler, after they were thrown in prison. I have no real memory of my parents. I later found out that my father was in the underground, fighting for Palestinian independence. My mother knew of his deeds but did not participate in any of the underground's activities."

"You mean suicide bombings?" Sabaya asked. He was thoroughly familiar with the fatal Palestinian technique.

"Bombings, kidnappings, murders and the like; my mother's only crime, I came to find out, was that she was guilty by association, by being married to my father."

"After my parents were arrested, I lived with my aunt and her husband. I grew up believing that I was their son. I had a happy childhood and went to a university. It was during that time that my aunt told me that she was my aunt, not my mother. Israel has stolen my homeland and killed my family. Those are sins that I cannot forgive, and it is why I fight."

"So why are you in the United States?"

The Angel smiled.

"That is such stupid question from an intelligent man… unless you already know the answer and want to judge my response."

The Angel paused for a moment.

"The United States supports both the Philippines and Israel. Israel would not even exist today without financial and military support from the United States."

Sabaya was satisfied with the Angel's reply.

"How did you know I was here and what my plans were?" Sabaya continued his queries.

"After I discovered what Israel had done to my parents, I dropped out of school and went in to hiding. I did not know how, but I knew that I would fight against the oppressors of my people and the killers of my parents. I was not interested in strapping a bomb to my chest; I intended on killing many more than could be killed with just one bomb blast. My first target was an Israeli policeman. After killing him, I shot a minor government official. With two killings under my belt I gained a reputation among the local people; a reputation of fearlessness that brought me in contact with others who had other contacts. I became an assassin and was very good at it. I won't discuss how many I have killed. Some you probably have heard of. I will say that I was paid quite handsomely. I was also involved in a high-profile kidnapping of a member of the Saudi family. I am paid by several members of the Saudi royal family not to kidnap them, so I am quite well off."

"Why?"

"The Saudis, with their resources, continually play one side against the other. By that I mean, depending on which way the wind is blowing, they will support either the United States and Israel, or our Muslim brothers. They have no principles and I have nothing but contempt for them."

"This was all before I had heard of al-Qaeda; mind you, though I did share many of its goals."

"Now I was contacted by al-Qaeda and became a part of their network. Unlike Carlos, the Jackal, who said he was a terrorist, but demonstrated that he was, in fact, a capitalist, by keeping the money he extorted; I willingly gave most of the money I earned to representatives of al-Qaeda. This one act gave me instant credibility with the powers in al-Qaeda."

"You have not explained how you found me," Sabaya said.

"I told you that I have quite a bit of influence with several important people in al-Qaeda. I knew that certain others had access to radioactive material and, when it was determined that Chicago would be hosting the Olympics, I had the foundation for a plan. I knew that you had spent time in Iraq, and were one of several who had training in the use of dirty bombs. I inquired where each of your dirty bomb cadre members was located and, through Allah's will, I found you."

"Where did you get radioactive material, and how was it transported into America?"

The Angel stared blankly at Sabaya. A moment later Sabaya understood. The Angel would not say because it was need-to-know and Sabaya did not need to know how the material got here; only that it was here.

Seeing that Sabaya realized that he was not going to get an answer to his last question, the Angel was ready to continue.

"So, my brother, are you ready to listen to my plan?"

"Yes, please continue."

AGENT Scott Ramsey was in the middle of his three-to-eleven shift guarding Mohammad, who was still in a coma. Mohammad still required 24-hour surveillance, with the day divided into 8-hour shifts. It was a typical shift, and, as all the shifts had been—uneventful. Mohammad was still lying in a bed and, since there hadn't been any indication of a recovery, was going to be transferred from the hospital intensive care unit to a permanent facility specializing in comatose patients.

All of the medical staff was perplexed as to why Mohammad's stigmatic wounds refused to heal and continued to bleed. Each of the wounds was bandaged daily. The flow of blood was neither continuous, nor severe, but the wounds would not form a scab; they did not get infected. No one on the staff had an explanation for the symptoms. Ramsey knew that no medical explanation would be found because the explanation was spiritual, though Ramsey hadn't discussed the matter with anyone.

A new nurse came into the ICU, rolling a cart with various prescription medicines, for each of the patients. She had dark skin very similar to that of Mohammad's.

"Hi, I'm Leah. You must be one of the guards?" The nurse asked Ramsey.

"Hi Leah, I'm Agent Scott Ramsey. You must be the new nurse?"

"My first day here, I was working across town."

Mohammad lay in his comatose state. During the weeks that he'd been in ICU he seemed to have the ability to foresee events; he was aware of his stigmatic wounds and the significance of them. He didn't feel that he was worthy of the wounds. He didn't consider himself pious, in fact just the opposite. He knew that God would bring him out of his coma, though he did not know when. It did not matter to Mohammad when it would happen; it only mattered that it would. He knew God had a purpose for him and it was to deliver His message about hell. He did not know how exactly God intended for his message to be spread, but that would be revealed to him at the proper time. He did not know the child who appeared to him in his present state, but he knew she served God also and she had a purpose in His plan.

At that moment a holy apparition appeared to Mohammad. It was not the young child, who God had sent to communicate with him, but the soldier who Mohammad had murdered, Christian Welter.

*Wake up Mohammad! You are not to die by the sword! It is not your time to die! Wake up!*

"IT'S a pleasure to meet you Leah. It's unusual to see a new nurse in the middle of a shift."

Leah laughed. "The new person on staff gets stuck with the mundane tasks. I'm to give the patients their meds, change bed pans and such."

"Don't let me keep you then Leah. Again it is a pleasure to meet you."

"Likewise, Agent Ramsey."

Leah began at the far end of the ICU and said hello to the patients, introducing herself, checking the charts to make sure that the correct medication and correct dosage was being distributed. Most of the patients were conscious and enjoyed the few minutes as she repeated the procedure with each of them.

After Leah finished dispensing each of the patient's medication, she rolled her cart to Mohammad, whose bed was in a corner, positioned away from the conscious patients. The FBI guard was standing about 20 feet from the bed. It would be over before he could stop her and she would have her revenge! No one would even know that Mohammad Baghai, the murderer, had been murdered!

Her plan was simple. She would administer Mohammad's insulin using a syringe, injecting it in his stomach. Thirty units was the prescribed amount. Afterwards she would measure his pulse rate, finding his carotid artery in his neck. Finally, she would use the syringe and inject air into his artery. The air bubble, inside the blood stream, would travel to his brain and cause a fatal embolism. The wound would be virtually undetectable and the cause of death, unless a doctor knew what to look for, was equally untraceable.

*WAKE up Mohammad! God commands you to wake up now!*

Welter, the murdered soldier, the soldier Mohammad murdered was attempting to aid Mohammad. Though Welter did not say, Mohammad got the sense that his life was in peril. Welter placed a hand on each of Mohammad's shoulders and shook Mohammad violently.

*Wake up Mohammad! God commands you!*

LEAH had finished taking Mohammad's pulse and recorded it on his chart. Seventy-two beats per minute. She was about to insert the syringe into his neck and inject a fatal air bubble into his artery when he started to convulse. Ramsey immediately raced to Mohammad's bed. Leah, not knowing what the cause of the seizure was, put the syringe on the tray and pretended to aid him.

Perhaps Allah, in His infinite wisdom, had decided to take this murderer's life and she would not have to. In a minute, a team of nurses was at Mohammad bed. A "code blue" had been called, meaning that a patient was in a life-threatening situation.

After a minute, for no apparent reason, Mohammad's convulsions ceased. His eyes opened. Mohammad's vital signs returned to normal. A doctor, several nurses including Leah, and Ramsey were standing by the bed.

"You just gave us quite a scare Mohammad," the attending doctor said.

"Doctor, I am happy to be among the living again," Mohammad replied.

The immediate medical concerns to Mohammad no longer relevant, the nurses returned to their duties. Leah rolled her cart out of the ICU.

"Doctor, please run any and all the tests that you feel necessary, but I suspect that you will not find anything abnormal; the cause of my seizure was spiritual, not medical."

"In any case, we still need to check you out."

"Check me out? I am not sure I understand you doctor."

"Check you out, examine you Mohammad."

"Oh, I see. I have a favor to ask from you."

"What is that?"

"I would like to speak privately to the Persian nurse who was here just a minute ago."

"We can arrange that."

The doctor turned to Leah, as she was about to leave.

"Nurse, would you come here please?"

"Me, doctor?" Leah responded. Though her plan was foiled, she had not done anything that could be construed to be hostile to Mohammad.

"Yes, our patient would like to speak to you for a moment."

Leah returned to Mohammad's bed as everyone else dispersed. Perhaps she would get another chance to carry out her plan, perhaps not. It was not Allah's will for Mohammad Baghai to die today and she accepted that.

"Yes, what can I do for you?"

"Please forgive me of my sins against you and your family."

Leah visibly flushed despite her swarthy complexion.

"Malekah, I know you have no reason to do so, and I have no reason to expect it, but I will ask again for your forgiveness for killing your father."

Malekah Pakravan was the daughter of the old man Mohammad had beaten to death for stealing in Iran.

"You know who I am and you know what I intended to do to you?" She asked Mohammad in a tone slightly above a whisper.

"I had your father killed for trying to feed his family. As for your motives, I know Hassan Nassiri sent you to kill me, but let us not speak of that again. No one will learn of this from me. There is too much blood on my hands already. I will not be responsible for any more."

Leah was crying. A moment ago she was seconds away from killing her father's killer, now she was contemplating forgiving this man for his crime.

"Malekah, I owe you a debt that I can never repay. I cannot return your father to you and I can't take away the pain and anguish I have caused you. I can only say that I am sorry and ask for your forgiveness. Malekah, please forgive my sins against you and your family."

Mohammad reached out with his right hand in a gesture to give her a hug. His left hand was handcuffed to the railing of his bed.

After a moment of hesitation, Leah bent down to Mohammad and wrapped her hands around his neck as he hugged her torso.

"Malekah, I want you to write your phone number on a card. I am going to have my attorney call you."

"Why?"

"No questions. Her name is Isabelle Franks. She will explain herself when she calls."

MOHAMMAD, handcuffed to his bed, was taking a moment to speak to Scott Ramsey.

"I am happy to see you again Scott."

"Mohammad, you have no idea what's been going on in the world while you were in a coma."

"Would you please give me a summary?"

"Sure, after you collapsed in the court room and taken here, the doctors determined that you were in a diabetic coma. You had no idea that you had diabetes did you Mohammad?"

"No, I didn't."

"The Reverend Casey Edgars, the one who first suggested that you be pardoned, has really turned up the heat on President Hays to pardon you."

"Turning up the heat? I am not familiar with that term Scott."

"It means to apply pressure, to force one to submit."

"Oh, I see."

"Anyway, he has suggested, and initiated a campaign, to have her impeached if she doesn't pardon you."

"Incredible. I had no idea."

"He's set up a web site, with the sole purpose of collecting electronic signatures of people who support him and his campaign, and forwards them to Congress."

"Has it been successful?"

"It's been successful enough that a delegation from Congress met with Hays in the Oval Office, but not successful enough that she felt compelled to pardon you."

"No, Scott, I mean the President hasn't been impeached has she?"

"No, Mohammad, there hasn't been a resolution of articles of impeachment introduced into the House of Representatives yet, though there are all sorts of rumors that one will be. No one knows for sure exactly how credible the rumor is."

"Scott, how much longer will I be in the hospital? I need to speak to Reverend Edgars. I do not believe that God wants President Hays impeached."

Ramsey was visibly surprised at Mohammad's question.

"Mohammad, as soon as you're medically cleared, I expect that you'll be transported back to Delmont and sentenced shortly afterwards. Perhaps you may be transported from here directly to court for sentencing. In either case I wouldn't expect you to be here more than 24 to 36 hours."

"Have my attorney and my priest been notified of the change in my condition?"

"Yes, Mohammad, I contacted them a few minutes ago. I expect that both of them will be here shortly."

"Thank you, Scott. I will get one of them to contact the Reverend for me."

"Mohammad, if you'll excuse me, I need to take care of some business before my shift ends."

"Of course, Scott, it is good to talk to you again my brother. I don't think I ever told you but your kind words to me when I was in isolation were an inspiration to me when I was in despair. It was if God was speaking to me through you."

Ramsey stared at Mohammad dumbfounded.

"Did I say something to offend you Scott?"

"No, Mohammad, Reverend Edgars claims that you should be pardoned because God chose you to speak his message. It struck me funny that you used the words you did concerning me. Anyway, I need to do some things before I get off work."

"Take care Scott."

REVEREND Edgars turned off CNN in his office. A special report has just announced that God's Prophet, Mohammad Baghai, had regained consciousness, just as he predicted. The topic of his next sermon had just been determined. Perhaps now President Hays would submit to the will of almighty God? His web site had collected over 750,000 electronic signatures and he was told that he could probably count on around 100,000 signatures a week for the next few weeks. Would that be enough pressure to convince her to grant a pardon? He didn't know, though he hoped it would. He did know that he didn't want the President impeached. She was a decent and God-fearing woman; just misguided.

Edgars detested the politics that he was using, he detested the politicians he was using and he was using them to accomplish God's plan. He had done everything that he could conceive of to free Mohammad, but somehow, because he had not been successful, he had the feeling that he should be doing more. It was an empty feeling, a feeling of inadequacy. This feeling left him feeling emotionally depleted.

It was at these times that he would pray and God, through his grace, would fill the void. He felt that now was such a time. Was Mohammad Baghai's recovery such a sign from God? If it was he didn't feel spiritually fulfilled. He definitely wanted, definitely needed, a recharge of his spiritual batteries.

Edgars' intercom buzzed.

"Reverend, there's a gentleman from FBI who wants to speak to you."

"Not right now Brenda. Take a message, please."

Edgars was contemplating more important matters.

"He says he's one of Mohammad Baghai's guards and it's urgent that he speaks to you now."

"Very well Brenda, connect me."

"Hello, this is Reverend Edgars."

"Reverend Edgars, this is Agent Scott Ramsey of the FBI. I am guarding Mohammad Baghai."

"Yes, my assistant told me that. What can I do for you Agent Ramsey?"

"I spoke with him shortly after he woke from his coma and he wants to speak with you as soon as possible, but I thought it was important to speak with you first."

"Thank you for relaying Mohammad's desires to me Agent Ramsey. I will make arrangements to visit him at my earliest opportunity. What do you want to discuss with me?"

"I need to speak with you face-to-face Reverend. Years ago, you had an unusual encounter with my father, Jacob Rabin."

"Yes I did. We should talk as soon as possible."

JAY Books, Cal and a cameraman were in the officer's mess, aboard the Gaffney; Books, a CNN journalist was given this assignment. Though human-interest stories were not what he intended to make a career of, the assignment got him out of New York and to the Middle East, where the action was. He hadn't any real interest in the Muslim-Jew angle; rather, he wanted to question the Muslim Petty Officer concerning his feelings about another Muslim, equally devout, renouncing Islam and converting to Christianity, though both themes integrated with each other.

Petty Officer Intavan seemed a pleasant enough fellow and was forthcoming about his personal life, his choice to join the Navy and his faith. The interview was going well; the young man was intelligent and articulate and the interview would probably get airtime back in the States, a Sunday morning "feel good" puff piece probably. Now Books wanted to discuss Intavan's feelings about Mohammad Baghai's conversion and the political maelstrom, surrounding the efforts to have him pardoned.

"Petty Officer, are you familiar with Mohammad Baghai and his current situation?" Books queried, hoping that Intavan was. It would be a quick end to the discussion if he wasn't.

"Somewhat sir, he was a terrorist that surrendered to the FBI, in New York City."

"That's him. Are you aware that he renounced Islam and terrorism, converted to Christianity and is seeking a pardon from the President?"

"Yes, it's been on the news."

"I was wondering if you had any thoughts on the issue. Specifically, how do you personally feel about a fellow Muslim becoming a Christian, and do you feel that he deserves a pardon?"

"Mr. Books, my opinion on whether he deserves a pardon doesn't matter. The only opinion that does matter is the President's. I also believe that certain members of Congress and vocal Christian religious leaders should let the President decide on the issue, without political pressure."

"So you're saying that you oppose the impeachment movement that's being generated against her?"

"That's correct sir. President Hays is a good person and I believe that whatever decision she makes, will be based upon her faith and character. She was elected to make those type decisions and America should let her do her job."

"Petty Officer, how do you personally feel, as Muslim, about Mohammad Baghai becoming a Christian and do you believe his explanation of the events leading to his conversion?"

"Islam teaches that the Jewish people, though devout and well-intentioned, became misguided and strayed from Allah's will, so Jesus Christ was sent to reaffirm the divine message. Thus, Christianity was created."

Cal neglected to mention that Jesus was only regarded as a prophet in Islam, because he was attempting to avoid a long religious discussion.

"Eventually, Christians, like the Jews, also corrupted Allah's message so another prophet was charged with spreading the divine message again. This was the Prophet Muhammad; Allah's greatest prophet. I believe that Mohammad Baghai is misguided and has strayed from Allah's will."

"Are you saying that he has strayed when he renounced terrorism?"

"Not at all, there are certainly plenty of non-Muslim terrorists and terror organizations. One doesn't need to look any farther than Northern Ireland and the IRA. Terrorism in any form is evil. What I am saying is that Mohammad Baghai has lost his faith; for what reason I can't say. It would be speculation on my part."

"So you don't believe that he has gone to hell and is a prophet?"

"Allah can certainly place anyone in, and remove anyone from, hell as he chooses. Islam teaches that not only is Muhammad Allah's greatest prophet, Muhammad is Allah's final prophet. So the answer to your question is no, I don't believe that Mohammad Baghai is a prophet."

"Petty Officer, it's been a pleasure speaking to you. Thank you for your time." Books said.

# Chapter 21

Isabelle and David Franks and Father Paul Stewart were chatting with Mohammad. It was about 9:30 a.m. the morning after Mohammad woke from his coma. Scott Ramsey had called David and Father Paul after he spoke to Reverend Edgars. The Franks were not able to visit him until the next day because Isabelle was in court and David was babysitting Tori and could not get a baby sitter on short notice.

Mohammad was still handcuffed to his bed. He appeared to be embarrassed to have his friends see him in his present state of incarceration and that he had bloody bandages on his hands and feet. The Franks brought a bouquet of balloons with a get-well theme.

Now that he was conscious and no longer in immediate peril, Mohammad had been moved to a private room. This was the best arrangement for the hospital, the FBI and Mohammad as well.

Beds in the ICU were at a premium and Mohammad, now conscious; his diabetes under control, no longer warranted continuous medical supervision. In a private room Mohammad's guards also had a much easier task guarding their prisoner. No one seriously thought that another ICU patient would threaten him, but all scenarios had to be considered. When Mohammad was having a confidential discussion, such as now, the FBI guard could simply step outside and close the door.

Since both his attorney and his priest were present, the guard was standing in the hall and the door was shut.

"My friends, I am so glad to see you," Mohammad said.

"Likewise, Mohammad," Franks replied.

"Everyone, please bring a chair over to the bed so you don't have to stand," Mohammad requested.

A moment later everyone was seated around the bed.

"Mohammad, we need to get you up to speed on your legal status."

"Up to speed? I'm not familiar with that term," Mohammad asked.

"I'm sorry Mohammad. Up to speed is an American slang term. It means to update. I am going to update you on your situation."

"Oh, I see. Please go on."

"I'm told that you'll be transported back to Delmont as soon as you've been released and arrangements made for your transportation. You'll be sentenced sometime next week. I don't have an indication as to what it will be."

Isabelle did not want to allude to the death penalty, though everyone present understood that it was a possibility.

"What is your sense of the situation Isabelle?"

"Given the current political atmosphere, if you had to make me say, I would guess life."

"I see."

"I have presented a pardon application to the President, and David, and I had a discussion with her about it. Though she has not commented on it publicly or privately to me, I believe it was well received."

"She'll have to deal with it very soon. Casey Edgars, the televangelist, has made it his purpose in life to have the President pardon you," David added.

"Yes, Scott Ramsey, one of my FBI guards mentioned that to me yesterday. Isabelle, could you arrange a meeting between me and Reverend Edgars?"

"Probably, but why do you want to speak with him Mohammad?"

"I want to thank him for his efforts on my behalf and ask him to stop his campaign to have the President impeached."

"Mohammad, my superiors have contacts with Reverend Edgars. I can take care of that, provided that you're sure that's what you want to do," Paul spoke up for the first time.

"Mohammad, I would advise against it. Though Reverend Edgars and I have not spoken, he has created a lot of favorable publicity for your cause," Isabelle commented.

"And I am grateful for it but I can tell you that God does not want the President impeached. She is a Christian and doesn't deserve that. Paul, would you please contact Reverend Edgars?"

"Certainly, Mohammad."

"David, I had some incredible experiences when I was comatose that I need to discuss with you. I am sure that it would make an excellent story and Isabelle, I can guarantee you that if it is published it will create favorable publicity and, more importantly, the faithful need to hear it."

"Mohammad, when you're ready to tell it, Paul and I will certainly listen. Someone will want to print it also." David told his friend.

"Fine then, can you and Paul come to Delmont after I am moved back?"

"Of course we can Mohammad," David said.

"Paul, the doctors tell me that the wounds on my hands are defying medical technology. Scott, tells me that you and he believe they are something called stigmata. I know you are familiar with it; could you give me the sixty-second summary?"

"Mohammad, I brought you some material on stigmata but, assuming you do have the stigmata, which are the wounds that Jesus Christ bore during his crucifixion, it means that God considers you to be a pious and just man, and the wounds are his symbol of that. Stigmatic wounds don't heal but don't get infected either. There is antidotal evidence that the blood of a stigmatic wound has healing powers also," Paul said as he gave Mohammad the literature.

"We can discuss this at length when you are back at Delmont."

"Interesting," Mohammad said with a pensive look.

"What's that?" Paul asked him.

"Paul, it was something that I 'dreamed,' if it can be called a dream when I was in a coma. It was revealed to me that I was to be 'marked.' Now I would argue that I am not, and have not been, 'pious and just' but do you think that these wounds are 'marks'?"

Paul smiled.

"Mohammad, God decides who is pious and, if someone is to believe your claims about hell, then the stigmata is not such a reach. I'm anxious to hear of your dream. My superiors will be anxious to learn about it also."

Mohammad reached under his covers and handed a slip of paper it Isabelle.

"Would you contact this lady for me Isabelle?"

"Certainly, for what purpose Mohammad?"

Mohammad paused for a moment.

"My friends, what I am about to say I do not want repeated beyond this room."

"Mohammad all of us here are bound by privilege," Isabelle retorted.

"I understand that Isabelle, but I don't want what I am about to say repeated to anyone; Paul, not to your superiors, David, not to your any of your associates and Isabelle, not to a member of your law firm. Can I count on all of you to honor my wishes?"

Mohammad received nods from everyone.

"Isabelle the lady that I want you to contact is Malekah Pakravan. She is an Iranian national and a nurse here. I want you to contact her and make arrangements to pay her one million dollars from the account that I set up."

"I don't understand Mohammad. Who is she?"

"She tried to murder me yesterday."

"What?" the three of them exclaimed.

Mohammad laughed as if he'd pulled a prank on his friends.

"My friends, God woke me up as she was attempting to kill me. I forgave her of her sins against me, for my sins against her are far greater."

"What were your sins Mohammad?"

"Paul, I had her father killed for stealing from me when I was living in Iran. I hope all of you understand why I want secrecy in this matter."

"Mohammad, how do you know that she won't try again?"

"I looked into her eyes Isabelle. Her eyes were those of someone seeking justice for a wrong against her, not those of a killer, like I was. She will not attempt to harm me again while I am still here. Isabelle will you call her today and make arrangements?"

"I will, Mohammad."

"My friends, I am happy to see all of you and, despite your concerns, I believe everything will work out in a favorable result for me."

"Let's hope so Mohammad."

"I have faith in our Lord Isabelle," Mohammad replied.

"We'll see you after you're moved back to prison, but before you're sentenced Mohammad." Isabelle said.

CASEY Edgars got up from his desk and met Scott Ramsey at the door of his office. Ramsey had taken a couple of days off from work so he could drive down to the Christ Ministries Church in rural Maryland.

Ramsey was not a man easily intimidated. Standing six feet tall and weighing a muscular 200 pounds, he stuck an imposing figure. However, he was uncomfortable meeting Reverend Edgars. His father, Jacob Rabin, had told him of the encounter with Casey Edgars and why Rabin had converted from Judaism to Christianity.

"Agent Ramsey," Edgars said as he opened the door to this office and shook his guest's hand furiously.

"It is an honor and a privilege to meet you."

"Reverend, please call me Scott."

"Only if you agree to call me Casey, come, let's sit down," Edgars said as he escorted Ramsey to two overstuffed wing chairs.

"Fine, Casey."

Scott sat down facing Edgars.

"Can I offer you some coffee?"

"No thank you, I'm fine. I've already had two cups."

"Scott, you were the last person on earth I expected to call me.

You have no idea of the volume of phone calls I'm getting from the White House, Capitol Hill, the various media outlets and even just supporters of my ministry. All of them want my time, either to support my efforts, or to dissuade me from continuing my mission.

Edgars, in addition to his efforts to have Baghai pardon continued to work 60 to 70 hour weeks doing his normal duties at the CMC. He had daily requests for interviews, television and radio appearances, rallies in support for Mohammad all over the country and personal meetings with anyone of influence who might be able help him in his cause.

"So, Scott, in light of our present circumstances, why did you decide to contact me? And, how were you able to conceal your identity and location from the very resourceful United States government?"

Ramsey smiled.

"Casey, you might say that I was hiding in plain sight."

"I can see that."

"Specifically, my father was Mossad. He, by his profession, knew a little about counter-intelligence and hiding identities. As you may have surmised, from talking with my mother, my father was in the habit of doing things without explanation. He instructed me and I learned. To answer your question though, I did some research, during my senior year of high school, at my father's insistence and found an obituary of an infant child born around the same time I was; a Scott Ramsey. With his name I was able to obtain his social security number and, with a social security number, I was able to obtain identification. Forging false high school transcripts was not a problem. I went to college as Scott Ramsey, not Jacob Rabin. Going to work for the FBI was coincidence."

"Why did your father insist on your taking such extraordinary measures Scott?"

"I asked him that."

"What did he say Scott?"

"He didn't, other than that one day it would be beneficial. I don't know if this is such a time or not. Now let me address your first question. I was assigned, by coincidence or providence, to guard Mohammad while he was in prison and while he was in the hospital. He and I got to know each other on a first name basis. I was present when his stigmatic marks came to be and when he regained consciousness from his coma. He and I chatted after he was examined and I filled him in on the events concerning him. It was then that he mentioned that he wanted to meet you. He didn't ask me to contact you on his behalf; I think he's going to have his attorney do that, but I thought that the time was right for me to speak with you."

"Scott, did he indicate what he wanted to discuss when we meet?"

"Reverend, it's my understanding that he's going to ask you to terminate you efforts to have President Hays impeached."

"Scott, it is not my intention to have the President impeached. I think you know already, and I have stated on numerous occasions, that I want Mohammad Baghai, God's Prophet, pardoned for any and all of his crimes."

"I understand that Casey, but the two issues are intertwined. You can't separate one from the other."

"Scott, I understand that President Hays is in a difficult political position and I also understand that you don't represent her. The last time I spoke with her was when she awarded me the Medal of Freedom. At that meeting I made it clear, in no uncertain terms, that I intended to use any means at my disposal to ensure that Mohammad Baghai was pardoned for his crimes."

Edgars paused for a moment.

"Scott, I don't want to sound like a preacher to you. I get the sense that you basically agree with my position, but I know in my heart of hearts that my cause is just. That is the end of my sermon."

Ramsey smiled.

"I didn't feel like I was being preached at Casey. Yes, I do share your views regarding Mohammad, but you're blurring the line between church and state and I don't wish to see President Hays, a good person, destroyed in the process."

"Scott, I appreciate that you are concerned about President Hays being politically ruined. It is not my intent to do so, but let me correct a point you raised."

"Oh?"

"Your premise that I am 'blurring the line between church and state' is false and, since your argument is based upon it, your argument collapses."

"I don't understand."

"Scott, nowhere in the Constitution is the phrase 'separation of church and state' found. The implication by those who use it is that the founding fathers wanted religion out of government when the exact opposite is true."

"I'm not sure I understand you Casey."

"All of the founding fathers were God-fearing men. They had seen the religious tyranny imposed upon British citizens by the King of England. In fact, the Church of England and the English government were one and the same. I would argue that our founding fathers wanted government out of religion but welcomed religion in government. If President Hays really and truly believed in the separation of church and state would I be getting an audit? I don't think so."

There was a pregnant pause and Edgars continued.

"So, Scott, I am sorry that our first meeting degenerated to this. I apologize for my part of it, but I hope you see how passionate I am on the matter. Can we discuss more pleasant topics? I am very much interested in your father. I only met him twice, not much time at all considering the impact he's had on my life."

Ramsey was flattered by the way Reverend Edgars complimented his father.

"Casey, I really don't know where to begin. My father and mother were never married, but they lived as husband and wife. My father was a postman; my mother was a nurse. Dad and I went to Mass every Sunday. Mom went with us when she didn't have to work. I was expected to address my elders, as 'sir' or 'ma'am.' Dad's rules and instructions were to be followed and obeyed, not debated. Other than being a borderline religious fanatic, my father was, what I considered, a regular dad."

"Did you ever ask your father why he and your mother never got married?"

"Actually, it never really came up. My mother wore a ring for appearances. They were husband and wife in every facet but name. My dad watched me play football on Friday nights; little league baseball when I was younger. He taught me to say prayers when I was little and said them with me until I asked him not to."

"Why did you do that Scott, if you don't mind me asking?"

"Not at all, religion, to me is a private matter, my 'one-on-one' time with God. I have never felt comfortable, other than at Mass, publicly displaying my faith."

"I see, but you and Mohammad have no doubt discussed the religious context of his plight?"

Ramsey laughed.

"Did I say anything funny Scott?"

"While he was in his isolation cell at Delmont, he began preaching his message to his fellow inmates by draining the water from his toilet bowl and conversing with whoever would listen. It was sort of an old-fashioned party line. We discussed his epiphany and that I believe his story."

"That is a unique method of delivery. Scott, is there anything that Mohammad needs, or would like, that is permissible for me to bring to him after I make arrangements for a meeting?"

"Any kind of reading material, books, paperbacks and magazines; he has time on his hands."

"Well, Scott, it has been a pleasure. I assume that we may see each other when I come to visit Mohammad. Would you prefer to keep your identity a secret?"

"You mean do I mind if you inform the White House of my identity? Not at all, but I think I'm going to contact the White House myself, much like I did with you, though I haven't decided when. I've done nothing that I'm ashamed of and the White House was going to discover me at some point in time. It was a pleasure meeting you Reverend."

"Scott, would you do me a favor when you speak to the President?"

"What's that Casey?"

"You are aware of my ability to predict future events?"

"Yes, it is sort of a sixth sense isn't it?"

"For lack of a better word, yes it is. However, sometimes I am able to see things clearly and sometimes not. Right now my sense is 'tingling' but I don't know why. Would you please tell her that something significant is about to happen but I can't say what? I would tell her myself but I don't think I'm very popular in her camp right now."

"Of course Casey."

Ramsey got up and the two shook hands. Edgars was going to have a busy and interesting week.

ISABELLE was working in her office when the intercom buzzed. She had called Malekah Pakravan, as she had promised Mohammad, getting her voice mail. Leah returned her call the next day. Isabelle explained who she was and what Mohammad had instructed her to do. Greed being a universal motivator, Leah was anxious to meet her as soon as possible.

"Yes Cathy?"

"Leah Pakravan is here to see you."

"Send her in please."

A moment later Leah came into her office; Isabelle got up and shook her hand.

"Miss Pakravan, I'm Isabelle Franks, Mohammad Baghai's attorney. It's a pleasure to meet you. Come sit down."

Leah took a seat in front of Isabelle's desk and Isabelle sat back down.

"Thank you Miss Franks."

"Please call me Isabelle. May I call you Leah?"

"That's fine. My real name is Malekah. Leah is my American

nickname."

"Leah, I came to the hospital after my client awoke and apparently after he spoke to you. He told me why he wanted to pay you the money as compensation."

Isabelle did not complete the sentence that she was thinking: He told me why he wanted to pay you the money as compensation for the death your father.

Leah immediately got defensive.

"He told me that he wouldn't tell anyone."

"Leah, I'm his attorney. I'm bound by my professional ethics not to discuss conversations with my client with anyone. Your secret is safe with me. I don't know if you're aware of it, but Mohammad intended to murder my husband, before all this business started, so I understand completely your motivation. Besides, do you really think that I'd allow a million dollar withdrawal without an explanation?"

"No, I guess not."

As if turning on a light switch Isabelle changed personalities from a friendly confidant to litigation lawyer.

"Now Leah, Mohammad assured me that your actions were actions of frustration and desperation and that there would be no more attempts on his life. I want you to understand that if I feel that you're a threat to my client, I am not bound by privilege. In basic terms, Leah, if I'm not satisfied that you are not going to harm my client, the next time I pick up the phone will be to call the police and have you arrested for attempted murder. Do you understand what I'm saying?"

Leah was taken aback by the abrupt personality change and averted her gaze.

"I will not try to hurt Mohammad again."

Isabelle remained silent and stared at Leah until she looked back up. She continued to stare straight into Leah's eyes for several seconds, continuing the visual lock up, until she was satisfied that Leah was sincere.

"No, I don't believe you will."

And like that Isabelle switched off her intimidating lawyer mode and smiled again.

"Leah, I have a check for you. I am required by the IRS, State and City of New York to withhold taxes, so the amount is a little over $600,000. Attached to the check is an itemization of which government entity is receiving their part of your money. There are some documents for you sign, including a confidentiality agreement, which means that you agree not to discuss the terms of this transaction. Afterwards, I can give you a certified check. Do you have any plans for it?"

"I am going to pay all my bills, but after that, I am not sure. This is all so incredible."

Leah spent the next few minutes signing her signature to various documents and Isabelle slid over a check to Leah, which she briefly examined and put it in her purse.

"I would suggest putting it in your bank as soon as you leave this office Leah."

"Oh I am. Thank you," Leah said as he shook Isabelle's hand and left Isabelle's office.

ALL About Diving is Cumming, Georgia's only Scuba Diving Shop. Todd Alred, a retired paramedic who took a scuba certification course and fell in love with the sport, decided to become an entrepreneur and now owned and operated the shop and instructed its scuba classes. A free spirit, Todd, stood about six feet tall with thinning brown hair, once shoulder length. He'd cut the hair and shaved his fu-manchu mustache for a corporate hairstyle, as a concession to owning a business, though he played heavy metal as background music in his shop.

Ralph had seen Todd's dive shop dozens of times but had never entered it. He'd thought about taking scuba lessons before, though only semi-seriously, but now that he had a future son-in-law who dove, and Heather had expressed an interest in it, he decided to drop by.

"How's it going?" Todd greeted Ralph. He was wearing camo shorts, a brown tank top and hiking boots.

"Fine, thank you. I'm Ralph Twig," Ralph said as he extended his hand to shake.

"Todd Alred. Do you have the insurance agency in town?"

"Yes, I do. Tell me about scuba lessons. I saw your ad in the local paper. You can train someone to dive in a week?"

"Yes, Ralph, actually I can, if you want the super-accelerated program. Usually it takes a month."

"Todd, my daughter in college, she may want to take your course also. What about a discount for the both of us?"

Ralph was not afraid to wheel and deal.

Todd broke into laughter. "Tell you what, Ralph, if both you and your daughter buy your basic gear from me, mask, fins snorkel et-cetera, I'll give both of you 50 percent off the tuition. Now if you tell anyone that I made you a deal like that I'll call you a liar; I do have a reputation to maintain."

"Deal, show me the equipment I need and I'll take it with me now. I'll bring my daughter and her fiancée in this weekend for her gear. Her fiancé is already a diver. We can agree on a date for the class then."

"Cool. Let's go hook you up with your gear."

Ralph and Todd walked to the front of the store. Todd saw dollar signs circling around his head.

AIR Force One landed at the Pensacola Regional Airport. Anytime a President of the United States traveled anywhere it entailed a major move. In addition to the Boeing 767 carrying the President, an Air Force cargo plane always arrived before Air Force One. The President had to be transported in a bulletproof limousine, nick-named "the Beast," which was flown in ahead of the President and had to be ready for immediate use. The Beast also held the other cars needed to transport the additional Secret Service personnel and miscellaneous equipment necessary to protect the President.

Ron Thomas was the first one outside the hatch, descending the rolling stairs and quickly surveyed the area. After satisfying himself that all was in order, and there was no threat to the President, he spoke into his microphone to his associates still in the plane.

"Beach baby is clear to sunbathe."

"Beach baby" was a reference to Pensacola and Pensacola Beach. Usually code names were selected at random. This time the presidential detail picked the name, though it was only whispered in Hays' presence.

A moment later President Hays descended the rolling stairs, waved to the crowd which had gathered, shook hands with several local dignitaries and walked briskly to the limo. Hays' home, Scenic Bluff, was a 15-minute drive from the airport. The convoy parked in the driveway and President Hays, along with Ron, entered the front of the house. An advance team had already entered the house, searched it and the property, and set up a security perimeter.

Upon entering the house Hays entered her living room and gazed upon the bay, soaking in the panoramic view through the floor-to-ceiling window. Though it was not built to code, the window was the best-selling feature of the house and Hays had immediately fallen in love with it.

"I get weak in the knees every time I walk by this window Ron."

"It is a fantastic view Madam President," Thomas replied.

"I see a couple of small pleasure craft on the bay. How much do you want to bet that they've been rented by our friends in the press?"

The Secret Service, working with the Florida Marine Patrol, created a 500-yard security perimeter from the shoreline. Hays had no doubt that by tomorrow at least a dozen such pleasure craft would be rented by various members of the press corps, each with photographers, equipped with digital cameras and telephoto lenses. All of them would be lurking just outside the security perimeter waiting to take pictures of the President. With flash memory cards, wireless Internet and laptop computers, any photo could be posted within seconds. Hays and her staff had to be cognizant that they were under constant scrutiny outside the four walls of her home.

"There will be a lot more tomorrow ma'am."

"The boat owners around here will get quite a windfall. I know Dunston will want to sponsor a bill to tax them."

Hays was referring to the property owners on Escambia Bay. Virtually all of them owned small, motorized pleasure craft, most 12-20 feet in length. The press, not wanting to miss a moment of Hays' working vacation, would contact her neighbors and rent their boats for the purpose of staking out Scenic Bluff from the water. The transactions were always cash, much to the IRS's chagrin. There were rumors that owners of the larger boats commanded fees of $1,000 a day.

"From what I hear he has other things on his mind ma'am," Thomas said.

"You're right. He's scheming to have me impeached," Hays said pensively.

"I'm not sure it will come to that Madam President," Ron said, not really knowing how to reply. It was not common practice for the President to make small talk with one of her bodyguards.

"I'm counting on it Ron," Hays replied as she was formulating a plan.

# Chapter 22

Ralph, Heather and Charlie were up early Saturday morning and arrived early at All About Diving at 9 a.m. Todd saw and recognized Ralph when he walked in.

"Ralph, it's good to see you again!"

Todd and Ralph shook hands.

"Todd, this is my daughter Heather and her fiancée, Charlie Michaels. He happens to dive also."

More handshakes were exchanged.

"Good to meet you both of you. So, Heather, I've already sold your dad on my facilities and service, do you want me to show you around or shall we get you fitted for your basic gear?"

"Todd since I'm paying for the equipment and the lessons, let's just skip the sales pitch and buy the gear she needs and then nail down a date for the dive trip to Florida. You said the check-out dives were in Panama City? Can we set things up for next weekend?"

"Yeah, that's no problem Ralph; I have my students do three beach dives on Saturday and a two-tank boat dive on Sunday."

Todd was conversing in dive speak. Charlie understood, but Todd could see quizzical looks on Ralph's and Heather's faces.

"I guess I lost you. What I said, in English, is that we'll make three dives from Panama City Beach on Saturday then we'll take a 45-minute boat ride on Sunday and dive on a local artificial reef with two tanks. I have standing reservations with the Holiday Inn Express, which is in walking distance from the beach and less than ten minutes from the dive boat. You'll be responsible for bringing your gear, yourself and returning to me no later than the following Tuesday."

Heather spoke up for the first time, turning to her father.

"That's not going to work."

"Todd, we were planning to spend a few days in Panama City then go to Pensacola, to attend Charlie's college graduation, and then do some diving there. We won't be coming back to Georgia for a couple of weeks. What can we work out? I'm not going to pay rental fees on scuba gear for two weeks either."

"Understood Ralph, I wouldn't either. Why don't we do this? How many days were you going to dive in Pensacola?"

"Two, maybe three, days Todd; we are definitely going to dive the aircraft carrier and maybe a couple of other spots," Charlie spoke up.

"Great! I'll only charge you for the days you actually use my gear while you're in Pensacola. You can just let me know when you bring it back to me. Heather, I've already warned your father not to tell anyone that I'm a nice guy, but I'm going to make both of you a deal. If you and your dad decide that you both like scuba diving enough that both of you want to purchase your gear from me, when you come back, I won't charge you any rental fees."

Todd saw more dollar signs and was making another sales pitch, this time to Heather, knowing that a father rarely has the willpower to refuse his daughter.

"Will that work for you Ralph?"

"I think that's more than fair."

"Cool, let's get you hooked up with your basic gear."

A half-hour later Heather had her required equipment and her instructional material.

"So Charlie, do you have all your gear? Do you need your regulator serviced?"

Todd was always ready to generate business.

"Thanks, but I already have a full set and my regulator is good to go also."

"All right, then we can start your pool training tomorrow afternoon; let's say 2 p.m.?"

"We'll be here Todd," Ralph said.


THE gavel banged three times.

"The committee will come to order," House Judiciary Committee Chairman Cedric Wrangler bellowed. Mumbling between fellow members ceased as the committee came to order. Wrangler had received his "marching orders" yesterday, from Speaker Richt. As the committee chair, he could for a vote to subpoena the pardon application for Mohammad Baghai. There would be debate and President Hays' supporters would argue that the Judiciary Committee did not have the authority to subpoena the document. After the opposition's voices had been heard, Wrangler would call for a vote to authorize him to issue the subpoena. There would be a second to the motion and there would be a vote on the motion, which would be divided down party lines. Hays' supporters, being in the minority would lose and the subpoena would be issued. Hays would not stand for such an affront to the executive branch, and would refuse to comply claiming executive privilege and this would be the grounds for impeachment.

"It is the intention of the chair to conduct today's meeting in the following manner. In light of the growing concern of the American public over the issue concerning the possibility of a Presidential pardon for Mr. Mohammad Baghai, I am going to make some opening remarks, not to exceed ten minutes. Afterwards, Mr. Smith, the ranking member of the opposition, will be allowed to make opening remarks, not to exceed ten minutes."

"After the conclusion of those two statements, each member of the committee will be recognized for five minutes to make an opening statement."

Up to this point Wrangler's remarks were routine; remarks that he could recite by rote. Now he extemporized.

"The chair normally likes to be liberal on the five minutes, but today, I think all of you can understand that, with all the committee's members wanting to make an opening statement, as I expect, I will have to be strict on the time limit."

"Afterwards, I will entertain a motion to conduct hearings on the issue and to subpoena all relevant documents."

Both sides knew that there was only one "relevant" document; the pardon application."

"Each member will be allotted five minutes to discuss the issue. At that time the committee will vote on the issue to conduct hearings on the pardon issue. Mr. Smith."

Wrangler acknowledged the ranking member of the opposition party, John Smith of Ohio.

"Mr. Chairman, I concur with the procedure that you have outlined and I appreciate your concern for allowing each and every member to be here on this serious matter. Thank you."

Wrangler spoke again.

"The chair recognizes himself for ten minutes."

"It is well known by our fellow members of the House, and of the Senate, and much of the American public, that Mohammad Baghai, an admitted terrorist and murderer, currently sits incarcerated in Delmont New York correctional facility, awaiting sentencing. It is also well known that Mr. Baghai arrived in our country, literally sneaking into America, under the noses of law enforcement authorities. He has freely pled guilty to the charge of murder, not offering any defense and not negotiating for a reduced sentence. He could be sentenced to death by lethal injection or life in prison. Mr. Baghai has literally placed his life at the mercy of the court."

"Why did Mr. Baghai come to America and pursue such a suicidal course of action? He has not publicly spoken on the matter because, first, he was in a coma and second, his legal team has not allowed him to comment, though his actions have piqued the interest of the American public. In fact, pubic interest has been aroused to such an extent that hundreds of thousands of Americans have contacted their respective Senators and Congressmen to demand that the President grant Mr. Baghai a pardon for his crimes."

"The President has remained silent on her position other than to say that she has received a pardon application from Mr. Baghai's legal team, but will not make a decision on it until after the legal proceedings have concluded. This is the President's right under the Constitution and I do not challenge it. The Constitution clearly grants the power to pardon to the President. However, in light of the public outcry supporting Mr. Baghai and a pardon, and in light of the fact that the White House has remained virtually silent on the matter, I do feel that it is appropriate for this committee to hold hearings on the matter. The Judiciary Committee certainly is within its purview to subpoena Mr. Baghai and all relevant documents concerning the issue."

Wrangler meant the pardon application.

"There is a procedure for requesting a pardon. Each party usually must submit what is called a pardon application. Mr. Baghai's legal team has submitted a pardon application. It is a 12-part application that not many are aware of. Each category details specific data concerning the applicant. The application is comprehensive and this committee, without it, cannot intelligently question Mr. Baghai."

"I have concluded my opening remarks and now yield to Mr. Smith from the State of Ohio."

"Thank you Mr. Chairman."

Smith began his opening remarks and afterward a motion was made and seconded to hold hearings on Mohammad Baghai and his pardon. A second motion was also made and seconded to subpoena pardon application and any other documents related to the pardon. Each and every member of the committee was allotted five minutes to state his or her opinions. The arguments against holding hearing were predictable. A pardon was the purview of the President and the President alone. Congress had no business meddling in such matters. The arguments in favor were just as simple. Though, only the President could grant a pardon, Congress could investigate any matter it chose and issue subpoenas for witnesses and documents. The Judiciary Committee voted along party lines in favor of holding hearings and granting Wrangler subpoena power.

HAYS turned off the closed circuit television in her office. So the House was going to subpoena Baghai's pardon application, knowing that she would refuse to supply it. Richt was behind this, nothing happened in the House of Representatives without Richt's stamp of approval. Dunston also had his hand in this, she had no doubt. She had a number of questions. Dunston had designs on her job, would undoubtedly run for it again and would take measures to ensure his success. This smelled like such a measure, but what about Taylor? Even if this fight with the Judiciary Committee led to impeachment proceedings, which she expected that it would, how would it help Dunston? If anything, in the worst case scenario, her removal from office would only strengthen Taylor by allowing him to take the oath of office and becoming President. Dunston and Richt were both consummate career politicians and not only had a plan but a probably a contingency plan as well. At any rate, the game was on!

IT was 14:00, 2:00 p.m. local time. The Gaffney was patrolling the Persian Gulf, an area roughly twice the size of Lake Erie, whose shores touch eight different oil-producing Muslim countries, Bahrain, Iran, Iraq, Kuwait, Oman, Qatar, Saudi Arabia and the United Arab Emirates. The location was approximately 90 miles due north of the peninsular country of Qatar near the geographical center of the Persian Gulf.

During the time that the Gaffney had been cruising in these waters she had passed hundreds of oil tankers. Each of these tankers was carrying, or had carried, millions of gallons of oil from each of those countries, the length of the Gulf, around the geographical bottleneck of the Strait of Hormuz to oil-consuming countries around the world.

The Gaffney was an older, and relatively smaller, ship by U.S. Navy standards. Designed as an anti-submarine warfare (ASW) ship, she displaced only 3600 tons. She carried hangers and a landing pad for twin ASW helicopters in the aft (rear) of the ship. Against surface threats, within sight she had a 76 mm rapid-fire gun amidships. On the bow she had a twin missile launcher, which could fire a SM1 missile against either surface or air contacts, as far away as 30 miles. Her superstructure had an array of communication antennas attached and various radar receivers for air and surface searching, as well as fire-control targeting and sonar for submarine detection. In the event of a missile, fired by either a ship or aircraft, the Gaffney could defend herself with a combination of two techniques, aggressive and passive.

The passive defense was to fire explosive canisters of chaff, aluminum-coated plastic confetti, while simultaneously steaming away at flank speed. The idea was that the missile's tracking radar would target the chaff rather than the ship. If chaff was not successful and the missile continued to target the ship rather than the cloud, the last recourse was to attempt to shoot down the missile with "C-WIS."

C-WIS was an acronym for "close-in weapons system," though it was pronounced C-WIZ. On the top of the Gaffney's helicopter hanger was a dome-like structure, containing radar, shaped somewhat like wasp's nest. Protruding out from the dome was a six-barreled gatling gun. The gun apparatus, nicknamed "Phalanx," aimed by the radar, would fire uranium-depleted ball bearings, at a rate of 3,000 per minute at an inbound target. Though the C-WIZ system could only be used for short range, the one Phalanx gun provided anti-aircraft protection a thousand fold better than all of the gun crews of a World War II battle ship.

Her mission was vague in the sense that she was to show the flag and project strength. Basically she was an ornament. Other than defending herself against an immediate and direct threat, the skipper, Commander Hampton, could do virtually nothing against one air or surface contact attacking another, other than radioing for instructions. By the time a sit-rep, another acronym for situation report, was transmitted and orders transmitted back, a conflict had generally resolved itself and almost always someone, and something, were generally dead.

Cal was standing on the bow of the ship to get some air, though it wouldn't be for long. He was happy to have some free time from Mr. Books. Commander Hampton had agreed to allow the CNN cameraman to shoot some footage on the bridge and Cal didn't have any desire or business there so this was the best place to find some solitude. There was no such thing as privacy on a ship; the bridge could view Cal, but being at the bow allowed him the opportunity to clear his head.

The Gaffney appeared to be cruising at about five knots, not nearly fast enough to assuage the triple-digit temperatures and the nearly triple-digit humidity. The term "hot and hazy" took on a special significance on Camel Station, which was the nickname for the Persian Gulf. It had been a boring cruise so far and he hoped that it would continue to be uneventful. The Gaffney was scheduled to make port at Jebel Ali next week to replenish its groceries. Because Cal spoke Arabic, he could usually get better quality produce. Being able to communicate with a merchant in his native language had its advantages.

At the same time that Cal was taking a break, Lieutenant Peter Bauer, the Gaffney's tactical action officer (TAO) was in the combat information center (CIC). He had been tracking a several bogeys, unidentified and potentially hostile aircraft. About an hour earlier he'd received a report from the Bush's E2 Hawkeye aircraft, the Navy's equivalent to the Air Force's AWACs (Airborne Warning and Control System), which is essentially a flying radar platform.

An hour earlier, the Hawkeye had tracked an Iranian military jet, which had taken off from Ahwaz, Iran, flying very close to ground level. It crossed the Iraqi border, flew over the Iraqi city of Basra and became "feet wet," meaning that it was flying over the Gulf; flying directly at the Gaffney. Two Iraqi jets were scrambled and were pursuing the lone Iranian jet; they were over 100 miles behind and had no hope of catching it and returning to their base. There was another Iranian jet that had been patrolling the Iranian city of Bushire, but now was on, what appeared to be, an intercept course with the bogey. The Gaffney's radar picked up the aircraft at 200 miles. At that time Bauer phoned Commander Hampton, who was on the bridge, and apprised him of the bogey. Hampton acknowledged Bauer's report and ordered him to keep him advised. The bogey continued its flight path. At 70 miles Bauer phoned the bridge again.

"Skipper, that bogey is still closing. It's at 70 miles now."

"If it breaks 50 miles phone me. We go to general quarters then."

"Aye, aye, Skipper."

Five minutes later, Bauer called the bridge again. "Skipper, the bogey is at 50 miles and closing."

"Go to general quarters, send out the standard warning."

"Aye, aye, skipper."

A moment later a boatswain's pipe echoed over the ship's loudspeakers, alerting the crew of an important message.

"General quarters, general quarters; all personnel to your battle stations!"

A klaxon sounded afterwards to emphasize the urgency of the order.

"Mr. Books, you and your man stay here, there's not enough room for you in CIC." Hampton said as he departed the bridge.

"Right, Commander," Books replied.

"Keep shooting," Books instructed his cameraman.

Bauer ordered Pat Thomas, the petty officer manning the surface radar, to generate the standard warning message on the international distress frequency.

"Unknown aircraft, this is U.S. Navy Warship Gaffney. Request you identify yourself."

Every member of the Gaffney's crew immediately dropped what he, or she, was doing and reported to a predetermined position on the ship, be it weapons, damage control or some other duty. Commander Hampton entered the CIC to direct the battle, should it come.

The executive officer occupied the bridge and would command the ship should Commander Hampton be killed or injured. Cal's battle station was manning a gun at the stern of the ship. His post was intended to prevent personnel from boarding the ship. Upon reporting to the gun station he donned a life jacket, a Kevlar helmet and loaded his weapon. Locked and loaded, he was ready but, since he'd been on the bow and was presently on the stern, Cal had seen that there were not any surface contacts in sight. He would not be repelling boarders today.

IRANIAN Air Force Major Ali Moghadam was tracking the American warship as planned. His F-4 Phantom, with Iraqi Air Force markings, was performing wonderfully and he was executing the plan to perfection. The Prime Minister had personally briefed him and stressed the mission's importance. In a nutshell, Moghadam was to fly his plane, carrying an AM-39 air-to-surface missile, at an American warship and launch the missile. Afterwards, Moghadam was to turn toward Basra, but eject in international waters, to be picked up by an Iranian gunboat. The idea was that, by flying out of, and back to, Basra, it would lead the world to believe that Iraq had attacked the American warship. If the wreckage of his F-4 was retrieved from the bottom of the Persian Gulf, the Iraqi markings would confirm that Iraq, and not Iran, had conducted the attack.

Moghadam launched his anti-ship missile at 2,000 feet; it quickly dropped to sea level and began racing towards the Gaffney, about 10 feet above the water at 500 miles per hour. Petty officer Thomas immediately detected the launch and barked out the attack.

"We have an inbound missile bearing 315 degrees!"

Hampton immediately began issuing orders.

"Weapons free! Come to bearing 045 degrees, all ahead flank! Start popping off chaff!" Hampton gave permission for all of the Gaffney's weapons to engage the missile. SM-1 missiles would be fired almost immediately. If they missed the mark, the 76-mm cannon would engage the incoming missile and continue firing approximately one round every three seconds until the target was destroyed, or it struck or missed the Gaffney. Finally, at about one mile out, the Phalanx gatling gun would engage. He also ordered the Gaffney to steer on a course perpendicular to the missile so that each of the three weapons systems could easily be brought to bear. The Gaffney would launch exploding canisters of chaff, with the expectation that the missile would track and target the confetti rather than the ship, which was steaming away at full speed.

"Weapons free, bearing 045, all ahead flank, launch chaff. Aye,

aye!" The order was repeated.

A missile traveling at 500 miles per hour covers 44,000 feet in a minute. In the three minutes that it took the Gaffney's crew to come to general quarters the missile had covered half the 50 miles distance between the Gaffney and the launch point. The Gaffney launched two SM-1 missiles at the approaching anti-ship missile. The closure rate between the opposing missiles was almost 17 miles a minute.

Approximately 90 seconds after the SM-1 missiles were launched from the Gaffney, Cal saw an explosion. Petty officer Thomas noted that the bogey had disappeared from the radar screen.

"Target destroyed!"

Everyone in the CIC congratulated each other with high fives and slaps on the back.

"Are there anymore threats on the screen? Everyone pipe down," Hampton ordered.

"Skipper, there are no missiles in the air, bogey aircraft retreating. It looks like another aircraft is tailing it skipper," Thomas replied.

"Very well, secure from general quarters. Keep tabs on both of the aircraft."

"Aye, aye skipper."

The cameraman was able to get footage of the missile launch, its path towards the inbound missile and the subsequent explosion. There was a roar from the bridge, with the crew giving each other high fives and back slaps when the bogey was destroyed.

"Did you get that?" Books asked his cameraman.

"Every bit."

"Great! We need to go to the stern and shoot an introduction, and then try to get off the ship as soon as possible."

Books did not have a satellite feed to transmit the digital footage. They had to take the camera to a location with that capability; probably Jebel Ali.

MOGHADAM, his mission 50 percent complete, turned his Phantom back towards Basra. He had done his duty and all that was to be done now was to locate the gunboat, eject, and wait for a pick up. Hopefully he would not have to spend much time in the water.

IRANIAN Air Force Colonel Asadollah Oveissi was flying an F-16 Falcon, patrolling the Iranian coast near Bushire. It was an uneventful patrol and, though his Falcon was armed with four American sidewinder heat-seeking missiles, he had no reason to believe that he would have to use them. Though the F-16 was an old platform, and had been replaced in the American Air Force by the F-22, the Falcon was a wonderful aircraft to fly! Without notice, his radio transmitted.

"Ghost Rider 21, you are ordered to intercept a bogey bearing 125. Your target is at 5,000 meters, vector to bearing 180 to intercept and destroy."

The order was to intercept and destroy a hostile aircraft. Did he hear the order correctly?

"Ghost Rider 21, vector to 180 for intercept and destruction of hostile aircraft. Acknowledge!" The voice on the other end of the radio had an edge of agitation to it.

"Roger, vector to 180. Attack and destroy hostile aircraft at 5,000 meters," Oveissi repeated. He turned his Falcon due south.

MOGHADAM continued to fly towards Basra. In another 10 minutes he would descend to 2,000 meters and eject from his aircraft, parachute to the water, inflate the life raft and wait to be rescued.

OVEISSI eased the Falcon's throttle to full military power, the fastest the aircraft could fly without thrusting it into afterburner. Within a minute, he was behind and within sight of the enemy aircraft. It appeared to have Iraqi markings. The Iraqi pilot apparently had no idea that he was being followed. He began to descend from 5,000 meters. Oveissi launched two heat-seeking missiles. Missiles were always fired in pairs, in case one of them failed. Seconds later the bogey was transformed into a ball of flames.

"Skipper, the second bogey just fired on the first! I mean the one that attacked us! It's gone," Thomas exclaimed.

"The admiral isn't going to believe this," Hampton said in a sardonic voice.

# Chapter 23

The "Bat Phone" phone rang in President Hays' office, which was next to her bedroom. The Bat Phone was Hays' nickname for a direct hotline to the White House. The phone glowed and beeped just like the phone in the Batman television series. It was the encryption techniques that she didn't completely understand, but she'd been assured that the line was 100 percent secure. Hays didn't know exactly what time it was, but she knew it was very, very early. Normally the procedure, when it rang while she was asleep, whether in Florida or some other location, was for the Secret Service to answer the phone and then wake her. This time she heard it and was putting on a robe when a Secret Service agent, she couldn't remember his name, knocked on her bedroom door. Hays was concerned; nothing good happened in the early hours of the morning.

"Thank you. I heard the phone; be right there," Hays answered the tap on the door.

"Yes ma'am."

Hays tied her robe, walked barefoot into her office and picked up the phone.

"This is the President."

"Mrs. President, there has been an engagement in the Persian Gulf," the Secretary of Defense, Scott Patton informed her from Washington.

"Go on, Scott."

"Less than an hour ago the USS Gaffney was attacked. An anti-ship missile launched by, what we believe to be, an Iranian aircraft."

"How many casualties? Who attacked us, Scott? You're not sure what nationality the plane was from?"

"No one was hurt; the Gaffney launched a SM-1 missile, which destroyed the inbound missile. Preliminary reports indicate that the aircraft took off from an air base near Ahwaz, an Iranian city near the Iraqi border, crossed into Iraq, flew over the Iraqi City of Basra and out into the Gulf towards the Gaffney. The hostile aircraft then closed to about 50 miles of the Gaffney and launched its missile. The Gaffney went to battle stations and, as I said, launched a SM-1 which destroyed the Iranian anti-ship missile."

"Where did the attacking plane land?"

"It didn't Mrs. President."

"What do you mean Scott?"

"This is where things get confusing. After the hostile aircraft launched the missile, it turned around and was on a course heading towards Basra but was intercepted and destroyed by an Iranian Air Force aircraft."

"We know this, how, Scott?"

"The entire battle was tracked and recorded by the Navy's E-2 AWACS from the aircraft carrier Bush."

"So, we definitely know that the plane that attacked the Gaffney was Iranian and not Iraqi?"

"Not definitively, no ma'am. We know it took off from Iran, and your assumption is the one any reasonable person would make."

"The Iraqi coast is pretty narrow, where it touches the Gulf. Is there any chance that it was headed towards Iran?"

"You are correct ma'am. The attacking jet could have quickly changed course at the last opportunity and landed in Iran. However, at the time it was destroyed, it was headed towards Iraq." Patton replied.

"What about the plane's wreckage?"

"The Gaffney sent out a helicopter to look for survivors and reported that there was an Iranian gun boat already there, collecting any debris still floating."

"So if I understand this correctly, an Iranian jet took off from Iran, entered Iraqi airspace, then flew over the Persian Gulf, attacked the Gaffney and was shot down by another Iranian jet?"

"That is correct ma'am."

"And an Iranian boat was Johnny-on-the-Spot to pick up any wreckage?" Hays asked rhetorically.

"Scott, I am going to get dressed and have a cup of coffee. I want you to call me back in an hour with an update."

"Yes ma'am."

Hays heard a click on the other end of the line, hung up the phone and decided to check her email. Whatever drowsiness may have lingered dissipated when she opened an email from FBI agent Scott Ramsey. Hays immediately got on the phone to Jim Scarboro.

"Jim, Mohammad Baghai has an FBI guard named Scott Ramsey. I want him in Florida tomorrow."

THE plan had worked perfectly! Hassan Nassiri was on Iranian Public Radio again, as well as national television. The F-4, with Iraqi Air Force markings, had launched its missile at the American warship. The fact that the missile had been destroyed didn't matter. The goal was to show the world that Iran was taking the high moral ground.

The jet was shot down by another Iranian jet fighter as planned. Dead men tell no tales! The "gun boat," was actually manned with divers ready to enter the water. They recovered enough debris to positively identify it as an Iraqi jet, which, in fact it was. The crash site would be marked, so the sunken wreckage could be recovered at a later time. But, there would be a little surprise waiting for the Americans, should they try.

Nassiri knew what American radar planes were capable of, and they'd probably tracked the entire flight. It didn't matter. There was an American expression, "Possession is nine-tenths of the law," and he had the debris from the jet. By announcing that pieces of the Iraqi jet had been recovered, and by displaying them to the media, Nassiri would manipulate the western media, and world opinion, in favor of Iran. The ignorant would believe what they heard first, regardless of the degree of truth. The ones who knew otherwise would be slandered and ridiculed to inconsequence.

HAYS was on her second cup of coffee, and watching CNN, when Scott Patton called again.

"Yes Scott."

"Madam President, not much has changed in the last hour, other than the fact that Hassan Nassiri is now speaking about the incident in front of the Iranian media."

"Yes, I am watching him now."

"So, what's the current status in the area?"

"AWACS planes indicate that both Iran and Iraq have planes patrolling their borders, though it appears neither is taking aggressive postures at this time. Navy helicopters at the crash site report that the Iranian gunboat has collected all the floating wreckage and is returning to shore, escorted by Iranian fighters."

"Nassiri said in his speech that he welcomed us, meaning the United States, to recover the sunken wreckage. How difficult would that be and could this be some kind of propaganda play?"

Hays' sixth sense had been aroused by Nassiri's invitation.

"The Persian Gulf is, on an average, 150 feet deep, 200 feet max. Yes, the plane could be recovered. I'd have to check to see exactly what assets would be required to do the job, where they're located and how long it would take to get them in place. Yes, knowing Nassiri, he has something up his sleeve, but that's just my opinion."

"Okay, what do you suggest?"

"Right now I don't think we should do anything more than maintain a heightened state of alert. Maybe double air patrols in the Gulf. That plane is not going anywhere. It can be recovered at a time of our choosing."

"I agree. Get back to me when you know what it'll take to recover that plane and I'll make a decision at a later time."

"I will Mrs. President."

Hays hung up the phone.

FBI Agent Scott Ramsey relinquished his weapon to Secret Service Agent Ron Thomas before being allowed to enter President Hays' office. Though both agents were federal law enforcement officials, only the Secret Service had the charter to protect the President and was allowed to carry weapons in the presence of the President.

Hays was on the phone, Ramsey had wait outside and cool his heels—a tactic many presidents have used to let their visitors know, who exactly was important and who was a "lower priority." Ramsey and Thomas exchanged chitchat, war stories and such. Thomas was impressed by Ramsey's G-man demeanor and Ramsey, a college football fan, knew of Thomas' University of Florida's football background. After a few minutes, the President walked out from her office.

"Agent Ramsey, come in, we have plenty to discuss," Hays said in a surprisingly warm voice, as she stood at the threshold.

"Of course," Ramsey replied and walked past Hays and into the office.

"Have a seat. Would you like some coffee?"

Hays motioned to one of the two chairs in front of an ornate mahogany desk.

"No, thank you, Mrs. President," Ramsey replied as he sat down.

"You have been the object of the most intense search by the FBI during my administration. If we had started looking for you right under our own figurative noses, we would have saved a lot of money," Hays said as she sat down on the other side of the desk.

"Mrs. President, I've been in the FBI for seven years and you've been looking for me just a few weeks," Ramsey retorted not trying to sound defensive.

"Agent Ramsey, I'm told that you are an excellent agent and I'm not interested in debating you on your justification for falsifying your employment application with the bureau."

Ramsey did not state that he'd been known by another name.

"I'm also not interested in debating with you exactly when you knew that my administration was looking for you, though I suspect that you knew shortly after your mother was visited by your associates, Agents Giles and Fox. It seems that you got some phone calls on your cell from various pay phones."

Hays could see that her guest was on the defensive, which was what she wanted. She didn't care about this man's past, but she was going to discovery everything he knew about his father's life and everything he knew about Mohammad Baghai, or she was going to destroy this man.

"Currently, there is a pardon application before me for Mohammad Baghai. I don't know if you were assigned to guard him by chance or providence and, frankly, I don't care. What I do care about is the relationship between Mohammad Baghai, Reverend Casey Edgars and your father, Jacob Rabin. Now, let me be perfectly clear Agent Ramsey, though it has not yet moved to the limelight, a movement has begun to remove me from office using Mohammad Baghai's pardon application as the leverage to pry me out of the White House. I don't intend to let that happen. If it means ending the career of a mid-level government employee, in order to squash this movement, I will do so without hesitation. Do I make myself clear?"

"Absolutely, Mrs. President, which is the reason I am here. What do you want to know?"

"You've been guarding Mohammad Baghai. Let's start with him, shall we?"

"Certainly, Mrs. President. I can't speak of him before he came to America, but I had ample opportunity to observe him while he was in his cell. He would read a bible at least an hour a day. He has developed a unique way of preaching the message."

"Yes, I have reports of his communications via the prison toilets," Hays said.

"I have also had conversations with him ma'am. He is sincere. He knows that he's likely to be sentenced to life in prison and yet he believes that God has designed a greater plan for him."

"Which involves me and a pardon?"

"He doesn't dwell on it, but yes he believes that God didn't throw him in hell, and then retrieve him, just to stay in jail."

"You believe his explanation?"

"Yes I do. Mrs. President, you're familiar with my father's unique circumstances?"

"You mean your father's epiphany? Yes, I've read the files."

"My father discussed it at length with my mother and me many times. I believed everything he told us. So yes, I believe Baghai. His stigmatic marks are confirmation, as far as I'm concerned."

"I understand that you were present when they manifested?"

"Yes ma'am, I was. He was lying quietly, one moment, a moment later he went into convulsions and, after the seizure stopped, the marks appeared on his hand and feet. The wounds were not inflicted by anyone. Representatives of the Catholic Church have examined the wounds also."

"The Church hasn't commented on them," Hays said.

"No ma'am, but I've been told that an announcement will be forthcoming."

Hays seemed placated at Ramsey's explanation so far. She didn't dislike this man but likes and dislikes didn't mix well with politics and she was going to extract every iota of pertinent information from this man.

"Let's talk about Casey Edgars. Why did you finally decide to contact him? If you hadn't contacted him you wouldn't be here, in front of me, now."

"As I said, Mrs. President, I wasn't trying to hide from you specifically. My father originally suggested that I change my identity. I can't say why, but he had the same type of epiphany that Mohammad had, so I didn't rock the boat. He, my father, had a background in counter-intelligence, among other things, so instructed me on what needed to be done."

Ramsey paused for a moment.

"Mrs. President, I realize that I haven't directly addressed your question. I hadn't decided to contact you until Mohammad recovered from his coma and stated to me that he did not support Reverend Edgars' attempts to coerce you into pardoning him. Before I contacted you, I met with the Reverend personally at the CMC campus and told him of Mohammad's wishes."

"What is your sense of the man?"

"You're referring to Reverend Edgars?"

"I am," Hays replied.

"He is a man of the highest morals and convictions. He told me that he doesn't want you impeached, though he doesn't regret any of his actions. He believes, without equivocation, that Mohammad is God's Prophet and that God does not want him to die in prison, be it from a lethal injection or old age. Furthermore, he sees himself as God's instrument to help Mohammad to fulfill God's plan. That is why, I believe, he is unwilling to compromise. As Reverend Edgars sees things, compromise is not with him, it is with God. Compromise is unacceptable and not even to be considered."

"So if I refuse to pardon this man, what is the end game?"

"Mrs. President, I don't think he believes that it'll come to that. He truly believes that, ultimately, God's plan will be fulfilled. He, as do I, also believes that you are God-fearing and that you fit into the plan, so, in the end, Mohammad will be pardoned."

"You feel that way, because?"

"Mrs. President, I am not a politician and I don't have an answer for you from that standpoint. From a spiritual perspective, if you or anyone else believes in a Supreme Deity, then one has to believe in a grand scheme. My father instilled that into me, and Mohammad's actions support that notion. There isn't any other rational explanation for Mohammad's actions, wouldn't you agree?"

Ramsey had become at ease enough with Hays to ask her opinion.

"Agent Ramsey, perhaps you are correct, but that's not my concern presently. I am concerned how all these unrelated pieces fit together. I can assure you, Reverend Edgars, Tim Dunston, Mohammad Baghai and even Jesus Christ that I am not going to make any decision unless, and until, I feel that I know all the facts concerning this issue."

"Mrs. President I think it all comes down to one's faith in God."

"I appreciate your candor Agent Ramsey."

"Oh, Mrs. President, Reverend Edgars asked me to relay a message to you."

"What was that?"

"He asked me to tell you that he believes some sort of crisis is rapidly approaching."

"I think that's an understatement."

Hays didn't know how prophetic she was.


CASEY Edgars, Tim Dunston and Jim Richt were enjoying lunch in the Christ Ministries Church's private dining room. The men from Capitol Hill wanted Edgars to meet them in Washington, but he refused. Edgars knew what Dunston and Richt were planning and Edgars wasn't playing their game on their home field.

The conversation was casual during lunch and only turned to the serious topic after plates were cleared and coffee was served.

"So gentlemen, you didn't drive here to talk about the weather; what can I do for you?"

Edgars knew their agenda but was forcing his guests to initiate their proposal.

"Reverend Edgars, Speaker Richt and I would like to thank you for inviting us here and, yes, we didn't come here to discuss the weather. Your campaign to have Mohammad Baghai pardoned has infinitely increased the American public's awareness of his unique circumstances. The American public, through your efforts, Reverend, has contacted each and every member of the Senate and the House in support of you and your efforts to secure a pardon for Mohammad Baghai," Dunston began.

"Yesterday, the House Judiciary Committee initiated proceedings to 'encourage,' shall we say, President Hays to pardon Mohammad Baghai."

"What was that Mr. Speaker?"

Edgars knew about the subpoena.

"Committee chairman Cedric Wrangler has been authorized to issue a subpoena for Mohammad Baghai's pardon application. We hope that by bringing to bear the power of Congress, the President will reconsider her obstinate position," Richt said.

"Both of you didn't drive here from Washington just to tell me that."

"No, we didn't Reverend. The two of us can maneuver the President into pardoning Mohammad Baghai. It involves some political risk on our part, but we do feel that it's worth our effort, provided that you remain committed to your cause."

It was Dunston's turn to speak.

"I'm listening," Edgars said.

"My colleague, Mr. Wrangler has been authorized to issue a subpoena, for the pardon application, but I advised him to wait until we had a chance to speak with you Reverend."

"You want to know if I support your efforts to force the President into pardoning Mohammad Baghai. Gentlemen, my position is, has been and will be, that Mohammad Baghai is God's Prophet and that he must be pardoned of any crimes that he is charged with. I'll support any effort which achieves that goal."

Edgars emphasized his last sentence to make his position crystal clear.

Dunston and Richt both heard what they wanted to hear from Edgars.

"Reverend can you keep what we are about to discuss in confidence?" Dunston queried.

"I am a minister aren't I? Virtually everything I discuss with anyone is kept in confidence Senator."

"Good, tomorrow I will advise Chairman Wrangler to subpoena the pardon application. At some point in time you will be called to testify before the committee and comment on the application, as well as give your reasons for wanting Mr. Baghai pardoned," Richt said.

"What happens if the President refuses to provide the pardon application?"

"I don't think that will happen Reverend. The President would be in contempt of Congress should she refuse and I don't think the President wants to travel down that path," Richt lied.

"Gentlemen, perhaps I'm a little slow, but what's in this for you?" Edgars asked.

It was Dunston's turn to lie.

"Reverend, I'm sure you've heard numerous public servants, the Speaker and me included, say that they are motivated to serve. There is some truth to that cliché but there is an even greater motivation in each and every public servant that none will publicly admit to."

"Oh? What is that Senator?"

"A politician doesn't go a day without thinking about being re-elected. Be it while raising money at a fundraiser or sticking our figurative finger in the political wind to see which way it's blowing, every politician, from the city council on up to the President wonders what it'll take to remain in office. When a ground swell movement, such as this, acquires the momentum that this one has, politicians listen—at least the ones that intend to retire. I haven't seen anything like this since 2008 when the American public demanded immigration control and rejected amnesty for the illegal aliens."

Dunston and Richt hadn't mentioned their agreement to anyone for obvious reasons.

"But President Hays isn't running for re-election Senator," Edgars replied.

"No, but her hand-picked successor, Vice President Taylor, is."

"I don't follow."

"Though he hasn't officially announced that he's running for the White House, he will soon, believe me. Since the President and the Vice President are connected at the hip, in a figurative sense, Taylor will want this issue put to bed as soon as possible and will demand that President Hays pardon Mohammad Baghai."

"I see. So, gentlemen, what do you need from me?"

"All we want from you, Reverend, is your support. We can provide you with a list of Senators and Congressmen who support you; perhaps you could post their names on your web site? Perhaps a press conference at the appropriate time will be helpful. Nothing major, all we really need is to know that you are on board," Dunston replied.

"Gentlemen, I've already told both of you, and I'll be happy say so publicly, that I'll support any effort which secures Mohammad Baghai a pardon."

"I think we are in agreement then," Richt said.

"Gentlemen, it's been a pleasure speaking with you today. I pray that you will have a safe trip back to Washington."

Edgars walked his guests to their limousine. Afterwards, he returned to his office and picked up the phone.

"Good morning, this is Reverend Casey Edgars. May I speak to Isabelle Franks?"

A moment later, Edgars was connected.

"Mrs. Franks, this is Casey Edgars. I was planning to visit Mohammad Baghai the day after tomorrow. I thought it would be a good idea if you could join us at the meeting…"

Edgars had a plan of his own; he could tell that Dunston thought that he was a dumb country pastor. Edgars was going to show the Senator who really was the dunce.

"UNDRESS, Julie."

"Yes, Master."

The Angel commanded his slave, Julie Stewart, a high school physical education teacher he had met, and had become intimate with, while he was staying in Chicago. They were at her apartment. He had used her body for his sexual gratification for several months and was actually a little sad that this would be the last time he would sample her pleasures.

Julie was wearing an elegant red evening dress; this one bought by her master. It was a wraparound garment, which accentuated her curves, and was kept from falling off of her body by an ornate brooch just above her left breast. She had been instructed to wear that dress and to wait for his arrival. As a slave she only had to be instructed once.

Julie was standing in front of the Angel, who was sitting on the sofa, as she removed the brooch. Her dress immediately fell to the ground. She was wearing a matching set of red Victoria Secret undergarments, a strapless lace bra and thong.

"Very nice, now remove the bra."

Julie unfastened the catch on the front of the bra. It fell to the floor revealing her perfectly proportioned breasts. She then crossed her wrists at the small of her back as she had been trained and awaited her master's attentions.

The Angel got up from the sofa and walked behind Julie, who was still standing at attention. She knew better than to move unless instructed to do so. He reached around her torso and caressed her left breast, giving it a gentle squeeze and whispered into her right ear. She could feel his hard features as electricity raced through her body. She couldn't resist him, even if she wanted to.

"Are you excited, my slave?"

"Yes, Master."

"Do you want to know what I have planned for you tonight?"

The Angel moved his hand from her breast and slid it inside the front of her thong, touching her most sensitive area.

Julie gasped.

"My desires are not important Master. It is only important that I please you."

"I have something especially delicious planned tonight."

The room was silent except for the ratchet sounds of the handcuffs, which he put on each wrist.

# Chapter 24

Bam. Bam. Bam! Charlie wasn't sure if the pounding was inside his head, or his apartment's front door, or both. What time was it? Only eight o'clock? PM not AM? It was getting dark outside so it must be PM. Hopefully he wouldn't be sick.

He wasn't very enthusiastic about working earlier today, leaving the office in mid afternoon on the pretense of 'cold calling, soliciting business by knocking on doors, passing out business cards and selling one's self as much as selling an insurance policy.

After two half-hearted attempts, Charlie decided to call it a day and went home to his apartment in Dawsonville, collecting his mail at the apartment's mailbox, but not examining any of it. Then he started consuming a twelve pack of beer, which was in his refrigerator. After number 7 he graduated to a bottle of Crown Royal. He was going to have a hell of a hangover tomorrow but at least he was sleeping it off, at least he was until who ever it was started pounding on his door.

"Yeah, who is it?"

Charlie slurred as he got out of bed and put on a bathrobe, on the way to the bathroom to get 2 aspirin.

"Charlie it's me. Open the door," Heather shouted to her fiancée through the door.

"Hold on, give me a second."

Charlie unlocked the door and was greeted by Heather, with a hug and a kiss. She immediately smelled the alcohol on his breath and knew that he had not been content with his usual adult beverage or two but had been drinking heavily most of the afternoon and evening.

"Charlie, what's wrong? I tried to call you on your cell and got your voice mail. Why have you been drinking?"

"I didn't realize that I turned off my cell. I'm sorry. Today is not a good day for me Heather," Charlie said as he broke the embrace.

Heather had never seen Charlie like this before. She didn't know that it was possible to be drunk and pensive simultaneously. She knew that he liked to drink beer. He had not been concerned about having one every now and again, when the mood struck him. He had an 'adult beverage' the first time that met her parents and he was in a fraternity. Fraternity members always had a keg on tap; it was an unwritten law, wasn't it? But she had never seen Charlie in such a state.

"Charlie you sit down. I am going to make some coffee after I call Mom and Dad. They were worried as much as I was. You want decaf?"

"Yes please."

Heather started a pot of coffee and then called her parents.

"Mom, hi, I am here at Charlie's. He is okay."

She was speaking in a physical sense and not an emotional one, but didn't elaborate further because she didn't know what Charlie's explanation was and didn't want to play 20 questions over the phone.

"He didn't realize that his cell phone was turned off. Okay, fine Mom. I'll call you tomorrow. I love you too. Bye."

Two minutes later Heather brought Charlie a steaming cup of coffee and sat down next to her man on the sofa.

"Take a sip of this, and tell me what's wrong. Mom is relieved that you are all right. I don't like lying to her."

"Thank you love."

Charlie took a couple of sips.

"I don't feel good."

"No wonder. How much did you drink and why?"

Heather asked not in accusing tone, but rather one of concern and perhaps, empathy.

"I started with beer and broke open a bottle of Crown," Charlie said as if he was in misery.

"Why Charlie?"

"Heather, did it ever occur to you that, we almost never met?"

"I hadn't thought about it Charlie. I know that you had to win your paint ball match to qualify to come here."

"Heather, our team was down to our last man, me against two others in a tie game. Whoever captured the flag was going to win the game and the match. If we didn't win I would never have come to North Georgia and met you. Do you know how often one man is able to kill two others in paintball? Never, that's how often. One man can pin down the opposing man, with suppressing fire while the second maneuvers for the kill. That's what they did to me, yet I got them both. Why do you think that happened?"

Charlie's headache was beginning to subside and he took another sip of coffee.

"I guess God wanted us to meet and fall in love with each other Charlie. He had a plan. What does paintball have to do with you being drunk?"

Heather was not mad, but didn't see where Charlie was going

with this.

"Precisely."

Charlie wasn't enunciating well. Precisely actually came out pre-cizely.

"Heather, my brother John, died in Iraq on this day. What was God's plan? What purpose did his death serve? I don't even know the circumstances. The Army said it was classified. What was God planning when my mother and father died in a car crash? How many other brothers are going to die in Iraq? What happens if you get orders over there after you graduate? Everyone in my family seems to die."

Charlie was all over the map, but she instantly saw his point. Either chance or fate brought them together. If it was strictly by chance, then what was to prevent another terrible random act from hurting him? If there was a divine plan from a Supreme Deity, why was he being so cruel to Charlie?

"Oh Charlie, I didn't know! Mom and Dad had no idea either," Heather said as she gave him a reassuring hug, but decided it was better not to address his last concern, at least until he was sober and raised the subject again. Perhaps her pastor would have satisfactory answers. She had none right now.

"I had always put flowers on my family's graves on this day each year. I wasn't able to do it this time."

Charlie completely broke down in tears.

"Charlie, why didn't you say anything? We all love you. Mom and Dad think of you as a son. When you are hurting, we hurt too. We will go visit your family's graves when we go to Pensacola," Heather said as she gave her man another embrace.

Charlie, having a cantharis was feeling a little better after purging some of his emotional demons and even managed to crack a smile.

"I feel like death warmed over."

"You look like warmed over death. Come on, you'll feel better after you have had a shower."

"Only if you take one with me."

Charlie's eyes widened with hopeful expectation.

This time it was Heather that had a wicked smile.

CASEY Edgars, Isabelle Franks and Paul Stewart signed in on the visitor's sheet at Delmont Correctional Facility. Like his meeting with the FBI agents several weeks earlier, rather than discussing matters in a booth, separated by plexi-glass, where conversations could and probably be recorded, the group met in the same 'cage'. Inside it was the same collapsible table with folding chairs.

Edgars and Franks were sitting when Mohammad was brought in.

"Isabelle, my sister, Paul, I am so glad to see you again!"

Mohammad, Isabelle and Paul exchanged hugs. Mohammad made sure that his bandaged hands did not touch his guests clothing.

"Mohammad, this Reverend Casey Edgars. He has taken an interest in your case," Paul introduced Mohammad's third visitor.

"Mohammad, it is a privilege to finally meet you for the first time."

Edgars offered his had to shake not concerned about touching his bandaged hand. Mohammad, instead, gave Edgars a hug like his two other visitors.

"Reverend, my friend Scott Ramsey has told me of your efforts on my behalf. I want to thank you."

Mohammad sat down at the table.

"Mohammad I wanted to meet you and discuss my plans with you and your team. Agent Ramsey has told me that you have issues with some of my tactics."

"How is Scott? I haven't seen him in the last few days," Mohammad asked.

"The FBI has suggested that he take some personal time off. Apparently, his superiors were not happy when he revealed his true identity," Isabelle replied.

Mohammad paused a moment. There appeared to be a bit of disappointment in his face; Ramsey had mailed a letter to Mohammad, explaining who he actual was when he left to meet the President.

"I am sorry to hear that. He was a friend and a true believer."

Mohammad paused another moment to compose his thoughts.

"Again, Reverend, thank you for your concern about my plight but, I do not feel impeaching the President is the correct method to resolve this matter."

"Mohammad, I have the greatest respect for the President, both as a government official and as a person. It is not my intention to be the instrument of her impeachment, only to be the instrument to allow you to complete God's plan. Ultimately that is the only thing that really matters. Wouldn't you agree Father?"

"Reverend, both you and I are duty bound to obey God's wishes," Stewart said.

"Exactly Father, though we have different reasons all of us have the same goal, to have Mohammad released from prison. That is why I asked to meet with Mohammad and his attorney. I should have thought to invite you also. Isabelle, I am glad that you did invite Father Paul to attend our meeting."

"It made sense for Paul to attend Reverend," Isabelle said.

"If I make a suggestion, let's dispense with the formalities and address each other by our first names, shall we?"

Edgars got nods from everyone at the table.

"Now let me summarize the situation before we go any farther. All of you please stop me at anytime, if I mis-speak," Edgars said as he looked at the three others, getting nods.

"Mohammad, you had an epiphany and because our Lord revealed to you the error of your evil ways, felt compelled to travel to the United States and answer for your crimes. You contacted your former captive David Franks, announcing your intentions and hired his wife Isabelle to represent your legal interests and to obtain a pardon from the President. After arriving in America you were baptized by Paul and then turned yourself in to the FBI and basically threw yourself at the mercy of the US justice system. I understand you are to be sentenced at the end of the week and you are likely to receive life in prison. Am I correct Isabelle?"

"That is what I anticipate Casey," Isabelle replied.

"Now Mohammad, partly because of my profession and partly because of my background, I was one of the first and to proclaim you a prophet of God. Certainly I have been the most ardent supporter of your cause. Isabelle, I am not attempting to detract from your efforts. I think it is fair to say that we are taking different roads to the same destination."

"Yes, yes of course Casey," Isabelle replied.

"Now Paul, can you tell us what the Catholic Church's position is regarding Mohammad?"

"Casey, I have relayed Mohammad story to my immediate superiors, who believe it, but had to push it up the hierarchy, his epiphany, his stigmatic marks, everything. Unfortunately, the Church is a bureaucracy, much bigger than the US Government and eventually, Mohammad's case will be investigated by the Vatican before the Church will comment on it."

"Do you have a sense on the position that the Church will take?"

"Eventually I believe the Church will support Mohammad, but no time soon," Stewart said.

"Fortunately, I don't have to deal with all the red tape. Mohammad, you have been quiet so far and this meeting is on behalf; do you care to add anything?"

"Reverend, thank you for your efforts, Jesus, by revealing hell to me, has saved me from suffering in Hell for eternity. I believe most jihadists will ultimately spend eternity there. I am also confident that he is using all of you as his instruments to carry out his will. The worst that can happen to me is that my life ends on Earth and I spend eternity in Paradise. I don't believe that will happen immediately but I am not fearful if it does. All of you have read Psalm 23 haven't you?"

Mohammad smiled. He knew all present were familiar with the passage, 'the Lord is my shepherd; I shall not want…Yea, though I walk through the valley of the shadow of death, I will fear no evil…'

"Mohammad, you said earlier, that you do not want to see the President impeached; neither do I. Earlier this week I secretly met with Tim Dunston and Speaker Jim Richt. They wanted my support in the impeachment proceedings. I sort of misled them, God forgive me."

"What did you say to the Casey?"

Stewart astonished, asked his fellow man of the cloth.

"Paul I didn't lie to the men. I told them both that I supported whatever it took to secure a pardon for Mohammad. I am sure they thought that I was an old country pastor and assumed that I supported them, when in fact I believe that the people here can stop the impeachment movement in its tracks, have Mohammad pardoned in such away that she does not appear to succumb to pressure."

"We are listening Casey," Isabelle said.

"This is what I was thinking…"

ST Andrews State Park, in Panama City Beach Florida, is a mecca for local scuba divers that do not choose to dive on any of the several offshore locations, which are only obtainable via a charter boat. A half a dozen pavilions each covering 8 concrete picnic tables allow visitors to picnic when not enjoying the sun or water. Approximately 100 yards from the closest pavilion, is the beach where scuba divers can dive rock jetties and sunbathers can tan themselves. The parking lot is only feet away from the tables and park visitors can easily carry coolers, cook out paraphernalia and scuba gear from a car to a table. A concession store was also within walking distance for anyone who might need ice, sun block, or other sundries. All in all, the facilities were ideally suited for a diving instructor teaching a small group of students in a class. Todd had made this trip dozens of times before, teaching hundreds of students and had the routine down to a science.

Charlie and the Twigs had driven down to Panama City Friday afternoon and checked into a local motel. Charlie was in heaven when they dined at a local restaurant on fresh Florida seafood. He ordered a dozen raw oysters on the half shell as an appetizer and red snapper as an entree'. Heather gagged when she tried an oyster, vowing never to eat one ever again. Ralph and Jo Ann, having the benefit of previous taste experience declined to eat the seafood delicacy, both smiled as their daughter managed to stomach the oyster. Charlie gobbled down the other eleven.

Heather, Ralph along with 4 other students were completing their fifth and final check out dive of the weekend, to obtain their coveted 'C-cards', otherwise known as scuba diver certifications. Charlie was accompanying the group, strictly as a guest. It was Sunday. The weather was overcast with scattered showers. Originally, the class was supposed to take a charter boat to an offshore artificial reef but, because of the nasty weather, the Gulf of Mexico was too rough for the charter to journey outside the bay, so the class was conducted for the second day, at the jetties just off St. Andrews Beach. Because the jetties were inside St Andrews Bay, the water was relatively calm despite the less than optimal weather.

Between 30 and 40 feet deep the rocks and boulders of the jetties act like an artificial reef for various fish sea urchins, star fish and many more forms of marine life. The class practiced the scuba diving techniques which, were learned in the pool. Ralph and Heather practiced buddy breathing on each other for a few minutes, until Todd gave the signal to the class that training was over and the class could spend the remainder of the dive investigating the marine life. Charlie, Ralph and Heather explored the rock formations.

Jo Ann, because of the overcast conditions, could not get a sun tan as she had hoped, was content to sit on a chair, reading a book on the beach.

After completing the final dive, surfacing, swimming to the beach, the group walked to pavilion took off their gear and showered at on of the public showers. Todd had brought hot dogs and had lit charcoal, on a grill in-between the fourth and fifth dives and intended to cookout to celebrate the new diver's certifications. With the training completed, Ralph and Heather, as well as the rest of the class were qualified to scuba dive without supervision.

The hotdogs cooked in about 2 minutes and the entire group enjoyed a few minutes of camaraderie with each other before checking out of the motel and driving back to Georgia. Charlie and the Twigs were heading west towards Pensacola instead of north to attend Charlie's graduation and take a vacation. Todd walked to where Heather and Ralph were eating and both of them a temporary diver certification card.

"Ralph, you and Heather will need these if you plan on diving in Pensacola. Your regular certification cards should arrive in my shop in about 3 three weeks. I'll call you when the come in. You all have a safe trip."

"Thanks Todd, we will."

"Todd, can I help you clean up before we part ways?"

"Appreciate that Charlie, but there is not much to do. I am already loaded up and all that we need to do is throw the paper plates in the trash. Thanks though."

After the Twigs and Charlie drove back to the motel, checked out and packed their Expedition, Ralph drove to a convenience store to gas up for the trip to Pensacola.

---

## RESOLUTION

Impeaching Jennifer Hays, President of the United States and Thomas Taylor, Vice President of the United States, for high crimes and misdemeanors.

Resolved, that Jennifer Hays, President of the United States of America and Thomas Taylor, Vice President of the United States of America are impeached for high crimes and misdemeanors and the following article of impeachment be exhibited to the United States Senate.

Articles of impeachment exhibited by the House of Representatives of the United States. of America in the name of itself and of the people of the United States of America, against Jennifer Hays, President of the United States of America and Thomas Taylor, Vice President of the United States of America, in maintenance and support of its impeachment against them for high crimes and misdemeanors.

Article I

In their conduct while President and Vice President of the United States of America, Jennifer Hays and Thomas Taylor, in violation of their constitutional oath to faithfully execute the offices of the President and Vice President of the United States of America, respectively and to the best of their ability, preserve, protect and defend the Constitution of the United States of America and in violation of their constitutional duty to take care that the laws be faithfully executed, have purposely defied Congress by refusing a lawful the subpoena of documents and testimony pertaining to a congressional investigation.

---

# Chapter 25

## US District Court

Mohammad and Isabelle were seated at the defendant's table. Isabelle was in a three-piece business suit with a white blouse; Mohammad in prison coveralls, tennis shoes and bloody rags covering his hand wounds. The bleeding was continuous, but light, requiring bandages to be changed every 4 hours or so. Mohammad's wounds on his feet, though noticeable, did not bleed significantly and didn't require bandages. He was also hand cuffed at five points, at each wrist and ankle, as well as around the waist.

After Casey Edgars and Father Paul left the meeting at Delmont, Isabelle and Mohammad discussed his next appearance before Judge Stephen Cobb.

"Mohammad, the drill will be pretty much the same as the last time…"

"Drill, you are certainly talking about the electric boring device Isabelle?"

Mohammad was definitely not up to speed on American slang.

"No, drill can also mean a procedure. The procedure will be the same as before, only the judge will sentence you."

"Do you have an idea what that will be?"

"I believe that you will be sentenced to life in prison Mohammad. As you know there is no parole for federal prisoners. So unless you are pardoned, you will spend the remainder of your life in a federal correctional facility," Isabelle said in somber voice.

"Only if it is God's will Isabelle."

"Mohammad, I appreciate your attitude, but I don't think you appreciate that while you are incarcerated, which could be another 30 or 40 years, that you will be in a prison cell 23 hours a day. Your entire life will be regulated from the time you wake up in the morning to the time you go to sleep at night. Because of your notoriety, you will be a marked man, especially by the Muslim inmates, so you will spend your time in solitary confinement. It won't a pleasant experience."

Isabelle did not mention the prison gangs and their propensity for sodomy.

"Isabelle, my sister, you have forgotten that I spent 23 minutes in Hell. Believe me, 23 minutes in Perdition is the same as a thousand life times. I am not concerned. I do believe Jesus has other plans for me."

Isabelle, not having a satisfactory reply just nodded.

Jack Gant was sitting at the opposite table, representing the US Government. He was smiling like the cat that swallowed the canary. His presence was only a formality, though he would undoubtedly get his share of face time on national television after the sentence was imposed.

"All rise! This court is now in session. The honorable Stephen Cobb presiding," the bailiff cried as all the occupants in the room rose.

"Be seated," Cobb said in a somber voice.

"Is the government ready to proceed?"

Cobb asked Gant.

"The government is ready your honor."

"Is the defendant ready?"

"We are ready your honor." Isabelle replied.

"Very well, Mohammad Baghai please stand."

"Mr. Baghai, immediately after you pled guilty to the murder of Christian J. Welter you collapsed in this court and entered a comatose state, which created even more controversy than you had, when you entered this country and turned yourself in to authorities."

"I am well aware of your claims of an epiphany and as a fellow Christian, I commend you, whatever your motivation, for taking responsibility for your crimes. As to the authenticity of your claims, that is an issue of faith, not an issue of law. It doesn't have a bearing in this court and it will not."

Cobb's last statement caused a disturbance in the courtroom.

"Silence in this court room," Cobb pounded his gavel.

After a few moments the audience became silent again.

"It is my understanding that you have been involved in other murders, which you have not been charged with. These alleged crimes are also not an issue which has a bearing in this court and it will not."

"The judicial branch of government is by design un-elected and is intended to be non partisan. My job is to impose a sentence upon you which is fair and just based upon the laws of this nation and not be swayed by factions, with their own agendas and I was not."

"It is my opinion that you are sincerely repentant of your crime. Your actions of surrendering yourself, speaks to that and your conduct while in prison has factored into my decision," Cobb paused a moment.

"I think that may be a good sign Mohammad," Isabelle whispered to her client quickly.

"Mohammad Baghai, I sentence you to prison, in a facility to be determined, to a term equal to the remainder of your natural life."

The court erupted with Judge Cobb pounding his gavel for order.

"That is the best that we could hope for under the circumstances Mohammad. I will speak to Jack Gant and see is there is any flexibility in where you will serve your sentence."

"Thank you Isabelle, my sister," Mohammad said as he was led away by his guards.

THE University of West Florida Campus, in Pensacola, Florida consists of 1600 developed acres, in the middle of over 20,000 undeveloped acres of rolling hills and streams in Escambia County, Florida, adjoining US Highway 90. The student body of 10,000 is large enough to give the university a true collegiate ambiance, yet small enough to allow professors to give undergraduates individual attention as needed. One reason Charlie decided to attend UWF, rather than another university, though he would never admit it is that the undergraduate population is 60 percent female, which gave him plenty of opportunities to 'socialize', before he met Heather.

Charlie and the Twigs arrived in Pensacola and checked into a hotel near by and after getting settled, Heather insisted that Charlie give a tour of the University. Charlie, because of the heat, humidity and the campus size, insisted that the tour be done in the car. The Twigs and Heather didn't appreciate how large UWF was.

"Charlie, this place is huge," Heather exclaimed.

"It's incredibly pretty and serene as well. Charlie, you said the campus had a nature walk? I would love to see it," Jo Ann said.

"Yes Mom, it's actually not far, with in walking distance, even though it helps to have a bicycle to get around," Charlie said to Jo Ann, before he turned to Ralph.

"Ralph, over there is the visitor's center, where you can get a parking permit. Then we can park and I can give you a short tour. First, I want to go to the Common's and get something to eat; I'm starving. We can discuss what we want to do while we are eating."

The Commons, also known as the student center, is a two-story building, which houses a post office, various student affairs offices, the campus book store, a game room, a bank and most importantly, as far as Charlie was concerned, the cafeteria.

The meals were served buffet style and the food was surprisingly good. The four found a table and were enjoying their meal and conversation. Students were just beginning to enter the Commons for the evening meal.

"Ralph, my graduation ceremony is a few days away; would everyone like to go to the beach tomorrow or checkout the diving?"

"Are you sure there will be a charter tomorrow Charlie?"

"The dive boats go out almost every day during the summer, when the weather is nice, Ralph. I will have to call to see if the boat captain I use is going to the aircraft carrier."

"Charlie, how far is the dive shop from here?"

"It's about twenty minutes or so Heather."

"Let's go to the dive shop after we leave here, make reservations for later in the week but go to the beach tomorrow."

"Sure if it is all right with everyone."

Charlie got nods.

"We need to go to Wal-Mart, or someplace to buy plenty of sunblock, drinks and ice for the beach. There's one not to far away. Excuse me a second, I see a friend of mine that I want to introduce you to," Charlie said as he popped up from his chair.

"Chris," Charlie yelled as he grabbed O'Callahan's shoulder.

"Charlie! When did you get in town?"

"I got here earlier today man. I want to introduce you to Heather and her family." Charlie said as he guided his friend to Heather's family.

"Heather, Ralph, Jo Ann, this is my friend, Chris O'Callahan. He was on our paintball team. Chris, this is my fiancée Heather Twig and her parents, Ralph and Jo Ann."

"Hello," Chris said.

"How are you doing son?"

Ralph said as he shook hands with Chris.

"I am fine sir and you? Hey look, Charlie I got to run. If you have time, why don't you and Heather come by the house tonight? It was a pleasure meeting all of you," Chris said.

"It was a pleasure meeting you Chris." Jo Ann said.

"I'll talk to you later," Charlie said as he sat down again.

"How do you know your friend Charlie?"

"Mom, he is a fraternity brother, a year behind me. We actually met for the first time at an AAMO meeting on campus."

"Ammo, as in ammunition?"

"AAMO as in Americans Against Military Occupation," Charlie said.

Jo Ann gave Charlie a quizzical look.

"It is an anti President Hays organization Mom," Heather said.

"It's not anti Hays per-se, though, if there is one person that hates her policies more than me, it would be Chris. We are against any and all politicians and organizations that support American occupation forces in Iraq, under any circumstances," Charlie said.

"It is anti Hays. Don't insult our intelligence Charlie," Heather said with a look of consternation at her future husband.

"Oh? I never told you Heather, but Hays had the FBI investigate me, because I don't happen to agree with her idiotic policies. Ask your dad, he spoke a FBI agent about me a few weeks ago. Am I telling the truth Ralph?"

Charlie was beginning to get worked up.

"Heather, Charlie, if the two of you want to discuss between yourselves fine but don't include Ralph and me. We don't want to hear it. It's neither the time nor the place for such an argument right now. We are down here to watch you graduate Charlie and to take a vacation," Jo Ann said.

"Agreed, that is a pretty silly topic to get mad at each other," Ralph said.

"You're right Ralph. This is a hot button issue for both Heather and me. Unfortunately, we are on different sides of it. I didn't mean to jerk your chain Heather," Charlie said as he squeezed Heather's hand and looked into her eyes. He could see that all was forgiven.

"Is everyone finished? If so, let's go take a trip to Charlie's dive shop, make reservations and then stop by Wal-Mart, to get some beach supplies. I want to buy a paper too."

"Ralph, you can drop me off at the hotel. I think I want to lie down," Jo Ann said.

"Are you not feeling well dear?"

"I got up early and the trip just caught up with me. I'll be fine after I take a nap."

WHILE Charlie, Heather and Ralph were at the dive shop, Jo Ann was laying down reading a book in the room when the telephone rang.

"Hello?"

Jo Ann said, not really expecting a phone call. Ralph would have called on the cell, rather than via the hotel.

"Hello, I am not sure I have the correct room. I am tying to reach Charles Michaels. Is he there?"

"This is not his room but I do know him. Who is this?"

"Ma'am, my name is Casey Edgars and I would like to speak to Mr. Michaels. May I ask who I am speaking with?"

"This is Jo Ann Twig. Is this Reverend Casey Edgars, the televangelist?"

"Yes ma'am."

"You have been on television a lot lately Reverend. Charlie Michaels is my daughter's fiancée. Why do you want to speak with him?"

"It's a pleasure speaking with you Mrs. Twig. The reason I would like to speak to you Charlie has to do with why I have been seen on TV as of late. Is he in Pensacola with you?"

"Yes Reverend, he is with my husband and daughter. They should be back later. Would you like me to have him call you?"

"Please, if you would. Let me give you my personal cell number. Please have him call me."

"I will Reverend."

"Thank you Mrs. Twig. Please have Charlie call me regardless of the time. Thank you again."

FBI Agent Martin Scrader had made a new discovery concerning Charlie Michaels. His telephone interview with Ralph Twig, during Michaels' background investigation basically confirmed his suspicions that Charlie was an intelligent, law abiding and opinionated young man and was not a threat to the President. Scrader still believed that but a deeper investigation of Michaels' ancestry revealed an anomaly, which raised a red flag. Scrader still didn't think it was significant, but that wasn't his decision to make. He would have to send an email to his superiors, with an attached file, containing the documentation. Eventually, it would cross the desk of James Scarboro, the Attorney General, who would forward it to the Secret Service and they would make the ultimate decision. Undoubtedly, young Michaels would, at the least get a visit and an interview from the Secret Service; at the most he would be detained until after the President left the graduation ceremony. In either case the procedure was probably unnecessary and would only cause Michaels embarrassment, but the Secret Service couldn't afford to take that chance.

Scrader opened his email browser and began to compose a memorandum that was certainly going to cause plenty of aggravation to plenty of people.

RALPH, Charlie and Heather arrived back at the hotel and meet Jo Ann. Like their accommodations in Panama City, the four shared two adjoining rooms, with a connecting threshold. Ralph, Jo Ann and Heather sharing one room with two double beds and Charlie was in the other room. Charlie as usual, was hungry again Heather was interested in seeing a movie, though she didn't really have clue as to what she was interested in seeing. Ralph, being the regimented personality in the family wanted to plan the week's activities. The only three activities that were cemented in concrete were Charlie's graduation, the dive trip, which could be fitted into the week's itinerary and tomorrow a trip to the cemetery at Naval Air Station Pensacola to visit the grave of Charlie's brother, John. A couple of days on the beach were definitely on the agenda but nothing was planned and loose ends like that drove Ralph nuts. Jo Ann decided to put an end to what she perceived as non-sense by changing the subject an informing Charlie about her phone call with Reverend Edgars.

"Charlie, you had a phone call while you were away. It was from a man named Casey Edgars. He asked me to have you call him back."

"I don't know anyone by that name. Did he say what he wanted?"

"It was the Reverend Casey Edgars on TV and no, he didn't say but asked for you to call him when you came back. He gave me his cell number and told me it was important for you to call him regardless of the time."

"Why would he want to speak with you Charlie?"

"I don't know Heather. I've never met the man."

"Son, why don't you call him and find out what he wants? Afterwards, we can go somewhere and find something to eat. I am starting to get a little hungry,"

Ralph said.

"Here is his number Charlie," Jo Ann said as she handed him a slip of paper.

Charlie dialed the number on his cell.

"Hello?"

"Yes, this Charlie Michaels calling Casey Edgars."

"This is Reverend Casey Edgars Mr. Michaels. Thank you for returning my call. I am guessing you would like to know why I am contacted you."

"Yes Reverend, since I don't know you and have never met you the thought occurred to me. And call me Charlie."

"I will Charlie. Thank you. Charlie, I spoke with your future mother in law earlier and I didn't want to get into the particulars of my interests with her over the phone. It is important that I speak to you personally. I will be traveling to Pensacola tomorrow and I was hoping that we could speak face to face."

"What about Reverend?"

"Charlie, I would rather not say over the phone."

"Why not?"

"The matter that I must discuss with you is much too important, much too urgent and much to complicated to converse over the phone. Charlie, please take me at my word that I will not be wasting your time and that it is imperative that I speak with you as soon as possible. Can I speak with you tomorrow evening?"

"Reverend, I am down here with my family to graduate from school and to take a vacation. Tomorrow, we were planning to go to the beach and to visit the Navy Base. I really wasn't planning to have covert meetings with people that I don't know. You can meet with me and my family and discuss whatever is on your mind."

"Thank you Charlie. Your future mother in-law sounded like a delightful person. I would love to meet your family."

"Good. You can call me on my cell phone tomorrow and we can agree to meet at a convenient location."

"Thank you again Charlie. I look forward to meeting you and your family tomorrow."

"What did he want Charlie?"

"He didn't say Heather. He did stress that was important to speak with me in person and not over the phone.

"And what did you say Charlie?"

"That he could call me tomorrow and we could meet. By us I meant all of us; not just him and me."

"Why did you say that son?"

"We are down here for a vacation Ralph. Some television preacher, which I don't know suddenly calls and says that he must speak with me immediately but won't say what about. I'm sorry but I don't take that type of introduction seriously and I am not going to interrupt my quality time with you all just on his say so. I'll speak with him but I am not going to allow him to impose his agenda on me or us."

"Charlie, because of his reputation, I am sure that he believes that it is important," Jo Ann said.

"Fine Mom but whatever he has to say he can discuss with all of us. I don't keep secrets from my family. Now is anybody else hungry? I know several good restaurants."

KEN Shugart and Jim Richt were sitting in the America Today, about to tape Shugart's interview concerning the Mohammad Baghai pardon issue. Richt, possessing the acumen of a career politician, knew he had the opportunity to strike political gold with, this interview. Political gold in this case equated to the Presidency. Dunston had conceived a brilliant political game plan to 'overthrow' the current administration and though Richt had tacitly agreed to select Dunston as his vice president, he felt no obligation to do so.

Promises and political alliances were made everyday on Capital Hill and they both had two things in common. Both were temporary in nature and both were subject to be broken due to any change in the political winds. Power was very much like sex in that men wanted it and there was no such thing as enough. In his younger days on the Hill, Richt had no hesitation about using his powerful position as a US Congressman to satisfy his sexual appetite, only prudence was required to keep his conquests out of the papers. Now he was much too old to be dipping his pen in anyone's ink well, so now political power was the only thing that excited him. He would give Dunston consideration when the time came but no guarantee.

Richt had called Shugart to beat President Hays and her public relations spin machine to the punch. She would undoubtedly frame this confrontation as nothing more that a political vendetta against her. Richt would make this a Constitutional issue, taking emotional reactions out of the equation. There had been other impeachment resolutions submitted to the floor of the House by the lunatic, Representative Kuykendal and all of them had been tabled by the yes man Representative Wrangler according to instructions because they were superficial. Hays, had never given any of them a second notice, a mosquito buzzing around and annoying a sweaty landscaper and Richt assumed that she would believe that this particular one was more of the same. Richt would emphasize that the resolution was legitimate, the reasons for resolution were legitimate and that the checks and balances of the Constitution, conceived by the founding fathers were indeed legitimate.

"Today we have Speaker of the House Jim Richt with us. Yesterday a resolution calling for the impeachment of the President and Vice President was introduced onto the floor of the House. This isn't the first time such a resolution that an impeachment resolution has been brought to the House. This is the first time that such a resolution against the President has been forwarded to the House Judiciary Committee and has been given serious consideration. Speaker Richt will discuss the resolution and why it is not likely to die in committee. Mr. Speaker thanks you for sharing time with us today."

"It's a pleasure to be here Ken," Richt replied.

"Mr. Speaker a resolution was recently introduced and sent to the Judiciary Committee, calling for the impeachment of both President Hays and Vice President Taylor. There have been other resolutions introduced calling for the President's impeachment previously and every one of them didn't get any traction, if I can use that term. Why is this one different?"

"Ken you are correct other resolutions have been introduced and every one of them have died in committee. Without getting into the specifics of any particular resolution, I can say that the charges, either did not rise to the level of 'high crimes and misdemeanors' and/or did not have sufficient evidence to support the charges."

"How is this resolution different from the others Mr. Speaker?"

"Representative Kuykendal had introduced a resolution previously, which claimed that Hays administration, had 'cajoled' members of the intelligence community to generate intelligence reports, which meshed well with, with the administration's policy in the Middle East and particularly our prolonged and continued occupation in Iraq. President Bush 43 had similar impeachment resolutions introduced against him. None got anywhere because there were legitimate questions as to if the charges rose to impeachable levels and if the charges were even provable at all. That was, in my opinion the case, here against President Hays and the resolution suffered a similar fate. In this case, one can legitimately argue that both the President and Vice President, by refusing subpoenas are both in contempt of Congress. President Nixon was cited for contempt and an article was voted out of the Judiciary Committee to the full House before he resigned."

"Mr. Speaker it is not a secret that contempt of Congress stems from the administration's refusal to surrender the pardon application submitted on behalf of Mohammad Baghai and its refusal to allow the Vice President to testify before Congress concerning the matter. Now it is clear that the authors of the Constitution did not intend for the President of the United States to testify before Congress, hence the subpoena of the Vice President. However the administration claims that Congress does not have any claim to neither the materials nor the Vice President's testimony, due to executive privilege. What is your answer to that argument?"

"It is entirely true that the decision and the power to pardon belongs entirely to the President. That is clearly prescribed in the Constitution. Congress does not dispute that. What we do dispute is that pardon application is and any other materials related to the pardon belong exclusively to the executive branch of our government. There is certainly nothing in the Constitution about a pardon application. If documentation related to a pardon is not exclusively the domain of the executive branch, then testimony related to it is not exclusive either. George Washington did not have a pardon application, when he granted the very first Presidential Pardon. It is merely a tool to expedite a pardon, nothing more."

"Why is Congress taken such an interest in this particular issue

Mr. Speaker?"

Richt smiled for a moment.

"Ken you, as well and the American public knows the answer to that question, but let me preface my answer if I may. The first three words of the Constitution are 'We the people'. Members of the religious community; one man in particular has been instrumental in raising the American public's interest in Mohammad Baghai's case. Reverend Casey Edgars, a man of the cloth, with which he and I don't agree on any issue, has gone so far as to call the Mr. Baghai a prophet of God. Ken, don't ask me to comment on that claim, but a sufficient number of American citizens do to believe that Reverend Edgars' claims are valid. The President and members of Congress are servants of the American people and as servants of the people; it is our obligation to examine this issue."

"Define the word examine Mr. Speaker."

"Ken the enormous volume of hits on Reverend Edgars' web site has sent a clear message to Congress and it should have sent the same message to the President that the American people want Mohammad Baghai pardoned, regardless of his crimes. As I said earlier, the power to pardon belongs to the President of the United States and not the Congress. However, Congress is within its rights to investigate issues and subpoena appropriate documents and witnesses when public opinion demands it."

"Are you saying that this issue would evaporate if the President pardoned Mohammad Baghai?"

Richt chose his next words carefully.

"Ken nothing has reached the point of no return at this point. If the President chooses to pardon Mohammad Baghai, the desires of the American public will have been satisfied. Congress may still choose to investigate the issue, but I think you would agree that the pardon application issue would be moot there is no reason that I can conceive of that the President wouldn't be reluctant surrender it to Congress."

"Mr. Speaker, I would be remiss if I didn't mention that should the President and Vice President both be impeached and removed from office, after a trial in the Senate, you, as Speaker of the House, would be next in line to take the oath of office."

Richt shifted in his chair and faced the camera lens, giving the appearance that he was speaking directly to the American public and not to Shugart.

"Ken, I knew you were going to address this issue and yes you are correct that the Speaker of the House of Representatives in third in line for the Presidency. Let me state or the record that I have not sought and am not seeking to become for the next President. I have publicly stated that I am going to seek one more term as my district's representative and after serving it I intend to retire from public service."

"Now during my years of public service, I have always done my duty as public servant. If circumstances dictate that I take the oath of office of the President of the United States, I would do so willingly and with a clear conscience. However, three years from now regardless of what position in government might be I intend to retire and live my remainder of my years quietly, God willing of course."

Richt had just made a promise, a political promise, which he would break without hesitation should he decide he want to run for his own term as President. He would make that decision in a couple of years.

"Speaker Richt that is all the time we have today. Thank you for coming."

"Ken it's always a pleasure. Thank you."

TIM Dunston used the remote to turn off the TV in his office. That bastard Richt was trying to double-cross him. Richt was on the verge of being handed the Presidency on a silver platter and he was playing political games. Did Richt think that he was a fool? He didn't get to be Senate Majority leader by being stupid or naïve. Dunston understood political double talk and knew Richt that knew that he would be watching this show. Richt was attempting to send a message to Dunston, one that said 'I am running the show now'. Well Dunston had planned for that contingency. He was running the show and not Richt. Dunston had an ace in his back pocket. Dunston had hoped that he wouldn't have to play the card this soon, if at all. He would make Richt play ball or he would ruin him.

CHARLIE parked the Expedition in the parking lot and he and Heather entered the Delta Kappa Alpha Fraternity house through the front door. As usual, there was a keg of beer on tap, inside a keg cooler, with a stack of plastic cups beside it. Charlie helped himself to a cup of beer downing half of it in one gulp.

"Would you like a cup Heather?"

"No thank you, but I'm not driving back to the hotel so you watch how much you drink."

"Kevin! What's going on man?"

Charlie shouted to Kevin Black, the judge in his PW trial.

"Charlie! Good to see you again!"

Kevin and Charlie gave each other a bear hug.

"Kevin, this is my fiancée Heather Twig. Heather this is Kevin Black."

"Oh, so you are the one that stole Charlie away from us? It's a pleasure to meet you Heather."

"Thank you, I'm pleased to meet all of Charlie's fraternity brothers."

"Well we do have some redeeming traits but we are doing our best to eliminate them," Brown said in jest.

"Come one in, a few of us are watching TV."

"Sure, but we can't stay long. We left Heather's parents at the hotel. I wanted to show Heather our frat house and talk to Chris. Where's he at?"

"I think he is in the dungeon. I don't know what he's doing though."

Charlie introduced Heather to the brothers watching TV. An episode of 24 was on and Jack Bauer was saving the life of the President, from an assassination, by jumping in front of the shooter.

After the perfunctory hellos Charlie and Heather descended a spiral staircase to the dungeon. Chris was standing at a workbench, working on his paintball gun. Charlie thought he smelled a faint aroma of hash.

"What's up bro?"

"Nothing man! You made it. Heather, it's good to see you again."

"Thank you. Good to see you again Chris." Heather replied.

"What you working on?"

"I'm making my paintball gun into a paintball pistol. Here let me show you." Chris motioned Charlie and Heather to the workbench.

"I sawed off the stock and I've attached a hopper that only holds about a dozen pellets. I've also got a machine shop to find me a miniature air tank, which is only about a quarter of the size of the smallest tank on the market today. After I finish the modifications, I'm going to have a leather maker make a holster for it."

"So why are you making these modifications Chris?"

"Charlie, you know I like to dabble. Heather, you're going to be in the military; would you like to test it out?"

"Do you mind?"

"Not at all, here step up to the line and fire at the bull's-eye. I haven't put any sights on it yet but give it try."

Heather stood about 25 feet away and started firing rounds and after a couple of shots she consistently found the bull's-eye. The gelatin ball exploded on the plywood backstop.

"Thanks Chris," Heather said as she gave the gun back.

"No problem Annie Oakley," Chris said.

"Charlie did I tell you that I have a job working for the university?"

"No, what are you doing?"

"I work for the banquet staff, serving the big wheels, when the university president wants to wine and important alumni or other VIPs."

"Cool, how does it pay?"

"Not much, but I'm not going to be doing it forever. I got a gig after the graduation ceremony."

"Hey Chris, Heather and I need to get back. It's great to see you again."

"No problem, great to see you too. Heather, it was a pleasure."

# Chapter 26

"**M**rs. President the issues are coming to a head. Mohammad Baghai has been sentenced. The House Judiciary Committe will soon be holding hearings on articles of impeachment, the public seems to favor a pardon and you have not commented on it publicly. Furthermore, we haven't even discussed how the White House will respond to these bogus articles or the Speaker's television interview," Shephard said to Hays via secured telephone.

Shephard was in Washington, running the day today operations of the administration, while Hays was in Pensacola. Vice President Taylor was scheduled to travel to Chicago in two days to attend the opening ceremonies of the Olympics.

"Yes, I am aware of that Andy. I am considering the pardon application. No, I have not made a decision no, these ridiculous charges against me will not factor into my decision and no I don't have a timetable for a decision. You can have C.C. tell that to the White House press corps. Oh, also, she can state my position on her regular press conference. I don't want a special one scheduled."

"When do you plan on returning to Washington? Your presence in Florida will give the Washington press some meat to bite into, in light of these circumstances."

"How is that Andy?"

"We are hearing, through our sources that you are being portrayed aloof and indifferent towards the issues. Nothing significant thus far because the buzz over Richt's interview hasn't died down yet, but you can expect to hear more before long."

"I have a commencement speech to make but I plan to return to Washington afterwards."

"I need to touch base on our position against Iran in the Persian Gulf. Nassiri as you know is rattling his sword and he is on the propaganda offensive. He claims that our assertion that the downed fighter, which attacked the Gaffney was Iranian and not Iraqi, is an 'imperialist lie' and that our claims that the wreckage is radioactive is an American attempt to overthrow his government."

"Is anyone paying attention to him Andy?"

"Just the international press, all they are doing is parroting his claims."

"Good. I am tired of that third-rate dictator. He has become quite an annoyance. Let's see what he has to say when we put an aircraft carrier in his back yard."

"Do you think that is wise Mrs. President? The Navy will not like putting the George Bush in such confined waters."

Shephard was referring to the Navy's dislike for placing an aircraft carrier battle group in the confined waters of the Persian Gulf.

"I know but that is the Navy's problem. The last time I checked I am still Commander in Chief. Nassiri is a loose cannon and Alan Reynolds at the CIA has told me that there is intelligence that Iran has sufficient materials to manufacture dirty bombs. I think it is time for Mr. Nassiri to realize that he is not speaking very softly and I carry a bigger stick than he does," Hays said.

"Very well Mrs. President. Is there anything specific that you would like C.C. to discuss about Nassiri?"

"She is not to mention a word about him personally. She is to re-iterate that the plane was Iranian, and that the wreckage is radioactive. Furthermore, we consider the attack to be orchestrated by Iran against the United States and that though no life was lost we consider the attack a provocation against the United States by Iran and the United States will act accordingly should a similar situation arise in the future. Make sure that when she is asked a follow up question that 'accordingly' means that the United States will act 'proactively'. Is that clear Andy?"

"When you say proactive, you mean we will be taking the first shot?"

"Yes I will communicate that to the Joint Chiefs immediately after I finish speaking with you. Any captain, that feels his ship is in danger may take whatever steps he or she feels appropriate to defend it, including taking the first shot."

"Do you feel that such a directive is wise Mrs. President?"

"Andy, we can discuss that when I come back to Washington, but my position is firm."

"Very well Mrs. President."

Shephard didn't agree with her boss but he would support her.

Hays hung up the phone and dialed Isabelle Franks' cell phone.

"Hello, Isabelle Franks."

"Isabelle, this is the President. How are you?"

"Mrs. President, if I didn't recognize your voice, I would believe this was a prank call. I'm fine ma'am. What can I do for you?"

"Isabelle, I need to hire you. When can you come to Pensacola to discuss my issues?"

"I'll be on the next available flight ma'am."

"Good. Call me when you know your flight so I know when to

expect you. Let me give you my personal number, as you can understand, I don't want it to become public."

"Of course not Mrs. President."

ABU Sabaya, formerly known as Benino Marcos and Malikul Mawt, AKA the Angel of death and AKA Yasser Saleem were at the deserted warehouse, where the two first met.

"Tell me Abu, what was your plan to infiltrate the Olympic security and attack the Vice President?"

"Very simple, I had a tailor make a uniform of the Philippine Team. I was going to join the team as it assembled outside the Olympic stadium and blend into the crowd, then as the team approached his seat I would draw a pistol and kill him."

"And you would be killed also," the Angel remarked.

"Probably, but only if it was Allah's will."

"Of course, but I believe Allah will help those who help themselves. Why do you feel the need to sacrifice yourself at so young an age?"

"If I die while I am in jihad I am guaranteed a place in paradise. You know this already Malikul. Why do you ask me such a question?"

"You are a devout in your faith, are you not Abu? You follow the precepts of Islam?"

"Yes, of course."

"Then Abu, you know that at the time of judgment Allah will judge your good deeds against your sins and so long as the scales tip in your favor, you will have a place in paradise."

The Angel put emphasis on the entire sentence.

"Yes every Muslim knows that. I don't understand your point."

"Allah made paradise for his faithful as a reward for the faithful, but didn't he make all of creation as well? Did he not create man, woman and the Earth as well? Of course he did. The Angel Jibr'il told his greatest prophet Muhammad this. Why shouldn't the faithful enjoy Allah's creations here on Earth? When we have finished Allah's work here, I intend to enjoy his creations until he calls me for judgment. I do not intend to die here unless Allah wills it. I believe he has much more for me to do," the Angel said as he uncovered the tarpaulin draped over the motorcycle, that Sabaya had noticed the first time he had visited the warehouse. It had Chicago Police Department markings.

"I see Malikul and how do you envision completing Allah's work?"

"The day after tomorrow you will be a police officer and with

Allah's blessing, we will make history."

"WOULD you all give me a moment please?" Charlie asked the Twigs.

"Are you sure Charlie?" Heather asked her fiancée.

"Yes I'm fine Heather. Just give me a minute with my parents and John."

Charlie and his family from Georgia were at the cemetery by John's grave. It was 9:00 in the morning. Everyone got up early ate a complementary breakfast at the hotel breakfast bar and then went to a Wal-Mart where Charlie purchased some flowers, ice, cold drinks, suntan lotion and snacks. They were planning to go to Pensacola Beach afterwards. They had it all in a cooler in the back and everyone was wearing their swimsuits underneath their clothes.

The Twigs stood a respectful distance away from the graves while Charlie laid flowers by each marker and then knelt on a knee and had a silent conversation with his family.

Charlie stood up wiped his tears from his eyes and turned towards his family. The Twigs walked over and met him at the by the gravestones. Each stone was an 8X12 granite marker with names and dates chiseled into it.

Heather gave Charlie an embrace, lasting for several seconds, while Ralph and Jo Ann each placed a reassuring hand on his shoulder.

"Do you want a tissue Charlie?" Jo Ann finally said

"No Mom, I am fine."

"Son I don't mean to sound insensitive but I have a stupid question," Ralph said.

"What's that Ralph?"

"The names on the grave stones aren't the same."

The markers for Charlie's parents said Hugh and Linda Michaels respectively, but John's marker had 'Christian J. Welter' chiseled into it.

"Oh, I guess I never thought to mention it. My parents adopted John when they couldn't conceive. He was 10 or 11 I think, when my parents adopted him, but they didn't change his surname. He was old enough to know that he wasn't their real son and my parents decided that a name change wouldn't be beneficial to John's adjustment. They had me afterwards."

"No Charlie you never mentioned that," Heather said.

"I'm sorry; I just never thought to mention it."

"Let's go the beach. I want to see just if the sand is as white as you say it is Charlie," Heather said as she gave Charlie another hug.

"Cool let's go."

Pensacola Beach lies on Santa Rosa Island, one of several barrier Islands, screening the Florida panhandle from the Gulf of Mexico. The weather was very hot and very humid. Both the temperature and the humidity were in the 90's. The beach wasn't overly crowded at this time and Ralph was able to park near the boardwalk. Charlie carried the cooler, Ralph carried folding lawn chairs and the women had a stack of beach towels and a radio. Heather was impressed; the sands were white as sugar.

The group found a spot near the water and set up shop. There was a wind, which made the temperature feel a little cooler and the surf was about 3 feet. Everyone stripped down to their swimsuits, though Ralph and Jo Ann left their shirts on. Charlie was wearing his favorite yellow and black nylon suit that hung from his hips to just above his knees. Heather wore a new red bikini, which was not thong, but it didn't cover much flesh. She turned every young male head in the immediate area. Charlie's eyes nearly popped out of his head. Ralph gave his daughter a look of fatherly consternation but refrained from comment. Jo Ann, never one to remain silent, when she had an opinion, did not.

"Heather, when and where did you get that bikini?"

Jo Ann asked, also showing her disapproval in her daughter's choice.

"Mother, take a look around you. It's not anymore revealing than most of the other swimsuits, people here are wearing. I got it so I could get plenty of sun."

"You certainly will, wearing that," Jo Ann said.

"Heather that may or not be appropriate for the beach; you and your mother can debate that, but it is not appropriate for dive boat. I hope you brought a one piece suit to wear." Ralph said.

"Yes Dad, I brought another one," Heather said to her father as she rolled her eyes.

"You know, I won't be just your daughter for much longer. I will also be Charlie's wife soon and his opinion on what is appropriate will carry just as much weight as yours."

Heather kissed her father on the cheek as a sign of placation and independence also.

"Charlie will you put lotion on me?"

"Sure, but first I am going to go jump in for a swim. Will you join me Heather?"

"Of course."

"Heather you be careful that the surf doesn't wash something off," Jo Ann warned.

"Okay Mom."

Charlie and Heather ran off to enjoy a swim while Ralph and Jo Ann applied the sun block to each other and sat down on lawn chairs. After a few minutes Charlie and Heather returned, toweled off and then applied sun screen to each other, before lying down to absorb the Florida sunshine.

"Heather how is the water?"

Jo Ann asked after the two returned and toweled off.

"Fine Mom, it's very warm. You and Dad should go in."

"We will before we leave dear. Charlie did you come here often, when you were living here?"

"Almost every weekend during the Summer Mom, though I went down the road a few miles to Navare Beach.

"Charlie, besides going diving and the beach, is there anything else would you like to do while you are down here? It is your time and your graduation present," Jo Ann asked.

"There is one place we have to go to before we leave."

"Where is that?"

"Seville Quarter."

"What is that?"

"It's an entertainment complex, in historic Pensacola, on Government Street, encompassing a series of themed bars and restaurants under one roof. I think it is listed as an official State of Florida tourist attraction. It's quite a site. One of the bars is called Pheneas Phogg's and on Monday nights, it serves quarter beer. My fraternity brothers and I spent many a Monday night there." Charlie remembering the festive Monday nights and the not so festive Tuesday mornings even more rolled his eyes and shook his head.

"I think I'll pass on the beer," Jo Ann said.

"That is only one of several bars and one of the restaurants is five stars. You would like the whole complex Mom."

"Well we will make a point to visit there before we leave Charlie," Jo Ann replied.

Charlie and his family laid down and tanned themselves for about an hour and a half when a military helicopter approached, at what seem to be an abnormally slow rate of speed, from the West following the shoreline, just offshore about 300 feet in the air. It hovered for about 30 seconds before it continued eastward. Heather sat up and peered at the helicopter.

"What was that about?" Heather asked Charlie.

"That was a Navy helicopter pilot that, who, without a doubt, wishes he had your cell phone number," Charlie said, unable to contain laughter.

"What do you mean Charlie?" Heather could tell that Charlie and her parents all understood something that she was missing.

"Heather, NAS Pensacola is about 5 minute's flight time away from here, that way." Charlie pointed west. He was referring to Naval Air Station Pensacola.

"The pilots have to log their required flight time to keep up their qualifications so they fly up and down the beach during the summer and check out the women sunbathing. Usually they just fly by and wave, but this pilot hovered for a while in front of us. How much do you want to bet that he and his crew had a pair of binoculars and was checking you out in your band-aid of a bikini? I bet everyone had some really powerful binoculars," Charlie said gravely, as he emphasized he last sentence and flashed another one of his wicked, evil grins at Heather and then winked at Jo Ann, who gave a nod of approval.

"That's perverse," Heather, horrified at the truthfulness if Charlie's assertions, disgustedly exclaimed.

"Do you think you accidentally flashed him? He'll be back in a bout 20 minutes for a second look, after he flies the entire length of the beach." Charlie was rolling over with laughter now. Ralph and Jo Ann were also having a chuckle at Heather's expense also.

"All he'll see is me with more clothes on."

Heather was seething in anger and disgust as she gave Charlie a jab to the ribs with her elbow.

"Speaking of which, we have been here a little over 2 hours and I'm not sure you fair skinned Georgia peaches should be out here anymore today. The sun is brutal" Charlie said.

"I think that is wise. We can come out again every day if we want but I can tell you from experience, sun burn is no fun," Ralph said.

"The showers are right over there."

Ten minutes later with the sea salt washed from their bodies and after toweling off the Georgia visitors loaded up the Expedition. Ten minutes later Charlie's cell phone rang.

"Hello?"

"Hello, is this Charlie?"

"Yes, who is this?"

"Charlie, this is Casey Edgars. We spoke yesterday."

"Yes Reverend. I remember. How are you today?"

"Fine, I arrived in Pensacola this morning and checked into a motel. I wanted to know what time later today I could speak with you privately."

"Reverend, I am with my fiancée and her parents returning from the beach. Today is not a good day. In addition, we are on a vacation and I consider your insistence on meeting me, without revealing the nature of the meeting under these circumstances an imposition and to be frank, a little rude. Furthermore, I don't keep any secrets from my new family. Anything you want to discuss with me can and will be done so with them present. Now do you want to tell me what is so important that you must speak with me today?" Reverend Edgars did not intimidate Charlie and the others in the car were surprised by the tone of his voice and that he was being so blunt.

Edgars was taken aback by Charlie's directness.

"Yes Charlie, perhaps you are correct. I certainly apologize if I came across as ill mannered to you; that was not my intent. I also meant no slight against your family either. I hope you will take me at my word when I say that it is urgent that I speak with you today because a man's life and another person's reputation hang in the balance."

"No offence was taken Reverend, but you still haven't answered my question. What do you need to speak to me about?"

"It is important that I speak to you about your brother John. It's not appropriate from me to discuss it more deeply than that until we speak in person. If you feel comfortable with your new family present, then I would be delighted to invite all of you out to dinner. Would that be all right Charlie?"

Charlie felt like he had just been awakened from a deep sleep by a cold glass of water. What did John have to do with Reverend Edgars and why was the good reverend being so evasive? Charlie didn't know but his curiosity had been piqued.

"Where are you staying Reverend?"

"I'm at the Hilton downtown. Why?"

"Good, one of the people at the desk can give you directions to Seville Quarter on Government Street. It's only about 2 miles from where you are staying. I am going to take you up on your offer of dinner for my family and me. You might need to call for reservations. Let's say 6:00. Call me if you can't confirm a table for 5, otherwise we will see you at 6:00."

"Charlie thanks you for agreeing to meet me and I look forward to meeting you and your family," Edgars said.

"Charlie what was that all about?"

"Heather I am not completely sure but Reverend Edgars wants to discuss my brother. I do know that he is taking all of us out to dinner tonight at Seville Quarter tonight."

# Chapter 27

"Boss, I'm telling you; I've met this kid. I've had a lengthy political discussion with him concerning the President. He actually saved my life when I was scuba diving with him. Charlie Michaels is not a threat to the President, " Ron Thomas emphatically implored his Secret Service superior, George Hickey, at the guesthouse on President Hays' property, where the President's detail stayed when she was in Pensacola.

Hickey, the head of President Hays' detail had received the email referencing Charlie, originating from the Gainesville Georgia FBI field office. The correspondence stated that the FBI uncovered the fact that Charlie was the adopted brother of murdered soldier Christian John Welter. It was the same soldier that Mohammad Baghai recently pled guilty to the murder. That, along with Charlie's vocal anti-Hays rhetoric and his membership in AAMO, immediately raised a red flag with the President's protection detail. Though, as the memorandum stated, Michaels was probably not a legitimate threat against President Hays, however, the Secret Service was not in the business of taking chances. Since Michaels and the President were going to be in the same building, procedure demanded that he be interviewed by the agent in charge, Hickey, to satisfy that there was in fact no threat whatsoever. Otherwise Michaels would be detained until the President left the city, which would mean that he would not be able to participate in the graduation ceremony.

"I don't care who the hell he is. You know the drill. I want him picked up for an interview at Pensacola PD Headquarters. I will make the arrangements with the locals. You just get him there. He is staying at the Holiday Inn near the campus, which is about 15 minutes away from here and I want him sitting if front of me within the hour. Do you have a problem with doing your job?"

Thomas, realizing that he was not going to win the argument, decided that discretion was better served.

"You know better than that boss. I'll take one of the black and whites with me and I'll call you when we are on the way to the police station."

"Good. If this kid is an a straight an arrow as you say he is, I'll be able to tell and all that it will cost him is a couple of hours of his time," Hickey said as an offer of reconciliation.

Fifteen minutes later Thomas and the police officer were at the front desk of the hotel.

"Good afternoon, what room is Ralph Twig in?"

Thomas said to the clerk as showed his badge.

"He has 2 connecting rooms, 105 and 107. I can buzz the room if you want to speak to him?"

"Thank you but that won't be necessary. I'll go knock on the door," Thomas said.

Thomas walked down the hall leaving one police officer with the clerk and taking the other with him and knocked on the door.

"Yes?" Ralph asked through the door. Everyone was taking a nap after the stay at the beach.

"This is the Secret Service. I need you to open the door," Thomas shouted through the door.

"Secret Service? Show me your badge," Ralph said as he looked through the spy hole.

Thomas held his bade up to the viewer. Ralph satisfied that it was legitimate, in part because he saw the uniformed officer in the background, opened the door. Jo Ann was sitting up in bed with a concerned look on her face. Charlie and Heather were watching TV in the connecting room was now standing next to Ralph at the door.

"Good afternoon sir, I am Secret Service Agent Ron Thomas. I need to speak to Charlie Michaels. Is he here?"

"Ron, I am right here. What's going on here?" Mom, Dad, Heather, this is Ron Thomas, the Secret Service Agent I met while I was diving," Charlie said offering his hand to shake.

Thomas didn't see Charlie initially was startled for a moment before taking Charlie's hand. It wasn't exactly professional under the circumstances but Thomas acted instinctively with his friend and not professionally.

"Charlie I need you to come with me," Thomas said.

"Why? What's the matter Ron?"

"There are some issues that have arisen that my superiors want to discuss with you Charlie."

"What kind of issues?"

Ralph demanded, speaking forcefully, in a raised voice. The police officer was poised to draw his weapon.

"Sir, don't escalate this situation. Charlie has to answer some questions about his brother, his association with an organization called AAMO and his feelings about the President. I have been instructed to invite Charlie to come down to the Pensacola Police Department for an interview, if he refuses I have been instructed to detain him and if you interfere with me I will arrest you," Thomas said calmly.

Because of his size he usually didn't have to raise his voice. He then turned to Charlie.

"Charlie, don't make a scene; it will turn out badly if you do. I want you to go with this officer to his car while I speak with your family for a minute. I'll ride with you and give you the details on the way over to the police station."

The police officer took his hand off his weapon seeing that the situation had been diffused. Charlie didn't know what to say. Ralph and Jo Ann were silent also. Heather was in tears and though Charlie tried to console her, it was a lost cause from the start.

"It'll be all right Heather. I haven't done anything that I am ashamed of."

Charlie said as he gave her a hug.

"I know you haven't Charlie," Heather said in between sobs.

"We will follow you to the police station Charlie. That is allowed isn't it?"

"Mr. Twig, I'll instruct the officers to drive slowly enough so you can follow," Thomas said to Ralph. Turning to Charlie, he continued.

"Charlie, follow this officer to the patrol car. I am going to have a short chat with your family. Afterwards I will ride in the back and tell you what I just discussed with them."

"Thanks Ron."

Charlie walked out with the officer, while Thomas spoke with the Twigs.

"I'm sorry that we had to meet under these circumstances, as I said before I am Ron Thomas."

"I am Ralph Twig. This is my wife Jo Ann and my daughter Heather. Mr. Thomas would you please tell me what this is all about?"

"Mr. Twig, a red flag was raised on a threat assessment and Charlie was perceived as a possible threat to the President and since he and she are going to be at the commencement ceremony, he is going to be interviewed by my superior."

"Charlie is not a threat to anyone. How did the Secret Service determine that? Someone from the FBI conducted a telephone interview with me a while ago about Charlie. I told him then and I am telling you now, Charlie is not a threat to the President."

"Agent Thomas, what is your boss attempting to determine with this interview?" Jo Ann asked.

"Ma'am, the usual procedure is just to detain a suspected threat, such as Charlie until after the President is left the city. I persuaded my boss to speak to Charlie and then make a determination. It's his decision, which is why I am going to ride with Charlie and instruct him not to fly off the handle. Assuming he keeps his cool. He will be riding home with you this evening. If he doesn't, he will be spending some time in the Pensacola jail."

"Is that legal? Can you hold Charlie, without charging him with a crime?" Heather asked

"I am not an attorney, but I am told the procedure is completely legal," Thomas told Heather, who had managed to stop crying.

"Do you think I should contact an attorney Agent Thomas?" Ralph asked.

"Sir, that is up to you, but I am confident that so long as Charlie minds his Ps and Qs everything will be fine. He will come home with you tonight and be able to graduate. I will stress that to him in just a minute."

"Thank you sir," Heather said, unable to conceal her relief and gratitude.

"You're welcome ma'am."

"Agent Thomas we appreciate what you have done to help Charlie, but I have a question," Jo Ann asked.

"What is that ma'am?"

"Surely this is not the first situation like this that you have had to deal with; why are you being so good to Charlie?"

"Charlie told you that we met scuba diving when I was on vacation here. We had plenty of time that to discuss a lot of things during the trip to the site and on the trip back. I have a good sense of people. Charlie has strong opinions on a number of issues and he is not afraid to express them, but he has too much going for him to do something stupid like attacking the President."

"Yes we know that and he did tell us about you, but you are still doing quite a lot for him considering the circumstances."

"Did Charlie tell you that on the dive trip he saved my life? I sort of owe him a favor."

"No, he didn't! We had no idea," Jo Ann exclaimed.

"I had an equipment malfunction about 80 feet down. My regulator stopped working properly and I couldn't breathe. Charlie was right there and let me buddy-breathe with him until we got to the surface. Mr. and Mrs. Twig, I need to escort Charlie to the police station now. I'll make sure that the patrol car doesn't lose you on the way there."

"Thank you Agent Thomas. We'll be right behind you," Ralph said as he shook hands with the Secret Service Agent.

Thomas walked out to the patrol car, after calling Hickey and sat in the back seat with Charlie, who was waiting patiently. The two officers were in the front seat and the car started the journey to Pensacola Police Headquarters.

"Ron will you please explain all this to me so it makes sense? I haven't done anything to deserve this."

"Charlie, be quiet and listen to me. I work for the United States Secret Service. My job, my team's job is to protect the President regardless of the consequences. I am even supposed to take a bullet for her. You know that."

"So?"

"So, instead of stepping in front of a gunman to save the President's life, we prefer to check out perceived threats and if necessary take them into custody."

"Are you saying that I am a threat to the President Ron?"

"No, I know that you aren't, but people above me think you may be and the Secret Service doesn't take chances with the President's life. We proactively remove any perceived threat whenever possible. Your circumstances have sounded the same type of alarm bells. People above me will make the decision as to whether you are a threat or not. It's up to you to convince them that you aren't."

"What do you suggest Ron?"

"My immediate superior, George Hickey will ask you a number of questions about your murdered brother, AAMO and anything else he considers pertinent. Answer his questions truthfully and directly. Don't be evasive. I have already vouched for you Charlie but my boss has the finial decision on your immediate future. Don't lose your head and chances are you will ride home with your family rather than being detained."

"Ron what does my dead brother, who died in combat years ago, by the way, has to do with me being a threat to the President? That makes no sense to me at all." Charlie asked.

"You mean that you don't know Charlie?"

"He died when I was 6. That was years ago. All I know is that he died in combat."

"Charlie, I've read the reports concerning your brother. He was captured and killed by Mohammad Baghai. The same man who is asking President Hays for a pardon for your brother's murder. Are you telling me that you weren't aware of the circumstances of your brother's death?"

"Ron, I was 6 years old at the time. My parents only told me that John died. Later, when I was older, they said that he died in combat. No I didn't know. As for me being a member of AAMO, I could give you at least a half a dozen names of AAMO members that will be graduating besides me."

"You weren't aware that Baghai had traveled into the country and turned himself in?"

"Sure I was, but I didn't pay it a lot of attention; I had other things, which were much more important to me going on in my life."

"Charlie we are here now. My boss will try to push your buttons during the interview to see if you will lose your temper. Don't. Keep your head and tell him what you told me and everything should be fine."

"Ron, thank you for your advice, I'll do what you say."

Ralph, Jo Ann and Heather were following the patrol car carrying Charlie. Jo Ann was using Charlie's cell. She had the presence of mind to remember to call Casey Edgars to cancel their dinner reservations. Though she could attempt to contact him via the hotel desk, either speaking him directly or leaving a message, though she correctly decided to use Charlie's cell and retrieve the number from the memory.

"Hello?" Edgars answered.

"Hello is this Reverend Edgars?"

"Yes."

"Reverend Edgars, this is Jo Ann Twig, Charlie Michaels' future mother in law. We spoke briefly yesterday."

"Yes, how are you Mrs. Twig? I'm looking forward to meeting you and the rest of your family later this evening."

"Thank you Reverend, but I am afraid that we won't be able to have dinner with you tonight. Something unexpected has come up."

"Oh? I am sorry to hear that is everyone all right?"

"Reverend, I don't want to impose but I suspect that your desire to meet with Charlie is somehow intermeshed with our problem and we're not sure we understand the whole picture. Perhaps you might be able to help us to understand it?"

"What happened Mrs. Twig?"

Edgars asked; his concern resonated from the phone.

"Reverend, about 20 minutes ago, the Secret Service came to pick Charlie up to ask him some questions; something about being perceived as a threat to the President. They are taking him to police headquarters now. We are following them now. Do you know anything about what is happening Reverend?"

"Mrs. Twig, I'm certain that I do. I'll meet you and your husband at the police station as soon as I can catch a cab, tell you everything that I know and help Charlie in anyway I can. Now if you can speak to Charlie, tell him to request to speak to me in my capacity as a spiritual advisor. I will see you all in a few minutes."

"Thank you so much Reverend," Jo Ann said.

Edgars hung up the phone and called to the front desk and asked the clerk to call him a taxi. Afterwards, he used his cell phone to call Andy Shephard via speed dial. Shephard wasn't answering for whatever reason so he left a voice mail.

"Andy, this is Casey. I am in Pensacola, Florida right now and I need to speak to you when you get this message. Call me regardless of the time."

While Edgars was waiting for a taxi, Charlie was getting moral support from the Twigs, before entering the City of Pensacola Police Headquarters.

"Charlie we will be waiting for you when you are finished," Heather said as she gave him an embrace.

"I called Reverend Edgars and he is on his way over to meet us here Charlie. He asked me to ask you to request that he be allowed to speak to you as your counselor. Will you be sure to make that request?"

"Sure Mom," Charlie replied.

"Charlie, the sooner we get the wheels rolling the sooner this will be resolved," Thomas told Charlie.

"Okay Ron. No problem, but I am having a pastor come to visit me. His name is Casey Edgars. I would like to speak to him when he gets here."

"Okay, that won't be an issue."

Charlie, the Twigs, Agent Ron Thomas and Charlie's Police escort all walked into the police station. Charlie was taken to an interview room, complete with table, 2 chairs and an extremely dirty pane of one-way glass, while the Twigs were taken to a lounge area.

"Charlie, my boss, Agent George Hickey, will be conducting the interview in a few minutes. Just answer his questions completely and accurately. I know it is a cliché' but tell the truth, the whole truth and nothing but the truth," Thomas instructed his friend.

"I will Ron."

"He will be here in few minutes. Sit tight."

"All right."

Thomas left Charlie, in the room alone with his thoughts. Charlie reflected on his predicament. He was suspected as being a threat to the President. Though he knew that he wasn't and hadn't done anything that he thought could be remotely construed as menacing, Charlie thought long and hard about the course of his life, which led to him sitting in this interrogation room. Though it was called an interview, he knew that he was going to be interrogated.

Charlie hoped the 'interrogation' would be over this evening. He hadn't done anything to deserve this treatment and hadn't sought any publicity either. He was just a victim of circumstance. All that he really wanted was to graduate, enjoy a little more of the Florida sun and then continue his life in Georgia. Charlie got up from his chair, walked over to the pane of glass and wrote 'Let's get on with it' backwards on the pane of glass with his index finger, flashed one of his wicked smiles, before walking back to his chair. Charlie knew that there were probably at least 6 people on the other side of the glass, including George Hickey, the man who would be doing the 'interview'.

"Let's get on with it," Ron Thomas managed to chuckle as he read Charlie's message.

"Sorry about that Charlie. I am going to let you stew for a while," Hickey, a 50ish man with thinning hair that was about half blonde and half gray, said.

"Can I ask why?"

Thomas asked in a respectful tone not designed to challenge Hickey's domain or authority. Thomas usually didn't question his boss's methodology, but Charlie was his friend and he wanted to see this through.

Hickey understood Thomas's investment in the situation and was not offended.

"Two reasons. First, I want to observe his demeanor under a little stress, though so far, if his little message is an indicator, it doesn't appear that he is rattled. Second, this young man wants to speak to a pastor and I don't want to be interrupted once I get started."

Casey Edgars paid the cab driver entered the police station and asked the desk sergeant to direct him to Charlie and the Twigs and was directed to the lounge where Charlie's family was staying.

"Reverend Edgars, thank you for coming so quickly," Jo Ann said, recognizing him immediately.

"Reverend, I am Ralph Twig, you have already spoken to my wife, Jo Ann and this is my daughter and Charlie's fiancée, Heather," Ralph introduced himself and his family as he shook hands with everyone.

"Reverend can you please tell me what this is all about?" Jo Ann asked.

"Please Reverend Edgars, Charlie hasn't done anything to deserve to be treated this way," Heather said.

"I know he hasn't young lady. Let me go speak to your fiancée and offer him some words of encouragement, since he may need some. Afterwards I will be happy to discuss all I know with you and your parents."

At that moment, Thomas entered the lounge.

"Reverend Edgars, I am Secret Service Agent Ron Thomas. Charlie Michaels has requested to speak to you. Would you follow me?"

"Certainly," Edgars said as the shook hands with Thomas. He then turned to the Twigs.

"I won't be long."

The two walked down the hall into the observation room, where Thomas introduced Edgars to Hickey.

"It's pleasure to meet you Agent Hickey."

"Likewise Reverend," Hickey said.

The group could see Charlie sitting patiently at the table.

"Gentlemen, I won't be long; I know you have a job to do and I don't want to delay you conducting your duties. However since I am going to be speaking to this young man in a religious capacity, my conversations are privileged, so can I assume that no one will be eavesdropping?"

"Yes you can Reverend. No one will be listening in."

"Thank you."

"You can enter through this door Revered."

"Thank you," Edgars said as he walked into the interrogation room.

Charlie stood up as Edgars walked over to him.

"Charlie, I am Reverend Edgars. I'm sorry that we had to meet here in this room, under these circumstances, but I am pleased to meet you just the same."

"Thank you for coming Reverend," Charlie said as the two shook hands and then sat down facing each other.

"Charlie, I don't think it is a stretch, even excluding these circumstances, that you are wondering why I insisted on meeting you while you were with you family on vacation, here in Florida."

"Yes Reverend but that was before someone decided that I might be a threat to the President. Do you know what this is all about?"

"Yes I do Charlie, which is why I had hoped to speak with you before the government did. Charlie unfortunately, you have become a pawn in God's plan. You have heard of Mohammad Baghai and my efforts to have him pardoned?"

"Yes, I have heard of him, though I really haven't paid a lot of attention to you and your movement. I was told, just a few minutes ago, that he was the man that killed my brother," Charlie said with a hint of disdain in his voice.

"Charlie, do you know that I have stated on a number of occasions that Mohammad Baghai is a prophet of God?"

"It seems to me that God has chosen a pretty evil person to do his work."

"Yes it does, but that is God's decision to make and he is far wiser that either you or me. Did you know that I have recently spoken to him? He wants to speak with you and to ask your forgiveness."

"Reverend, I have already told you that until today, he wasn't on my radar screen and why would I forgive him? Would you mind telling me why you think he is a prophet?"

"I'll be happy to Charlie, to you and your family, after you leave here. Right now I want you to know that God knows of your plight and he will not forsake you."

"Reverend, can you tell me why God decided to leave me in a lurch like this?"

"God hasn't left you in a lurch Charlie. He has sent me here to help you. I know that you don't have any hostile intentions towards the President just as I know that your brother's killer is God's Prophet. God will work his will through men like me and you and Mohammad Baghai. Judging by the way that you have conducted yourself, I suspect that you will be going home with your family later this evening. In any case God will not desert you in your time of need. All that is required is for you to have a little faith in him. Have faith Charlie."

"Reverend, I appreciate you coming here to lend me moral support, I really do, but I hope you understand if I am not ready to aid you to free my brother's killer from justice. I certainly don't want to meet him."

"Charlie, you believe that every person has a soul don't you?"

"Yes, of course."

"And you believe that souls are eternal?"

"Yes."

"Charlie, John spoke to Mohammad. As a matter of fact, he saved Mohammad's life."

"Oh? What did he say to him?"

"Charlie, Let me tell you and your family about this whole affair when you are released. Right now I want you to know that God has plans for Mohammad Baghai and it appears to me that you fit into his grand scheme. Everything will be fine; I can assure you of that. Would you mind if I lead a prayer before I speak with your family?"

"Please, if you would Reverend."

Charlie and Edgars bowed their heads.

"Father, our Lord in Heaven, we pray to you today to strengthen your child Charlie with the courage to face the challenges, which lay ahead of him. Father, we know you have a plan for us all. We ask that you guide Charlie through his perilous journey. Grant him the foresight to make wise choices, the correct choices. We ask that you bless Charlie and his family and that Charlie will find it within himself to forgive people who have sinned against him as you forgave the sins of mankind by allowing you Son Jesus to die on the cross. For these things we pray in Jesus' name, amen."

Both men raised their bowed heads and stood up.

"Charlie, I am going to speak to your family now. We will all be waiting for you when you are finished answering the Secret Service's questions."

"Thank you for coming Reverend," Charlie said as he shook Edgars' hands.

Edgars left the room and spoke briefly to Hickey.

"Gentlemen, thank you for patience. I am going to speak to the Twigs now. Are they still in the lounge?"

"Yes they are Reverend," Thomas said.

"Good. I know the way."

Edgars walked the length of the building and found the Twigs all sitting in over used, uncomfortable looking furniture, obviously distressed that they were in a police station under vexing circumstances. Ralph noticed Edgars first and met him at the door. Jo Ann and Heather were right behind him.

"Reverend, how is Charlie, is he holding up well?"

"I just spoke with him Ralph; I hope you don't mind me calling you Ralph and everyone please call me Casey. He is in good spirits and I assume that the Secret Service will begin questioning him shortly. He hopes that the interview now will put an end to this affair. Come let's sit down shall we?"

The group sat down and arranged the chairs in a circle.

"I don't think that Charlie will object if I discuss our conversation with his you. Let's see, where is the best place to start?"

Edgars began to relate his story, when his cell phone rang. Edgars immediately recognized the number.

"Ralph, Jo Ann, Heather, I apologize. I wouldn't normally let a phone call interrupt me in a situation like this, but this is Andy Shephard, the President's chief of staff and I believe he can help us."

"Certainly Casey," Jo Ann said.

"Hello Andy? Thank you for returning my call," Edgars set his cell phone to speaker mode.

"Casey, what's the matter? Your voice mail had a sense of urgency," Shephard replied.

"Yes I am in Pensacola. I am in the city's police head quarters as a matter of fact."

"What happened are you using your one phone call for me to bail you out?"

"No, I haven't gotten myself arrested," Edgars laughed.

"Andy, I have just spoken to fine young man named Charlie Michaels. Presently, he is being questioned by the Secret Service, in a city police interrogation room. It seems that someone there believes that he is a threat to the President."

"Casey how are you involved in this and what do you want from me?"

"Andy, I can tell you from speaking to Mr. Michaels and from my God-given talents, which you and I have discussed that he is not a threat to anybody."

"My involvement with him is intermeshed with my efforts to have Mohammad Baghai pardoned. Mr. Michaels is an unfortunate casualty in this business, collateral damage is the buzz phrase, I think. I want you to make a phone call and have Charlie's file either faxed or emailed so that you can examine it and call back in an hour or so."

"Casey, that's impossible."

"Andy, I know that as the President's chief or staff, you wield an incredible amount of power. So far as I can determine all that he is guilty of is having a brother, who was killed by a terrorist, turned prophet. I would like you to inspect the file and either confirm my suspicions or, if I am wrong tell me specifically why he is being detained."

"Casey, the White House doesn't owe you any favors and the Secret Service doesn't fool around with the President's life. Why don't you let them do their job?"

"I am letting them do their job and your assertion that the White House owing me a favor can be debated at another time. Right now, after you look into this for me ASAP, I can and will help the President with her political plight. If not, I can call a press conference and state that a honors student, who is engaged to a future soldier, who just wants to graduate from college is being detained by the Secret Service, as a threat to the President, only because his brother was killed by a terrorist years before President Hays took office. Andy, don't you think such a press conference would create even more headaches for the President?"

"Is that a threat Casey?"

"I don't make threats. That is a promise though. Andy though it doesn't appear so, I don't want to be adversarial. I know you can have the file in question on your desk in ten minutes and it would take about ten minutes to review it. Don't you think that our relationship is worth 20 minutes? Don't you think President Hays would want you to take 20 minutes to examine it?"

"All right Casey, let me make phone call and I will get back to you," Shephard said in resignation.

"Thank you Andy."

Edgars concluded the call and related his conversation and spoke to the Twigs.

"I'm a bit of a mentor figure to the President's chief of staff and I can push his buttons, though I only do it when I do the Lord's work," Edgars said in a humorous tone of voice.

"Reverend, we appreciate everything that you are doing for Charlie," Heather said.

"I suppose all of you are curious to know why I have such a special interest in Charlie."

Edgars gave his explanation to three attentive listeners.

WHILE Reverend Edgars was counseling the Twigs as guests of the Pensacola Police Department, Andrew Shephard, the White House Chief of Staff, was reviewing the file on Charlie Michaels, compiled by the FBI. While not an expert on security, it appeared to him that Michaels was not a threat to anyone, but rather just a loud mouth, know it all college kid, who was just caught in the wrong place at the wrong time.

Edgars was correct though. The White House did not need the bad publicity from this and Casey was just the man to stir the pot, if he didn't get what he wanted. This was a non-political dilemma with political consequences and disaster was written all over it.

HICKEY was standing in front of the one-way glass window, sizing Charlie up. It had been 30 minutes since Reverend Edgars had left the interrogation room. He intended to "sweat" Michaels at least another 30 before he walked in and questioned him, only Michaels appeared cool and calm and he wasn't co-operating. He had been offered food and water, with the expectation that he would have to answer nature's call. Refusing to allow a suspect to use the facilities was a tried and true interrogation tactic. It caused stress, obvious discomfort and gave the suspect tangible incentive to co-operate. Michaels knew the drill and refused.

Hickey had reviewed the dossier on Michaels and except for his membership in the anti-Iraqi war group called AAMO; there was really nothing out of the ordinary. The only real red flag that was raised were some blogs. In them, Michaels said some uncomplimentary things about President Hays, wondering if her IQ was one point above or below George Bush's, how many more Americans would she let die in the Middle East, while she was commander in chief and the like. If the man who was seeking a pardon from the President hadn't murdered his brother, Michaels wouldn't even be a blip on the radar screen, not to mention in an interrogation room. In fact, other than being a ladies man, this kid seemed to be an All-American apple pie type.

Hickey walked into the room and sat down at the table facing Charlie, who remained seated. Both men stared at each other in silence, not even blinking, for about half a minute. When it was obvious Hickey was not going to intimidate him by stare-down, Hickey began, using an alternate strategy to get a feel for this young man.

"Charlie, I am George Hickey and I am the one you have to convince that you are not a threat to the President. You don't look like much of a threat to me." Hickey carefully studied Charlie's response. He wanted to see if Charlie would feel affronted by his comment.

"No, I'm not. To be honest, President Hays hasn't been much interest to me since I moved to Georgia."

Charlie recognized Hickey's challenge as an attempt to bait him into losing his composure and did not react to it, partly because he didn't want to give the man any more reason to detain him and because Hays didn't interest him anymore.

"Come on, Charlie, you are a member of AAMO, an anti-Hays organization. You have said some derogatory things about the President. You had a brother, who was killed while 'occupying' a Middle Eastern country. You have recently written some very unpatriotic things about this country in blogs."

"Mr. Hickey my membership in AAMO is a right, freedom of speech, guaranteed me by the First Amendment which I choose to exercise, so anything I have written or said in my capacity as a member of AAMO is not by definition, unpatriotic. My brother, as you know, was killed before the President took office so you as well as any other reasonable man should be able to see that I don't hold her personally responsible for his death. I haven't discussed anything on a blog that a reasonable man like you, would consider threatening to the President ever."

"What about these?"

Hickey handed over hard copies of his most recent blogs, the ones insulting Hays' intelligence and holding her accountable for American blood spilled in the deserts of the Middle East, which Charlie read.

"Mr. Hickey, while these transcripts reflect my feelings, I did not write them and I take issue with the fact that they are unpatriotic.

They are certainly not threatening."

"You didn't write them? You're lying. You signed your name to both of them."

Charlie suspected that Hickey was attempting to bait him again by giving him these transcripts and took a breath before he replied.

"Mr. Hickey, each of these was written on a computer, with an Internet connection, only a couple of weeks ago. Each of these connections has an Internet Protocol address. My IP address is now in Georgia and you will see that I haven't visited this blog in months and certainly not since I have been living in Georgia. You will also see that I am telling the truth as soon as you have someone check it out," Charlie said in a calm and deferential tone.

Hickey was momentarily surprised but he didn't show it. Charlie's assertion should have been investigated. Damn the FBI, sloppy work. It would be investigated by the Secret Service, but Hickey already knew that Charlie was telling the truth.

"Tell you what. We'll come back to that. Let's talk about your brother and Mohammad Baghai. You know that Baghai murdered your brother?"

"Yes sir and you know that he was murdered before the President took office and I don't hold her responsible for his death."

"The President has been pressured to pardon Baghai for the murder of Americans, your brother included, now you can see, in light of your animosity towards the President, how that would be a concern to people charged with her safety?"

"Until a month ago, I hadn't heard of the man and I didn't know that he killed my brother until a few minutes ago, when Reverend Edgars told me. My brother was killed when I was child and my parents, for obvious reasons didn't tell me the circumstances. So if we follow your logic, I wasn't a threat to the President until a few minutes ago, but we both know that's what's not going on here right now."

"Prove it."

"How do you prove a negative? You can't. You judge the circumstances. You judge the character of people involved, what they say, what they do, how they act. You judge what people say about someone, you judge their background, what they have done in the past and how they did it. Undoubtedly I've been thoroughly investigated and the only things that I am aware of that is a concern of the Secret Service is that I oppose one of the President's policies and I have a murdered brother. Is there anything else? If so, let me hear it," Charlie said in an even tone, careful not to lose his temper.

Hickey had one ace in the hole and Charlie opened the door for him.

"All right, tell me about this."

Hickey handed over a picture of his modified paintball gun, complete with a rifled barrel mini-scuba tank and round lead slugs for bullets.

"It's my paintball gun, a modified Tipman, which was in my apartment in Georgia." Charlie replied with a note of irritation in his voice. Since the Secret Service had it, it meant that someone was in his apartment to retrieve it.

"We had a search warrant if that is what has got your boxers all wadded up."

"So you took my paint ball gun because?"

"A paintball gun has a small tank of air and shoots plastic balls with jelly inside. This gun has a rifled barrel and a mini-scuba tank attached to it, which propels a lead slug at a lethal force, with accuracy."

"And if I wanted to kill the President with it, I would have brought it with me, hid it under my graduation robe and shoot her as I received my diploma. I may have even been able to escape during the confusion. It sounds reasonable to me. What do you think?" Charlie had regained control of his emotions.

"I think you have a vivid imagination, probably from watching too many James Bond movies."

Hickey cracked a semi-sardonic smile.

Charlie had deftly diffused all of Hickey's suspicions and had maintained his composure while doing so. Hickey still wasn't completely sold on this young man, his intellect told him that, but his instincts told him that Michaels was clean. At that moment someone tapped on the one way glass, probably Thomas and probably important. Everyone in the presidential detail knew better than to interrupt an interrogation without damn good cause.

"Excuse me for a moment," Hickey said as he left the room.

"Mr. Hickey, before you leave, let me just say that, I understand that you are doing your job, but I am not, have not and will not be a threat President Hays. I don't like her. I think she has been a lousy President but I have never thought about harming her. I think you sense that. Is there anything that I can say or do to convince you of that?"

"Let me see why we were interrupted and we'll discuss that some more."

Hickey left the room.

"Yes what is it Ron?"

"Boss, the White House Chief of Staff called on your cell and expects you to call him back immediately boss."

"Did he say what it was concerning?"

"No he didn't but I think you and I both can guess."

"Right, I want to speak to him privately."

Thomas and the others left the observation room as Hickey clicked the redial button on his cell.

"Agent Hickey?"

"Yes, Mr. Shephard, this George Hickey."

"You have been interviewing Charles Michaels?"

"Yes he is in an interrogation room in Pensacola Police Headquarters and I am just outside the room speaking to you."

"I am sorry to interrupt you Agent Hickey, but it is important that I speak with you before you make a decision as to detain him or not."

"I appreciate your interest in the matter Mr. Shephard. I am in the process of interviewing him now."

"So I did interrupt you?"

"Technically yes, you did but I was planning to divide the interrogation into parts and we had reached a stopping point sir."

That was a lie but Hickey knew that telling the chief of staff the truth was pointless at this stage, at least until he knew exactly what was going on.

"What's your sense of the boy thus far?"

"He is an intelligent articulate and level headed young man. I haven't formed a definitive opinion yet, but my sense is that he is a victim of unfortunate circumstances and is not a threat to the President."

"Agent Hickey, I don't want what I am about to say to be misconstrued. Would you please listen to me carefully?"

"Certainly, Mr. Shephard."

"You are aware that the President is being subjected to considerable public and political pressure currently, involving a possible pardon for Mohammad Baghai?"

"Yes I am."

"And the reason your are interviewing Mr. Michaels is in part, because Mohammad Baghai murdered Michaels' brother and that Michaels may resent the President granting a pardon and that Michaels is supposed participate in the college graduation ceremony, in which she is speaking?"

"Mr. Shephard, that is correct, but I don't see where you are going with this."

"Agent Hickey again let me be clear, the President's safety is your responsibility and if you are not completely comfortable with the notion that Charles Micheals is absolutely not a threat to the President, I want and expect you to detain him until after the graduation ceremony. The White House and I will back your decision 100 percent, be that the case. I know it is your job to err on the side of caution, but it would benefit the President immensely from a public relations stand point if Mr. Michaels is released and allowed to participate in his graduation."

"Mr. Shephard you are not giving me the full story. I need the truth, the whole truth and nothing but the truth about these circumstances in order to make an informed determination."

Hickey wasn't sure if was being used a pawn in some political power play or not.

"Of course, it wasn't my intent to sound or appear deceptive. About an hour ago, I received a phone call from Reverend Casey Edgars, during which he told me that you were questioning Michaels for the reasons what we discussed. Is he with the family?"

"Yes."

"He also asked me to personally review his FBI file. He also informed me that he was inclined to call a press conference and announce that Mr. Michaels, a honors student was being unjustly detained by the Secret Service, at the White House's direction because he had a brother, a soldier was murdered by a terrorist seeking a pardon. You can understand why the White House would like to avoid that kind of publicity?"

"Mr. Shephard, the Secret Service doesn't play politics, especially when the President's safety."

"Absolutely, I understand completely Agent Hickey. Obviously, from a public relations standpoint, if Michaels is determined not to be a legitimate threat, he needs to be released. The President doesn't need the bad publicity, but the White House will support what ever decision you and the Attorney General make," Shephard said.

He hoped that Hickey understood the implications and that he had 'massaged' Hickey enough to avert a public relations disaster, if Michaels wasn't deemed a threat. However, if Michaels was in fact a potential threat to the President, he would be detained until after the President spoke and the scenario could be spun in a beneficial light. After all, the President's safety was at stake.

Compromise is other side of the coin called politics and in the political world of Washington, there is seldom a win-win situation. A good political compromise is constructed when neither proponent of an issue is completely happy with the solution. Though Hickey, as head to the Presidential Protection Detail, was not supposed to involve himself infighting and in a perfect world he wouldn't be, he could see that the situation demanded concessions, both by him and The White House.

In Utopia, from his perspective, the Secret Service would detain Charlie Michaels simply because he vocally opposed the President and there were some miscellaneous circumstances floating around him that raised some eyebrows. However, in Utopia, there wouldn't be a need for a protection detail either. Since Hickey was dealing in the real world and he didn't believe that Michaels constituted a hazard to the President, but he was not willing to risk his career on his instinct, he was deciding upon how to reach a solution, which would make all parties equally unhappy.

With that Hickey understood that though, he had the final say on if Mr. Michaels participated in his graduation; it was clear how the White House felt about the matter. Now he had to decide how and when he would be released. He could give Michaels a blank check and release him, detain him, which really wasn't an option or compromise. Damn, he wasn't a politician and shouldn't have to act like one! Now, what to do about Mr. Michaels? Hickey walked out of the observation room and found Thomas, who was standing just outside the door.

"Ron, get a bracelet from my car. I'll be back in the interrogation room with Michaels. Come on in when you get it."

Hickey didn't wait for Thomas to acknowledge his instruction and walked into the interrogation room again.

"Sorry to keep you waiting for so long Charlie. It seems that some important people are interested in your status and welfare."

"Other than Reverend Edgars who else would that be sir?"

"Andrew Shephard, the White House Chief of Staff."

"I don't know him. I've never met him. Would you mind telling me exactly what is my status and welfare?"

Charlie emphasized 'status and welfare'.

"Charlie, I told you the first time I walked in here that you had to convince me that you were not a threat. I don't believe that you are."

Hickey ignored Charlie's last question.

"So I can leave then?"

"Not so fast. Charlie you asked me before I left if there was anything that you could do to convince me of that you didn't intend to harm the President. There is."

"What's that?"

"As I see it Charlie there are three options. Option one is for you to spend time in the city jail until the President leaves town. Option two is for you to travel back to Georgia. I can see from your face that though each of them would be acceptable to me, that they aren't acceptable to you."

Thomas entered the interrogation room and stood by the door. Hickey didn't bother to look up. Charlie saw his friend enter but didn't acknowledge him.

"What's the third option?"

"Compromise." Hickey motioned for Thomas to come over to the table where placed a bracelet on the table.

"What's this?" Charlie asked

"It's a bracelet for you wrist to wear while you and the President are both in Pensacola at the same time. It has a chip that can be tracked by global positioning satellites. It is tamper-proof and waterproof and looks like a piece of jewelry so you can still continue your vacation without attracting a lot of attention. After you or the President leave town you can take it off."

Hickey paused for a moment.

"It's decision time. Those are your three choices."

Charlie flashed one of his wicked smiles realizing that he was going to be leaving shortly and get on with his vacation and his life.

"This is a no brainer, how do I put this on?"

"It has a tamper proof rivet Charlie and can only be secured and released with a special tool. Here let me attach it," Thomas said as he attached the rivet.

"Charlie you to keep your cell phone with you at all times, so we can communicate, if I decide I need to speak to you. We will take the bracelet off immediately before the graduation. Do you have any questions?" Hickey asked.

"Nope."

"There are some ground rules" Hickey warned Michaels.

"I'm listening", Charlie said.

"One, you will have your cell phone with you at all times and answer it immediately when we call you. We can track the cell you are in when you pick up your cell phone and your GPS coordinates had better be in the cell. If they don't match, you can plan on spending some time in jail. Understand?"

"Completely."

"Two, don't go anywhere, where hand guns are sold. No gunsmiths, gun clubs, no hunting stores, no flea markets. If you violate this rule, you can plan on spending time in jail. Three, if this bracelet comes off your wrist, for any reason, before we take it off, plan on spending some time in jail. No exceptions what so ever. Understand?"

"Loud and clear Mr. Hickey, there won't be any issues," Charlie said.

"Good. Charlie, a lot of people have gone out on a limb for you; Ron included. Don't disappoint them."

"Thank you sir, I won't."

"Ron, why don't you escort Charlie to his family?"

Both Agent Thomas and Charlie had broad grins as they walked out of the interrogation room to greet four very concerned people waiting on Charlie.

# Chapter 28

Across the back of the Seville Quarter Complex is an open-air Victorian style courtyard, complete with gas lighting and dozens of wrought iron patio tables and chairs, suitable for weddings, receptions, family, class reunions and other similar functions. Around the periphery of the courtyard is a barrier, part stone wall and part iron fence, constructed in such a way at to allow Pensacola's cool evening summer breezes to flow through the premises, while buffeting outside noise, allowing guests to dine outside in peace and comfort.

Reverend Edgars, Charlie and the Twigs were had enjoyed a belated dinner and were having coffee. After leaving the police station Edgars insisted on honoring his dinner invitation and the group drove, in the Twig's Expedition to Pensacola's famous social complex. The conversation before and during the meal was casual, with everybody just getting to know each other and carefully avoiding the topic, which was on everyone's mind.

"Charlie, I'm sorry we missed our dinner reservation, but I enjoyed our meal here out in the courtyard. On the way here I was struck by the architecture of the building and the others in the area. Do you know much about it?"

"Not really Casey, but if I had to guess it is either Spanish or French. Pensacola is called the City of Five Flags because at one time five different countries ruled it. This is the historic area of town, and several of the street names are French."

"What were the five countries Charlie?" Edgars asked.

"The Spanish settled Pensacola first, then the French and British, followed the United States, the Confederacy and then the United States again. The city incorporated parts of each culture."

"Charlie, I've imposed upon you and your family and to whatever extent that I've aggravated your plight I apologize."

"Nonsense Casey, our family owes you our gratitude for helping us. Your phone call to the Chief of Staff seemed to tip the scales in Charlie's favor," Jo Ann said.

"Absolutely Reverend, I can't begin to thank you enough for helping Charlie," Heather added.

"Thank you both, but if Charlie had really been a threat, nothing I could have said or done would have been able to help him. It was you, young man that impressed the right people. In any case I have spoken to both Charlie and to the rest of you briefly about my agenda. Let me discuss it in detail, if I may. I hope you will understand and support my agenda," Edgars said.

"Certainly Casey," Ralph replied.

"All of you are aware of who exactly Mohammad Baghai is, what he has done, what he claims and my efforts to free him, I assume."

"He is a terrorist and has killed American soldiers, surrendered to American authorities and his legal team is seeking a pardon from the President. You are supporting an independent movement to though I haven't paid it a lot of attention," Ralph said in a disdainful voice.

"Ralph, I understand that you served in the Air Force and from the tone of your voice, I don't think I am wrong to say that you are against it and under normal circumstances I wouldn't blame you. Heather, I understand that you will be serving our country also, but these are not normal circumstances and if everyone will keep an open mind and hear me out, I believe you and your family will understand and support me."

"Reverend, the least we can do is listen to what you have to say," Jo Ann said.

"Thank you, Jo Ann. Let me start by saying that as Christians we know that all we have to do to have our sins forgiven is to ask God to forgive them. Mohammad has done that, but as you know he was a Muslim and accepted Jesus Christ as his Savior, so he has been saved and thus his sins have been forgiven."

"Casey, everyone present knows that, from their first Sunday school class. I am concerned with the secular rather than the theological. He can be forgiven for his sins by the almighty but as far as I am concerned he has to answer for his crimes via our legal system," Ralph retorted.

"Ralph, Mohammad is serving time as we speak for the murder of Charlie's brother; John and he may face murder charges for his other victims. On a personal level, if Charlie can forgive Mohammad for John's murder, certainly you can?"

"I think execution, if what you say is correct, is a more accurate term Casey and no, I'm not ready to make that leap."

Edgars paused a moment.

"Charlie you did know that while Mohammad was in a hospital, in a coma, he received the holy marks of Stigmata? God doesn't mark just anyone with them. I'm certain that he has a purpose for him."

"I read about them but I'm not conceding that they are holy. I understand that there are several explanations for similar marks."

"I'm not familiar with the term Casey. Would you mind explaining the term to me?" Heather asked.

"Of course Heather, a Stigma is term referring to wounds on a person, corresponding to the wounds of Jesus. I have inspected them Charlie and I am convinced that they are authentic and I believe that you will feel the same way."

"Will? I don't have any desire to meet the man," Charlie said.

"Charlie, he desires to meet you and beg your forgiveness."

"Casey, I just said a minute ago that I'm not prepared to do that."

"Charlie, you wouldn't know, but while Mohammad was hospitalized and comatose, someone tried to murder him?"

"No, I didn't. I don't remember it being in the papers" Charlie replied.

"It wasn't but it happened and would have happened except for the intervention of your brother. A nurse tried to inject air bubbles into Mohammad's bloodstream, using a syringe, causing an embolism, when John woke him."

"John woke him? Casey you are becoming bizarre now and why did the nurse want to kill him?"

"Charlie let me answer your second question first. I know that I sound that I am way out in left field, but never the less what I say is true. You see, Mohammad, when he was about your age, living in Iran, had the nurse's father killed for stealing money to feed his family. You can understand her motivation, for wanting him dead. Your brother John, or the spirit of John, I should say, woke Mohammad from his coma, as she was about to kill him because God has a plan and it wasn't Mohammad's time to die."

"Casey, please don't be insulted, when I ask how you know this?"

"Not at all Jo Ann, now believe me when I say that there was not a valid medical explanation for Mohammad's miraculous recovery. I understand doctors will tell you that sometimes comatose patients will, on occasion, just wake up and one could argue that's what happened. On the other hand, I would argue, for good reason, this was definitely a case of divine intervention. God used the spirit of John to wake Mohammad, so that he could complete God's plan. I asked him about the circumstances and Mohammad told me as such. He doesn't have any reason to lie."

"On the contrary, he has every reason to lie. I think he would say or do anything to save his neck," Ralph said as Charlie nodded in agreement.

"Ralph, the point is that Mohammad voluntarily turned himself in and even though he knew a nurse attempted to kill him with a clever method, he refused to raise the issue. He had a FBI guard in the room and all he had to do is speak up. Instead, he asked to speak with her alone and begged her forgiveness for his sins against her family, as he wants to do with you Charlie."

"Talk is cheap Casey," Charlie said. It was obvious that he was still unimpressed with Edgars' persuasion.

"Money talks and bull shit walks," Edgars said.

The others at the table were visibly shocked at the reverend's choice of words.

"Please forgive the crassness of my last comment but yes Charlie, talk is cheap and Mohammad has put his money where is mouth is. I didn't tell you that when he spoke to the nurse, her name is Maleaka Pakrahvan, he made arrangements to pay her a million dollars, as he has done for all the other family members of the American soldiers Mohammad murdered. He made everyone of the family members sign a confidentiality agreement because he doesn't want any publicity. He wants to do the same for you Charlie, but you were a little tougher to locate since you and John have different last names."

Everyone at the table was visibly shocked tenfold from a minute ago.

"The point is Charlie is that Mohammad Baghai is a prophet of God. I knew it the second he arrived into the country and I have made it my purpose to have him pardoned because I am certain of my beliefs. However there are still many people that are either unconvinced or do not believe it at all. That is fine. There are dozens of prophets that were mocked by such people, but Mohammad Baghai is different."

"Oh? I can't wait for you to tell us how," Charlie said.

"Let me start from the beginning so everyone understands the context. Only once has God appeared to a prophet; that was Moses and God manifested himself in the form of a flaming bush, which didn't burn. In every other instance, communicated via an angel or spoke. Mohammad, before he intended to murder the journalist, David Franks was thrown into the pits of hell and suffered as the lost souls do. After 23 minutes, Jesus raised him out of hell and directly charged Mohammad to tell the world that hell exists. This is the first time since Jesus' time on Earth that he has appeared to anyone. It was at that time that John appeared with Jesus and forgave Mohammad. So Charlie, if John forgave Mohammad, certainly you can also?"

"Casey, this is all too convenient. This Mohammad Baghai wants to stop running from the authorities like Dr. Richard Kimball, from The Fugitive so he creates an incredible story about Heaven and hell and flashes cash around. No, I don't hate the man, though I feel that I should. No, I don't believe him about my brother waking him from a coma and no I am not going to be bought off to join his bandwagon. I don't care what kind of money he has," Charlie said empathetically.

"Charlie, before Mohammad turned himself in, he met with David Franks, his wife, Isabelle, who is an attorney and a Priest, named Paul Stewart, who baptized him as a Christian. They met in a hotel room and Mohammad explained his actions, why he spared Mr. Franks' life why he turned himself in, he recounted his experience in hell and his encounter with Jesus and your brother. A recording was made and I have a copy of it on CD with me. Ralph, I noticed that your SUV has a CD player would everyone like to hear it and judge Mohammad's sincerity? Charlie, I assume that you are OKAY with that?"

"I owe my indulgence Casey. Let's go listen," Charlie said, though he was becoming uneasy.

Edgars paid the bill and the group of five walked out to the Expedition Ralph and Jo Ann sat in front bucket seats, while Charlie, Heather and Edgars sat in the middle row bench seat. Ralph inserted the CD into the player and the group listened to the terrorist, murderer and Prophet Mohammad Baghai recount his 23-minute ordeal in Hell. About 10 minutes into the narrative, Charlie became visibly upset. Heather clasped her fiancé's hand with her own.

"Stop it. I don't need to hear anymore. I said stop it now," Charlie screamed as Ralph ejected the CD.

Everyone's eyes were on Charlie. Heather dug her fingernails into Charlie's hands.

"Heather, you're about to draw blood, I'm fine now. Would you loosen your grip?"

"Charlie, I'm sorry but you were scaring me," Heather replied.

"I'm sorry," Charlie said as he gave her an embrace.

After a moment he turned to Edgars.

"Casey, five minutes ago, I didn't believe your story. I still don't want to believe it but in my heart, I now know what you say is true."

"Charlie, let's drive to my hotel and we can talk about this more. I have a conference table in my room, which is definitely more user friendly than Ralph's car."

"Let's go. Your hotel is only about 10 minutes away and we still have plenty to talk about."

Fifteen minutes later the group was sitting around a circular conference table inside Edgar's suite. Though it was only one room, it was spacious and ornate. At one end was a king-sized bed, a dresser and a kitchenette, stocked with ground coffee, fruit and bottled water and at the other was a desk suitable for a traveling business man, complete with a telephone and Internet connections. The conference table was off to the side, with a half dozen chairs, which all but one was occupied. Heather sat next to Charlie facing the three older members of the group.

"Heather, Mom, Dad, I can't thank you enough for your support of me under these circumstances. Years ago I had a family that was taken away from me. I had forgotten what the meaning of family really meant until I met all of you."

"Ralph, from day one you called me son. I knew then that it was just an expression that you use, but you treated me with kindness and respect, even when I could tell that you didn't agree with my opinions, but you made me feel like one of your own. I am referring to my views on the war and the FBI's investigation of me. Now I want you to set aside you feelings concerning the man that murdered my brother. I will explain why in a moment."

"Jo Ann, I felt like a square peg inside a round hole when I was in your company, until we had our conversation, while returning my U-Haul truck. It was then that I began to feel like I had a mother and father again."

"Heather, I don't know if I could ever truly express how I feel about you. You were just another conquest for me when we first met. I was disappointed when you didn't fall for me immediately and I only tried harder when you didn't. I've told you before that I fell in lust with you right away but I'm glad that our team stayed in Dahlonega the entire week so I could fall in love with you. There is a God in Heaven. I know this because he has blessed me with my new family. All of you have supported me so far and I want all of you to continue to support me now. I don't know what lies ahead but I do know that it is bigger than me."

"Charlie, you said in the car that you knew what Baghai said is true. My question is how," Ralph asked.

"Dad, on the CD Mohammad mentioned something concerning the image of my brother, when he said he was in the presence of him. It was a minor detail; something that he couldn't possibly have known to mention about him unless he was telling the truth."

"What was that?"

"John gave me shooting lessons, with his Marlin .22 rifle when I was a small child. He would take me out in the boon docks and let me shoot it. There wasn't much of kick to the rifle and for a boy my age it was pretty heady stuff. With all gun lessons, safety can't be stressed enough and John did so as well only, he emphasized the point of showing me his left pinky finger, which was partly missing. You see John lost it in a shooting accident and wanted to show me what can happen if you aren't careful. Mohammad mentioned that John was missing a digit so I knew he wasn't fictionalizing everything. It's a minute detail that validates his claims and Reverend Edgars' assertions as well. As incredible as it sounds to me, I accept the reality that Mohammad Baghai did communicate to the spirit of my brother and Jesus Christ, so by extension, I also believe that he is God's messenger." Charlie paused for a moment for the situation's gravity to manifest.

"Casey, where and how do I fit into this?"

"Charlie, Mohammad does want to meet you and ask your forgiveness. His attorney Isabelle Franks wants to speak to you to discuss a check she has for you and I would like to enlist your support to obtain a pardon. Are you willing to help?"

"Yes, I'm willing to meet the man when my schedule permits, though I really haven't given thought as to whether to accept that kind of money."

"Charlie, are you sure you want to become involved?"

"Mom, I don't have any doubts that this is bigger than all of us. It's not that I want to get involved; I feel compelled to."

"Charlie, right now the House of Representatives is using this business as an excuse to impeach President Hays and Mohammad has said that he is opposed to that, regardless if he is pardoned or not. I have spoken to Speaker Richt and Senate Majority Leader Dunston on the issue. Believe me, men like them are the reason politicians have such terrible reputations. However, Mohammad his priest and his attorney have discussed the situation and have a plan."

"Casey, is this something that should be discussed between you and Charlie privately?" Ralph asked.

"Absolutely not, you, Jo Ann and Heather are my family and I don't keep secrets from any of you." Charlie asserted.

"Ralph you and your family are welcome to remain. This won't take long and there isn't anything top secret either," Edgars said.

"Okay," Ralph cracked a smile.

"Shortly, I am going to hold a press conference, in which I am going to play this CD and simultaneously launch it on my web site. I would like you to attend Charlie and basically reiterate what you have just said."

"Casey that doesn't sound like very much to me," Charlie said.

"No, but I also have in my possession a letter authored by Mohammad, which he states why he converted to Christianity and that President shouldn't be impeached. At the press conference, I am going to release the letter and on the web site as well. Ralph and

Heather, as former and future military officers, both of you are welcome to participate; that is if you both are comfortable doing so. If not I understand."

"Casey, I won't speak for my father but I support whatever Charlie agrees to," Heather said.

"That goes for me also," Ralph added.

"Good. I can make the arrangements for a press conference tomorrow or the next day. I expect that when everything is brought to bear, with God's help Mohammad will be pardoned and begin God's work. Charlie, Heather, Ralph, Jo Ann, it has been a pleasure meeting you, though I apologize for us meeting under these circumstances. I hope you enjoy the rest of your vacation. That's all I have to offer at this point but I will remain in contact. Now if you will excuse me, I have some other affairs that need my attention."

"Casey thank you again for helping Charlie and yes we intend to," Ralph said as he shook hands with Edgars as he escorted everyone out o his room.

As soon as he was alone, Edgars used his cell phone to dial Andy Shephard again.

"Casey, thank you for calling me back."

"No, Andy, I wanted to thank you for assisting me. You probably already know that Charlie Michaels has not been detained by the Secret Service. He has to wear a bracelet with a GPS chip, but the young man is happy that he can get on with his life."

"My actions were all for selfish reasons. Casey."

"At any rate I wanted to thank you again and give you a heads up."

"Oh?"

Shephard's internal radar just got aroused.

"Yes Andy, I am going to be holding a press conference, here in Pensacola, as soon as I can arrange it, on Mohammad Baghai's behalf."

"Casey, you made a promise that you wouldn't hold a press conference disparaging the President's policies, if I was able to help you."

"And, I'm not, however I remain steadfast in my efforts to have him pardoned. Andy, you know that I am a man of my word and nothing derogatory about the President will be discussed; in fact, if things unfold as I expect, my press conference will be very beneficial for her."

"How so?"

"Andy, I'm not going to get into that with you, but as I said, my goal has never been to harm the President, but it is to secure a pardon for God's prophet. I hope you will take me at my word."

"I do Casey, but I'm afraid of unintended consequences."

"You believe that there will be some?"

"In Washington, there are unintended consequences all most every day. You know that I will have to inform the President?"

"I expect nothing less."

DUNSTON entered Richt's office again for another late night encounter. Dunston had called earlier that day and requested the meeting, which Richt readily agreed to after his staff had left for the evening.

"Senator, come in," Richt said as he Dunston entered Richt's private office.

"Would you care for a drink?"

"No thank you Mr. Speaker, I won't be staying long."

Richt's political acumen instantly was alerted.

"Oh?"

"Mr. Speaker, may we speak frankly?"

"Is there any other way?"

"I wasn't happy with your double speak on your television interview."

"Senator, since when is a politician ever 100 percent happy?"

Richt retorted with hint of a smile.

"The problem, Mr. Speaker is that as a politician, you and I know that double speak often leads to double cross and that is not going to happen in this case. You will bring articles of Impeachment against President Hays and Vice President Taylor to the floor of the House and they will be voted to the Senate for a trial. I will then ensure that they are removed from office. After you take the oath you will nominate me to become the next Vice President."

"That's what we discussed Senator."

"Yes, and that is what will happen. Do you want to know why I am so confident?"

"I'm sure you are going to tell me."

"I didn't get to be majority leader by being naïve or stupid. I attained my position by knowing which strings to pull and exactly when to pull them."

Dunston handed Richt a manila folder with several 8X10 pictures.

"Mr. Speaker I've never had the pleasure of meeting your lovely wife, but I'm guessing the woman in those pictures with you isn't her."

"Where did you get these?"

"Does it matter? You can have those, I have plenty more."

"How do I know that you won't release these after you are sworn in as Vice President and force me to resign?"

"You don't, but I hadn't intended to publicize them before your feeble attempt to renege on our deal and as long as you follow the script, I'm not inclined to make changes in the play. Do we understand each other Mr. Speaker?"

Dunston asked in a matter of fact tone, knowing that Richt didn't have a choice in matter.

"Yes we do," Richt said in resignation.

"Mr. Speaker, there's no need for that tone. In a matter of weeks I will be addressing you as Mr. President." Dunston said in a manner, which let it be known that he was the president's puppet master.

CAL was looking forward to fresh fruit and vegetables for the next meal and shore leave afterwards. The boat transporting the Gaffney's produce was approaching from the stern, as he viewed it with binoculars. Because of his heritage and his fluency in Arabic, Cal was designated as the Gaffney's liaison, translator and troubleshooter at any and all ports in the Persian Gulf or the Arabian Sea. Cal chuckled to himself. Though it wasn't in his 'job description' Cal was pleased to assume the role.

As the boat approached, an inboard fiberglass craft, about 25 feet in length, which had been used to deliver, produce on previous occasions; Cal noticed that the fiberglass hull had been repaired since their last visit. The boat's skipper had crashed into the Gaffney accidentally, so hard that the hull was cracked, even with the old tires and boat fenders cushioning the blow that a three foot by 1 foot section of the gunnel was left dangling. During his visit to the produce merchant Cal joked that he hoped the same boat skipper wouldn't be attempting to ram the Gaffney again.

Cal also noticed something peculiar. There were four men onboard, when only two men had been manning the boat every other time. In addition, the boat appeared to be riding higher in the water than normal, which could only mean that the entire produce order had not been filled, the lighter weight not causing the craft to displace as much and reveal more of the hull above the waterline. That in itself was not unusual; produce and dry good orders were sometimes transported in several trips, but why were there twice the normal crew for a partial shipment? Something was not quite kosher, to borrow a Jewish phrase. Cal continued to inspect the craft, through his binoculars for another minute or so, still perplexed, when the gravity and seriousness of the situation dawned on him and immediately grabbed the microphone to the bridge to speak to the officer of the bridge.

"Bridge, Lieutenant Bauer," Bauer said when he picked up the hand receiver.

"Lieutenant, this Petty Officer Intavan. Sir, this ship is about to be attacked by the produce boat. We need to go to general quarters."

"What makes you say that Intavan?"

"Several things sir, no one thing by itself, but added up the total equals an attack on the ship."

"You can explain yourself to the captain."

"Captain, Petty Officer Intavan in on the line and claims that the ship is about to be attacked," Bauer said as he handed the handset to Commander Hampton.

"Intavan, what is going on?" Hampton demanded.

"Sir, three things, first, the transport boat is riding extremely high in the water, indicating her cargo is light. Two, I could see twice the normal crew onboard. Why does it have twice the crew for only half the normal load? Three, it is the same boat that accidentally rammed us, the last time that we were here in port, but there is not a bumper or boat fender to be seen. That boat is going to ram us again!"

Hampton didn't even bother to reply to Cal.

"Officer of the bridge sound general quarters, order all weapons to engage hostile craft approaching us! Alert harbor patrol to intercept the produce boat! Make emergency preparations to get underway!"

"Aye aye! Bowswain sound general quarters," Bauer echoed the captain's order.

"Aye aye!" The order was repeated as the bowswain sounded the klaxon.

Cal immediately ran to the stern of the Gaffney and manned his gun. As soon as the produce boat heard the klaxon, it immediately increased speed, knowing that its mission had been discovered. Tactically the boat was attacking at the Gaffney's weakest point, the stern. The missile launcher and the gun turret were ineffective because both weapons were blocked by the ship's super-structure. That left the deck gun on the stern and the C-WIS as the only defense until the Gaffney got underway and that wasn't going to happen until the issue had already been resolved.

While attacking from directly astern was the correct decision, attacking at the weakest point, it also made Cal's task of aiming the gun considerably easier. Instead of having to lead a moving target, Cal only had to center the gun's sight on the target and then make a slight adjustment to account for gravity.

The boat opened up on the Gaffney with small arms fire, but

was ineffective, with the rounds falling well short of the ship. Cal on the other hand, opened up on the boat and after a few rounds falling short of the target began to hit its' mark. Every fifth round of the gun was a tracer and Cal could see that his rounds were beginning to have an effect. He was hoping that one of the tracer rounds would strike the fuel tank, igniting the fuel and causing an explosion. A moment later the C-WIS opened up, firing its 1-inch titanium slugs and a moment after that the produce boat produced a giant fireball, with flaming pieces of fiberglass raining down on the harbor of Jebel Ali.

Twenty minutes after the attack, the Gaffney had cleared the harbor and was crusing in the Persian Gulf. Commander Hampton was on the bridge and felt comfortable now that he could maneuver his and defend his ship. In another 10 minutes he would order the crew to stand down. There were still men left behind in port but that couldn't be helped. They would be on board as soon as they could be rounded together and taxied to the ship by the helo.

"XO, I want a head count to determine exactly how many of the crew are still in port and then I want them picked up ASAP! I wanted a report from damage control yesterday! Send a flash message to the fleet informing them of the attack." Hampton barked.

"Aye, aye skipper! I'm on it."

The damage control officer called the bridge immediately after Hampton issued his orders, as if he was clairvoyant. Hampton picked up the receiver himself.

"Bridge, this is the captain."

"Skipper, this is Lieutenant Martin, I have a damage report. No casualties no damage; we got lucky."

"Good."

"Skipper, we are picking up higher radio-activity readings than we should. It's nothing dangerous, but definitely higher than they should be. I think that boat was packing a dirty bomb."

Hampton didn't bother to respond and hung up the phone.

"XO, start the radio-active counter measures and pass out the badges."

"Aye, aye skipper!"

Hampton ordered the crew to give the Gaffney a bath from bow to stern, with the premises of washing away any radioactive particles. It was an arduous task. The crew would have to have to wear protective suits, known as MOPP and drag heavy water hoses. The heat and the humidity would further compound the task, but there was not alternative. The ship would have to be sunk, if it absorbed lethal doses of radioactivity. Every member of the crew would wear a badge, which would show his exposure to radioactivity.

HAYS was at her desk, getting an early start on the day when the Bat Phone rang again. She could see that from the caller identification screen that is was the Secretary of Defense. It was not usually a good sign when he called on this line.

"This is the President."

"Madam President there has been another attack on one of our ships in the Persian Gulf."

"How many casualties were there?"

"We were lucky ma'am; no one was killed or hurt."

"All right, tell me what happened Scott?"

"The Gaffney, a guided missile frigate was anchored in the port of Jebel Ali, in the process of replenishing its supplies, when a produce boat, loaded with explosives, attempted to ram her."

"The Gaffney, wasn't that the same ship that was attacked by an Iranian Jet?"

"Yes ma'am, the same. As I said we got lucky. One of the ship's petty officers noticed that something was fishy and alerted the captain, Commander Hampton, who ordered battle stations and the crew destroyed the suicide boat. The Gaffney immediately got under way and exited the harbor. She is currently in the Gulf."

"How long ago did this happen Scott?"

"It happened less than a half hour ago Mrs. President."

"So we don't know who is behind this?"

"Not at this point. The FBI is sending an investigative team and will be there is 12 hours." The FBI investigated all terror attacks on Americans, regardless of where they occurred.

"Very well, I expect a briefing as soon as we have determined the facts."

"Of course."

Hays didn't need the briefing though. She already knew that Hassan Nassiri was some how behind this.

To my brothers and sisters in Jesus Christ:

    I am writing to you today to explain my reasons for my choice to renounce my previous actions as a jihadist, to renounce my actions of violence and murder, to renounce my previous life as a Muslim and to announce and to explain my conversion to Christianity.

    Several weeks ago I converted to Catholicism, renouncing my Muslim faith, by being baptized by Father Paul Stewart. I must confess that I did not reject Islam by questioning its precepts, over a period of time and being unable to obtain satisfactory answers. Indeed, until my conversion, I hadn't met a more fervent practitioner of Islam than myself. Instead, my conversion was realized, by divine grace, when the Lord Jesus Christ appeared to me. Let me repeat myself to my Muslim brothers and sisters. The Lord Jesus Christ and not the prophet Jesus Christ appeared to me. Though he did not say so, I knew implicitly and immediately, when I was in his presence that Jesus was indeed the Son of God and not a prophet of Allah, though while in our Lord's presence I could clearly see the wounds of his crucifixion. For those ignorant in the doctrines of Islam, I would say that Muslims believe that Allah took the prophet Jesus Christ to Paradise and that he did not die on the cross for our sins, as all Christians believe. The wounds were proof enough for me that at least that Islamic belief is incorrect.

Since my conversion and my confinement I have been the target of death threats and death sentences by numerous Islamic terrorists groups. Islamic clerics and leaders have legitimized these death sentences by labeling me, through fatwas (Islamic judicial verdicts), an apostate, an enemy of Islam, a liar and vilifier and someone who wants to harm Islam. These are the same groups that I once belonged to and I pray for them each and every day, for I believe that it is time for radical Muslims to end violence, intimidation and abuse of those who do not share their views of religion and do not respect man's inherent freedom to choose. There are thousands of converts to Islam, who live and practice their new faith in peace, while there are certainly as many Muslim converts to Christianity who must practice their new religion in secrecy for fear of assassination by extremist, such as I once was.

Both believers and non-believers would naturally ask why Jesus would choose to appear to me. To those who would ask such a reasonable question, I do not have an answer and can only reply that he did appear to me, entrusting me to deliver a message and it is not my place to question his motives or his wisdom. The same people certainly would ask why am bearing the wounds of Stigmata? Again it is not for me to question the wisdom of God. I only accept it to the best of my ability.

To the believers, I want you to know that my wounds do not cause me pain, but only the embarrassment of bloody bandages. To the skeptics and non-believers, I can only say that these wounds were not self-inflicted, since I received them while I was still in a coma under the guard of the FBI and still, after several weeks have not healed. Father Stewart has told me that, according to legend, the blood from Stigmatic wounds has divine power. I can not say to the affirmative or the negative to the validity of that assertion, and will leave it to faith.

Delivering his message is the purpose of my letter and I want to be perfectly clear about my motives. I am guilty of committing numerous murders and I am presently serving a life sentence in an American correctional institution for my crimes, though I may be charged with other offenses, which I am guilty. If so, I will plead guilty to them. My legal team is currently seeking a pardon of my crimes from the President and I understand that there is a movement, initiated by Reverend Casey Edgars, to have the President removed from her office because she has not granted me a pardon. I want to thank Reverend Edgars for his efforts. I have had the privilege of meeting him and I sincerely believe that not only is he a man of God, but a man of principle and integrity. However, even though his efforts have the best intentions, I can not in good faith support them.

Let me state clearly and unequivocally that I do not support any movement, which has the goal of removing the President from office because she is reluctant to pardon me for my crimes. I also believe that she is a woman of principle and integrity and her decisions must not be made under the political pressure applied by those having immoral ambitions. God's will be done, regardless, if am to remain in prison or freed to deliver the message entrusted me by Jesus Christ.

Now let me address the purpose of my letter, to proclaim the message that our Lord Jesus entrusted to me. It is a simple one but as important as anyone will hear in a lifetime.

Both Muslims and Christians believe in hell, with only one major difference between the two religions' concept of the domain. My former faith teaches that hell is a place of temporary suffering. Lost souls, after sufficient suffering for their sins may enter paradise and I believed that precept, without question while I was Muslim. I now know that the lost souls of hell suffer damnation for eternity, as my Christian faith teaches. I know this because immediately before I intended to commit another gruesome crime against an innocent man, David Franks, who I now call my friend, Jesus hurled me into hell, where I suffered for only a few minutes as the lost souls have suffered and will continue to suffer for all of eternity. I have described hell in detail to David and Father Paul and both transcripts and audio recordings will be released so I will not waste words describing it here, but please believe me when I say that no one wants to spend one minute there.

After spending just a few minutes in damnation, Jesus lifted me out of my fiery torment; he charged me with telling the world that hell does exist and that he doesn't want any soul to reside there. Again, though he did not say, I knew implicitly and immediately that lost souls reside there for eternity and have no hope of relief, as my former religion teaches. Jesus did say that he was saddened by each and every soul that were suffering in Hell and that he did not desire for any soul to suffer.

My bothers and sisters in Jesus Christ, take heed in what I say, for our Lord also revealed to me that he was coming very, very soon and it is my hope and desire that all of God's children will one day join me in Paradise. Weather I am released or remain in prison for the remainder of my life; I will proclaim Jesus' message to anyone who will listen, through all means available to me. God blesses all of you.

Mohammad Baghai.

Edgars scanned the letter and created a HTML file of it in his laptop's hard drive. He would post this document to his web site as soon as all the other arrangements for his press conference were made. Afterwards it would be in God's hands.

# Chapter 29

Reverend Edgars was pleased after receiving a phone call from a member of the hotel's staff. The Hilton's conference room was filled with dozens of journalists, both print and television. Edgars had spoken with the hotel manager the previous morning to make the arrangements for the press conference for the following afternoon. He posted the press conference announcement on Mohammad's web site, just listing the date, time purpose and place. Less than an hour before, Edgars had created a new page on Mohammad's web site, which contained Mohammad's letter and his description of Hell.

Charlie and the Twigs were in his room with him enjoying some light refreshments, while waiting for the appointed time. The five of them would shortly leave the suite and walk to the conference and take a seat at a meeting table, beside Edgars while he conducted his business.

Charlie and Ralph were in coat and tie, while Heather and Jo Ann were both wearing the dresses, which they intended to wear to the graduation ceremony. Edgars was impeccably dressed, as always, in one of his dozens of tailored suits, Italian dress shirt and styled hair. Everyone appreciated the event's decorum and formality.

Edgars looked at his watch.

"It's just about time. Why don't we get this little show going?"

Several dozen steps and a couple of minutes later the group entered the conference room and took their seats as Edgars stood in front of the podium. There was a lap top computer and a projector set up for a power point presentation next to the podium.

"I want to thank all of you coming here this afternoon. As you can see, I've invited some guests. To my right are Ralph and Jo Ann Twig, of Cumming, Georgia. To my left, are their beautiful daughter Heather and her fiancée Charlie Michaels, formerly of Pensacola, now also living in Georgia. Charlie will be graduating, with honors, later this week from the University of West Florida. I'll make a statement and then we will take questions."

Edgars took his reading glasses from inside his coat and put them on and began speaking extemporaneously, occasionally referring to a note card.

"As all of you are aware, I am sure, I have championed a grass roots effort to have Mohammad Baghai pardoned by President Hays for his crimes. You are all also aware that I have called Mohammad a prophet of God and have demanded the President's removal from office should she not choose to grant a pardon in a timely manner."

"To this end I launched a web site, www.pardonGod'sprophet. com which collected electronic signatures of Americans supporting Mohammad's pardon and forwarding them to their respective Senators and Congressmen. If national opinion polls are correct, a majority of God fearing Americans support a full and unconditional pardon. Influential members of Congress have paid attention to the American public and articles of impeachment have been introduced onto the floor of the House and have been moved on to the House Judiciary Committee for hearings."

"I've called this press conference for 3 reasons. First, I call again on the President to pardon Mohammad. Second, I am going to release a recording of Mohammad's explanation of his divine experiences and summarize again why he should be pardoned, so he can spread God's message. Third, I want to explain why I am calling upon the Congress not to consider articles of impeachment against the President and Vice President."

Edgars paused for a moment for effect.

"I will explain myself in a moment."

PRESIDENT Hays paused, in front of a computer monitor, not quite sure if she heard Edgars correctly. She was viewing the press conference via the Internet. Andy Shephard had warned her of Edgars' press conference and she was watching it in her office. She expected another attack upon her from Edgars, but this was completely unexpected. Undoubtedly the next few minutes would be very interesting. Hays opened Edgars' web site on her computer and began to navigate through it. She had visited it before. After a minute she walked outside her office, where Ron Thomas was standing, at his assigned post.

"Good afternoon Mrs. President."

"Ron, I understand that you know this young man?"

"Yes ma'am. He and I met while I was on vacation here and as you know my boss interviewed him a couple of days ago. He was deemed a possible threat to you, but it was determined that his isn't a threat after all. He's intelligent and very opinionated. He doesn't agree with your policies, but I never believed that he was a threat. "

"I hope not because I'm going to invite him and his family to visit."

"When Mrs. President?"

"He's participating in a press conference with Reverend Edgars.

I'm going to leave the good reverend a voice mail, inviting him and his guests for a visit. Since you know him, I'd like you to take some one go downtown and extend the invitation personally."

"Mrs. President, this creates a number of personnel irregularities directly affecting your protection. I need to clear this with Agent Hickey."

"Ron, inform him but I just cleared it."

Hays just gave the Secret Service, via Thomas, a reminder of who was ultimately in charge.

"I expect you and a driver to be rolling in 10 minutes."

"Yes ma'am."

"LADIES and gentlemen, I have said on numerous occasions that the Lord has given Mohammad Baghai a divine message and that Jesus wants him to spread it far and wide and not to spend the rest of his life in prison as the situation stand presently. Even a blind man can see the logic in this. Therefore, the issue is whether Mohammad's message is to be believed or not and to that end I would like everyone present as well as all Americans to judge for themselves. I'm going to play a recording of Mohammad's explanation for his actions. This recording can be downloaded from the web site, www. pardonGod'sprophet.com."

Edgars played the recording of Mohammad's meeting with The Franks and Father Paul Stewart and sat down. For the 10 minutes the room was absolutely silent. Edgars got up and again stood at the podium after the recording was finished.

"Ladies and gentlemen, this is the first time that this recording has been released to the public. You all have heard his explanation for surrendering himself. You have heard his message about and description of hell and all of you can judge his sincerity. Now if you believe Mohammad's explanation, then you must believe that Jesus has forgiven him of his sins as the Bible teaches and the spirit of Christian Welter has also forgiven Mohammad of his murder."

Edgars paused again for moment to judge the audience's reaction, before continuing. He wasn't sure he could articulate what exactly he was looking for, but he was sure that he would recognize a sign when and if he saw it. He started his power point presentation, though he wasn't sure if one page qualified as a presentation.

"I now want to show you a letter that was written by Mohammad Baghai, by his own hand writing. Again a copy of this can be down loaded on the web site. Here are some copies of it. Now each of you can read it so I'm not going to insult your intelligence by reading it to you so take a few minutes and afterwards I want to make a few remarks."

After a short pause, Edgars began.

"Ladies and gentlemen, all of you have read Mohammad's open letter to God's believers. I believe that God wants Mohammad to spread his message about hell and the lost souls in Perdition. I realize that this is an incredible story but true believers, be they Catholic or Protestant, who possess faith know the truth in Mohammad's words. For those that have lost faith God invites you to renew it through him. God has given a sign of faith. Consider it carefully."

"Now let me address some of the secular concerns surrounding Mohammad's plight. Mohammad has committed terrible gruesome crimes. He has admitted that and is presently serving a life sentence, for the murder of Christian Welter, an American soldier. As things stand now, Mohammad Baghai doesn't need to be charged with another murder, since a prisoner, serving a federal life sentence is imprisoned for the duration of his or her entire life. There is no such thing as parole."

"Now I want to re-introduce my guests. On my right is Captain Ralph Twig of the United States Air force retired and his wife Jo Ann and on my left is their daughter, Cadet First Class Heather Twig, a senior at North Georgia College and State University. North Georgia is Georgia's military college and Heather, after her graduation next year will be serving our country as a commissioned officer. Beside her is her fiancée Charlie Michaels."

"My guests have a unique perspective on this matter. You see, Mohammad pleaded guilty to the murder of Charlie's brother, Christian Welter."

The audience's interest, already piqued by the press conference, now increased a hundred fold.

"Charlie, though understandably reluctant initially, wasn't in a forgiving mood, but he believes Mohammad's story but now has forgiven him and believes she should be pardoned. Ralph, as a former military officer, understandably was reluctant about a murderer of American soldiers being pardoned. His daughter, Heather a future military officer also has the same sentiments but they are both agreeable to the concept of forgiveness and a pardon."

"I can see that most of you have questions and all of us here are available to answer them."

"Reverend Edgars, why are you reversing your position and no longer supporting the President's removal from office?"

"That's an excellent question. Truthfully, I had a high and mighty opinion of myself and I felt that I was the only one who could engineer Mohammad's pardon. Calling for the President's impeachment was a tool to that end. I had forgotten that God's will, would be done. I realized that God was humbling me just a little when Mohammad, expressly asked that political pressure not be applied to the President, to secure a pardon. As such, I am even more confident that the President will grant him a pardon."

"Charlie, why does your brother have a different surname from you and what exactly are your feelings about your brother's killer being pardoned?"

"My parents, when they couldn't conceive, adopted John when he was a young boy. Because of his age, they decided not to change his name. Afterwards, my parents became pregnant with me. To answer your second question, initially I didn't make the connection between Mohammad Baghai and my brother and to be honest, he was just another terrorist nutcase, so I didn't pay his plight a lot of attention. A couple of days ago, when Reverend Edgars first contacted me, I was reluctant. However, the first time I listened to recording we you just heard, I knew, beyond a shadow of a doubt that Mohammad's account of was true and accurate. Given that, I believe that God chose him to deliver a message and that he did speak to the spirit of my brother."

"How do you know that Mohammad's explanation isn't just a hoax?" The same journalist asked a follow up question.

"Mohammad said on the recording that John's left pinky finger was missing a digit. John lost part of his finger in a shooting accident. It was just too much of a coincidence for me not to believe his story."

"How do you feel about him personally?"

"I've never met the man and to tell the truth, I'm not sure that I want to. However, I believe him, so at some point I will and the chips will fall where the may."

"I have a question for Ralph and Heather." Another journalist asked.

"Since both of you have ties to the military, what are your feelings about a murderer of American soldiers getting off scot-free?"

"My daughter can certainly speak for herself, but I swore an oath, when I received my commission to defend this country against all enemies. Mohammad Baghai certainly qualifies as one and as far as I'm concerned he is right where he belongs, but if my future son in law supports a pardon for him, then I can and will respect his position."

Ralph looked over to Heather.

"I will take that same oath also a year from now and as a 2nd lieutenant and I will expected to follow orders and not offer opinions.

If my commander in chief pardons a terrorist, then I will give her a salute and carry on. Personally, I haven't lost a loved one so I support Charlie's position."

"When are you getting married and how did you and Charlie meet?"

Heather's demeanor changed and she lit up the room with her aura.

"December 16th. We met on the North Georgia Campus. His team was participating in the In Inter-collegiate Paint Ball Championships and I was the team's escort."

"Actually, we met off campus in the lobby of the hotel where our team was staying," Charlie said as he reached for Heather's hand.

"You're right Charlie, it was in the lobby of the Days Inn in Dahlonega" Heather said to Charlie. She turned to the audience.

"Dahlonega is the city where the North Georgia campus is located."

"She was so dazzled by me that she can't remember the events correctly," Charlie said as he flashed one of his smiles. The group laughed.

"I tried to put some moves on her when we met and she gave me a cold shoulder," Charlie said while being animated.

"I'd never been given the cold shoulder before; no one gives me the cold shoulder, so I kept trying. Eventually I managed to eliminate all of Heather's objections with my 'forward' personality and got her to converse with me. I just wore her defense mechanism down."

Charlie leaned forward the audience as is he was sharing a secret and then winked, while flashing a smile. The audience was in stitches and Heather was blushing.

"Heather, what are your plans after graduation?"

"I'm going to be a Marine, though I haven't decided on a billet," Heather said after regaining her composure. "I'll have to spend several weeks in Quantico, Virginia, then maybe flight training, here in Pensacola."

All new Marine officers went to Quantico for orientation and training and all Naval Aviators, be they Navy, Marine or Coast Guard took their basic flight training at Pensacola NAS.

"Charlie, what do you do now and what will you do when Heather graduates?"

"I work for Ralph, as an insurance agent and after Heather gets her commission, I'll probably sell insurance wherever Heather is."

"Heather, do you plan to make the Marines, a career?"

"Probably not."

"Charlie, have you thought about what you will say to Mohammad when and if you finally meet him? Also, what would you say to the President, to encourage her to grant him a pardon?"

"I haven't thought that far ahead. I'm sure it would be incredibly awkward. He was a really bad guy in his previous life and I'm glad that he has changed. People can change."

Charlie emphasized the last sentence.

"My close friends will all tell you that I'm not the same person I was 6 months ago, so if I get the sense that he is sincere, then I suppose I can forgive him. I am not, have not and will not be a fan of the President. Her policies have caused others to lose family members and I would encourage her to pardon Mohammad and to get our soldiers out of the Middle East. Maybe she has changed too."

Charlie got a chuckle out of the audience.

Another female journalist asked a different question. This one was for Jo Ann.

"I have a question for you Jo Ann. You have been silent thus far and perhaps you are, because you are the farthest removed from this issue and best prepared to voice an objective opinion on this whole affair. Do you have any comments?"

"Certainly, when Heather first brought Charlie to our home, to meet us, my husband and I were both impressed with his integrity and maturity. We thought Charlie was wise beyond his years and we quickly accepted him as a member or our family. The events of the last couple of days have confirmed our impressions of Charlie. We all are proud of him and proud of the way he has carried himself. I also, support Charlie's position."

"As a mother, how do you feel about your daughter potentially having to go into combat?"

"I think bringing our troops home from the Middle East is an excellent idea," Jo Ann quipped.

The questions continued for a few more minutes but the press conference ended and after the room cleared of most the people present; Ron Thomas approached Edgars at the front of the conference room. Charlie and the Twigs were happy to see their new friend again.

"Reverend Edgars, I've been instructed to invite all of you to visit the President. She left a message for you on your cell phone."

Edgars took his cell phone and listened to his voice mail.

"Is this a back handed way of saying we are all under arrest again Ron? I still have my bracelet on," Charlie said to his friend with a smile on his face, while raising his left hand.

"No this is purely social. The President was watching the press conference on the Internet and wants to meet all of you."

"Agent Thomas is correct. I had my cell turned off during the press conference and she left a message inviting us to her home. Do you have any other immediate plans?"

"She sent her limousine to take us. I know none of you have traveled in it before. We call it 'the beast'," Thomas said.

Inside the belly of the beast, Thomas and his five guests made themselves comfortable. Inside the vehicle, were all the amenities, one would expect of a 'tricked out' limousine. Plush black leather upholstery, carpeting, a huge L-shaped leather seat, a mini bar, satellite telephone and television and interior mood lighting all embellished the interior.

"I feel like I am going to the prom again," Heather remarked.

"You didn't go to the prom in a vehicle like this Heather. The entire limo is built to withstand a RPG round and have the body remain intact. The windshield alone weighs 1,500 pounds and all the windows are bullet proof. The tires are filled with a soft rubber compound, instead of air, so they can't be shot out. Basically, it is designed to withstand a bomb blast and be able to drive away, at high speed, to escape the danger. You can call anyone in the world on that phone and watch anything that's on television on the TV. The Vice President rides in one exactly like this one also by the way," Thomas said. All of guests were impressed.

"Ron, how many agents typically ride with the President in here?" Charlie asked.

"Planning an assassination attempt Charlie?" Thomas joked.

"Two usually, a driver and a guard in the passenger area and there is always at least one chase car behind the President."

"Agent Thomas, a President of the United States just doesn't invite guests on the spur of moment for chit-chat; would you know what she wants?" Edgars asked.

"No sir, I can tell you that she was watching your press conference and asked me to invite all of you to her home, but you can ask her in just a minute. Now ladies, for security reasons, I'm going to have to look into your purses to look for weapons and everyone will have to walk through a metal detector."

"Certainly," Jo Ann replied as both she and Heather gave their purses.

After the limousine stopped in the President's driveway each of he occupants walked through a metal detector after they removed all their metal objects. Charlie's bracelet sounded a warning so a portable wand was used on him and afterwards, they were ushered into the President's home and were seated in her den, which was decorated in earth tone colors and plush leather furniture.

"The President's on the phone but she will be with you shortly," Thomas said.

Everyone was admiring the view of Escambia Bay, when the President concluded her business and greeted her guests. Edgars was the first to see her.

"Reverend Edgars, it's a pleasure to see you again," Hays said. She was dressed casually, in simple dress and low heel shoes.

"And you also Madam President," Edgars replied, not exactly sure if she was sincere or not.

"I want to thank all of you for visiting on such notice. I'm Jennifer Hays."

"Mrs. President, I am Ralph Twig, this is my wife Jo Ann, my daughter Heather and her fiancé Charlie Michaels. Thank you for inviting us."

Everyone shook hands.

"Reverend, I was watching your press conference and I thought that since we were in the same city, it might be a good idea to meet all of you and discuss the issues of the day. Shall we sit down? Can I offer any of you refreshments? Would some iced tea be all right?"

Hays asked and received affirmative responses.

"Make yourselves comfortable and I'll be right back," Hays said as she walked into her kitchen.

A few minutes later she returned with a picture of tea and six glasses. Everyone was seated.

"I'm supposed to have a staff here, but I refuse to allow it in my own home, so I'll beg your indulgence for leaving you."

"Heather and I would have been glad to help you ma'am," Jo Ann said.

"I wouldn't hear of it Jo Ann and while you all are guests in my home, call me Jenny. I'm from Wisconsin originally and until I moved to Florida, I have never heard of iced tea. Now I don't think there is not a day that goes by that I don't drink a glass. I miss being able to relax on my deck and daydream and gaze upon the bay. I miss teaching even more, I think. That's what I intend to do at the University here after I leave Washington."

"It is a magnificent view Mrs. President. We have a house on a lake with similar view. Ralph and I love it," Jo Ann said.

"Jo Ann, every guest in my home is on a first name basis with me."

"I'm sorry, I'll try to remember that Jenny," Jo Ann replied.

"As I said earlier, I saw the press conference and I thought it would be a good idea if we talked. Charlie, I understand that you and I will be participating in UWF's graduation ceremonies?"

"Yes, that's why I'm wearing this," Charlie said, showing his bracelet.

"Yes I understand. The Secret Service takes their responsibility to protect the President very seriously. Sometimes they are overly zealous. Ron?"

"Yes Mrs. President?"

Thomas appeared from the next room.

"Find the tool that will take this bracelet off of Charlie's wrist and remove it before he leaves, will you?"

"Right away Mrs. President."

"Thank you," Charlie said.

"No, thank you Charlie, you certainly had the stage earlier today to make a stink about being detained and having to agree to be placed under electronic surveillance in order to graduate from college and you didn't. You could have used that same stage to rail against my policies and you didn't do that either. That says a lot to me about your character and besides, I've been getting a lot of bad press lately and I don't need anymore."

"You are aware of my position?"

"Yes, I know you are a member or AAMO and a vocal opponent of our presence in the Middle East. I get briefings on anything I want Charlie."

"A majority of the Arab population doesn't want us there. The attack on the Gaffney is the latest example of that attitude," Charlie replied.

"I would disagree but the data that I would use to support my position is classified, so why don't we have that discussion on another day?"

Hays turned to Edgars.

"Reverend, I invited all of you today to have a discussion with all of you in confidence. Can, I count on everyone present not to discuss this subject with anyone outside this room?"

Hays got nods from everyone.

"Good, now Casey, I wanted you to be the first to know. Though I'm not going announce my intentions immediately and I haven't decided upon a date, but I want you to know that I intend to pardon Mohammad Baghai. I am going to meet with his attorney tomorrow and communicate this message to her as well."

"Thank you, why are you being so furtive and not going to do it immediately?"

"Casey, you opposed me on principle and though I didn't like it I certainly respected you for doing it. However, certain people on Capital Hill decided you jump on your bandwagon, for purely political purposes. Soon articles of impeachment will be voted out of committee to the floor of the House. Though Speaker Richt is on point, Senator Dunston is orchestrating this. You see he still feels that I stole the Presidency from him and wants to run again. I believe that he thinks by eliminating me and the Vice President will give him a clear path to the White House."

"I'm going to deal with him first before I issue a pardon, otherwise it would appear that I am being forced to grant a pardon to save my skin."

"So Mohammad is just a pawn in the political struggle between you and Senator Dunston?"

"No, Casey, it is always been my position that I wouldn't make a decision on a pardon until after his legal proceedings were concluded and it is a little known fact that I am opposed to the death penalty. I had already decided to commute his sentence to life if he had been sentenced to lethal injection. I also made the decision early on to wait until everything shook out before I made a decision. At any rate, you have the word of the President of the United States, that Mohammad Baghai will be pardoned. In the mean time, please continue your crusade and take all the credit you feel appropriate when I announce my decision."

"Thank you. You are being very magnanimous. I hadn't any idea that you were opposed to capital punishment," Edgars said.

"Years ago, I lost my husband and my unborn baby within a matter of a few weeks. I learned from those experiences that life is precious and no one alive has any idea how much it distresses me when I have to order our young men and women into combat situations."

Hays glanced at Charlie, understood the President's reference.

"Heather, I understand that you will be a Marine after you finish school."

Hays changed the subject.

"Yes, Mrs. President." Heather as member of the military chose not to address her commander in chief by her first name, feeling that it was entirely inappropriate.

"The Vice President is a retired Marine; perhaps I can introduce you to him sometime in the future?"

"It would be my pleasure ma'am."

"I want you to email me when you start your senior year and keep me apprised of your progress. Will you do that for me?"

"Of course ma'am."

"Here, let me give you my personal email address. Please don't give this out to anyone."

Hays wrote it down on a piece of paper.

"I won't ma'am."

"It's been a pleasure meeting all of you and I do appreciate everyone taking the time to visit with me, but the American taxpayers are paying my salary so I need to get back to work."

"We understand. Thank you for allowing us to visit," Jo Ann replied.

"Charlie, don't forget to have Ron remove that bracelet."

"I will. Thank you again."

After bidding her guests goodbye Hays walked back to her office and used the Bat Phone to call the Vice President's office. Taylor was scheduled to leave for Chicago for the Olympic Opening Ceremonies and then return to Washington immediately afterwards. Hayes wanted him to make a detour to Pensacola.

"Yes Madam President."

Taylor picked up in his office in the White House.

"Tom, I've made some decisions on some relevant issues, which you need to be in the loop, before I announce them and I have some ideas, on other issues, because of your military background, I want to bounce off you."

"You should be able to arrive here by 6 PM and we will discuss it over dinner; I'm cooking and we'll be having seafood. You can leave for Washington afterwards."

Hays knew that Taylor preferred Texas beef.

"Certainly Madam President, report at 1800 hours. I'll be there."

Hays hung up the phone. Tomorrow she would meet Isabelle Franks in the morning and the Vice President in the evening. Both would be surprised to learn of her plans.

AGENT George Hickey was sitting at a desk inside the guesthouse at the President's home, investigating AAMO's web site. Charlie Michaels wasn't lying when he said he didn't write the blogs, derogatory of the President. The IP address was from a UWF router and server, which meant that any student possessing a laptop, a wireless connection card and a password could have authored them and if the laptop was unregistered, as most computers were, the blogger could be almost anyone. Assuming that the author was another AAMO member, and the Secret Service didn't make assumptions, there were still at least two dozen possible threats to the President. That left too many names to be investigated and the protection detail wouldn't have the authority to detain any of them without any more proof than conjecture and innuendo. Though the President over-ruled him by ordering it removed, Hickey knew in his gut that Michaels was not a presidential threat, but his gut also told him that someone or something was not kosher. Unfortunately, the Secret Service didn't act on gut instincts and that left the team holding an empty bag. Hickey opened a bottle TUMS and swallowed two to curb his heartburn. He had a feeling that he would consume many more in the next few days.

THE Angel also swallowed two TUMS. Over the last few months, he had suffered, what he thought was an ulcer. He probably should've seen a doctor to treat it, it would leave a paper trail, which the FBI would eventually find and that was something that he couldn't afford. He had remained alive so far by being wise and cautious, taking calculated risks, which the benefits of these risks were worth taking. Contacting and enlisting Sabaya had been such a risk.

To begin with, the burning sensation in his stomach was nothing more than an annoyance, but over time, the pain grew progressively worse, but nothing compared to the degree when he was a prisoner in Israel. Though the KGB of the former Soviet Union enjoyed the reputation of unjust imprisonment and torture, it was the Mossad, which were the masters of it. Additionally, because every several months a Palestinian brother would blow himself up to kill a few Israeli citizens, the Mossad were able to ply their techniques and still be able to fly under the international media's radar.

Another such risk, though objectively, the rewards didn't justify it was Julie Stewart, the schoolteacher, whom he had been seeing while he was residing in Chicago, for the past year. Objectively, he should never have gotten involved with her, though his carnal desires precluded that. Objectively, he should have killed her immediately after fulfilling his lusts, with her body, their last night together, though he would have to dispose of her body, which would involve other risks. She was just a whore, with no morals and didn't deserve the dignity of a quick death. Instead he decided that the whore would suffer a miserable death. After subjecting her to the indignities and sexual perversions that no woman of faith be she Christian, Jew or Muslim, should have to endure; indignities and perversions, she craved and begged for like a drug addict craving for a fix, he gave her a gift. It was a trinket attached to a thick gold chain, suitable as a necklace. A local jeweler spot-welded the trinket to the gold chain foor him. The trinket however, was deadly, since it was a nugget made radioactive by Strontium 90, both alluring and now lethal.

Both he and Sabaya were reviewing the final preparations for tomorrow's attack in Chicago. The plan was simple. Sabaya, dressed as a Chicago policeman and riding the motorcycle, which carried the dirty bomb, would follow the Vice President's motorcade. As a motorcycle cop, Sabaya would be wearing a helmet and sunglasses, obscuring his face. As the Vice President's limousine approached the Olympic stadium Sabaya would race ahead of the motorcade and park his bike near where the Vice President would exit he vehicle and walk a safe distance away. After the Vice President exited Sabaya would detonate the dirty bomb from a safe distance away, killing Taylor, his protection detail and innocent bystanders in the area, contaminating the area with radio-active debris. Sabaya would escape in the confusion and would both men would escape separately. The Angel would be nearby with a second detonating device should Sabaya's device fail. The Angel had prepared a contingency plan, which he neglected to inform Sabaya, and with the help of Allah, there wouldn't be any surprises.

"Do you have any questions Abu? Make sure you are on the far side of the limousine when you detonate the bomb so it will shield you from the blast, then escape as quickly as you can. No one will question you so long as you are dressed as a policeman."

"None at all, it is a good plan and if Allah wills it, we will both escape and see each other again."

"You will be wearing a second set of clothes, so you must find a secluded area and remove your uniform. You will have $5,000 in cash and a fake passport in your pockets. Take a bus to a different city and check in to a hotel for several days before purchasing a plane ticket out of the country. We will meet another time, in another place."

The two jihadists both felt confident; one, more so than the other.

# Chapter 30

"**G**ood morning, the President will be with you shortly. Please have a seat," Thomas said perfunctorily.

"Thank you."

Isabelle laid her briefcase on the floor and sat down. Though she didn't say, Isabelle assumed the President wanted to discuss the pardon issue and her laptop, as well as, Baghai's thick file was stuffed into the zippered leather laptop bag. However, since she didn't specifically say that Mohammad Baghai was going to be the topic of the discussion, Isabelle was prepared for that contingency, as best she could be as well. She had pencil and paper, for notes and her Blackberry to access the Internet, should it be necessary. Isabelle could hear the President speaking in her office, assuming that he was on the phone, though she couldn't hear the one-sided conversation clearly. After a few minutes the President was silent and moment later she came out of her office and greeted her guest. Isabelle stood up as soon as she saw her.

"Isabelle, how are you? It's good to see you again. Come in and let's talk."

Hays motioned her to enter to enter the office.

"I'm fine Mrs. President. Thank you for asking," Isabelle replied as she walked into the President's office.

"Come sit down." Hays said as she motioned her to sit in a leather-winged chair. Hays took a seat in an identical chair facing her.

"Thank you for coming on such short notice."

"Your welcome Mrs. President, it was no trouble at all."

"Non-sense! You have a small child and I know that it is no small feat to juggle schedules of two working parents, while accommodating the need of a 3-year-old. How is Tori by the way?"

"She is fine ma'am; and says hello. David is babysitting today."

Isabelle didn't want to discuss Tori's nightmares with her.

"Will you please give him my best?"

"I will Mrs. President," Isabelle replied.

"Isabelle, I asked you here for 2 reasons. Now we are speaking under the umbrella of attorney client confidentiality?"

"Technically, you're not my client ma'am and since I represent Mohammad Baghai, there may be a potential conflict of interest representing you, but you have my word that, unless I am subpoenaed, I will not reveal whatever we discuss today with anyone."

"That's good enough for me Isabelle. Now first, I want you to know that I have decided to pardon your client in the near future, though I have not decided exactly when and I don't intend to publicize my intentions at this time. You may inform your client of my decision, but officially, the White House's response to any questions concerning the issue will be that I still haven't made a decision. In fact I probably won't give you a head's up when I do decide to announce my intentions. Am I making myself clear and do you have any questions?"

Isabelle momentarily was at a loss for words. She had hoped that this was why the President invited her to the White House on the bay though a phone call could have sufficed if that was the only point of the visit. Why was she being so secretive? Since a majority of Americans, according to most opinion polls, favored a pardon, Isabelle thought that the President would want to generate as much publicity from this as possible. There was definitely, much more to this than met the eye. The President was playing politics; that was obvious, but she didn't understand the point.

"Thank you ma'am but may I ask why you want to keep your decision to yourself? You certainly could have communicated this to me over the phone."

"Actually, I have also informed Reverend Edgars of my decision yesterday, making the same stipulations to him as I just did with you. But the answer to your question to involves the second reason why I asked you here. Yes, if I had only wanted to inform you of my decision, concerning your client, I would've telephoned you, but one day this week, I expect the House Judiciary Committee to send articles of impeachment against the Vice President and me to the House floor. If so, I am going to need legal representation. Your firm has some expertise in Constitutional law and litigation and since I have already seen and had been impressed with your work, you seemed like a natural choice. Tell me, what is your sense of the articles against the Vice President and me?"

Again Isabelle was dumbfounded. Did she just hear the President say that she intended to confront the impeachment proceedings, which were stalking her, much the same way a great white shark would stalk a seal for its' next meal? By immediately announcing her intention to pardon Baghai and soliciting support from prominent religious figures, Casey Edgars in particular, she could probably avoid the debate and vote in the House, or at least ensure that the vote on impeachment would be defeated. This didn't make any sense at all. Why didn't the President try to nip this in the bud?

"Mrs. President. It would be a privilege to represent you. However, I'm not sure I understand your motivation? Any trial attorney will attempt to keep a client from being exposed to risk, i.e. going to trial. Why not announce your intentions and pardon my client immediately? That would cut the impeachment movement off at the knees and minimize, if not eliminate your exposure, to the risk. As to the articles themselves, or article, I should say, I'm not sure it would pass constitutional muster. A sitting Vice President has never had to face impeachment ever. This single article encompasses charges against both you and the Vice President. It seems highly irregular, if not completely unconstitutional. Perhaps it could be challenged in the judicial branch; in any case it would definitely require research."

"I see. That is interesting. Isabelle certain members of the Legislative Branch, you can figure out who they are, are blatantly attempting to hi-jack this government by usurping powers, specifically designated to the President, by the Constitution. That is why I have refused the subpoenas and I haven't allowed anyone in the Executive Branch to appear before the Judiciary Committee to testify concerning this issue. As far as I am concerned, to do so, would tacitly admit to Congress's authority over the Executive Branch's domain. I won't stand for it!"

Hays slapped the arm of the chair, startling Isabelle.

"I am not going to allow the opposition party in Congress run rough-shot over my administration, the way George Bush 43 allowed it to happen to him for his last two years in office. Impeachment and pardon are two unrelated issues. Mohammad Baghai will be pardoned for his crimes at time of my choosing and not before! Basically, assuming the article is passed, I expect to pardon him sometime after the House has taken a vote on the articles against the Vice President and me, but before the Senate begins debate. That is assuming that the article passes. If it doesn't then he can expect a pardon in short order. Your job of course, is to make sure the article doesn't pass. Now can you handle the job? It will be more complicated than you expect or do I need to contact another law firm to represent me?" Hays asked, though she already knew the answer to her question.

"Mrs. President, on behalf of myself and my firm we would be delighted to represent you."

"Now let me ask you your opinion Isabelle. Here is a copy of the single article against the Vice President and me and as you can read it is very word specific. It names me as President and Taylor as Vice President. Now if I was to resign my office, obviously, I would not longer be President and therefore unimpeachable. Would Taylor, as the new President be insulated, shall we say for lack of a better word, from the charge against him, since he is no longer Vice President?"

For the third time in 5 minutes Isabelle couldn't believe what she heard. Did the President just say that is intended to resign from office? After contemplating a moment, she answered the question.

"I believe another article would have to be drawn against Mr. Taylor naming him as President, but charging him with crimes while, he was Vice President. It is a point that certainly is an issue, which could be litigated. Are you really considering resignation ma'am?"

"That is my fail-safe Isabelle. I will not be only one of three Presidents to be impeached. I want you to be prepared to argue that point, should the worst case scenario come to fruition. Can you do that?"

"Certainly."

"Good, you may prepare a press release as soon as the articles are voted out of committee. Isabelle, I expect you to be lead counsel not a senior partner; rely on as many others as necessary, but you are my 'woman'. The buck stops with you. Make that point plain to your fellow partners. I will personally call you again to discuss strategies. Do you have any questions?"

"None at all Mrs. President."

"Isabelle, it was a pleasure to see you again. Thank you again for coming down to speak with me," Hays said as she and Isabelle got stood up.

"Thank you again Mrs. President, I'll be in touch."

Hays sat down at her desk and took a moment to reflect before she called Shephard. So Dunston and Richt wanted to play hard ball and remove her from office? Well she wasn't a political neophyte either. She wasn't going to resign the Presidency; it was necessary for Isabelle to believe it was a contingency. The talk of resignation was a smoke-screen to conceal her real plan. She was going to throw Dunston and Richt a huge political curve ball and they would be called out on strikes. All she need now was right opportunity spring her trap.

MALIKUL Mawt, formerly known as Yasser Saleem, AKA the Angel of Death and carrying identification identifying his as Giovanni Batista, was dressed in jeans and a polo shirt, un-tucked. He was also wearing a souvenir Olympic ball cap, bought from a kiosk and a new pair of Nike athletic shoes. His outfit, designed to blend in with the thousands of other spectators, in and about the Olympic stadium, was completed with a pair of an overpriced pair of sunglasses, purchased from the same kiosk, which he placed on his ball cap.

It was a few minutes before 10:00 AM and it had already been a long day. Both he and Sabaya had been up since 4:00. The night before, in his condo, they had destroyed every piece of paper with either of their names on it, leaving a monstrous pile of shredded paper in the middle of the floor and then they wiped virtually every surface free of finger prints. Finally, they stripped the bed sheets and did a final load of laundry, removing any traces of DNA.

After cleansing his home, he and Sabaya spent the night at his 'safe house', Julie Stewart's apartment. She had left him several voice mails for him, the first explaining that she was in the hospital. The others implored him to visit her, which he ignored. He had answered her first message and dutifully, brought her a bag of hospital necessities. She was still wearing her necklace and looked awful and her doctors didn't have a clue as to what her illness was. They would soon see dozens, if not hundreds of similar symptoms, nausea, diarrhea, fever and chills. By that time the whore would be dead and he would be out of the country.

After arising the two terrorists drove to the warehouse, where Sabaya would change into a police uniform, the two prepared the bomb's detonator. There was nothing more to do than to wait, until the appointed time. Both men were tense, but confident, keeping their thoughts to themselves. They had reviewed the plan and its contingencies a thousand times already; there was no need for another review. It was up to Allah's will now.

As the first rays of the sun revealed themselves, from the eastern horizon, both men washed, knelt facing Mecca and began the Salat ul Fajr, the Morning Prayer ritual. Sabaya prayed for success and that Allah would have mercy upon the infidels, hoping that Allah would forgive their sins out right, or at least, there sins would be purged, after suffering the fires of Janannum (Hell).

After finishing his fajr, Sabaya exclaimed, in conversational tones, a salutation.

"Oh Allah forgive me of my former and later sins, what I have kept secret and what I have done openly, what I have done extravagantly and what you know better than I do. You are the advancer and the delayer. There is no god but You."

"You quote the Prophet Muhammad," The Angel remarked.

"I thought it was appropriate," Sabaya replied.

"Yes it is. Come we have time to share a meal before we initiate our battle."

They both sat down and ate a simple meal, afterwards, Sabaya put his police uniform on, placed the bomb in a saddlebag, designed for a motorcycle and left. The Angel repeated Sabaya's salutation.

Sabaya 'patrolled' various parts of the city until the time Air Force

Two arrived, staying in contact with The Angel via radio. Blending into the motorcade was not difficult. Sabaya parked his motorcycle at the airport and merely walked around the vicinity, never stopping, always appearing that he had a purpose in his step. After Force Two touched down, The Angel merely remounted his cycle and used his flashing lights to catch up to the end of the motorcade.

IT had been an uneventful flight and hopefully an uneventful ceremony. Taylor had always said that the office of Vice President was ceremonial office, with the Vice President, not much more than a figurehead and he didn't feel different today.

Taylor boarded Air Force 2, at Andrews Air Force Base after his limousine picked him up from his home at the Naval Observatory. He was wearing a suit but as soon as the plane was airborne, he changed into khakis and a white open collar-oxford shirt, much more comfortable for traveling. He put on his suit after the plane landed, maintaining the appearance and aura of his office.

Normally there would've been a welcoming delegation at the airport, consisting of the mayor and other locally important officials. But since he would meet these people at the Olympic Stadium, so Taylor deplaned and walked, without delay to his limousine and his motorcade of three cars proceeded to the stadium, escorted by Chicago PD motorcycles.

Taylor had more important things on his mind today. After making a cameo appearance, he would fly to Florida and meet the President. Though she didn't say, he assumed that the President wanted to discuss the Baghai pardon issue and probably the upcoming impeachment battle. What did she plan to do? Pardon that murderer? That would solve a lot of headaches. That would be the smart political move, but there was a mutual disdain between the President and the Senate Majority Leader and it wasn't within her character to avoid a political fight.

He wasn't concerned about bogus charge made against him. Anyone with a double-digit IQ could tell that the charge was baseless and just a political play against him to damage his chances for election in the next campaign. The President had the right to refuse to allow testimony from other members of the Executive Branch and he might consider resigning his office, if things came to that. However, the charge against her—refusing to turn over the pardon application to Congress was serious and probably legitimate. What were plans? How did she intend to combat the charge? How did he fit into her plan? Tonight's dinner conversation would nothing, if not interesting.

THE Angel was sitting at park bench, near the entrance of the stadium, pretending to be reading a newspaper. He had noticed two surveillance cameras and there undoubtedly many more. His beard was a week old to conceal his features and he would shave it using an electric razor as soon as he left the scene.

"I am in position. ETA twenty five minutes," Sabaya said to The Angel over the radio.

The message was coded. The motorcade was actually five minutes away from the stadium and Sabaya was at the rear of the motorcade.

The Angel clicked his microphone twice to acknowledge he received the message. Then he got up from the bench and hid the remote detonator inside his folded newspaper and walked to a semi-secluded location about location about 200 yards away from where he expected the motorcade to turn into the stadium's underground vacant parking deck. The entrance was located away from where the general public was entering the stadium, which was unfortunate, but unavoidable. Casualties from shrapnel would be light, but the point of the attack was to contaminate both property and personnel with radiation.

He could see the motorcade approaching and Sabaya had overtaken the motorcade and just ahead of the Vice President's limousine.

"Oh Allah, forgive me of my former and my later sins," The Angel said as he detonated the bomb.

TAYLOR'S Secret Service bodyguard immediately leaped on him, pushing the Vice President to the floorboard.

"Get back to Air Force Two now! Initiate jailbreak procedures," The agent instructed his associate, driving the vehicle, in a calm and professional voice. The driver radioed their intentions to their escort.

'Jailbreak' was the code name for emergency evacuation protocol. The protocol called for Air Force Two to be idling at the entrance of the runway, waiting for the limousine to drive straight to the plane and the take off immediately after the Vice President and the protection detail boarded the plane. All other air traffic would be diverted to other airports while Air Force fighters would circle the airport and provide an escort to a location, to be determined, only after the Vice President was airborne.

"Young man, I appreciate your endeavors to ensure my safety, but you can get the hell off of me," Taylor ordered his bodyguard, using his authoritarian voice.

"Not yet sir, we haven't cleared the kill zone yet and we don't know what we are dealing with."

"Your knee is in my ribs."

"Sorry, Mr. Vice President."

The Secret Service Agent shifted his weight and repositioned his knee. Taylor used his strength and leverage to right himself as his bodyguard shifted his weight.

"Mr. Vice President this is not a good idea. We don't know what other threats we might be dealing with," The agent replied, with consternation in his voice.

"Duly noted, but I just vetoed you son, so let's get to Air Force Two as quick as we can. Shall we?"

The agent picked up the satellite phone and notified his superiors.

BENINO Marcos saw a mangled corpse of a motorcycle policeman lying on the ground next to an equally mangled police motorcycle. Both legs of the body were dismembered and were laying about two dozen feet from the bloody torso, pointed in opposite and unnatural directions. The policeman's left arm appeared to be broken and the lenses of his sunglasses were wedged in between his forehead and the helmet. Blood was drenched all over the man's face, making him unrecognizable. Marcos found it peculiar that despite the obvious carnage he couldn't hear any sounds. No one was in the immediate area. What had happened? This whole scenario was so strange.

Finally, a paramedic came to attend to the body. He placed a finger to the policeman's throat to check for a pulse. His lack of urgency confirmed his death. The paramedic took a cloth and wiped the blood away from the policeman's face.

Marcos was incredulous to see that the dead man's face was his! It also became apparent that Marcos seemed to be floating over his own body! Did that mean that he had died? How? What happened? The bomb, which was secured to the motorcycle, must have gone off prematurely, but he had an intuitive sense that Malikul Mawt had exploded it.

Marcos now took critical evaluation the events immediately after his apparent death. As a former Christian, he knew the differences between the Islamic and Christian doctrines of the afterlife.

Islam taught that there were four stages of life. Life in the womb, life on Earth, life in the grave and the afterlife, according the teachings of the prophet Muhammad, the Angel of death, Malikul Mawt was charged by Allah to remove the soul or ruh from a recently deceased body and allow the soul to hover over it. Marcos found it ironic that Malikul Mawt, the man took his life and he was waiting for Malikul Mawt, the Angel to take his ruh.

Shortly afterwards the ruh is taken before Allah, who commands that his or her name is either written in the registry of Heaven, the Illiyun, or the registry of hell, the sijjin. After the name is recorded in the proper register, the ruh is taken back to earth and resides in the ground where the body is buried until the Day of Judgment or Youmul qiyamah.

At the Youmul qiyamah Allah would judge all the souls that had lived on Earth and determine which ones would be sent to Heaven and who would be sent to Hell.

Marcos didn't remember the Malikul Mawt removing his soul from his body, but obviously it had since Marcos was hovering over it. When would it take him to Allah? He died while on jihad so paradise was guaranteed to him on the Youmul qiyamah. In addition, even when he was a Christian Marcos had made a point to live a virtuous life. Where was the Malikul Mawt now? Why was the Angel of death waiting to complete its mission?

A moment later, without any warning, Marcos found himself engulfed by a brilliant light and discovered that he was standing, at a distance, in front the gates of paradise. Marcos, for a peculiar reason thought of the Book of Genesis in the Old Testament of the Christian Bible. 'How awesome is this place! This is none other than the house of God; this is gate of Heaven'. He also noticed that his legs were attached to his body and the he didn't suffer any disfigurement from the explosion that had killed him.

Marcos noticed a crowd of souls standing outside the gilded, ornate gate. He wasn't sure exactly how far away they were, time and distance didn't seem to apply here, in the same way they did on Earth. As they approached, Marcos recognized faces in the crowd. He saw his Christian mother and father, friends from his childhood, other family members, who had passed away. Everyone was happy to see him and gave him embraces. Marcos was equally pleased to see his them as well.

All of the members of his welcoming committee were Filipino, his race, with one exception, an American. Marcos recognized him immediately. He was the American missionary, whom the terrorist group Abu Sayef kidnapped, along with his wife in the Philippines. The missionary was killed in a fire fight between Philippine Marines and Abu Sayef on the island of Basilan. The group wanted to rape his wife. Marcos was outraged refused to allow it and threatened to kill anyone who attempted to harm her.

"Benino, thank you for protecting my wife," the missionary said as he embraced Marcos.

Marcos also found it peculiar that he thought of himself by his Christian name and the every soul present was addressing him by his Christian name also. What did that mean?

"I personally meant you no harm to your wife."

"I know and I thank you again. My wife is alive and happy again. I prayed to our Lord Jesus to forgive your sins because you saved her from defilement."

*Our Lord Jesus, not the prophet Jesus, Marcos thought to himself.*

"Yes Benino our Lord Jesus."

The missionary read his mind.

"You were misguided on Earth but even now you already know the truth.

Come; let us enter the gates of Paradise."

Marcos understood the truth in missionary's words.

"Yes I will follow you by brother," Marcos replied.


GEORGE Hickey opened the door to the President's office and walked in unannounced. Hays immediately knew that there was an emergency and a confirmed attack or threat against her or another high government official.

"Madam President, there has been an attempt on the Vice President's life. He's unharmed and his limousine is in transit to Air Force Two."

Hays used a remote to turn on CNN.

"What happened?"

"I don't have any details ma'am but, according to an agent of the Vice President's protection detail, a bomb exploded outside his limousine, showering it with shrapnel, as it was nearing the underground parking deck at the Olympic Stadium."

"Do we know how many casualties there were?"

"No ma'am. The protection detail instituted the 'jailbreak' protocol, which calls for the limousine to immediately evacuate the area, drive directly to Air Force Two, which is standing by for immediate take off and then depart. The pilot is ordered to a fly to a designated location, only after the plane is airborne."

"Have there been any other attacks?"

"Not at this time ma'am."

"Very well keep me advised," Hays ordered.

"Yes Madam President," Hickey said as he exited the office.

"Oh George?"

"Yes Madam President?"

"I'm taking an unscheduled, unannounced trip to Tampa tonight."

"Ma'am?"

"Central Command, McDill Air Force Base. I am going to pay General Norman a visit. We will be returning to Pensacola afterwards. George this trip is strictly under the radar. Keep a low profile when you make your preparations."

"Yes ma'am."

Hickey left her office a second time.

Hays used the Bat Phone and called Scarboro.

"Yes Mrs. President," Scarboro answered.

"Jim you know about the attack on the Vice President?"

"Yes ma'am, the Secret Service notified your cabinet and advised us to be ready to relocate, if necessary."

"How soon will it be before we know that particulars Jim?"

"The FBI is begun its investigation, though it's way to early to determine anything substantive."

"I want you to call me in an hour with what ever you have. Understand?"

"Yes ma'am."

Hays hung up the phone and then called Shephard.

"Andy, I want you to contact the networks. I am going speak to the nation tonight."

"About the explosion?"

"You can tell the press that."

"What time? Do I need to have the speech writer contact you?"

The Presidential speechwriter was a paid staff position in the White House. The President would normally give the talking points to him and inform him of the desired duration of the speech and the speechwriter would compose the President's oratory.

"No Andy, I'm going to write my own."

There was pregnant pause over the line. Both Shephard and the President realized the significance of her last statement. By allowing the speechwriter to compose her speeches, any President was tacitly allowing the points, supporting the speech's theme to be sanitized, molded and polished. In other words, a proposed speech was made 'politically correct'. The President would review and edit the speech, as she felt appropriate; omitting sentences and adding others and there would be, on occasion, negotiation on the verbiage and sentence structure. In the end, no government, religion or person was likely to be offended—unless that was the intent of the message. By choosing to write her own speech the President was cutting everyone out of the loop, which could and probably would become, considering the political climate, very contentious.

The only question was who would suffer the President's wrath? She was under fire from several different directions. The Iranians had been giving her headaches on the international theater. Edgars was still calling for a pardon for Mohammad Baghai and Dunston appeared to be conspiring with Richt to orchestrate the impeachment proceedings against her.

Later in the week the Judiciary Committee would pass the impeachment resolution and send it to the House floor. There it was only a fifty-fifty bet if the resolution would be defeated. Anyone or all of them could become a legitimate political target but Shephard couldn't conceive a positive endgame in any scenario.

"Are you sure Mrs. President?"

"Yes, I am. Andy, I appreciate your concerns but don't attempt to dissuade me. Is that clear?"

"Very well, I'll call you when I've made the arrangements."

"Very good."

Fate had presented Hays with the circumstances she needed to crush Dunston.

AS explosions went, this one, judging from the destruction appeared to be ordinary. Battalion Chief Stan Gabreski, of the Chicago Fire Department had seen more powerful ones when he was a probationary fireman, while he was still in firefighter's school. Even those explosions at 'Firefighter U' were also insignificant compared to the ones he had seen, when he was aboard the Missouri, during Desert Storm. No one could fully appreciate the destruction caused by an explosion until they saw and heard a 16-inch round impact a target. The 'Mighty Mo' pounded its' targets in Iraq to rubble with ease and Gabreski never forgot the destruction the shells created.

There was only one dead body, a Chicago PD motorcycle cop. Both he and his bike were both mangled messes. Shrapnel from the bike sprayed the crowd and other motorcycle cops injuring dozens, some seriously, but this terrorist attack, if that what it indeed was, appeared to missed the mark. The Vice President was alive and there was relatively little carnage.

The Chicago Cops would want to take the lead on this high profile investigation, especially since one of their own was dead and Chicago's finest had clearly been caught with their pants down on this attack, but that wasn't going to happen. This clearly fell under Chicago Fire Department domain. The head cop in charge hadn't stopped by to attempt to assert his authority over the scene yet but that was coming. Gabreski would dispose of him in short order, quoting city ordinances and inviting the cop to look them up in the manual, which always carried in his fire-engine red command car. The FBI might be more difficult to deal with but he would address the issue with them when the time came.

He saw a cop with gold braid on his uniform walking in his direction, which he assumed, would start a pissing contest over jurisdiction. The cop was about a dozen steps from him when a fireman from one of his stations, Joe Robinson, blew past the cop, just before he and the cop were about to exchange introductions. The cop seemed irritated that a junior fireman would interrupt him. Gabreski got an inner laugh from the cop's expression just before his adam's apple sank to his stomach.

"Chief, we got a big problem."

"What do you have Robinson?" Gabreski said ignoring the cop, a captain, he judged by the silver eagles on his uniform, which irritated him even more.

"Take a look Chief."

Robinson took out a hand-held radiation detector from the right pocket of his jacket and plugged it in to a palm-pilot, which was retrieved from the left pocket and then showed Gabreski the readout.

"Holy Mary, mother of God! Where did you take these readings?" Gabreski demanded from Robinson.

"At the blast site sir."

"You, what's your name?" Gabreski asked the cop, but not waiting for a reply; he saw that his last name was Freeman, from the name badge on his uniform.

"Captain Freeman, this is a hand-held radiation detector. Basically, this says that the explosion was a dirty bomb and this area has been contaminated by radioactive debris."

"What do you need from me?" Freeman asked. Clearly he was as shocked as Gabreski was a moment ago

"First, have someone notify Homeland Security. They have a response team trained for this. Also, notify all the hospitals to be prepared to treat patients for radiation exposure. Second, clear everyone away from any debris; it's radioactive. The response team will remove it. Third, any casualty has to be stripped of their clothing." Gabreski saw the dismayed and shocked reaction from Freeman.

"Captain, anyone who has been showered with shrapnel has also been showered with radioactivity. Men get stripped to their boxers, women down to their bras and panties. No exceptions. I'll have my men gather the clothing in a pile for removal. Robinson we're going to need plenty of blankets for the casualties." Gabreski ordered his subordinate.

"You can't just burn them Chief?"

"Yes but burning won't destroy the radioactive particles—they're sub-atomic."

"Anything else?"

"Yeah, I'm ordering every pumper truck I have here to hose down the area to wash the particles into the sewers and into Lake Michigan. I need plenty of room for the trucks and a separate space for portable showers. Anyone wounded who can walk needs to be washed down to remove any radioactive particles that may be on their body. Also, the television and radio stations need to make announcements to the public. People who were here and left need to place their clothing in a plastic bag, place it outside for retrieval and thoroughly shower."

"I'm on it," Freeman said.

"Robinson," Gabreski spoke to his subordinate.

"Yes Chief."

"Break out the MOPP suits we have here. I'll have every suit in the city here in 30 minutes."

MOPP is an acronym for Mission Oriented Protection Posture. A MOPP suit covers someone head to toe, complete with boots, gloves, hood and gas mask and is designed to protect its wearer from radioactive contamination. It was originally designed for the military to allow soldiers to perform their duties in a nuclear fallout environment. The Chicago firemen would wear them to gather the discarded clothing, identify 'hot' debris and use their hoses and pumper trucks to hose down the infrastructure, around the blast site.

"It has been done already Chief."

Gabreski didn't hear Robinson's reply as he was on the radio ordering every MOPP in the city suit to be delivered to his command post.

YASSER Saleem, AKA Malikul Mawt and now known as Giovanni Batista was driving a used Chevrolet Impala, which he purchased several months ago, using a false identity; this one, the name of Pope Paul VI. He smiled to himself when he thought the irony of a Muslim, in a state of jihad, having struck the most devastating blow against America since 9-11, using the name of an infidel Italian Catholic Pope, as a false identity to make good his escape. He looked Italian and spoke the language well enough that anyone but a first or second generation Italian wouldn't be able to recognize his accent. He wouldn't travel near anyplace named 'Little Italy', while he was on the run. During his drive he used the electric razor to cut and shave his beard. He would do a more thorough job later.

He had planned to kill Sabaya all along; he never left loose ends and Sabaya, like Julie Stewart knew him personally. Both could connect him to the attack and both were gullible and naïve.

'Batista' knew that the blast would not likely damage the armored limousine, much less kill the Vice President; instead he detonated it while Sabaya was still riding the motorcycle, as it passed the largest group of pedestrians visible. Sabaya's death was assured and hopefully the death dozens of other infidels.

After detonating the bomb Batista removed the sunglasses from his ball cap, put them on and walked approximately a mile to his car which he had parked in a rented parking space, paid for in cash two months in advance. No one paid any particular attention to him; many were going in the same direction as he was, in fact.

His plan was to spend the next five hours driving down Interstate 55 to St. Louis and spend the night there, paying cash for all of his expenses. Then, depending upon what his instincts told him he would either stay there for several days, changing motels daily, drive on to Memphis, continuing on I-55, or board a plane in St. Louis, which would eventually take out of the country. He had plenty of money for whatever course of action he chose--$5,000 in a fanny pack and another $5,000 hidden in the trunk. He also had plenty of time and he would use it wisely. He had his cruise control set at 62mph. He wouldn't be caught speeding and there wouldn't be any of his fingerprints found when he decided to abandon the car since he was wearing driving gloves. In any case he would be out of the country by the end of the week.

AIR Force Two was in the air flying in a circular pattern over the plains states. Jailbreak was executed without incident. The limousine pulled directly onto the runway beside the rolling stairs and the Vice President, in the middle of a human shield was hustled up the stairs and into the plane. Air Force Two was rolling 30 seconds later and airborne 30 seconds after that.

Taylor was in a conference room speaking to Hays.

"Tom, I'm glad that you and your detail were unharmed."

"Thank you Mrs. President but I feel embarrassed actually. I didn't realize it was it was an explosion until my bodyguard jumped on me. It was nothing compared to Iraq."

"I'll take your word for it. Tom, I know you were supposed to visit here but as soon as the Secret Service thinks it is safe, I want you to go to Tampa."

"Tampa?"

Taylor knew that something huge was up.

"Yes, I am going to fly to there and meet you and General Norman there after I make the speech, but you don't need to announce that, then I'm flying back here to Pensacola. He can give you a preliminary briefing.

"Yes ma'am, a briefing? You're not going back to Washington?"

"No, I'm going to address the nation tonight and I'm going to call General Norman after I hang up with you. That was a terrorist attack on American soil by some Muslim cell. Scarboro called me a few minutes ago, one of the Chicago motorcycle cops was an imposter; he hasn't been identified yet but I'll wager he has links to al-Qaeda."

"Aren't you making dangerous assumptions ma'am?"

"Tom, I think that's a very reasonable assumption."

"Very well, I'll look forward to speaking to you after your speech Mrs. President."

Taylor knew something big was about to happen and he also knew not to ask her any questions.

Hays hung up the phone and then she phoned to Central Command.

"General Norman, this is the President…"

# Chapter 31

The camera crews assigned to President Hays, while she was in Pensacola, were assembled inside her three-car garage. There were camera technicians, from each network, attempting making finial adjustments on their equipment, endeavoring to capture a perfect image of the President, when she began her speech. Lighting and sound technicians were doing the same.

A podium, with the presidential seal and a curtain, serving as a backdrop, was at one end of the garage and faced the cameras. Several microphones protruded from it. The media wanted to set up for the speech in the President's office, inside her house, but Hays vetoed that idea, since it wasn't practical. She had to work, so the garage was the only other practical choice. Since Hays was going to speak in an area large enough to accommodate spectators, a request was made for her to take questions after the speech, but was refused. Hays would have more important issues to deal with immediately after her speech.

Earlier in the day, she had contacted CENT COM commander, Army General Frank Norman and ordered him to give her a briefing over the phone of the readiness of his forces. Hays found it a little ironic that virtually all of the military forces currently available to Central Command were naval, which was the task force in the Persian Gulf. Other than storage posts, where hardware, such as tanks, trucks and artillery, located on a few insignificant islands, in and around the Gulf, guarded by Army personnel, there were no 'ground ponders' in the Middle East.

Hays smiled. It wasn't often that a President escaped the scrutiny of the national media. She was about to. George Bush 43 did it one year at Thanksgiving. The press thought he was going spend the holiday with his family in Crawford, Texas, but he pulled a fast one and showed up in Iraq, to spend it with American Servicemen.

Hays was going to do him one better tonight. Immediately after the speech she was going to ride to the airport and board Air Force One. The press may notice her departure but she would be in the air before anyone would have a chance to follow her and be on the ground in Tampa within the hour. After a conference with General Norman and his staff, she would return to Pensacola. With any luck she would be back in time for the opening monologue of Letterman.

Earlier Scarboro had called her with a situation report on the terrorist attack. The dead motorcycle cop was an imposter, identified by his picture as Abu Sabaya, AKA Benino Marcos, and a former member of the Philippine separatist group Abu Sayef. He was Muslim, with connections to al-Qaeda. Al Reynolds confirmed all of this. The explosion dispersed radioactive material but because of the quick action of the Chicago Fire Department disaster had been averted. She would make a point thank the man who took charge of the situation, Chief Stanley Gabreski.

Sabaya had an accomplice and apparently was double-crossed by someone. Sabaya had a remote detonator on his person and undoubtedly intended to detonate the RDD Taylor exited his limousine. He wore civilian clothes underneath the uniform and there was several thousand dollars on his person, at the time of the explosion. The FBI was investigating and had some leads, thanks to several security cameras, but Hays suspected that since he had obviously planned to tie up all his loose ends he had planned a foolproof extraction plan. He was probably long gone. The FBI would find his trail until he was out of the country and unreachable.

"George, are we set?" Hays asked Hickey who was standing outside her office.

"Yes Mrs. President, as you enter your garage, the driver will enter the limousine and watch your speech on television. After you conclude you will immediately be escorted to the idling vehicle and the motorcade of two cars will depart to the airport. Air Force One will depart to Tampa, escorted by Two F-22s from Eglin."

Eglin Air Force Base was approximately 50 miles east of Pensacola, located in-between the cities of Fort Walton Beach and Niceville.

"After your conference, you will return to the Pensacola airport and be escorted back here."

"Fine, let's do this."

Hays, after speaking with Isabelle Franks, had constructed a political mousetrap for Dunston and Richt and she needed the correct circumstances to set it. Fate had provided the circumstances with the Olympic terrorist attack and this speech tonight would be the bait.

The garage was originally a stand alone building, 60 feet from the main building, but a hallway was built, connecting the two buildings when Hays became President. She had conducted press conferences in the garage on occasion, so the media wouldn't suspect her escape plan. The media would be kept 'hostage' in the garage for a couple of minutes, just long enough for her to depart, though they probably wouldn't even be aware of the their captivity, since they would begin to disassemble their equipment.

Hays entered the garage, walked to the podium, where she was given a cue and a countdown from five.

"Good evening my fellow Americans. Earlier today America and every peace-loving nation of the world were deliberately and viscously attacked by terrorists. The cowardly and dastardly attack was designed to kill as many people as possible by means of a radioactive dispersal device, better known as a dirty bomb. The cowardly and dastardly attack was also an assassination attempt on the Vice President. A Philippine terrorist, named Benio Marcos, with links to al-Qaeda and Iran, disguised as a Chicago Policeman, wearing civilian clothes underneath the uniform, while riding a police motorcycle, approached the Vice President's motorcade, as he was traveling to the Olympic stadium where the bomb was exploded. He was also carrying several thousand dollars in cash on his person. It is clear that he intended to escape after exploding the bomb and killing the Vice President, as well as innocent by-standers. "

"I am pleased to report to you that casualties were extremely light and the contaminated area has been cleaned, due in large part to the immediate and decisive actions of the Chicago Fire Department and Chief Stanley Gabreski. Chief Gabreski, the firemen and paramedics of the City of Chicago and every other public servant, who helped save lives and maintain order, during this time of crisis, on behalf of a grateful nation, I say thank you."

"A response team from Homeland Security has already removed the contaminated debris and has been cleaning up the contaminated area. The area in and around the Olympic stadium is free from contamination. To the citizens Chicago, the Citizens of the State of Illinois and guests visiting Chicago to view the Olympics, let me emphasize that this cowardly and dastardly attack will neither stop, nor even delay the games."

Hays had concluded the fluff portion of her speech now she was about to bite into the red meat. It would be short and sweet.

"Since the days before Christ, in ancient Greece, warring city-states, such as Athens, Sparta and others would cease combat during the ancient olympics. Peace between armies was expected and was maintained during this time. This cowardly and dastardly attack during the games was deliberate and designed to cause terror, international mistrust and conflict and it can not and will not be tolerated."

"In addition to this cowardly and dastardly attack, Iran has also twice attacked an American Naval Frigate, the USS Gaffney in the Persian Gulf. Once, an Iranian military aircraft launched an anti-ship missile at the Gaffney. Fortunately, the missile was shot down and no one was hurt. Less than a week later Iranian suicide terrorists also attacked the Gaffney at the port of Jebel Ali by attempting to ram a boat packed with explosives and radioactive material into the ship. It was the same radioactive material that was used in the attack today. Again the enemy was engaged and destroyed before anyone was hurt though radioactive fall out was released in and around the area."

The nationality of bombers hadn't been confirmed but Hays wasn't about to let the facts stand in the way of the truth.

"Furthermore the United States has visual evidence, in the form of satellite imagery that Iran has supported al-Qaeda terrorism in the past as well as this attack on American soil. An al-Qaeda terrorist training camp is located near the town of Furg, Iran, as well as a stockpile of Strontium-90, the radioactive material used in both the attack on the Gaffney and today's explosion."

Again the type radioactive material had not been confirmed and again the facts clouded the truth.

"Terrorist attacks and the countries which support terrorism are today's moral equivalent of Nazi Germany, Stalinist Russia, Mao's China or Saddam Hussein's Iraq. Iran is such a country and its' hostile acts can not and will not be tolerated by this President. They can not and will not be tolerated by this country and they can not and will not be tolerated this community peaceful nations."

"To that end, earlier today, I ordered a cruise missile attack by American Naval forces in and around the Persian Gulf and the Arabian Sea to destroy this terrorist base in retaliation for the attack earlier today in Chicago. Furthermore, I am ordering the Iranian Prime Minister Hassan Nassiri to capture and detain every member of the al-Qaeda terrorist network, within Iran's borders, until they are transferred to American custody. Failure to comply with these demands within 48 hours will result in the severest consequences for Nassiri and Iran. Thank you and good evening."

Hays immediately left the podium and walked backed through the hall out through the door directly to her limousine. She just jumped out of the frying pan and into the fire. Hopefully the fire wasn't as hot as the fires that Mohammad Baghai claimed to experience.

Hays placed a call to Andy Shephard on the secured phone, after Air Force One was airborne.

"Andy, I assume that my speech stirred the pot back in Washington."

"Mrs. President I have taken calls from the Secretaries of State,

Defense, Homeland Security and several members of Congress. They all want to know what you are doing. I didn't have an answer for them. What are you planning?"

"Andy, I'm flying to Tampa to confer with General Norman. Afterwards I am flying back to Pensacola. I'll call you when I am back."

"Mrs. President, I strongly suggest that you return to Washington as soon as you conclude the meeting with the General. There are a lot of bruised egos that need to be soothed and you will be able to do it."

Shephard was referring to the inside the beltway mind set of 'decision by consensus'. Ever cabinet secretary thought that he or she was the most intelligent person in the world and every senior Senator thought that he or she should be the next President and could definitely do a better job than the current occupant of the position. Navigating through dozens of immense egos made efficient government all most impossible and created chaos when a president took immediate and decisive action.

"Andy, Washington is the last place I want to be right now. I will discuss the issues with you when I return to Pensacola."

That was the end of the discussion.

PRESIDENT Hays, Vice President Taylor and Army General Frank Norman were in a large room viewing an electronic map of the Persian Gulf and the surrounding countries.

Norman was a second generation West Point graduate and an infantryman by trade. He was the same age as Taylor and had graduated in the top 10percent of his class.

Except for age Taylor and Norman had nothing in common. Norman, an excellent soldier, a trait that Taylor respected, was also was a public relations master. He was equally at ease at a black tie cocktail party as he was in combat fatigues. He was knowledgeable every current political topic and made it a point to be an authority of all branches of the United States Armed Services, since Central Command was a multi-branch command.

He was as eloquent articulate and intelligent as he was dashing, with Fred Astaire good looks. Norman never seemed to have a hair out of place or wrinkle in his uniform. Questions had been raised concerning he future after his retirement, which was scheduled for next year. Norman had been silent on the issue, except that he made it clear that he had no interest in politics.

Because of their polar opposite personalities and that both men were infantrymen by trade, Taylor and Norman got along very well.

Taylor had recommended Norman to Hays to fill the Central Command vacancy three years before. After interviewing Norman, Hays also impressed appointed him to the position.

"Madam President earlier today, we launched 10 BGM-109 Tomahawk missiles, carrying 500 kilogram warheads at the al-Qaeda base, near Furg. Five were from the attack submarine Indianapolis and five were from the missile cruiser Leyte Gulf. The Navy flew a reconnaissance flight, from the Bush over the target and as you can see from the photographs, it has been destroyed."

The before and after photographs showed a compound of half dozen buildings completely decimated, with huge craters pock marking the desert.

"Is there any way to confirm a body count General?"

"Not from not from the air ma'am. That would require intelligence assets on the ground, which we don't have."

"Very well, General I want you to draw up plans to destroy Iran's oil producing infrastructure starting with its' off shore drilling platforms and eventually its' inland rigs and refineries. I want the attacks to be conducted using cruise missiles and I want you to be prepared to attack with in 48 hours, if given the order. Gentlemen, I see confused looks on your faces. What are your thoughts?"

"Madam President, I can attack any GOSP, which is what we call offshore platforms, an acronym for Gas and Oil Surface Platform, with cruise missiles in an hour but, using them may not be the best tactic. Cruise missiles, such as the Tomahawk are excellent for targets on land, because can navigate via a digital strip map, in its' memory, but they are not always as effective on floating targets. A strike force from the Bush might achieve more effective results," Norman replied.

"Harpoons are available, aren't they General?" Taylor asked.

"Mr. Vice President we have both the RGM-84 Harpoon and the SS-N-12 Sandbox missiles. They are both anti-ship missiles, which both could be used against oil platforms. The issue is that they both use infrared or radar as guidance. Infrared guidance in a heat seeking tracking method much like an air to air sidewinder missile and could conceivably be defeated in the same way any missile counter measures defeat a hostile missile."

Hays had a confused look.

"I see that I lost you Madam President. An attacked plane releases a canister of burning phosphorous, which burns much hotter than the jet engines and canister is designed to attract the missile to itself instead of the target."

"Radar guidance systems can be jammed, which would cause

the missile to fly off aimlessly. My point is that if the Iranians know that we are firing cruise missiles at them, then they may be able to act accordingly and counter them. An air strike avoids these complications."

"General, I don't want one American pilot fired upon much less shot down. Cruise missiles are more expensive than a bomb but not nearly as expensive as a human life. That's why I want you to start with the off shore platforms, fewer civilian lives at risk. If the Iranians are able to counter act our cruise missile attacks then we can bring surface ships in close and fire on the platforms, can we not?"

"Certainly Madam President, I was playing devil's advocate. I don't expect the Iranians to able to effectively defend their GOSPs."

"Good. Iran, al-Qaeda and Prime Minister Nassiri were behind today's attack and I intend to eliminate the terrorist threat from Iran once and for all. If it means destroying Iran's ability to produce oil then so be it."

"Yes ma'am."

"General would you give the Vice President and me a few minutes please?"

"Yes ma'am," Norman said and he left Hays and Taylor alone.

Taylor glared at the President. He knew that this charade wasn't a military planning session, but a pretense for what was about to come. It had politics written all over it. Taylor had the feeling that he was somehow a pawn in the political battle, between the White House and Capital Hill, a puppet, whose strings were being pulled by puppet master Hays and he didn't like it. He agreed that Hays' retaliatory strike was appropriate and necessary and he liked her attitude concerning escalation, but there was more to this than met the eye. Taylor knew this and he knew that Hays knew that he knew this.

"What is going here Mrs. President? This isn't about Iran, though I like your methods for dealing with Nassiri."

"Do I need to call the Secret Service Tom? Your looks could kill."

Hays opened a briefcase and took out a document with the official presidential seal. It was folded into thirds.

"Tom this Mohammad Baghai's pardon; I want you to sign it."

"Mrs. President, you know how I feel about the man and even if I wanted to pardon him, I don't have the authority. You know that."

"You don't now Tom but soon you will."

Taylor wasn't sure he heard her correctly. Was she going to resign her office?

"Are you resigning Mrs. President?"

"Not in a million years Tom."

"I'm not following you."

"How familiar are you with the 25th Amendment?"

Taylor thought he knew exactly what she referring to, but he knew he was still missing something. The 25th Amendment provided a clear line of succession should the Presidency become vacated. It was ratified in 1967 as a result of President Kennedy's assassination. But unless Hays died in office or resigned, it didn't apply here.

"It has to do with presidential succession."

"Tom you and I both know that these impeachment charges against us are just bullshit."

"Of course I do."

"It's just a thinly veiled political power play by Richt and I suspect, Dunston. Dunston is going to run against you in the next election and wants you out of the picture. You can't be removed from the equation without taking me out first, which is why we are about to be impeached."

"I know that Mrs. President."

"I've hired Isabelle Franks represent me in the impeachment trial should it come and for practical purposes, she represents you also, unless you want to hire your own separate counsel, but I don't expect it to come to that."

"Again, I'm not following you ma'am."

"I've purposely left Washington, secluded myself in Pensacola and then basically declared war on Iran, without consulting you, my cabinet, or Congress. Do my actions sound like those of a sane person? Certainly I'm not able to discharge the duties of my office, wouldn't you agree?"

Taylor grinned. He now knew exactly what Hays had in mind. The 25th Amendment in part, stated that when 'the Vice President and a majority of the principle officers of the executive departments', the cabinet secretaries which had been so designated by Congress, 'transmit to the President pro tempore of the Senate and the Speaker of the House of Representatives their written declaration that President is unable to discharge the powers and duties of his office, the Vice President shall immediately assume the powers and duties of the office as Acting President.'

If Hays was unable to discharge the powers and duties of the office and removed from office, her cabinet would have to justify her removal. Undoubtedly her mental competence would be the reason and if she wasn't competent to be President, then she obviously wasn't competent to contribute to her defense at an impeachment trial. In fact it would be a legal question if a President judged unfit for office and legally removed via the 25th Amendment could be impeached at all? Furthermore, would the American pubic stand for it? If Casey Edgars could create a ground swell movement, strong enough to cause the President to be impeached, he certainly could orchestrate the same movement to call for the movement's cessation. He could but would he? In any case, the PR aside, the litigation could tie the issue up or years and Isabelle Franks' law firm was certainly capable of doing it.

As Acting President, Taylor didn't believe he could be impeached as Vice President, another legal conundrum, probably requiring years of litigation to sort out. By pardoning Baghai, an act he didn't want to do, but appeared to be a political necessity, he could take the moral high ground and would cut off the impeachment movement at the knees. Dunston and Richt would be left in deep dark political dog squeeze, if they continued a public vendetta against the President and the Vice President.

The only question was how soon after this impeachment movement ran out of steam would be how the President, want her job back. The 25th Amendment provided for the President, Hays, to transmit to the President Pro Tempore of the Senate and the Speaker of the House that no disability existed, she was able to discharge the duties and powers of the office and resume exercising her duties. There was more to the amendment, but Taylor couldn't recall all the specifics. There was something about that if the Vice President and the cabinet were of the opinion that the President still could not discharge the powers and duties the office, both Houses of Congress would decide, requiring a two thirds vote in each to remove her from office.

It was brilliant political stroke! Though a Senate impeachment trial required a two thirds vote to remove both of them from office, the House of Representatives required only a simple majority vote to send the charges to trial. Even as powerful as Richt was, he wouldn't be able to assemble that many votes to remove them, following the 25th' Amendment's provisions. That was the blueprint of the plan as Taylor saw it. He was sure Hays would outline it all in the next few minutes.

"Tom, you will undoubtedly be approached by members of my cabinet to discuss my actions of the last 24 hours. At some point my fitness for service will be questioned and you will be asked to support a declaration stating that I am temporary not competent to hold office. After what you feel is an appropriate amount of contemplation, keep in mind that I have given Iran 48 hours to meet my demands, I want you to support the declaration and remove me from office."

"That probably stops the impeachment proceedings dead in its tracks temporarily, but how soon do you demand your office back?"

"Tom in article IV of the 25th Amendment, the provision states that after you and my cabinet judge me unable to discharge my duties I can at any time notify the President Pro Tempore and the Speaker that I am able to perform my duties as President. Then if you and my cabinet still judge me unfit, the Senate and the House are both notified and they both vote on the issue, within 21 days. A two thirds vote in both chambers, judging me unfit for the office is required to have me removed permanently."

"Which is a stretch in the Senate and impossibility in the House; the real question is how soon do you demand your job back?"

"Exactly, the assumption is that I would immediately notify the appropriate people that I am fit to serve, triggering a constitutional crisis, but there's nothing in the 25th Amendment that doesn't say there is a time table for me to do so. As I see it, I can state publicly that I am fit to serve to anyone who will listen and so long as I do not notify the President pro tem and the Speaker of my intentions to reclaim my office, you and I are untouchable. Tom, the article of impeachment is very specific in its wording. It specifically names me as President of the United States and you as Vice President. I'm going to have my legal team argue that I can't be impeached since I'm not President and you can't be impeached as Vice President, since you are Acting President. Isabelle Franks should be able to tie that assertion up in litigation for months if not years, certainly longer than my remaining time in office. This move takes all the political heat off of us and places it on Dunston and Richt. The wind leaves their sails when you pardon Mohammad Baghai."

Taylor didn't reply immediately. He took a moment to size up Hays. She was playing poker but he couldn't determine if she was bluffing or not. Did she intend to take a powder from the Presidency or not?

"Mrs. President you are not going to just walk away from this office."

"Of course not Tom, but this scenario gives you a free hand to prosecute terrorism as de-facto President and effectively blocks out Dunston and Richt from power. Yes, I am planning to come back but I haven't decided when. I'll give you all the latitude you need to deal with this war, in whatever way you see fit. I've ordered Admiral McClain to assemble a second fleet and be prepared to sail to the Arabian Sea. It will be up to you to decide if you want or need it. You obviously won't be able to order ground forces to the theater because of political considerations, both domestic and internationally but strategic air strikes are an option, if you decide."

"At a future point in time I plan to announce that I am fit to serve. You will then have to decide if you will again judge me unfit."

"You know I'd never be disloyal to you Mrs. President."

"I know that Tom, that's one of the reasons I chose you as my running mate. Assuming that you win the election, I might even decide to come back just in time for your inauguration."

Hays and Taylor both laughed that joke.

"Mrs. President assuming your plan works, you have just outsmarted the two most powerful members of Congress. Congratulations."

"Tom I'm going back to Pensacola now, Godspeed to you on your trip back to Washington. Oh and Tom?"

"Yes ma'am?"

"Don't forget to pardon Mohammad Baghai as soon as you take over my job."

"I will Mrs. President."

Now she, Taylor, Dunston and Richt were all now in the fire. The heat was going to be too much for someone to stand and she wasn't going to be the first to jump.

RICHT was on his 4th Black Jack and Coke. His doctor had told him numerous times that a 79 year old man, 75 pounds overweight, such as himself, needed to follow Ben Franklin's adage—'early to bed early to rise makes a man healthy, wealthy and wise'. His doctor also told him that unless he started exercising to reduce his blood pressure and started taking care of himself, he was facing a heart attack or a stroke or both.

It was all most midnight so he wouldn't be to bed early. He probably wouldn't up early and he definitely didn't feel wise either. How did Dunston get his hands those pictures of him and that buxom intern? Hell, he didn't even remember her name.

Richt walked to his bar and freshened his drink. The only thing he liked about the South was its' booze. He thought there ought to be a national holiday in honor of Jack Daniels. How many political deals had been made over Jack on the rocks? Thousands? Hundred of thousands? Though Texas was considered a Southern State, Richt considered himself a Texan and not a Southerner. He would make it a point to wear his best pair of boots when he took the oath of office and then, as his first official act as President, celebrate with a shot of Jack, in a in a rocks glass. The next conscious thought Richt had been why he was laying flat on his back.

"ANDY, I'm not going to negotiate. Iran committed an act of war by attacking this country. al-Qaeda committed an act of international terror by attacking this country and both have to be dealt with. The training base has been destroyed, but who's to say when and where Iran will build another?"

Hays was in a heated discussion with her chief of staff. The flight home was uneventful and the media was waiting for her at the airport and she was bombarded by the typical inane questions, which she ignored without appearing rude. The drive was equally uneventful, which made Hickey and Thomas very happy and upon entering the house she called Shephard, knowing full well what to expect.

"Andy, Nassiri is going to turn over every terrorist in Iran's borders, which the CIA says are present, regardless of nationality or I'm going to start bombing their oil platforms. Right now he's just assuming all this is rhetoric and not taking the United States or me seriously. I've ordered General Norman to prepare a battle plan, with specific emphasis on their offshore oil platforms. Some will have to be destroyed just to get Nassiri's attention and let him know I'm mean business. I don't think it will take him very long to reach the correct decision."

"Madam President your actions will make the United States an international pariah. It will destroy all the credibility this administration has earned in the world community during your time in the White House."

"Andy, would the American public rather have our country perceived as an international pariah or be like the Israeli public, which is under continuous threat of terrorist attack? I don't think there is really a choice, do you?"

"Is the Vice President onboard with this ma'am?" Shephard asked, avoiding her question.

"What does Taylor have to do with this Andy? I am the commander in chief. He was there because I chose to keep in the loop. Make no mistake though; I am calling the shots here and not Taylor or have you forgotten what the Constitution says? Understand?"

Shephard could see that he wasn't making any headway. Perhaps tomorrow would bring better luck.

"When are you coming back to Washington ma'am?"

"I'll call you tomorrow afternoon after I decide."

Hays hung up the phone. She didn't like treating her most loyal subordinate like an insolent teenager but it was necessary; Andy deserved better than that. He would understand after everything came to light, but that didn't make her feel better. Everyone in her cabinet and inner circle had to believe that she was not thinking clearly, whether it was from the pressures of the job, her domestic problems, this terrorist attack or a combination of all three. If, Shephard was convinced that she was incapable of thinking this crisis through, logically and without emotion, then the rest of the cabinet would believe it also. She would know for sure some time tomorrow.

# Chapter 32

"Gentlemen, why have you called this cabinet meeting, without my knowledge and consent?"

Hays said from her office, to her cabinet, though she already knew its' purpose and had already acted proactively by calling Isabelle Franks and summoning her back to Pensacola. Taylor and Shephard, her entire cabinet and CIA Director Alan Reynolds were all present in the White House conference room and were communicating via secured electronic audio conferencing.

Everyone was seated at a long oblong conference table, directly facing the person directly opposite another, though all heads were turned towards the camera and monitor, transmitting their images to Hays and showing her image to them. Hays noted that the Secretary of State, Jefferson Longstreet was sitting at the near end o the table, across from Taylor. Scarboro and the Defense Secretary were paired, facing each other, up after Taylor and Longstreet and so on down the table. Shephard was sitting at the far of the table, directly facing the monitor. Immediately before him were Admiral Sidney McClain of the Joint Chiefs of Staff and Alan Reynolds of the CIA. Beyond the group was a computer and projection accessories, used when a PowerPoint presentation was required during a meeting.

"Mrs. President, your cabinet, your Vice President, your chief of staff and your countrymen are all concerned with your actions in response to the attack in Chicago. In short we have reservations with the disproportionate in severity of your counter strike to the attack. The casualties were extraordinarily light, while the retaliatory missile attack decimated the base. In addition, your stated aggressive intentions towards Iran will trigger jihad by every Muslim terrorist cell in the world against innocent Americans, both in the United States and abroad. Furthermore, it was inappropriate for you to make last night's speech without consulting the appropriate cabinet secretaries and the leaders of our allies for counsel. In addition, what does the term 'severest consequences' mean? The leaders of the free world want to know. Mrs. President, what I am trying to say is that you have stepped on a lot of toes," the Secretary of State replied.

Longstreet, an Ivy League educated diplomat, graduated with degrees in international studies and political science, was a descendent of the Confederate General James Longstreet, had deep Georgia roots and wasn't afraid to mention his ancestry, in the course of a conversation. Hays thought he should named be 'Longwind' instead, since he always managed to use at least 3 sentences to complete a thought, which should easily be completed in 2. If every cabinet secretary thought he was the smartest person in the country, Longstreet truly believed he was the most intelligent person to hold any cabinet position at anytime in American history! His unabridged oratory was an excellent complement to his knowledge in international politics and made him a logical choice for Secretary of State, though his arrogance and condescension occasionally made him a huge pain in the ass.

"Mr. Longstreet, thank you for expressing the concerns of what I assume is the majority of my cabinet. Now before I begin, I want to let it be known that what is about to be discussed is to be kept 100percent confidential; there will be no leaks what so ever. If anyone is discovered to have discussed this with another person outside this room, I can assure you that they will be prosecuted vigorously to the maximum extent of the law. Anyone who is not comfortable with this pre-condition may leave now," Hays said.

Hays paused a moment and saw no one had left the conference.

"Very well, for the record, as I am recording this conference, no one has left and they tacitly agree to my stipulations. Mr. Longstreet, yesterday America was attacked by a cell of al-Qaeda terrorists. I don't need to discuss the ramifications of another terrorist attack on American soil."

"Mr. Reynolds has shown me intelligence that Iran and Prime Minister Nassiri was instrumental in supporting this attack. Alan, without compromising any of your assets, please describe the intelligence that you have shown me in the Oval Office."

"Mrs. President we have satellite imagery of the terrorist training camp outside of Furg, which clearly shows masked men exercising, apparently to hone physical conditioning, firing small arms for target practice, and practicing military small unit tactics. All of these activities are consistent with a terrorist training facility. It is also significant that the men are masked. This indicates 2 things. First that they know when our intelligence satellites pass and these men do not want their identities known."

"We also have human assets, which inform us that significant amounts of ordinance is regularly transported to this base and this is a further indication that the base in Furg was a terrorist training camp. It's not anymore and its' occupants are with Allah now."

Reynolds got a laugh from a few of the room's occupants.

"Thank you Director Reynolds. Mr. Scarboro, what do we know about the dead man impersonating a Chicago Police Officer?"

The Attorney General spoke.

"Mrs. President, he is a Philippine national, linked to al-Qaeda born Benino Marcos to well to do Catholic parents, but changed his name to Abu Sabaya, after his conversion to Islam. He belonged to a Muslim separatist group called Abu Sayef, operating predominately in the Southern Philippine Islands. The group bombed ferryboats, kidnapped American Missionaries and the like, before the Philippine Marines decimated it in a surprise attack."

"Marcos/Sabaya survived the attack and is believed to have migrated to Iran, training with al-Qaeda and dropped from the radar until he re-appeared yesterday. It appears that he was a patsy in this attack."

"Thank you Mr. Scarboro. Gentlemen my counter-attack was a Band-Aid fix. Other terrorist bases will be built; the only question is when and where. Other terrorists will train at these bases; the only question is who and when. Nations which support terror have done so without repercussions. That stops as of now! It's to that end why I have ordered Admiral McClain to assemble a second battle group to the Persian Gulf/Arabian Sea area and last night I ordered General Norman to prepare a battle plan to destroy all of Iran's oil producing infrastructure, beginning with its' off-shore drilling platforms. That is assuming that Mr. Nassiri does not surrender the terrorists in his country."

The group collectively gasped.

"I am aware that many of you do not agree with my actions and I will give everyone present time to argue an alternative solution but this is the scenario as I see it. First, al-Qaeda is an international terrorist network, with cells embedded in dozens of countries. Virtually all of them are in a state of jihad against the United States. Second, the countries, actively supporting these terrorist cells do not support the United States or its' policies, but require our support, whether it is financial, technological, humanitarian or military. Basically these countries want their cake and eat it also. I consider Iran such a country. Finally, such countries, which I have just described expect our support, yet continue to not only despise us, work furtively to bring our downfall."

"If we continue to allow the status quo, then we can expect other attacks on our soil. In short, unless there are consequences, countries like Iran will continue to fight an undeclared guerilla-style war against us. That is why in 36 hours the United States Navy will begin cruise missile attacks on Iran's gas and oil surface platforms, unless they surrender all terrorists in their country and their remaining supply of radioactive material which could be used to construct a RDD. I want all of you to understand that, based upon our history in dealing with terrorism, I don't expect Iran comply with my demands so their platforms will be destroyed. After what I consider an appropriate amount of time, the United States Navy will attack Iran's remaining oil infrastructure, until my demands are met."

"Mr. Longstreet you will summon the Iranian Ambassador and inform him of the consequences of his country's refusal to satisfy these demands. Gentlemen that is all I have to say. The floor is yours."

Longstreet began again.

"Mrs. President, I feel compelled to protest your rash and outrageous decision. There are certainly other avenues short of war to be explored. Diplomatic pressure against Iran can be applied in the UN for instance. We can apply an economic embargo. A blockade could certainly be considered if other measures fail. This course of action will make the United States an international pariah in the world court of public opinion. The consequences will be disastrous," Longstreet continued to speak but Hays did not listen.

Harding, the Secretary in the Interior and a former Ohio Congressman of the opposition party was next.

"Mrs. President, American oil companies have invested in Iranian oil. I am talking about billions of dollars. That's money middle class Americans have invested. American capital goes up in smoke if the United States attacks the Iranian oil infrastructure. Additionally, the price of crude oil will probably double overnight, which will make the $5.00 a gallon price of gasoline back in 2008 look like chump change."

Each secretary made similar argument, all imploring her to not to be hasty, explore other avenues, allow diplomacy to work its' course. They were all talking in circles and it had been going on for over an hour. When she was convinced that no one was going to share an original thought Hays terminated the conference.

"Gentlemen I want to thank you for you counsel, however no one presented an argument, which I haven't already considered. Certainly, Prime Minister Nassiri can save his oil platforms and refineries by surrendering the terrorists and the radioactive material. I don't think he will, mind you, so the GOSPs will be destroyed, otherwise the United States will never be taken seriously again. The alternative is for our citizens to live like the citizens of Israel do, under constant threat of terrorist attack. Gentlemen that will not happen while I am President! Ever!"

Harding spoke up again.

"Mrs. President, as a former member of the House, I'm certain that both Houses of Congress will oppose you in every way possible, if you choose to pursue this outrageous course of action."

"Mr. Secretary, the House Judiciary Committee is about to vote a dubious article of impeachment against the Vice President and me to the floor. Are they going vote on another one? Everything that I have proposed is within the parameters of my constitutional job description and I intend to execute all of them. I expect congressional opposition, since Congress has opposed everything else I have attempted to accomplish since I took office. However I hold the moral and legal high ground in this matter and any effort to oppose me on this issue will fail. Thank you gentlemen."

Hayes left the view of camera.

There was a whirlwind of chaos in the cabinet room. Admiral McClain and Shephard excused themselves. McClain, because this was obviously a political matter and he was a military professional, which were mutually exclusive occupations as far as he was concerned and Shephard left because even though he disagreed with her decisions, he would not oppose them. Everyone else present had something important to say and demanded to be heard. It was Longstreet who took Taylor aside and spoke to him privately.

"Mr. Vice President, you were silent during this discussion. What exactly are your feelings regarding the President's position?"

"Mr. Secretary, I agree with the President that ultimately force will have to be used, but diplomacy is certainly preferable to bloodshed."

Taylor was playing fast and loose with his feelings. Hays wasn't planning to put any American lives at risk and because the GOSPs were fixed targets, they weren't going anywhere and could be destroyed after all civilian personnel were evacuated from them. The truth was that he would support any measure, which prevented terrorism on American soil.

"Mr. Vice President, I'm glad to know that you believe a moderate tact is the best course of action. You do realize how disastrous the President's plan will be for this country don't you?"

Taylor realized that Longstreet was attempting to maneuver him into a political corner with his questions. He played along.

"Mr. Secretary, I am a retired professional soldier. I abhor the unnecessary loss of life and believe that measures should be taken whenever possible to preserve lives."

More double-talk, Taylor could tell by Longstreet's facial expression and body language that the Secretary was pleased with what he was saying.

"Mr. Vice President, this is the first time that I have seen the President to act in such a heavy-handed manner, clearly she is not is not herself. Do you think that between her impeachment and this sudden attack, she has temporarily lost the ability to reason thoughtfully on important political issues devoid of emotion and personal bias?"

There it was, just as Hays predicted. Longstreet had just laid the groundwork to exercise the 25th Amendment and was backhandedly asking him if he would support removing her from her office. His next question would be direct. Taylor had to choose his words carefully.

"Mr. Secretary, you saw the same monitor I did."

Taylor pointed to the screen, from which Hays spoke to her cabinet. "I have never seen her so passionate. Is she thinking emotionally? Without a doubt she is. Are her conclusions correct? I'm inclined to say yes but I am in agreement with you that a course of action needs to be pursued which at least, has a chance to succeed without loss of life."

"Mr. Vice President, we are in agreement. Now I have an important question to ask you."

"What is that Mr. Secretary?"

"Mr. Vice President what I am about to ask you requires an immediate answer. I realize that as a retired Marine, it's not in your DNA to betray your President and though it appears that is what I am asking, would you support a motion, in the interest of national security, to have her declared temporarily unable to perform her duties as President under the provisions of the 25th Amendment? I am speaking only as long as it takes to resolve this current crisis."

"Mr. Secretary, would you refresh my memory on the provisions of the 25th Amendment?"

"Mr. Vice President, the short version is that if you, as Vice President and a majority of the President's Cabinet feel that the President is temporarily unable to perform her duties she is removed from office and you act as President until she feels that she is able to perform them. Hopefully, her cabinet will be able to convince her to exercise more restraint towards Iran before he reclaims her office."

"As long as it was a temporary solution I wouldn't object in principle, though I will need to review the Constitution before I definitively agree."

"I understand completely sir. May I suggest that you adjourn to your office for a few minutes to read the 25th Amendment while I discuss the matter with my colleagues? I will call you in a few minutes. Will that be satisfactory Mr. Vice President?"

"Of course."

TAYLOR took the short walk to his office in another portion of the West Wing and called the President.

"Madam President it's about to begin. Longstreet approached me about supporting your removal, according to the provisions of the 25th Amendment."

"Very well Tom, pretend you are on board and deal with Nassiri as you feel appropriate. Oh and Tom?"

"Yes Mrs. President?"

"Let me be the first to address you as Mr. President."

Hays hung up the phone with Taylor and immediately called Isabelle Franks again.

Isabelle picked up.

"Isabelle, this is Jennifer Hays again."

"Mrs. President, it's so good to hear from you again. What can I do for you??

"I wanted to call you again so you were not caught unaware. In approximately 30 minutes, maybe even less, I expect to be removed as President under the terms of the 25th Amendment. Are you familiar with it?"

Isabelle was at a loss for words. Did she hear the President correctly? She knew that she did. What was going on here?

"Yes ma'am I am. It deals with presidential succession, though I am not completely certain of all of the provisions. The Vice President and your cabinet have to agree that you are not capable of performing your duties. How do you know this?"

"Correct Isabelle, the Vice President just called and informed me that my cabinet is discussing the issue now. I instructed him to support the motion."

"Why in the world did you do that ma'am?"

"Since I am no longer President and Taylor is no longer Vice President, neither one of us can be impeached Isabelle."

"I'm not sure that argument has merit ma'am."

"I believe it does but we will certainly discuss it when you visit me tomorrow, but I want you to prepare a motion stating as such and be prepared to file it after we meet."

"I'll be on the next available flight ma'am."

THE Vice President was putty in his hands! Though he was being coy, Longstreet could tell that Taylor was ready to pounce at the chance to become President. It had all been so easy. He also knew what the President meant by the term 'severest consequences', which she used in her speech last night. She intended to take this country to war and crush Iran, which would have incredibly terrible international consequences for the United States and obviously had to be prevented.

He contacted Harding and several other cabinet secretaries after Hays' speech and felt them out concerning their feelings about an attack on Iran. All feared that the President would over react and that an attack would be premature at this time. A consensus was reached that the cabinet would meet and speak with the President, but Longstreet wanted an ace in the hole. He called Harding again both agreed that the President would probably not be dissuaded from her plan. Both agreed that she would probably have to be temporarily removed from office under the provisions of the 25th Amendment. It wasn't a hard sell. Harding and he were on the same page.

The Olympic terrorist attack was regrettable certainly, but didn't justify the economic destruction of a country. America would extract it satisfaction from Iran via political and economic methods and not military. That was imperative.

"Gentlemen, it's obvious that cabinet has quite a bit to discuss. Mr. Reynolds, would you excuse us please?"

Reynolds departed.

"Gentlemen we have a crisis on our hands. Would everyone agree that the President's course of action, attacking a country will risk war and at the very least create a domestic and diplomatic mess that will require years, perhaps decades for America to extricate itself?" Longstreet asked his associates.

Getting affirmative nods from everyone, including the Attorney General, who was in the President's inner circle of advisors, the Secretary of State continued.

"The question is what can be done about it? Personally, the President's threats of prosecution for media leaks rings hollow to me. There is much more at stake for me than a jail sentence. Not only is there a real threat of international isolation an attack, would likely double the price of gasoline and at the very least corrupt and distort global commerce. I don't need to discuss the possible consequences of such scenario. I am prepared to hold a press conference and expose the President's plans."

"Excuse me Mr. Secretary. There might be an alternative than you falling on your sword," Harding interrupted as if on cue.

"Oh? I'm certainly interested in another option to deal with this Mr. Secretary."

"Let me preface what I am about to suggest by saying that what propose is only intended as a temporary solution, but I think it is a viable one," Harding said while he was enjoying the moment. "It is obvious that the President either is unwilling or unable to assess this situation dispassionately. I'm sure she is, to a certain degree caught up in the moment, however our plight requires immediate attention. Perhaps the cabinet and the Vice President should declare her temporarily unable to discharge her duties?"

"You are referring to the provisions of the 25th Amendment?" Longstreet asked, already knowing what the script said.

"I am," Harding replied.

"Mr. Secretary, perhaps we could use a laptop computer to do an Internet search, load a copy of the Constitution, particularly the 25th Amendment, and project it on the screen, so everyone knows what we are referring to."

A few moments later the 25th Amendment displayed for everyone to view and everyone took few moments to read it.

Longstreet continued.

"I had briefly entertained that notion but not seriously considered it because first, it had never been implemented before and because though, it is obvious that many if not all of us here clearly do not agree with the President, does that mean she is unable to discharge her duties? I suppose that is an area of gray, which should be debated now."

"It doesn't matter," the Secretary of the Treasury spoke up for the first time. "The President's plan will mean disaster on several levels, which every one of us has already discussed with her earlier. If we stretch the interpretation of the wording to save the country, so what, my only question is that if the Vice President agrees with us and if we vote and have the President removed from office, it is only temporary. As I understand the Amendment, President Hays can immediately declare that she can resume the powers and duties of her office and reclaim her office. Then she can immediately carry out her plans."

"You are correct Mr. Secretary, but Article IV provided that if the Vice President and the cabinet still believe that the President is still unfit, the matter is then decided in both Houses of Congress, requiring a two thirds vote in each house to have her permanently removed," Longstreet replied.

"But Congress isn't required to address the issue for 48 hours and by that time the President could start World War III," The Secretary of Commerce added.

"I believe the Speaker's unfortunate condition and the President's location have provided a way to side-step that provision," Longstreet replied.

"Right now Speaker Richt is recuperating at Walter Reed. A letter is required to be delivered to the Speaker and President Pro Tem of the Senate and after the President reclaims her office another letter, stating the same, is required. Now because of logistics we can hand deliver the letter to the Speaker and because the President is in Florida she can't do the same when she wants to reclaim her office."

"There is such a thing as email or fax Mr. Secretary," the Treasury Secretary retorted.

"No sir. Article IV specifically states that the President has to transmit a written declaration to both the Speaker and the President Pro Tem that no disability exists. Not email, not fax. As long as we adhere strictly to the letter of the law we can demand that the President do the same. I'm sure the Speaker could be persuaded to be unavailable until we can resolve the issue before us. Does everyone here agree?"

Longstreet commented emphatically as he got nods.

The discussion continued for another 20 minutes or so until the Cabinet decided to vote. Scarboro voted against the declaration, but everyone else did.

"Gentlemen, I have a confession. Earlier I was playing Devils Advocate. I had discussed the issue with the Vice President and he is agreeable to what we are trying to accomplish. He is waiting in his office and is prepared to sign the appropriate documentation. Shall we invite him to our meeting?"

A document was drawn up, signed by the appropriate people and copies delivered to the Senator who was presiding over Senate and functioning as the Pro Tempore and to James Richt. In between the signing of the historic and possibly infamous document and its delivery, Longstreet and the remaining cabinet secretaries set up another videoconference with Hays.

"Gentlemen, what is this, a second conference? I haven't changed my mind. Is there anything else you wish to discuss?"

"Mrs. Hays, since you have chosen to pursue a radical course in dealing with a sovereign nation, a course of action that involves fighting an undeclared war, which would cause international condemnation, consternation and chaos. The Vice President and a majority of your cabinet have judged that you are unable to discharge the powers and duties of your office under the provisions of the 25th Amendment of the Constitution. The documentation is being delivered to the appropriate governmental officials as we speak. You are no longer President. Mr. Taylor is now the acting President," Longstreet said, barely concealing his glee.

"I see, Mr. Longstreet, when can I expect a copy of the document, which removes me from office?"

"We can email you a copy momentarily ma'am. Now as you may be aware, under Article IV you can reclaim your office by submitting in writing to the Speaker and the President Pro Tem, a declaration that you are able to resume your duties. To be in compliance, the original hardcopy has to be transmitted. An email or a facsimile will not suffice," Longstreet stressed that provision; assuming that given time Hays would reconsider her decision.

"We sincerely hope you will take time to reflect on your position and reconsider it before you reclaim your office," Longstreet continued his dissertation.

"Thank you Mr. Secretary. I will consider your counsel carefully," Hays terminated the videoconference.

Longstreet found Hays' reaction odd and was surprised. He expected her to be outraged at what certainly perceived as a betrayal by her cabinet. He was surprised that she didn't verbally assert that is intended to reclaim her office. In fact she took the news in stride. Perhaps he had misjudged her somewhat? If so, then surely it would be easier to convince her to allow other means to be applied to Iran to achieve her goals? At any rate, President Taylor would need to keep him advised as to when Hays was planning to return to Washington, so he could meet her at Andrews and talk some sense into her.

"Mr. President, we need to hold a press conference and announce what has happened and exactly why. The American public needs to know that their government hasn't been overthrown."

"I agree Mr. Secretary. I'll contact C.C. Frost to assemble the White House press corps in 10 minutes. We need to announce this before the media discovers what has happened on their own and we don't need rumors floating around either, but first I suppose I need to take the oath of office."

"I agree entirely Mr. President."

After swearing to preserve, protect and defend the Constitution, Taylor picked up the phone.

"CC. This is President Taylor."

Taylor emphasized his new title.

"President Hays has been removed from office under the provisions of the 25th Amendment. I want you to assemble the press corps in 10 minutes so I can announce what has transpired. I'll speak with you privately after the press conference."

Taylor hung up the phone.

"Gentlemen since the cabinet secretaries are here we need to have a short chat."

Taylor was about to assert much to what would be Longstreet's consternation, who was actually in charge. He sat down at the center of the table, which was traditionally the President's chair. The chair itself was raised 2 inches higher than the others were. Taylor used the symbolic gesture as a means to show the cabinet that he was now in command. He paused for a moment to look everyone directly in the eye before beginning. Again this gesture was designed to assert his authority over his new subordinates.

"Gentlemen, I intend to be completely up-front and candid about what has just happened here today and I expect everyone here to do so as well. I don't care about opinion polls and focus groups. We do not want and we can not afford for the American public to lose confidence in their government. Mr. Longstreet."

"Yes Mr. President?"

"I may not be President for very long but I am going to assume that I will be for the remainder of this term and I am going to run the Executive Branch accordingly. After the press conference is concluded, you will have your staff contact all our ambassadors and instruct them to immediately inform the appropriate government officials that I am now President and describe the circumstances of how I attained this office."

"Of course Mr. President."

"You will also personally contact the Iranian Prime Minister, explain what has happened and why and inform him that his country's oil producing infrastructure is not currently threatened. However you will make it clear that the United States will act proactively in combating terror and that we still expect his country to surrender any terrorists in Iran."

"Mr. President, may I ask how you intend to force Iran to produce any remaining terrorists? We aren't completely certain how many we are talking about." Longstreet asked.

"An excellent point Mr. Longstreet and I have a couple of ideas which, I'm not prepared to share until I consult with Admiral McClain and General Norman. Afterwards I will advise the appropriate people of my plans."

Taylor paused again to emphasize his last point and his next.

"Gentlemen, just so there are no misunderstandings, this is not government by committee. I am the President of the United States, don't any of you forget it. Mr. Longstreet, you are accompanying me to the press conference. Mr. Longstreet and Mr. Harding, I want to speak with both of you later today. Clear your schedules so both of you are available to me this afternoon."

Taylor rose from the table, signifying that the meeting was over.

JIM Richt was resting comfortably in the intensive care unit at Walter Reid Army Medical Hospital. Floral bouquets and get well cards had already started to arrive, from various well wishers. He had suffered a heart attack, which would require by-pass surgery, if the blockage couldn't be eliminated using non-invasive procedures, meaning clot thinning drugs. His doctors had informed him that he would be moved to a private room tomorrow and that though they would attempt to avoid surgery that he should be prepared for it.

He didn't care for the idea of surgery, but he knew that, in all likelihood, he would have to endure it, which meant an end to his political career. The American public didn't want and elderly politician, with a bum ticker running the country or representing a congressional district for that matter. And if he was able to assume the office, how long would his health allow him to do the job?

"Jim, can I get you some water?"

His wife Ruth asked.

"No thank you dear, I'm fine. Why don't you go home and get some rest? I'm in good hands here."

Ruth had been a saint to him, both here, at the hospital and throughout their 51 years of marriage, never once complaining about his bizarre hours and their time away from each other. Together they raised 3 children, though she deserved much more credit for the feat than he did. And though she didn't say so, after 50 years of marriage, both could sense what each other was thinking without saying a word, he knew that she wanted to return to Texas, retire to their ranch and enjoy their remaining time together with their children and grandchildren.

He didn't deserve such a woman and why did he ever contemplate cheating on her? Lord only knew. The decision, which he had reached about his future, was an easy one. Ruth had sensed it as well, though he hadn't discussed it with her. Again it was the 50-year matrimonial ESP at work, but Richt had pledged to retire after one more term, before this pardon and impeachment business began. Now with his health in doubt, he decided to resign his seat as soon as he was out of the hospital and return to Texas when he was healthy enough to do so.

Dunston would scream bloody murder, but it didn't matter. This heart attack was a blessing in disguise, allowing him a graceful political exit. Richt didn't care if Dunston released the pictures of him and the intern or not, but he didn't think they would be. An unwritten Capital Hill rule was that politicians never spoke ill of the dead. That also included the political dead as well. Dunston would lose immense political respect if he broke it.

Oh well. The articles against Hays and Taylor would be voted to the floor but they would never be sent to the Senate for trial. Only he could muster enough votes against the President, who Richt did admire and he wasn't prepared to do that now. The idea of being addressed as 'Mr. President' or 'President Richt' was exciting but perhaps never realistic.

It was then that a shipping envelope from the Executive Branch arrived. Richt opened and read the document.

"What is it Jim?"

"Ruth, we are going home very soon."

Richt refolded the single page letter smiled and affectionately squeezed his wife's hand.

THE walk from the conference room to the White House pressroom was a short one. Taylor knew his first and possibly only press conference, as President would be contentious. This was the first time an American President had been lawfully removed from office and the White House Media were going to scream murder. It wouldn't be because they were morally outraged; they weren't. Hays was not their most favorite person. She regarded the media as her tool to manipulate the political landscape in much the way Ronald Reagan did in the 80's and didn't hesitate to use them to suit her purpose. Instead they would be outraged because the biggest political story had happened in the same building as they worked, literally under their collective noses' and no one had a clue about it. They would all assume that only a 'code of silence' had kept them from discovering the story themselves. The messengers delivering the document probably were only now just arriving at their destinations. This would come as a complete surprise to everyone.

Taylor and Longstreet entered the room. Taylor stood in front of the podium, with Longstreet a step behind and a step to the side. Taylor began with a statement.

"Ladies and Gentlemen, a few minutes ago President Hays was removed from her office, under the provisions of the 25th Amendment of the Constitution. A majority of her cabinet and I signed a document stating that she was unable to discharge the power and duties of her office. President Hays was informed via videoconference of our action and I have assumed her duties as Acting President."

Several members of the press corps audibly gasped with surprise. All of them were typing text messages to their editors as quickly as their thumbs could push the keys of their keypads.

"Following the provisions of Article III of the 25th Amendment, copies of the declaration are being delivered to the President Pro Tempore of the Senate and the Speaker of the House of Representatives. For those of you not familiar with the provisions of the amendment, Article IV provides for President Hays to reclaim the office by transmitting a written declaration to both the Speaker and the President Pro Tem that no inability exists and resume the duties. I do not know when and if she intends to reclaim the office, but I intend to discharge my duties, as I see fit and to the best of my ability until I am relieved of them."

The questions were routine and expected, given the circumstances, though each was imbued with an understated tone of indignation. The White House press corps had been scooped and it was obvious that they were not happy. Why was the President removed? She was removed under the provisions of the 25th Amendment. How does a policy disagreement within the Executive Branch result in the Commander in Chief being removed from office? There was concern that her actions would start an armed conflict in the Middle East and possibly escalate. Did he or the cabinet initially proffer the notion of using the 25th Amendment? Secretary Longstreet did. Was Taylor reluctant to initiate the proceedings against the President? Yes, but he and the cabinet didn't feel armed conflict was necessary at this time. What was the vote count? A majority of the cabinet voted in favor of the declaration. Did Taylor intend to attack Iran's oil production facilities? Not at this time but nothing was being ruled out. Did Taylor feel like Benedict Arnold? No, Arnold was a traitor and betrayed his country. He was merely following the rule of law. Did he think the American public perceives this action as a coup? The rule of law was followed so by definition it was not a coup. How soon would President Hays reclaim her office? No idea. What was he going to do about the terrorist attack? The FBI was handling the investigation.

Taylor answered each and every question. Some questions were asked several times and were answered in the same way. He understood that every facet of this had to stand up to scrutiny.

"Mr. President, how does President Hays' removal affect the articles of impeachment pending against the both of you?"

"I'm not a constitutional lawyer, so I really don't have an informed opinion. It will all just have to be sorted out..."

"IT will all just have to be sorted out..."

Sorted out like hell! Dunston thought. What was going on here? The declaration had been delivered to the acting President Pro Tem and Dunston was immediately informed. Undoubtedly, Richt had received an identical document. After retreating to his office, he turned on the TV to watch Taylor's press conference. Was this a stunt by Hays or did her cabinet really declare her unable to perform her duties because they feared an armed conflict with Iran?

Dunston would have to sort things out. The article would be voted out of committee, probably in a couple of days; Richt had ensured that. It was unfortunate that Richt had a heart attack. That bastard had to live for a few more weeks, long enough for him take the oath and then appoint him as Vice President. He didn't care if he lived or died after that. All his plans would be meaningless if he died before his plans could be implemented, though it didn't appear likely. As heart attacks go reports indicated that Richt's was mild. He would have to take an aspirin each day, start eating healthy foods and exercise some to recover, which he would. Richt wanted to be President, even if it was just for a few months.

How would this coup by the cabinet and Taylor, he couldn't bring himself to address him as President Taylor, affect the impeachment proceedings? He wasn't sure but he would have his people investigate it. He knew that Hays could claim her office back as soon as she flew back to Washington and then it would be business as usual. Yes, things would get sorted out.

TAYLOR sat at the President's desk for the first time. The press conference had been contentious, even hostile just as Taylor believed. The press corps was pissed. Being assigned to the White House was a prestigious assignment given only to accomplished journalists. Every one of the corps had been hoodwinked by the event of this morning and because accomplished journalist never get the wool pulled over their eyes, there had to be a deliberate attempt by someone to conceal the story. They were only partially correct! Right now every Washington politician was expecting Hays to fly back and reclaim her office, but that wasn't going to happen right away.

This was the first opportunity that he had to review this whole business in the Persian Gulf. Taylor took a few minutes to examine the reports of the two attacks on the Gaffney. A Petty Officer named Kahlid Intavan was mentioned by name in one report, stating that his alert observations and actions saved the ship while it anchored in Jebel Ali. The Gaffney's skipper recommended him for a Navy Cross, for saving a fellow sailor as well and the sailor is about to receive orders to Pensacola to AOCS—Aviation Officer Candidate School. Taylor immediately decided he wanted to meet this young man and would have orders cut so he would he would receive his Navy Cross in the White House. Taylor would make a phone call to Admiral McClain to arrange the award, but now he had more pressing issues.

"Send in C.C. please." Taylor said to the intercom.

Frost entered the Oval Office.

"Have a seat C.C."

"Yes sir, err, Mr. President." Frost said as she sat at the desk facing Taylor.

"Sounds strange, doesn't it?"

"My error sir, it won't happen again."

"What we are about to discuss is to remain inside this room. Are you clear about that C.C.?"

"Certainly Mr. President."

"At some point in time, probably sooner, rather than later you will be asked some pointed questions, which directly relate to what we are about to discuss."

"I understand sir."

"C.C. I don't know when President Hays will be reclaiming her office, but it won't be right away."

"You're certain of that sir?"

"Yes she told me last night when we met with General Norman in Tampa. She suspected that her cabinet would vote to remove her and asked me to support the declaration, but you are not to speculate about that if asked."

"She did sir?"

Frost said, visibly surprised.

"Why did she do that?"

Taylor ignored her question.

"C.C., tomorrow I am pardoning Mohammad Baghai and you are going to announce it at a press conference; I am going to address the nation tomorrow evening. I wanted to give you a heads up because the press will probably figure out that President and I met last night and assume that she and I concocted this whole scheme."

"What scheme is that sir?"

"Baghai's pardon, this whole business about Hays' removal, my presence here, assuming her duties, is Hays' plan to defeat the impeachment movement against us, de-fang, shall we say, Nassiri and cripple al-Qaeda, but as I said that is confidential. That's all for now C.C."

Taylor next called Reverend Edgars. He dialed the number himself and after a moment was connected.

"Reverend Edgars?"

"Yes, Mr. President this is Casey Edgars."

"This is President Taylor. I'm calling to inform you that I am honoring President Hays' promise to pardon Mohammad Baghai. I will make the announcement tonight, but I wanted you to be the first to know."

"Thank you on behalf of myself and Mohammad, Mr. President."

"Reverend, don't thank me, if it were up to me, Baghai would sit in jail for the rest of his life. I'm honoring President Hays' commitment because it is a political necessity."

Taylor didn't mention that Edgars' efforts to obtain a pardon for Baghai were the reason.

"In any case, thank you again sir."

# Chapter 33

"**A**dmiral, I understand President Hays ordered you to assemble a task force hand have it sail to the Arabian Sea?"

Taylor asked McClain, while the two were in the Oval Office. They were also teleconferencing with General Norman in Tampa. Secretaries Longstreet and Harding were cooling their heels outside.

"Yes Mr. President. The 5th fleet will be arriving in 10 days. She also ordered me to re-supply the 3rd fleet, our current force deployed at Camel Station."

McClain was using the military vernacular for the Arabian Sea.

"Good. General Norman, I want you to prepare a plan to blockade every Iranian port and GOSP, with the goal of sealing Iran's exporting capabilities for an indefinite period of time."

Both McClain and Norman broke into huge grins. Taylor did not.

"Gentlemen, as a military man myself I appreciate you feelings. I also have the desire to bomb Iran back to the Stone Age, but as President I feel duty bound to achieve our objectives, without loss of life, if possible, both on our side and our enemy's."

"What is our objective Mr. President?" Norman asked.

"To secure all the radioactive material in Iran, which can be used to construct a radioactive dispersal device and to secure any al-Qaeda terrorists remaining in Iran," Taylor replied.

"Will a blockade be sufficient?" McClain asked.

"Given our available assets we only have two alternatives, one is a blockade and the other is either a cruise missile attack and/or an air strike. I am going to start with the least hostile option and increase the pressure as necessary. If we hurt'em in the pocket book bad enough Nassiri will come around."

"Should I have a contingency involving ground forces Mr. President?" Norman asked.

"No General, I don't anticipate infantry being necessary. We don't need to generate any 'American imperialism' or 'blood for oil' rhetoric that would be caused by anything resembling an invasion. I'm confident that the Navy can handle the task at hand."

"Very well sir," Norman said.

"Now I want it loud and clear to every ship captain that he or she is to act proactively. Nassiri is not going to take this action against him lying down, either politically or militarily. Once the blockade is in place, nothing goes in and nothing goes out. Each skipper is expected to aggressively defend itself against any and all potential threats and I expect that Iran's military will attack the blockading force."

"Yes, Mr. President."

"Now if both of you will excuse me, I have two members of my cabinet that are anxious to speak with me."

McClain exited through one door and Longstreet and Harding entered through another. Taylor got up and met them half way.

"Gentlemen, I trust I didn't keep you waiting too long," Taylor said.

"Not at all Mr. President," Longstreet replied.

All three knew that Taylor purposely kept them waiting, only to re-enforce the point that he was in charge.

Taylor motioned for his guests to be seated at the pair of matching sofas, which faced each other, in the center of the Oval Office. Longstreet and Harding sat on one and Taylor on the other.

"Gentlemen, I am going to address the nation this evening and I thought it was appropriate that I discuss the content with both of you since your departments will have to deal with the execution of my guidelines."

"Thank you for your consideration Mr. President," Longstreet replied.

"First of all, Mr. Longstreet, where do our embassies stand in regards to notifying the nations of the world how and why I am now President?"

"Mr. President, immediately after your news conference, I instructed my staff to notify all our ambassadors of yesterday's events and to notify the appropriate governmental personnel of the respective countries, they are now serving. The process is ongoing but because of the time differences between Washington and the various capitals should be completed no later than tomorrow morning. I also spoke to the Iranian ambassador personally, as you instructed and outlined the events and reasons leading to President Hays' removal. He thanked me for the explanation and asked me to thank you for exercising restraint under the circumstances. He sounded genuinely grateful and wants to thank you personally at a convenient time.

"Good, Mr. Longstreet you may contact him and schedule a meeting at 8:00 AM tomorrow. He will undoubtedly want to speak with me after my speech tonight."

"What are you going to be discussing in your speech Mr. President?" Harding asked.

"My speech tonight has three purposes. First, to explain to America exactly what has transpired. Second I am going to announce that I am pardoning Mohammad Baghai and third to announce how the United States is going to address the Olympic terrorist attack in Chicago."

"How do you intend to address that issue Mr. President?" Harding spoke for first time.

"Gentlemen, the attack in Chicago was an assault against America and every other peace loving nation in the world. We have indisputable evidence that it supported by Iranian Prime Minister Nassiri. The issue is how are we going to respond? President Hays ordered a missile attack to destroy an al-Qaeda training base, but if Nassiri had any inkling about the Chicago attack and I certainly believe that he did, he moved the facility's supplies and occupants to another location, so the attack accomplished next to nothing."

"President Hays proposed an additional series of attacks to destroy Iran's oil production and refining infrastructure to force Iran to surrender the radioactive material and terrorists and all of us here agree that such action is at least premature, if not complete overkill."

Taylor got affirmative looks from his guests.

"Iran will, of course deny any involvement and that is to be expected, however their protests will fall on deaf ears. The United States will apply economic pressure in the form of a naval blockade until Iran agrees to our requirements. Mr. Harding, this blockade will cause the price of crude oil, as a result the price of to rise. You will instruct your staff to immediately release the strategic oil reserve to counter the expected fuel shortage."

The strategic oil reserve was just that, a reserve of crude oil in the ground, most of which was in Wyoming and in the ANWAR preserve in Alaska.

ANWAR was a compromise between different factions of government. One side supporting the idea of drilling and refining the crude oil into gasoline and heating oil at once, while the other side did not want to drill at all, fearing an environmental catastrophe. Drilling but not piping the oil to refineries, but rather leaving it in the ground, unused except in time of national crisis, as determined by the President was the compromise worked out. Neither side was particularly happy with the bargain, which was a sign that it was a good one.

Longstreet and Harding were both visibly distressed.

"How much of it do you want release Mr. President?" Harding asked.

"All of it."

"Mr. President, I must advise against this aggressive action at this time. There are diplomatic remedies available, which should be considered before implementing a hostile response such as this one. There is no need to rush into a rash action; time is on our side here. The Iranian ambassador understands why President Hays ordered a missile attack on the base outside of Furg and he indicated to me that though his government will denounce the attack it will not attempt to retaliate against us because of it," Longstreet interjected.

"The Iranian government would be wise not to retaliate. Mr. Secretary, since any attack on any American Military personnel or assets will result in an appropriate and disproportional counter attack."

Taylor emphasized the word disproportional indicating that a counter attack would be an overkill of a corresponding target.

"May I remind you sir that earlier, you suggested a blockade as an alternative to bombing. The United States does not want lives lost or blood shed, but it can not allow an unprovoked terrorist attack on its' own soil to go unpunished. My solution avoids armed conflict and allows Iran to gracefully exit the diplomatic stage gracefully."

"I don't see how Mr. President," Longstreet replied.

"Simple Mr. Longstreet, before 9-11 the United States had dozens of terror cells, on our soil, actively operating to orchestrate our downfall and we didn't have a clue to their existence or their intentions. Why can't Iran round up all the al-Qaeda terrorists, the raw radioactive material and RDDs surrender them to us and claim ignorance of their existence? It gives them plausible deniability. We can certainly make their co-operation economically worth their while and I can guarantee you that their resistance will ultimately be to their detriment."

"Mr. President, these tactics are heavy-handed and not likely to achieve beneficial results," Longstreet retorted.

"Mr. Secretary this matter is not one for debate. I have made my decision. I appreciate your desire to work out a solution, which avoids armed conflict, but the American public demands action and not diplomacy or negotiations. You will accompany the Iranian ambassador to the meeting here in this office at 8:00 AM tomorrow and enthusiastically support my position. If can not or will not do as your President instructs, you may resign your position now."

Taylor just laid down the gauntlet and dared Longstreet to cross him. Longstreet decided not to fall on his sword.

"Thank you Mr. President, I serve at your pleasure and I will be here tomorrow."

IT was Shephard's and Scarboro's turn to cool their heels outside the Oval Office. Both of them felt like the captain on a sinking ship. When the cabinet voted on Hays' ouster, Shephard had to excuse himself, since he was not a member of the cabinet and Scarboro was the only cabinet official to vote against her removal.

"The President will see you now," Taylor's administrative assistant told Shephard and Scarboro.

"Gentlemen come in. We have a lot to discuss."

Taylor welcomed his guests and motioned them to be seated where Longstreet and Harding were earlier.

Both Shephard and Scarboro were taken aback buy Taylor's cordiality.

"You two both look like you were walking to the gallows."

"Are we Mr. President?"

"Jim, a lot has happened in the last 24 hours and I understand either of you could feel like you were unfairly caught up in this business. Unfortunately, politics doesn't always discriminate between the good guys and the bad guys."

"I'm not following you Mr. President," Shephard replied.

"I know both of your loyalties lay with President Hays and not with me. Hell, Jim you were the only one of Hays' Cabinet, which didn't vote against her. Andy, I know you called President Hays when the Cabinet was in the process of mutinying, but couldn't get to speak to her. The reason you couldn't was that she was on the line with me and I had beaten you to the punch."

Shephard was visibly surprised.

"I called both of you here to speak with me because both of you are loyal to her and to bring both of you into the loop. Unlike those slimes Longstreet and Harding, President Hays and I both have complete confidence in both of you. Andy, President Hays asked me to apologize to you for keeping you in the dark, but I'm sure you'll agree it was necessary."

"What are you saying Mr. President?" Shephard asked.

"Gentlemen, last night after her speech, President Hays flew to Tampa and suggested to me, in person, that her cabinet would pull the stunt they did this morning. She told me that she goaded them into taken this action, but because she knew I am as loyal to her as both of you are, she asked me to support the motion to remove her."

Taylor spent the next 10 minutes explain Hays' plans to defeat Dunston and Richt, by pardoning Mohammad Baghai and combat Nassiri and al-Qaeda, by manipulating her cabinet into having to support Taylor's methods. He also explained what he would discuss in his speech tonight and that Hays did intend to reclaim her office, but only after all her goals had been accomplished.

Shephard and Scarboro were both pleased with what Taylor told them.

"What kind of time frame are we looking at Mr. President?" Shephard asked.

"Depends how soon Dunston and Richt realize they've already had their ass kicked."

TAYLOR was standing in front of a podium, inside the East Room of the White House, having the last touches of make up applied to his face before his first speech as President of the United States. He had given the White House speechwriter a quite a challenge, constructing a cogent speech with his talking points on just 4 hours notice, but that is what he was paid to do. A manuscript was on his desk immediately afterwards, for his review. Taylor made a few minor revisions, but he was pleased with the initial work. The text was on a teleprompter now.

Taylor made a point to wear a navy blue suit, a white oxford suit and a deep red power tie, as a subtle patriotic theme. He also wore a United States' flag lapel pin, which wasn't subtle. He intended to pull the collective emotions audience and focus them away from the impeachment and towards al-Qaeda and Iran. With any luck both issues would be eliminated.

"My fellow Americans, the world has seen some extraordinary events initiated during the last 48 hours. A terrorist attack against the international community on American soil, a missile attack on a terrorist base in Iran and a president lawfully removed from office, for the first time in American history. Americans may yet witness other historic events in the near future. I am referring to President Hays lawfully reclaiming the office that she was removed from, articles of impeachment against this same President and her Vice President being voted to the floor of the House of Representatives, for only the fourth time in American history and a terrorist pardoned."

"Many Americans and even more citizens of the international community understandably, fail to comprehend how one cowardly attack on a non-military target, during an international celebration led to the downfall of the President. The explanation is simple, yet complicated. It is straightforward, yet convoluted and dramatic, yet anti-climatic. This evening I will address all of these paradoxes."

"Yesterday morning the innocent American civilians were attacked at the Olympic stadium in Chicago. One bomb was exploded, showering the immediate area with radioactive material. Fortunately, casualties were light and the only fatality was identified as a Philippine national, impersonating a police officer, with al-Qaeda links. Intelligence assets have placed him in participating in paramilitary activities in an al-Qaeda terrorist training facility, outside the Iranian City of Furg. Intelligence has also traced the source of radioactive material to Iran."

"Yesterday President Hays, in retaliation to the attack ordered an immediate cruise missile attack, destroying the base. I applaud her quick and decisive action. In her speech to the nation last night President Hays demanded that Iranian Prime Minister Nassiri surrender all the al-Qaeda terrorists, within Iran and the remaining quantities of radioactive material to the United States. Tonight I reiterate these demands. Prime Minster Nassiri will surrender any and all materials, required to construct a radiological dispersal device, also known as a dirty bomb, within Iran's borders and he will account for all al-Qaeda personnel and surrender anyone who survived the Furg attack immediately. There will not be any negotiations Iran will comply with the United States' demands."

"President Hays, in her speech last night promised Prime Minister Nassiri that Iran would suffer the 'severest consequences' for his non compliance, while not being specific as to the nature of the consequences. This morning, in a teleconference, with her cabinet and me, President Hays, who is presently in Florida, informed us that she intended to order General Frank Norman of Central Command to attack and destroy Iran's oil producing infrastructure. The attacks were to begin with Iran's off shore gas and oil producing surface platforms in the Persian Gulf and later oil refining facilities were to be targeted. They were to continue until Prime Minister Nassiri complied with the demands."

"While President Hays was within the scope of her constitutional duties, as commander in chief to order such an attack, her cabinet, myself included, cautioned against an immediate attack and suggested pressure be applied via diplomatic, economic and political avenues to achieve her goals. Clearly this is a superior alternative than the immediate destruction of millions of dollars of oil producing equipment and potentially an environmental catastrophe."

"Though President Hays considered her cabinet's counsel, it was clear that she was committed to her original plan, a plan with potentially dire results. International scorn, higher crude oil prices and probably more terrorist attacks against Americans, both at home and abroad and possibly armed conflict were foreseeable and reasonable consequences of an attack against Iran."

"It was the opinion of a majority of President Hays' cabinet and myself that risks of an attack at this time far outweighed the benefits. At that time a majority of her cabinet and I judged her unable to discharge the duties and powers of the office of the President and signed a document, which temporarily removed her from office. I immediately took the oath of office became acting President. President Hays, may, at any time reclaim an office by delivering a statement to the Speaker of the House and the President Pro Tempore a document stating that she is indeed to able to discharge the duties and powers of the office. Until that time, when and if it comes, I intend to exercise the duties of the Presidency to the best of my ability."

That was not true but mentioning that he and Hays had agreed to on a plan to remove her from office, since it would only confuse the issue.

"To that end, as President I will not tolerate terrorist attacks against the United States citizens at home or abroad. The United States will not tolerate governments, which actively support international terrorism. Iran is such a country and Prime Minister Nassiri is the leader of such a government."

"Tomorrow the Secretary of State and I will meet with the Iranian ambassador to reiterate the United States' demands. Unless he gives me immediate and satisfactory assurances that Iran will comply, I will direct that all-diplomatic political and economic pressures be brought to bear against Iran, including a naval blockade of every Iranian port. Any ship attempting to enter a port, for whatever reason will be turned away, using whatever degree of force required. This blockade is not limited to just oil carrying ships but every vessel. A blockade will accomplish the goals of economically isolating Iran without damaging its economic infrastructure."

"I am aware that because of the economic laws of supply and demand and possibly due to an embargo from other oil producing nations will cause the price of crude oil to rise. To counter the anticipated rise I am ordering the release of the United States' entire strategic oil reserve. I want to remind our citizens our strategic reserve is estimated to be at least the size of the known reserves of Saudi Arabia."

"I urge Prime Minister Nassiri to comply with the United States' demands and spare Iran's citizens unnecessary economic hardship. The United States is resolute in this matter."

"In addition to this cowardly and despicable attack, President Hays and I have, over the last several days, had to prepare to defend ourselves against superfluous, bogus and dubious contempt of congress allegations. President Hays' refusal to release a pardon application to the House Judiciary Committee and my refusal to testify before the same committee concerning my limited knowledge of the pardon application, which clearly falls under the Executive Branch's purview, is the genesis of these bogus impeachment charges against both of us. I have no doubt that history will show that the charges are nothing more than a thinly veiled masked attempt at a partisan political power play. The American public deserves better from their elected officials."

"Since President Hays' justifiable reluctance to consider a pardon for Mohammad Baghai, an al-Qaeda terrorist, until the legal proceedings were concluded is the origin of the baseless charges, I have decided to eliminate it. Yesterday evening I signed a document, granting Mr. Baghai a full and unconditional pardon for any crimes he committed against American servicemen. He will be released from custody tomorrow at 12:00 PM Eastern Standard Time. It is my understanding that President Hays intended to pardon Mr. Baghai before she was removed from office. Though I do not necessarily agree with her, I am honoring her wishes."

"Now, I want to call attention of the American public and the leadership of the House of Representatives to the single article of impeachment against President Hays and myself. The wording is very specific. It names Jennifer Hays as President of the United States and me as Vice President. Since Hays is no longer President and I am no longer Vice President, I believe that the article is no longer valid. Our attorneys intend to argue that contention in the courts and if necessary litigate it to the fullest extent allowed. I am told that the litigation process could potentially last years; longer than the remainder of the current presidential term."

"Furthermore, it is my understanding from a conversation I had with President Hays last night in Tampa, Florida, at Central Command Headquarters, that she does not intend to reclaim her office immediately. In fact she indicated that she might not reclaim her office until a month or so before the current presidential term expires. I want to state publicly that when and if President Hays decides to reclaim her office I will not vote to remove her a second time."

"I understand that it seems contradictory that I judged President Hays unfit for office one day and I am prepared to judge her fit the next. In fact the whole scenario smacks of politics and to anyone who makes that assertion, I would agree. I would also remind anyone that it was the opposition party, which initiated this political battle. Again I say that the American pubic deserves better from its' elected officials."

"Since the original reason for the impeachment proceedings no longer exists and it is doubtful that the House will be lawfully vote on the superfluous, dubious and bogus article against President Hays and me, without lengthy litigation, I now consider it a non issue. I call on the House Leadership to cease its activities on this superfluous, dubious and bogus article of impeachment and let it die in committee. There are much more important issues, which need to be dealt with. The American public deserves better from its' elected officials. Thank you and good evening."

Taylor exited the East Room and was given a letter by Shephard, who was waiting in the wings. The envelope bore the seal of House of Representatives.

"What's this Andy?" Taylor asked the chief of staff, though he was pretty sure he knew the writer of the letter and its' subject.

"It's a letter from the Speaker's office, sent by email."

Taylor opened the sealed envelope and began to read.

---

United States Congressman
31st District State of Texas

The Honorable Governor Mark Williams
1010 Colorado St
Austin, TX 78711

Dear Governor Williams:

Please accept this letter as my resignation as Congressional Representative of the 31st Congressional District of Texas. My resignation will become effective at 12:00 noon tomorrow EST.

My health no longer permits me to perform my duties as a United States Congressman or as Speaker of the House.

Respectfully,
James Richt
Speaker of the House

ccThomas Taylor
Jennifer Hays
Timothy Dunston

---

DUNSTON crumbled up the letter and threw it across the room in anger and frustration. He had just listened to Taylor's speech and then this letter was delivered to his office. That bastard Richt had just double-crossed him and he wasn't sure if he could do anything about it! He could release those pictures, but it wouldn't serve a purpose. Richt had just ended his political career and those pictures would only ruin a marriage and possibly make him kick the bucket. It certainly wouldn't advance his political career and could easily harm it.

Was Hays smart enough to manipulate her cabinet into removing her from office? Was Taylor in on it with Hays or was he just a minion? Could Hays and Taylor still be impeached under the current circumstances? That was an unknown. It was obvious that she wasn't in a hurry to reclaim her office and if she and Taylor were immune from impeachment under the status quo, then she wouldn't be demanding it back anytime soon. No doubt Hays' attorneys were already investigating that avenue already. And no, she didn't dupe Taylor; he was a part of this scam. He said in his speech that he spoke to her last night in Tampa; she informed him of her game plan then.

Hays appeared to have covered all her bases. She had beaten him to the intersection of preparation and opportunity.

"THANKS for dinner David and Isabelle," Father Paul thanked his friends.

Isabelle and David had invited Paul over for dinner, partly as a celebration for Mohammad's impending pardon. Isabelle had a red-eye flight to Pensacola to meet with Hays the next morning, while David Paul and Tori were going to drive to Delmont to visit with Mohammad and Casey Edgars on his impending release. Tori and Mohammad had never met and he had expressed a desire to meet her.

The adults were clearing the table, while Tori was in her room changing into her nightgown.

"No problem Paul, we're glad that you could come. Tori and I will pick you up at the rectory tomorrow at 8:00 and we should be at Delmont around 10:30."

Paul's cell phone rang.

"Hello?"

Paul listened for moment. Isabelle and David could tell that he was becoming distressed.

"Okay, I'll fly over as soon as I can get a flight. Yes, I'll call you back when I know a flight number and arrival time."

"Paul what's wrong?"

"Isabelle, I have to fly to Chicago tomorrow Isabelle. I have a cousin, which I haven't seen in several years. She's in the hospital and her doctors aren't sure if she is going to live. Her parents want me to come and administer the last rites."

"Oh Paul, I'm so sorry to hear that. Is there anything that we can do for you?" Isabelle asked.

"Just pray Isabelle. David, will you tell Mohammad that I'm sorry that I wasn't able to see tomorrow?"

"Of course I will Paul."

"Thank you now I need to go pack and book a flight."

# Chapter 34

"**M**r. Ambassador, do I need to remind you that my predecessor wanted to destroy all your oil production facilities to force your government to accede to our demands? Now of course you will agree that my solution is much more beneficial to your country?" Taylor lectured the Iranian ambassador, Manucher Eghbal.

It was just after 8:00 AM. Taylor, Longstreet and the Iranian ambassador were in the middle of an intense discussion in the Oval Office. Taylor had made a point to call the Iranian Ambassador for the early meeting; an hour before diplomatic protocol dictated to demonstrate that to Eghbal and Longstreet that he wasn't prepared follow the normal protocols and be heavy handed in this matter, if necessary. Taylor was sitting at his desk, while his guests were sitting in two chairs, in front of the desk, facing their host. All three men were impeccably dressed and formalities were exchanged. Taylor didn't wish to be pleasant, he was not a diplomat. The meeting was going to be a short one.

"Mr. President, my country denies it has radioactive material in sufficient quantities to manufacture so called dirty bombs in the quantities you claim. Furthermore, your country has no legal right to attack or even blockade a neutral country."

"Mr. Ambassador, I am not prepared to debate the issue with you. For the purposes of this discussion I am assuming that your government is purposely keeping you ignorant of the realities of this situation. The United States has solid intelligence supporting my assertions. I am not going to reveal it to you at this time, but rather at a time of my choosing, but rest assured that it exists. I have also ordered an additional carrier battle group to support our current one. Though I have pledged not to destroy your infrastructure, I will shut down your oil exportation. Completely sir; by that I mean if necessary, I will order any ship attempting to run the blockade fired upon so that is disabled."

"Now to address your argument, about the legalities of the United States' position, I will assert that under the Bush Doctrine. Mr. Secretary, would please refresh our memory on the doctrine's provisions?"

Longstreet had a reputation for elaborate oratory and Taylor expected no less from him now. Longstreet did not disappoint.

"Certainly Mr. President, President George W. Bush 43 instituted the Bush Doctrine, shortly after the September 11th attacks in 2001. In the strictest interpretation, the United States asserts its' right to secure itself from countries that harbor and/or give aid to terrorists groups. Later it was broadened to include additional elements, including the policy of preventative war, which held that the United States should depose foreign regimes that represented a potential or perceived threat to the security of the United States, even if that threat was not immediate. It also included a policy of spreading democracy around the world, especially in the Middle East, as a strategy for combating terrorism; and a willingness to pursue U.S. military interests in a unilateral way."

"Right now I am inclined to only to use the blockade at this time to secure the United States' interests and I don't presently regard Iran as a potential threat, but make no mistake sir, our demands are not negotiable. By not attacking your country I am taking the moral high ground. Since my country was attacked and is exercising restraint, you will not win the public relations battle."

"As of now your country's ports are now sealed and will remain so indefinitely by the United States Navy. There is not another navy in the world, which can dislodge us and I doubt any other would even try. I have also ordered the ships of our fleet to take proactive measures to defend themselves against any threats," Taylor said, stressing the word 'proactive'.

"Your job now sir is to communicate to your government the political realities of the situation of our non negotiable position and strongly suggest that you're Prime Minister that he should meet our demands."

"Mr. President, the Bush Doctrine has been rejected by the international community, as well as every American President since President Bush because it is it is perceived as unlawful. It is perceived as unlawful today. If the United States truly believed that the doctrine was legitimate, why hasn't it ever pleaded its' merits before the United Nations or the World Court?"

"Mr. Ambassador this is not a theoretical discussion, which I am not going to engage in. As a practical matter, your country is just become economically isolated and will remain so until your government surrenders the instruments of terrorism. Though you and your government claim that they do not exist, I know they do. I will release evidence of their existence to the American public and the international community at a time when it is most beneficial for the United States and least beneficial for Iran. All the rhetoric from your country, the Arab community or anyone else won't change our position and as I said before, there isn't a navy which can force us to release our grip on the area. You government can certainly put whatever sort of 'spin' it wants on the situation; I don't care. But in the end, your government will surrender the weapons and the terrorists to the United States before the embargo is removed."

"Very well Mr. President, I will communicate your message to my government," Eghbal replied sardonically.

CHARLIE, Heather, Ralph and Jo Ann were enjoying the free complementary breakfast in he motel's dining room. Jo Ann was enjoying fresh fruit and cereal while the rest of the family was enjoying self-serve waffles, prepared by Charlie, after he mixed water with waffle mix and poured the batter in waffle iron.

Today the group had planned another trip to the beach in the morning and some shopping in the afternoon at a nearby mall. They had dived the Oriskany other local dive spots earlier in the week. Tomorrow morning Charlie would graduate and everyone would leave for Georgia the day after. It had been a great vacation for everyone. Charlie had gotten to see many of his friends and introduce them to his new family. Heather had grown closer to Charlie, if that was possible. Her entire family had been impressed with the way Charlie had conducted himself after he was 'arrested'. Heather's intuition told her that her fiancé, in addition to his good looks, quick wit and intelligence, he had integrity. Now both Heather and her parents knew what she had suspected.

Everyone was sipping a cup of coffee when Charlie's cell phone rang. Charlie didn't recognize the number.

"Hello?"

"Hello, is this Charlie?"

"Yes it is. Who's this?"

"Charlie this is Jennifer Hays how you are?"

"Fine Mrs. President, and yourself?"

"Fine thank you Charlie. I was calling to see if you and your family had plans for lunch after tomorrow's graduation ceremony?"

"I think we were planning to go to a restaurant and near the university and eat ma'am."

"Charlie I wanted to invite you and your family to have lunch with me, the UWF president and a few other distinguished guests in the executive dining hall."

"That's very gracious of you Mrs. President. I'm sure it would fine with my family, but let me check. They're right here."

Charlie had everyone's attention.

"President Hays has invited us to have lunch with her and the university president tomorrow after the ceremony. Is that all right with everyone?"

Charlie got nods of approval.

"That would be fine ma'am. Thank you for inviting us."

"Charlie, one of my Secret Service body guards will track you and your family down after the ceremony. I look forward to seeing all of you again."

"Thank you again for inviting us ma'am."

Charlie hung up the phone.

"Well that came out of the blue," Jo Ann remarked.

"I'm surprised as much as you are Mom. I wonder why she decided to invite us."

"Apparently, despite your philosophical differences with her, she was still impressed by you to invite us as her dining guests," Heather told Charlie.

"Anyway, I'm ready to hit the beach again. Let's go back to the room and get the towels."

"MRS. President, when will you reclaim your office and assuming you do, will Acting President Taylor and your cabinet vote to relieve you of your duties again?"

Hays and Isabelle Franks were conducting a televised press conference inside her garage. Isabelle had flown down to Pensacola that morning and after checking into her hotel room drove to Hays' home on the bay. Together they discussed Hays' dilemma and her proposed solution. It was clear that Hays' was no longer President it was equally unclear if she and Taylor could be impeached. The article was specific. It named Hays as President and Taylor as Vice President, which they were not at this time. Would a new article have to be drafted, or could the House constitutionally vote upon as the article was currently worded? If a new article was drafted and Hays then decided to reclaim her office would the second article become invalid?

Hays wanted a temporary restraining order issued to prevent such a vote until a motion could be heard before a judge. It wasn't clear to Isabelle if the Judicial Branch could assert it's authority over the Legislative Branch like this but the right judge would issue a TRO anyway and hear the case, just for the publicity. And the issue would ultimately be decided in the court system. Hays' opponents had, for decades, attempted to stack the federal courts with judges, without compunctions to legislate from the bench. They weren't in a position to change course now.

With appeals, all the way to the Supreme Court, if necessary, the issue could be tied up for weeks, if not months, since the court was about to take the summer off. Hays just wanted time and this plan was designed to secure it for her. It certainly raised complex questions, which were, not only not easily answered, but also not even fathomed. This was the first time one part of the Constitution was being used to trump another; clearly this was neither what the Constitution's neither original authors nor the authors of the 25th Amendment had in mind.

"Yes, I intend to reassume my duties as President at some point in the future, but no, I haven't decided when. Technically I can't right now, even if I wanted to. I'm required to notify the President Pro Tempore of the Senate and the Speaker of the House in writing that I am now capable of resuming my duties. Since Speaker Richt has resigned, I will have to wait until the new Speaker is elected. As for how President Taylor and my cabinet will vote, when I do decide to become President again; well perhaps someone should discuss that with him."

"Isn't this whole business just another political game, between you, Acting President Taylor and Congress?"

"Absolutely correct, these are political games and beneath the dignity of people orchestrating them and to echo Acting President Taylor's sentiments, the American Public deserves better."

Hays paused for a moment and then continued.

"Let me remind everyone here and those listening, of the circumstances surrounding these political games."

Hays used a sardonic tone and reiterated the recent events and the paused for a moment.

"I introduced to you earlier, my attorney Isabelle Franks, who will be representing me when and if the Judiciary Committee votes the bogus article to the floor. Earlier today former Speaker Richt said in an interview that he didn't think that it was likely that the article would be sent to the House floor, due to the fact that several Congressmen will be seeking the Speaker's position. Our position is that the article can't be legally sent to the House floor, under the present circumstances. I'm going to turn the floor over to Isabelle to explain our position."

Hays took a step away from the podium and Isabelle stood where Hays was and adjusted the microphone.

"Good afternoon. I am Isabelle Franks. My law firm is representing President Hays. As you all know, some very extraordinary and unique events have recently taken and are about to take place. A President has been legally removed from office via the 25th Amendment for the first time in American history and the same President may face impeachment for only the fourth time in American history."

"I want to call your attention that impeachment proceedings in the House of Representatives and a subsequent trial in the Senate, is another methodology to remove the President or any other federal official from office. It is our position that since President Hays has already been removed from office, impeachment is redundant, unnecessary and unconstitutional. The single article of impeachment is specific, naming Jennifer Hays as President and Thomas Taylor as Vice President. At the very least it would need to be revised to reflect Acting President Taylor's new title. However we believe it no longer applies at all."

"President Hays and I call upon the House leadership to stop the impeachment proceedings immediately. It is redundant, unnecessary and unconstitutional. Furthermore, if the article of impeachment is voted to the out of committee and to the floor I will seek a temporary restraining order from a district court, prohibiting the House from conducting impeachment proceedings against President Hays and Acting President Taylor until the issue is heard before a judge. The motion is prepared, ready to submit and we intend to litigate this issue fully if necessary."

Every one of the two dozen journalists asked a question at once. Hays' revelation turned an orderly press conference into a feeding frenzy, with every journalist acting like a hungry shark with blood in the water, demanding that their questions be addressed first.

"Ladies and gentlemen, this press conference is about two seconds away from termination unless all of you can conduct yourselves as professionals," Hays said.

The chaotic mob of journalists suddenly remembered that they were adults again and acted as such.

"I'll answer questions for another five minutes," Hays said as she pointed to someone.

"Mrs. President, are you saying that you are not going to reclaim your office until the impeachment issue is decided?"

"As I said I haven't set a timetable but since Congress decided to stir this political pot, I'm going to be the one who decides how hot the stew gets cooked. So yes, exactly how the House deals with the bogus article of impeachment will be a factor in my decision."

"What would happen if the courts rule against you and vote on the impeachment article before you decide to reclaim your office?"

Hays laughed.

"Then it's time for more political games. Let me explain the provisions of the 25th Amendment that apply, when and if I decided to reclaim my office. After I transmit in writing to the appropriate officials that I am capable of resuming my duties, I immediately become commander in chief again. It is very likely, assuming that the conflict with Iran has not already been resolved to my satisfaction, that I will order the Navy to resolve the issue using my intended methods."

"Now assuming my cabinet and Vice President Taylor decide for the same reasons that I am still not capable of discharging my duties and vote as such, the issue of is decided in both Houses of Congress. The House and the Senate are constitutionally obligated to address the issue within 48 hours and a vote on my competency is required within 21 days. A two-thirds vote in each chamber is required to remove me. Any political pundit will tell you that 67 votes in the Senate and 290 votes in the House are impossible. What is very likely however is that my allies, whom I still have quite a few, will tie up both chambers for three weeks debating the issue. Is the scenario I described a political game? I wouldn't argue the point. I would, however argue that it is unnecessary and irrelevant if a pledge is made from the next Speaker not to pursue this bogus article of impeachment."

"Acting President Taylor has stated that he will not vote to remove you a second time when you do decide to reclaim your office. Wouldn't the scenario you described be irrelevant?"

"Of course it would, unless he reconsidered his position. Let me remind you that he has as much at stake in this impeachment business as I do."

Hays hinted by her tone and mannerisms that she expected Taylor would change his position.

"OF course he will reconsider his position damn it," Dunston said to no one.

He was alone in his private office again watching Hays' press conference, seething in rage.

How could everything fall apart so fast? In less than 18 months, he was going to be President of the United States and now due to events, unforeseeable and beyond his control; he was holding an empty bag. First Richt has a heart attack, then some rag head terrorist group explodes a bomb and as a result Hays' cabinet removes her from office. He had to give her credit though. A good politician recognizes and takes advantage of opportunity and she did. Certainly she wasn't smart enough to orchestrate this? He even had an ace in the hole, the pictures, to force Richt to follow through, which he couldn't use now, if he still wanted to run, for President again, which he would, only without all the advantages of running as Vice President.

Releasing those pictures wouldn't accomplish anything now. In fact their release would do more harm than good, though Richt deserved it. Even though Richt was leaving Washington, he still had plenty of powerful friends who wouldn't be pleased if they were released to the press, friends that could catalyze a presidential campaign or derail it. As angry as he was, Dunston knew Richt, was untouchable, at least for the moment. He would however, give Richt a reminder that he had them in couple of months. Richt would make several phone calls to solicit support and endorsements on behalf of the Dunston for President Campaign at the appropriate time, provided of course, he didn't have another heart attack and kick the bucket. In the mean time Dunston would have channel his anger towards other Hays instead.

WITH the press conference completed, Hays and Isabelle returned to the house.

"Isabelle, I have another favor to ask. You can make arrangements to stay in Pensacola one more day on business can't you?"

"Yes, of course I can."

"You are welcome to stay here overnight if you wish, but I want my will revised and tomorrow I have been invited to dine at the local university here, after I give a commencement address and I'm inviting you."

"Mrs. President, I couldn't."

"Of course you can and I insist. The university president, years ago, tried to have me fired here when I broke up a flag-burning protest and he owes me big time. Your attendance won't be an issue."

"Very well Mrs. President, I would be delighted, but I will need to call my husband and change my flights."

"Certainly Isabelle, use my phone, while I change."

"DAVID, I am disappointed that Paul couldn't be here and I equally disappointed that I couldn't meet your daughter. Will his cousin recover?" Mohammad remarked.

Mohammad, Franks, Scott Ramsey and Casey Edgars were waiting on Frank's car to be brought around. They had been listening to Richt's interview on a television. Mohammad was visibly pleased that Richt was going to recover. Ramsey was still assigned to guard Mohammad until he was released. Afterwards he was instructed to report to his field office.

Mohammad had changed from his prison jumpsuit into one of the business suits, which he had bought in Switzerland. The plan was to speak to the press outside when Edgars was staying and then fly to Washington. Mohammad still had not disclosed exactly what he intended to do there but Edgars was not concerned and only too happy to accommodate him.

"I'm not sure Mohammad, Paul was called suddenly to administer the last rites to her, so it doesn't appear good, but I do have a recent picture of Tori. Would you like to see it?"

Tori had another nightmare and woke her father up again the night before. Franks called Isabelle's mother to come over and baby-sit.

"Yes please."

Franks open his wallet and handed a wallet-sized family portrait to Mohammad. 'David, Isabelle and Mary Victoria' was written on the back of the picture. Mohammad showed surprise in his facial expression.

"David, may I keep this picture for the time being?"

"Yes Mohammad but why?"

"I will tell you another time, but I need it now. Are you sure it is all right?"

"Yes of course," Franks replied.

"Scott, my friend, I'm sorry that I have to leave shortly, but I look forward to see you again soon my friend," Mohammad said as he embraced his friend, being carefully not to get blood from his hands on Ramsey's clothes.

"We will meet again under better circumstances Mohammad," Ramsey replied.

"Casey, David, I need to travel to Chicago. David, will you call Paul and tell him I am coming?"

"Mohammad I always have time to do God's work. Let me make a call and have my office book a flight."

"Good, afterwards we will speak to the press," Mohammad said.

Ten minutes later, with a flight booked, the group stepped outside and conversed with the press.

There were about a dozen journalists and half that many cameras. The group walked out the double doors and to the group of microphones, where the press conference was conducted.

After the question and answer session, concluded, Franks drove the group back to Edgars' hotel room and said goodbye to each other. Franks drove back to New York, while Edgars and Mohammad waited to catch a flight to Chicago.

"Mohammad, I sense there is something on your mind, though I don't know what it is. Do you want to discuss it?"

"You are very perceptive Reverend. Perhaps we should, but I

would rather wait to speak to you and Paul together."

Mohammad was referring to Edgars' extraordinary abilities of perception.

"Of course Mohammad."

Mohammad and Edgars sat the small table and conversed about other things while they waited for the time to leave.

AFTER a nap Richt felt re-energized and decided to play politics one final time. Ruth had gone home to change and get some rest herself so except for the continuous stream of doctors and nurses checking in every few minutes, he was alone in his room.

Richt speed dialed Cedric Wrangler with his cell phone and attached a microphone to a digital recorder.

"Mr. Speaker! What a surprise! How are you feeling?"

Wrangler asked with surprising enthusiasm.

It was mid-afternoon so Richt was no longer Speaker or the House or even a Congressman but Wrangler was paying his respects to his former colleague.

"Better than I look Mr. Chairman," Richt replied, chuckling a little.

"To what do I owe the pleasure of this phone call sir?"

"Two reasons Mr. Chairman. One, to thank you for the flowers your office sent over and two, to ask a favor and negotiate a deal if necessary."

"Oh?" Wrangler asked.

"Mr. Chairman then I'm sure you know you are one of 3 people I think has a legitmate chance to replace me as Speaker."

"Mr. Speaker, I'm flattered that you think so highly of me."

Wrangler was being coy, as all good politicians did until they knew the parameters of the discussion.

"Shall we cut to the chase Mr. Chairman or would you prefer me to address you as Mr. Speaker?"

"That does have a nice sound to it."

"Yes it does and you and I both know a good politician seizes an opportunity, when it presents itself. Unless I completely misjudged you, I'm guessing that you have been personally calling at least a dozen senior Congressmen, soliciting their support for you as the next Speaker. How is your campaign coming?"

"Mixed results so far," Wrangler said after a pause.

"Do you think your results would be better if you told the fence sitters that you have my endorsement?"

"Certainly, but why are you so interested and what would your endorsement cost in return?"

"I would even be happy to personally call anyone you weren't able to persuade yourself."

Richt ignored Wrangler's question.

"That's very gracious of you sir," Wrangler was waiting for Richt to elaborate.

"Mr. Chairman, you and I both have been around long enough to know that the article against Hays and Taylor, if sent to the floor, wouldn't pass now under the present circumstances, so I'm asking you to table the impeachment article and let it die. In return, I will pledge you my endorsement and support for your efforts to become Speaker as I've described," Richt said.

"Mr. Speaker, I agree it would be very difficult for the new Speaker of the House, whoever it may be to create a consensus and sustain the article to a vote. That is assuming that there is a prolonged political fight for the office. There would be several influential Congressmen with bruised egos. By supporting me and making alliances before other potential adversaries can gain momentum you are actually making an impeachment vote more likely."

"This is why I am speaking with you now."

"Mr. Speaker you still haven't addressed my question as to why you are doing this."

"After a near death experience, one gains a new perspective. Taylor's assertion that the American public deserves better from its' representatives, in his address to the nation, rang true to me and this is my small contribution."

Richt paused for a moment.

"At any rate that is my proposal, are you interested in it?"

"Of course I am."

"I'm glad we came to an agreement."

Richt had just made his last political deal.

"THROUGH this holy anointing, may the Lord in his love and mercy help you with the grace of the Holy Spirit."

Father Paul dipped his right thumb into a chalice, which he was holding in his left hand, containing a small amount of olive oil, which he had blessed a moment before and made the sign of the cross on Julie's forehead.

"May the Lord who frees you from sin save you and raise you up."

Paul again wetted his right thumb with the olive oil again and rubbed each of Julie's hands with it, completing his cousin's anointment of the sick sacrament as prescribed by the papal document, 'Sacrum unctionem infirmorum'.

A few minutes earlier, Paul heard his cousin's confession and gave her Holy Communion in accordance with the Last Rites ritual. Julie confessed her sins as best as she could remember them. She confessed that she rarely attended church that she slept with Giovanni and submitted to his indignities; the litanies went on. Paul what shocked by Julie's revelations but he kept a straight face and forgave her sins.

Julie was visibly relieved that her burden had been lifted after Paul completed Last Rites and immediately dozed off. Though he was not a doctor, it was apparent to him at Julie didn't have much more time on Earth. Paul spent a minute prayed at her bed and then called the family back into the room.

---

CNN Washington—New York Congressman Cedric Wrangler, Chairman of the House Judiciary Committee will be the next Speaker of the House. A vote to elect the new Speaker will be taken tomorrow and Wrangler has collected enough votes to assure his election.

The position of Speaker of the House became vacant when the previous Speaker James Richt resigned due to health reasons. Richt appears to have tipped the balance, in what was predicted to be a bitterly contested election, though Richt had no comment when asked.

Wrangler will be the first African-American Speaker of the House.

---

# Chapter 35

"Intavan!" Lieutenant Bauer yelled across the galley.

"Yes sir." Cal relied

"The skipper wants to see you on the bridge ASAP!"

"I'm on the way lieutenant."

A minute later, Cal entered the bridge approached Commander Hampton and saluted. Hampton returned the salute.

"Petty Officer Intavan reporting as ordered sir."

"Intavan, let's go to my cabin. You just received new orders and I wanted to give them to you."

"Yes sir."

"Captain is off the bridge," an occupant of the bridge screamed in the background.

Hampton and Cal exited and walked the 10 feet to Hampton's cabin, which was directly behind the bridge.

"Close the hatch and take a seat," Hampton ordered.

Cal followed the order and took a seat at the side of Hampton's desk, a mini-sized office style, metallic piece of furniture. Hampton was already seated and removed an official envelope from his desk and handed it to Cal.

"The President wants to award you your Navy Cross at the White House."

"You're kidding me sir."

"Open the envelope and read."

Cal removed the document and took a moment to read his orders, which confirmed Hampton's remarks.

"The President is going to award you the Navy Cross in front of the press in the Oval Office in four days. Right now it's Taylor, but it might be Hays in a couple of days; I don't know but in any case you have orders to Washington for the ceremony and then two weeks later you are to report to Pensacola for AOCS. I assume that you would like to take some leave; maybe visit your family? Aren't you from the Memphis area? "

"Yes sir I am. Skipper I don't know what to say," Cal said to Hampton.

"Intavan, you've earned and deserve all of this. Do me proud."

Hampton stood and shook Cal's hand.

"Thank you sir, I will."

"Get your gear packed, the ship's helo will take you to the Bush at 1700 tomorrow. Then you will catch the hops to take you back to the States."

"What do you think is going to happen here sir?"

"Not a damn thing, if the Iranians are smart. Another battle group is on the way and I've been ordered, along with every other skipper in the fleet to act proactively to protect their boats. The Persian Gulf is now on lock down."

"I see sir."

"Intavan, I want to commend you on the way you have conducted yourself while you have been under my command, especially in light of the current political climate. I know that you have had to suffer certain amounts of prejudice and perhaps discrimination because of your religion and despite that you have displayed exemplary behavior. It's a privilege to command young men like you."

"Thank you skipper, but every religion has its' share of bad apples, which reflect badly on the whole. Muslims are not an exception. Fortunately there are many more honorable worshipers of Allah, the one and only God, be they Christian, Jew or Muslim, who follow the Ten Commandments and live repentant lives. I expect all of Allah's believers will be in paradise one day. Those that don't will suffer Perdition."

"Intavan I want you to stay in touch with me. Good luck to you. You have a great future ahead of you son."

"Thank you skipper."

"Dismissed."

---

CNN Tehran—Iranian Prime Minister Hassan Nassiri had reportedly agreed to surrender its' stock of radioactive waste material and has agreed to account for any people suspected by the United States as al-Qaeda terrorists.

Iranian ports in the Persian Gulf and the Arabian Sea had been under a naval blockade by the United States, authorized by Acting President Thomas Taylor.

"Very much like the United States wasn't aware of the terrorists inside its' borders before the September 11th attacks, Iran was unaware of the terrorists and the strontium 90 inside it's' borders." An Iranian official has been quoted.

---

IT was the early hours of the morning in Memphis, Tennessee. Batista, AKA, the angel of death had met a local woman at a club, near his motel and together they walking back to his room. Impressing her was easy. Wearing expensive jewelry and flashing several hundred dollars in cash accomplished the task. Batista would satisfy his deviant sexual urges with this whore, with or without her consent. He looked forward to several hours of un-interrupted sexual depravity at her expense.

"Hand over your watch and your cash now," an armed robber said to Batista as he jumped at him from the shadows and jammed a gun into Batista's chest.

Batista, caught unaware, instinctively attempted to disarm the man and the two men struggled. A gunshot, muffled buy clothing and flesh rang out. A female scream immediately echoed as her new acquaintance crumpled to the sidewalk, a hole in his chest where his heart was.

Batista hovered over his body and the woman he had just met. It took him a minute to realize that he had died. In a moment, he expected the Malikul Mawt to appear and take him before Allah, where his good and evil deeds would be judged. Batista didn't have any fear though. He was on Ji-had, his sins automatically forgiven! The ledger was in his favor. Batista found himself falling downward and a moment after that he found himself laying naked, flat on his back in some sort of stone dungeon. The temperature was incredibly hot, hotter than anything he had felt before, hotter than he should be able to endure.

Batista didn't have any strength to move. Suddenly two grotesque abominations appeared and attacked him…

THOUGH the sun was had just begun to reveal itself, Charlie, full of nervous energy, decided to take a run around the UWF campus and noticed the uniformed Campus and Pensacola Police were already setting up security for President Hays' on his run. G-men, in their department store suits, wearing their communication headsets were also going about their business. Charlie was surprised how many people were required to protect the President. He was equally surprised that there appeared to be significant cracks in the security blanket. After circling around the field house, where the graduation ceremony would be held and President would speak and where law enforcement officials of various jurisdictions were buzzing about, Charlie ran over to the President's Hall where no one guarding. The room was unlocked.

Charlie had never been in this building before; it was reserved for pretty exclusive company. Banquets, receptions, speeches and formal dances held periodically there. The room was already set up for this afternoon's lunch. Round dining tables, white tablecloths, crystal and china, sterling tableware and formal name cards occupied the room. 'Charles Michaels' was the name on his card. He never used 'Charles'. Charlie and Heather were would be sitting on the right of President Hays. UWF president Robertson would be to Hays' left at the head table, while Ralph and Jo Ann would be sitting on Robertson's left.

To the right side were double doors, which connected the hall to the kitchen and the refrigerated food storage area. The kitchen had no unique distinguishing features. Chris would be serving today and would be in and out of both rooms. Charlie had never seen him in a white dining jacket, which the servers would be required to wear. Charlie immediately decided to make a joke about the 'Good Humor' ice cream man when he saw Chris.

"Can I help you?" The university chef asked Charlie.

Charlie had seen him occasionally during his time at UWF.

"Oh… No." Charlie was startled but managed to flash a patented smile.

"My name is Charlie Michaels and I'm graduating today and I've been invited to dine here at lunch. You are here early."

"It's not everyday that a chef gets to prepare a meal for the President of the United States. This is a career maker for me," the chef said.

"I suppose it is. Hey, I didn't mean to interrupt you. It's just that the building was unlocked and I've never been in here before. I guess curiosity got the better of me. One of my friends is working as a server today."

"Oh? Who is he?"

"Chris O'Callahan."

"Yes, he's a strange one, but does a good job."

"How is that?"

"He doesn't think very much of the President and has said so, but insists on working the luncheon. I told him if he couldn't leave his feelings about her at the door, I didn't need him. As I said, this is a career maker for me and I can't have him ruin the luncheon by spilling hot coffee or something on her."

"No I suppose not."

Charlie laughed.

"Sorry to bother you."

"Not a problem. Congratulations by the way Charlie."

"Thank you."

Charlie left and ran back to the motel. He decided that he would take a quick swim when he got back.

"CHARLIE, are you going to leave any room for lunch today?" Jo Ann asked.

Charlie was on his second helping of waffles. He and the Twigs were having breakfast at the motel's breakfast bar.

"Of course mom, I always have an appetite and today I'm all wound up. I hope all of you have an appetite for broiled flounder this afternoon though."

"How do you know what will be served Charlie?"

"Heather, I ran to and around the campus this morning and by the President's Hall. It was unlocked, so I went in and saw the menu and spoke to the chef for few minutes. Raw oysters are being served as appetizers; I ordered you a double serving."

Charlie razzed her knowing that she didn't care for the shellfish and got an elbow to the shoulder as a thank you.

"What? I knew you wouldn't eat them so I was going to."

Charlie flashed another smile and Heather reached for and held her hand as a peace offering.

"The building was unlocked and you just walked in Charlie?"

"Incredible isn't it Ralph? The chef and I were the only ones in the building."

"No security was there at all? I hope someone didn't plant a bomb there last night," Ralph remarked.

"Me either. I'm too young and too pretty to die."

"And much too modest also," Jo Ann added.

MOHAMMAD and Casey Edgars were at the baggage claim waiting for the two bags of clothing to come out of the chute. Both men could have easily carried and stored the bags, since each only carried suits, shirts socks and underwear, but Mohammad raised red flags because of his swarthy complexion and because he had not yet obtained a legitimate form of Identification, his pass-port was forged. Edgars had to personally vouch for Mohammad. Mohammad was allowed to fly only because Edgars' celebrity status as a televangelist.

Paul was supposed to meet them at the gate but phoned stating that he was having difficulty finding parking space.

The flight was otherwise uneventful and both men managed a short nap. Edgars wanted to discuss the purpose of this trip to Chicago, but refrained from asking.

"Paul, my brother, I am so happy to see you again! How is your cousin?"

Mohammad and Father Paul embraced.

"Resting right now Mohammad" Stewart replied.

"Paul you remember my friend Casey Edgars?"

"Yes of course. Reverend it's a pleasure to see you again."

"Father, I wish we could have met under more pleasant circumstances. Is there anything I can do for you or your family?"

The two men of the cloth shook hands.

"Thank you Reverend, but right now we are just praying and trying to make Julie comfortable."

"Paul, Casey, I would like to pray with your cousin. Can we drive the directly to the hospital?"

"Certainly Mohammad."

The drive was a pensive one until Mohammad broke the silence.

"Paul, Casey I consider both of you my friends and both of you are both are the only Christian men of the cloth that I know. Casey you have gone so far as to call me a prophet of God, but I don't feel like a prophet; I am not well versed in the doctrines of Christianity. It would be a privilege if both of you will be my mentors. May I call both of you my teachers, in addition to calling you my friends?"

"Mohammad, it would be a honor to work with, advise and counsel you; I'm sure Paul feels the same way," Edgars said.

"Of course I will help you in anyway I can Mohammad," Paul added.

"Thank you both. I can't say that Jesus spoke to me as he had before because he hasn't, but I do feel that he communicating to me now and wants me to meet and pray for your cousin now Paul."

"It's not far now Mohammad. We'll be there is about 15 minutes or so," Paul replied

The 15 minutes turned into 30 but Paul Casey and Mohammad arrived outside Julie's hospital room. Paul entered the room and invited Julie's parents, Hugh and Betty Stewart outside in the hall, since no one wanted to disturb Julie.

"Hugh and Betty, these are my friends, Mohammad Baghai and Reverend Casey Edgars, they both wanted to come and pray for Julie."

Handshakes were exchanged. Mohammad had recently changed the bandages on his hands and put the old ones in his pocket.

"Mr. and Mrs. Stewart, I am Mohammad Baghai, you may have heard of me recently, since I have been in the news. Until recently I was Muslim and a terrorist but I had an epiphany and Paul baptized me a Christian. Now, if you will permit me, I would like to pray for your daughter and tell the three of you about my divine experiences."

Hugh man of dignity, about 5′ 8″ tall with hair that was more salt than pepper spoke. "Thank you for coming. Yes my wife and I have heard about you and Reverend Edgars. I didn't think very much of you previous life, but if Paul says you are a changed man, I believe him. I appreciate you praying for our Julie, but the doctors say that she doesn't have much time left. She doesn't have an appetite and anything she tries to eat comes back up. I'm thankful that she has made her peace with God though."

"Mr. and Mrs. Stewart, if you are aware of who I am and my background, you know what I have said about Mohammad. Though I am in no way shape or form minimizing the power of prayer, Mohammad is here for a reason. I have said publicly, numerous times that Mohammad is God's latest prophet and if anyone on Earth can help your daughter, it is Mohammad, with God's help." Edgars added.

"Why don't we go to the waiting room at the end of the hall since Julie is sleeping? Mohammad can tell you the story he related to me when I baptized him," Paul said.

Chairs were arranged in a circle, with all eyes on Mohammad. He began his story. A few minutes into it, Mohammad noticed others eaves dropping and invited them to listen.

"Jesus instructed me to tell his people," Mohammad told his original group and his new audience.

"Mohammad that is an incredible story, how are you sure it's true?"

"Mrs. Stewart, after I entered Switzerland, I had the same doubts you are having now. As real as my ordeal was to me at the time, I began to doubt it actually happened. I prayed to God to show me a sign that my experiences were real. He sent me back to Hell again, this time for only 20 or 30 seconds. So you see I am certain of my convictions. I would like to pray for Julie in her room. Mr. and Mrs. Stewart, I can't promise you that I can do anything more for her than her doctors already are, but I do feel that our Lord wants me to pray with her."

"Mohammad, Betty and I appreciate you and Reverend Edgars coming here. If you think God wants you and Julie to pray together, then go to her room and do so. We will be waiting here until you are finished," Hugh said.

"Thank you Mr. Stewart, I will return here when Julie and I are finished."

Mohammad walked down the hall and entered Julie's room. She was still sleeping. It was obvious that some of her hair had been falling out and there was a faint smell of vomit in the room. A moment later Mohammad noticed a bed pan which obviously was for when Julie had a bout of nausea. Julie's color was pale and her face was gaunt.

Mohammad walked to her bed knelt bedside Julie and began to pray silently. After a few minutes she began to stir.

"Who are you?"

Julie had fear in her eyes.

"Julie, I am Mohammad Baghai. Your cousin Paul is my friend. Both he and your parents are just outside. I wanted to pray for you, which is why I am here now, but if you are afraid I will call your family," Mohammad said as he rose and moved a chair to sit next to the bed.

Julie paused for a few moments.

"No, that won't be necessary. Are you Muslim?"

"Until recently, I was, but Paul baptized me, so like you, I am a now believer in Jesus Christ."

"You have such compassion in your eyes," Julie said.

Mohammad was at a loss of words for a moment. How could a vicious killer of men acquire compassion? Didn't David say that he had eyes without remorse?

"Julie, I was an evil man when I was a Muslim. I did some very terrible things to innocent people. If you see warmth and compassion in my eyes it is only because God put it there, but thank you for the complement."

"I was scared when you walked into my room but I'm not now," Julie said.

"Your doctors, say that you are very sick."

Julie began to cry.

Mohammad took some tissues wiped Julie's eyes.

"Julie there is no need for tears. There is a Heaven and a hell; I have been to both places. Paul has heard your confession, your sins are forgiven and if God chooses to call you, Heaven will be your destination. However, I do not feel that it is your time to die now."

"What do you mean that you have been to both places?"

"Julie, I have murdered many Christian soldiers when I was a Muslim and on jihad and was about to murder again, when God took me from this Earth, threw me into hell and then showed me Heaven. He made these marks on my hands and feet."

Mohammad showed Julie his bloody palms.

"Are those stigmatic markings?"

Julie asked remembering lessons from her catechism.

"That is what I am told. You see, I am a new to the Christian faith and you are probably more familiar with Catholic doctrines than I. I was in a coma when I received these so I don't have a memory of it. Julie, I understand you suffer from radiation poisoning. How did you get sick?"

"The man that I was seeing gave me a gold necklace which was radioactive."

"And you wore it around your neck?"

"Yes."

"Julie, would you point to me where around your neck and on your chest it hung?"

Julie made a motion with her finger to indicate the areas.

"Would you permit me to place my hands on those areas Julie?"

She nodded her consent. Mohammad removed the gauze bandages and then placed his hands around her neck and on her chest, where the necklace hung, and smearing small quantities of blood over the areas Julie had previously indicated. Mohammad then got on his knees again and prayed again. Though she did not communicate to him Mohammad saw the girl of his dreams in his mind's eye. She smiled in approval of his actions.

"Julie, tomorrow, when your doctors see you, they will see an improvement in your condition. I am going to call your family back into the room now. Excuse me for a moment."

Mohammad exited the room and walked down the hall to the lounge to four pairs of expectant eyes.

"Julie wants to see her family."

Hugh, Betty, Paul entered, the room with Mohammad, while Edgars waited outside within earshot.

"Mom, Dad, I'm so sorry."

"Julie, you don't owe any of us an apology. Hugh said as he held his daughter's hand.

"The only thing that is important now is that you rest."

"Julie dear, what is this around your neck?"

Betty didn't get an answer because her daughter dozed back off.

"Mrs. Stewart, it is my blood from my stigmatic wounds. Julie allowed me to place my hands on her body while I prayed for her. I can't tell you exactly how, but I can tell you that your daughter will be better the next time her doctors visit her. We will leave both of you to be alone with your daughter now, but Reverend Edgars and I will be back tomorrow," Mohammad said as he entered the room's threshold.

"Thank you so very much Mohammad," Betty said, fighting tears, as he gave Mohammad a hug.

"Paul would you and Casey accompany me to the cafeteria? I need to discuss something with both of you and I'm a little hungry right now anyway," Mohammad asked his friends.

Perhaps the one universal and common denominator of all hospitals is the food; it is bad and the hospital cafeteria food, which the three men were eating, was not an exception. The meal was silent one, not because of the banter of the others in the room, making conversation difficult but because Edgars and Stewart both knew that Mohammad wanted to discuss something but had not decided to raise the issue. Mohammad had re-bandaged his hands in men's restroom before ordering a 'rubberized' salisbury steak with 'pasty' mashed potatoes.

"Casey, thank you for buying me lunch I suppose that I make a withdrawal from my bank account and reimburse you for my expenses," Mohammad said as he poked at his food.

"Of course Mohammad, but your credit is good with me until then," Edgars replied.

"Paul, let me ask you a couple of questions," Mohammad said.

"Certainly Mohammad."

"How well do you know David and his family?"

"I married them and baptized their daughter. David and I have been friends since grade school."

"Paul, do you remember me telling you about the spirit of a young girl that I saw, while I had my I had my divine experience?"

"Yes, of course. You mentioned that communicates with you periodically when you are asleep. I'm sorry but I don't have an explanation as who she might be or why she appears to you."

Mohammad removed the family picture of the Franks from his pocket and showed it to his friends.

"She appeared to me while I was praying for Julie. Paul, the hair style is different, but this is the girl I have repeatedly seen in my visions."

"Mohammad that is impossible," Edgars jumped in the conversation for the first time.

"Yes I understand that Casey. But the young girl that I see, who gives me spiritual guidance and the girl in this picture, Mary Victoria are identical in appearance. Paul, did she have a twin that died?"

"No Mohammad she was an only child."

"Mohammad, are you certain that the child in your visions and Mary Victoria Franks are identical in appearance?"

"Casey, are you certain that I spent time in hell and spoke to Jesus?" Mohammad retorted.

"Excellent point Mohammad."

"Her parents call her Tori. Mohammad, if you think it is important, I can call David and we can discuss Tori and the child in your visions," Paul said.

"It is important but I don't think its urgent Paul. I was hoping either of you could enlighten me as to why I am periodically visited by this child."

"I have no idea Mohammad; Casey, do you?"

"No, I'm afraid not Paul, but I'm sure God will reveal his plan at the appropriate time." Edgars replied.

Hugh Stewart appeared at their table from out of the crowd, wearing an expression that was a combination of elation and confusion."

"Hugh, what's the matter?"

"It's Julie, she's gotten her appetite back and her color is good! Her doctors are looking at her now but her mother and I can tell that she is better already! Mohammad how can I thank you?"

"Let's go visit your daughter Mr. Stewart."

Julie was sitting up in bed and being fed soup and some crackers when the group returned to her room. A healthy flesh tone replaced her ghost-white complexion of before, making Mohammad ponder for a moment that Julie had returned from the dead.

"Oh Mohammad thank you so much for saving Julie, Betty said as she put down the soup and embraced Mohammad.

"Mrs. Stewart I was only God's instrument. Jesus saved Julie, not I."

"Yes of course, but thank you just the same. Paul, Reverend Edgars thank you both."

Betty broke Mohammad's embrace and gave hugs of gratitude to the clergymen.

CHARLIE and the Twigs arrived at the field house where the graduation would take place. Charlie took his place in line outside the field house, while the Twigs found seats inside. Each of UWF's colleges had a portion of the seats on the floor reserved for their respective graduates and as an honors student Charlie's place in line would allow him a seat was at the front of the College of Business.

At the appropriate time Hays UWF President Robertson and other distinguished guests walked from behind a curtain onto the stage at one end of the field house, while the students marched to the music of pomp and circumstance to their designated seats. Various local dignitaries spoke and then Hays approached the podium and spoke.

AS Hays was speaking, Chris O'Callahan was in the kitchen of UWF's President's dining hall, putting on an apron and rubberized gloves. He was helping to prepare to the meal for President Hays, university president Robertson and several other distinguished guests and had just finished pouring ice water in each of the crystal goblets, in front of each of the eight place servings on each of the eight circular dining tables.

The chef and his staff were putting the busy preparing the entrée, broiled flounder with asparagus and oysters on the half shell as an appetizer, in keeping with President Hays' preference for fresh seafood. He was helping to shuck the oysters, which would placate the chef and keep him occupied until the President arrived. The process required a stiff knife, suitable for prying the two halves of the oyster shell apart and gloves to protect his hands. Normally the meal would be nearly complete at this point but the chef insisted that everything being freshly prepared, he wanted it 'ultra' freshly prepared. He and his staff were so myopic about the quality of the meal they weren't paying attention to anything else. The Secret Service agents seemed to be more interested in securing the receiving line, which Hays would be standing.

AUDIENCES viewing graduation ceremonies are generally bored for hours by the wait time before the event, the endless speeches, of unknown school administrators and the endless procession of anonymous students receiving their diplomas. The boredom is justified and highlighted by a few seconds of pride and excitement as their loved one receives their proof if intelligence and perseverance from the appropriate school administrator.

The Twigs weren't an exception in this case either. Though President Hays' speech did break the monotony, overall it was a ho-hum affair until Charlie walked upon stage and received his diploma. Ralph had his 35mm digital camera with a zoom lens to capture Charlie's walk across the stage. As usual he had a huge smile when he shook hands with Mr. Robertson and accepted his diploma. Like some he raised his hands in victory, but unlike most he did the 'Rocky' victory dance as he exited the stage. Heather and Jo Ann bowed their head, proud of their new family member and his accomplishments but slightly embarrassed for him also. Ralph quickly switched his camera to streaming video and captured Charlie in all his glory.

After the conclusion, Charlie waited for the Twigs outside the field house, along with nearly every other graduate. As the friends and family of UWF's graduates flowed out of the exit of the field house, a sea of humanity immediately began to materialize in front of the building's entrance. It was close to 20 minutes before he found his family. Charlie got a congratulatory handshake from Ralph and hugs from Jo Ann and Heather.

"Charlie, I'm so proud of you," Heather said as she embraced and kissed her future husband.

"Heather, I'm proud that you and your mother and father could come to see graduate. I never thought that I could be so lucky to meet you! Sometimes I have difficulty believing all this is real."

"It's very real Charlie; dad got it recorded on his camera. He even got your victory dance on streaming video."

"Oh? I was considering doing a running flip, like I sometimes do in paintball but I decided I better not."

"I'm glad you didn't. The last thing we need to do is take you to the emergency room on your graduation day."

"Not a chance! I'm very limber and agile."

"Well I want to hang on to you for a while and I certainly don't to have to rush you to the hospital because you were showing off."

"Well you can hang on to me while we walk to meet the President and eat lunch; I'm sure the Secret Service is looking for us already and they have a much better chance of finding us the farther we are away from here and closer to the dining hall."

Ron Thomas found President Hays' guests as they approached the dining hall and re-aquatinted himself with the Twigs.

"Congratulations Charlie. Mr. and Mrs. Twig, Heather how are all of you?"

Thomas shook Charlie's hand.

"Thank you Ron. We've been on vacation all week and are going back to Georgia tomorrow."

"Agent Thomas, what a pleasure to see you again, I want to thank you again for vouching for Charlie."

"Mrs. Twig, I was happy to do it. Now I need to explain know the drill. It's pretty much the same as before. Basically, you will have to empty your pockets and walk through a metal detector before you enter the dining hall. Ladies, you will have to open your purses for a visual inspection. Afterwards the President will greet you and the other guests in the receiving line and each of you will be escorted to your seats. Do any of you have any questions?"

"None what so ever," Ralph said.

"Good, the President is looking forward to seeing all of you again. Now Charlie, if you give me your cap and gown, I will put them in a closet and you can put on your suit coat," Thomas said.

Charlie did as instructed, giving his graduation gown to Thomas and took his coat from Jo Ann, who was holding it. Together the group walked completed the walk to the entrance of the dining hall and took places in line to walk through the metal detector.

After passing through the security measures, Charlie and the Twigs joined the receiving line to introduce themselves to the dignitaries.

"Charlie, Heather, it's good to see you again. Congratulations Charlie," Hays said.

"Thank you Mrs. President," Charlie said as he shook Hays' hand.

"It's pleasure to see you Mrs. President. Thank you for inviting us," Heather added.

"You're certainly welcome Heather."

Hays turned to Robertson to get his attention.

"President Robertson, this is Charlie Michaels, one of your most recent graduates, his fiancée Heather Twig and her parents Ralph and Jo Ann Twig."

Handshakes and cursory pleasantries were exchanged.

The guests were escorted to their places with Hays and Robertson the last to be seated, next to Charlie and Heather at the head table. Charlie was seated to the right of Hays and to the left of Heather, with his chair positioned such that he could see the servers entering and exiting the kitchen through the double-doors. Robertson was seated Hays' left with Ralph and Jo Ann to the left of Robertson. Isabelle was to the left of the Twigs.

Again more idle chitchat was exchanged as the servers poured the white wine, expensive Chablis, suitable for the seafood being consumed and the appetizers. Charlie tried to make eye contact with Chris, but he seemed to avoid looking in his direction. That seemed peculiar to Charlie and mentioned his observation to Heather.

"Chris is acting strange."

"He's probably just focused on doing his job Charlie. There are some important people here."

Charlie ate his oysters with a miniature fork and would've loved to eat Heather's but refrained from doing so. Heather on the other hand managed to eat one, not wanting to appear rude but had no wish for any more.

"Heather you don't care for oysters? It is an acquired taste," Hays asked.

"No, not at all ma'am; it's just that I'm nervous dining with such distinguished company. I mean how often does a 21 year old get to dine with the President of the United States?"

Heather tried sound gracious in her fib.

"I understand, but feel at ease."

"Thank you ma'am, I will."

In the kitchen, O'Callahan was taking the plated entrée's and putting them chrome domes to keep the fish warm and putting them on large circular serving platters. In a few moments he and the other servers would bring these platters to the dining room and the meal would be served.

"So Isabelle, I saw your press conference with the President, would you mind telling me how you became the President's lawyer?" Ralph asked as both of them were eating their meal.

"Not at all Mr. Twig."

"Would you also call me Ralph? You're making me feel older than I am."

"It was an accident actually Ralph. A client, who has been in the news lately, hired me to apply for a presidential pardon. I met with President Hays at the White House to present my client's pardon application and make my pitch. She was impressed with my work enough have me and my firm to represent her."

Isabelle didn't mention Mohammad by name but Ralph did.

"Yes, I've been following Mohammad Baghai in the news. Whether you believe him or not, it is an incredible story. It is even more incredible when you integrate the politics and religion that were married to it. Didn't Baghai kidnap and release your husband before he came to the United States?"

"Yes he did. So Ralph, how do you know the President?"

"I'm sorry Isabelle, this probably isn't appropriate conversation under the circumstances and I was mistaken to lead it in this direction. However, to answer your question, my future son in law Charlie Michaels, who is sitting across from us, along with my daughter, was investigated by the FBI and the Secret Service as possible threat to the President, until she put a stop to it."

"Why?"

"Charlie's brother was Mohammad Baghai's first kidnap victim and some people thought that because the President was considering a pardon for him, Charlie might have an issue with her."

Isabelle immediately knew that Ralph was being delicate when he used the word 'kidnap' in lieu of murder or be-heading.

"Oh I didn't realize that was the case Ralph. I'm sorry."

"Charlie obviously doesn't have an issue with a pardon for Mohammad, so I don't either."

THE tension in the kitchen had passed. The meal had been served and the guests had enjoyed it. In a few minutes the plates would be collected and coffee served. O'Callahan and several other servers gazed at the guests in the dining hall with contempt. Outside were the representatives of all the institutions, which he despised, especially Hays. Prominent attorneys, businessmen, doctors even wealthy bankers were present to inflate each others ego and congratulate themselves upon their success in front of the President. All of them undoubtedly felt too superior to common men like him. UWF's President's dining hall was an example of a building erected by such men to establish institutional authority over its' students.

At the top of the pyramid was Hays, who established her authority over everyone. America wasn't a big enough stage for her, so now she was flexing her muscles in the Persian Gulf. Oh Taylor was technically running the show, but O'Callahan knew who was calling the shots from behind the scenes. Everyone knew the truth and she said as much in a press conference.

Charlie used to feel as he did but now, even he had lured over to the upper crust of capitalist society. The Charlie Michaels he used to know would never have sat in the company of such people, now he was sitting at a dining table at the right hand of the President!

O'Callahan remembered the paintball matches and the team's victories. It was perhaps the one of the happiest events in recent memory. Every member of the team became an instant celebrity on campus but did university president Robertson congratulate the team? No. Paintball wasn't a legitimate sport like football or basketball, he said. It didn't matter that not other team representing UWF in any sport, as done as well the paintball team had.

Chris O'Callahan was suddenly suffused with contentment. He knew what he must do and it would be easy doing it. The night before he had sneaked into the dining hall and hidden a .38 revolver, which he had bought from his dealer, who supplied him his hashish, in freezer of the kitchen. There were dozens of metal shelves and stainless steel pans in the room so a cursory sweep of the room with a metal detector would be useless. The only way the gun would be found would be if all the contents of the freezer were removed first.

Entering the premises was easy since he had a key as all employees did. The gun was a relic by modern standards, but lethal. He brought it with the intention of using it according to its' designed purpose, but wasn't completely sure of his commitment but now, high from the effects of smoking hashish earlier in the day, he found his determination steadfast.

"SO Charlie, when are and Heather getting married?"

"December 16th is the date ma'am but the year is still being discussed Mrs. President," Charlie replied, expecting a smack on the shoulder from Heather. He wasn't disappointed.

"I guess it has been discussed and decided that our wedding will be December 16th of this year ma'am."

Hays smiled in amusement and turned to Isabelle.

"Isabelle, have you met my guests Charlie Michaels and his fiancée Heather Twig?"

"No, but I just met Heather's father and mother and have been having a delightful conversation with them, how do you do?"

"It's a pleasure Isabelle," Heather said.

"Charlie, before you and you family leave, may I have a word with you privately?"

Isabelle asked. She wanted to discuss when she could give him a check from Mohammad.

Charlie seemed a little perplexed by the unusual request.

"Sure, but concerning what?"

"Charlie, I'll explain in due course but for reasons you will understand I do need to speak with you privately," Isabelle replied.

"Very well."

O'CALLAHAN carried a carafe of coffee in his left hand and the revolver in his right, holding it in a firing position, covered by a white linen napkin and walked through the double doors. By fate or just plain luck Charlie was looking at the doors when O'Callahan passed the threshold. Charlie immediately noticed the crazed; drug induced expression on his friend's face. He had seen it before when they were at the fraternity house after the visit to SAMMY'S GO GO. Chris's gaze was locked on to the President. Charlie was also familiar with it, having seen it when Chris was about to make a kill, while playing paintball. Recognizing his Chris's intent Charlie looked downward and saw the tip of what appeared to be a barrel of a gun. It was only about 20 feet from Chris to the President's table and he was walking quickly towards it.

Charlie grabbed the back of the President's chair, yanking it backwards and back flipping her to the floor simultaneously. Hays landed on her back unceremoniously.

"Gun," Charlie screamed as he jumped over Hays with cat like agility, honed by hundreds of hours of paintball matches and darted towards the threat.

O'Callahan, his senses dulled by the drug induced high was slow to react to the situation and slower to adjust his aim. Charlie tackled him as he fired a round, striking Charlie's stomach. The 2 tangled human bodies crumpled to the floor. The bullet stopped Charlie in his tracks; he groaned and rolled off of O'Callahan, barely conscious. Blood had already begun to pool around him. O'Callahan pushed Charlie off and aimed at Hays.

Charlie's scream took everyone by surprise; Hays' protection detail included, but only for a moment. Agent Thomas drew his weapon and fired three times at O'Callahan killing him instantly.

George Hickey and another agent grabbed Hays by the shoulders and dragged her to the limousine, which was parked in the back of the building. Hays' feet barely touched the floor. She was away from the kill zone in less than a minute.

The gunfire caused everyone to duck to the floor. Thomas, who was standing, kicked the gun away from the body and kneeled beside Charlie.

"Charlie!"

Heather screamed as she attempted to run to her fiancée but was intercepted by Ralph who held her far enough away from Thomas, who was applying pressure to the wound.

"I saw a first aid kit in the kitchen. Someone get it now," Thomas yelled.

"You hang in there buddy. An ambulance is on the way," he said to Charlie

"Where's Heather?"

"I'm here Charlie."

Ralph released his daughter and drew Jo Ann near him. Heather kneeled beside Charlie holding his hand with both of hers but she was unable to hold back her tears.

"Heather, you don't look so good," Charlie weakly managed to utter. His smile was even weaker.

"Charlie don't you leave me!"

Charlie didn't hear her plea; consciousness had left him.

UNIVERSITY Hospital is a 5-minute drive from the UWF campus, located on Davis Highway. Numerous Secret Service Agents surrounded the waiting area near the operating room. Its' occupants included Hays, who insisted on being with the family, the Twigs and Isabelle Franks. Thomas was present inside the waiting room as Hays' bodyguard.

Isabelle had called David to let him know what had happened, to say where she was. Hays and Taylor had had a short conference and the Twigs got a call from Reverend Edgars, to inquire about Charlie's condition. He was distraught to learn that Charlie had been seriously wounded and was in surgery.

Charlie had been in surgery for over an hour when the surgeon entered the room and was met by 5 pairs of expectant eyes. Not knowing whom to address.

"Charlie is in recovery now. We did exploratory surgery and he will have a pretty big scar, but fortunately the bullet went clean through without hitting anything vital. He will need to stay here for probably a week before he can be moved and then several more weeks' convalescence at home."

"When can we see him?"

Heather asked the doctor.

"He's being moved to a room and is still out from the anesthesia. Give us 15 or 20 minutes."

An hour later with the Twigs and Hays in the room, Charlie woke up to Heather smiling about 18 inches from his face. Thomas and Isabelle stepped outside when it appeared that Charlie was about to come to.

"I think I must be dead since I'm in heaven," Charlie said and flashed a smile and then grimaced when he tried to move.

"No I'm not heaven, because I hurt too much."

"Charlie, don't move; you might rip your stitches. Do you remember what happened?"

"Yeah, Heather, I forgot to duck," Charlie said, attempting humor. "Does anyone know why Chris to decided to shoot me?"

"Charlie the Secret Service thinks that it was a culmination of several things. He was high when he attacked me. Hashish was found in his room as well as some uncomplimentary material about me, written on his laptop computer. It appears he was the author of derogatory editorials about me though he used your name. He was also on academic probation and was in jeopardy of being thrown out of school. There may be some other things as well but that's all we know now," Hays spoke for the first time.

"Charlie, I owe you a debt of gratitude. Thank you for saving my life," Hays spoke again.

"It seemed like the thing to do at the time, Mrs. President."

"Charlie the doctors say you are going to have to be here for at least a week. Mom and I are going to stay here and Dad is going to drive to Cumming tomorrow," Heather said.

"And you and your mother are going to stay at my home while Charlie is in the hospital."

"Mrs. President that won't be necessary," Jo Ann said.

"Nonsense, Jo Ann, its' the least I can do for your family and don't concern yourself about renting a car either; I have several you can use."

"That's very gracious of you," Jo Ann replied.

"Is Ron outside? I think I owe him a debt of gratitude," Charlie asked.

"I'm right here buddy," Thomas said as he and Isabelle walked inside the room.

"Thanks man. I owe you huge."

"No, I was just returning the favor I owed you Charlie. How did you manage to leap over the President and close the distance so fast? It was close to 30 feet."

"Paintball man, it's a hobby of mine that I don't have any peers. I'm out of commission right now but later on I'll be happy to teach you or any of your Secret Service buds a dose of humility on a paintball field."

"You're on."

"Right now, the only thing you are doing is get well quickly. Do you read me?"

Heather said in a Marine voice.

"I think I've just been given my first order by my wife to be. Oh, everyone here is invited to our wedding; be sure to give Heather your address so we can send you an invitation. Ralph, is this what I can expect being married to a Twig?"

"Yep I take orders like that from Jo Ann all the time and she's not in the Marines. I just hope you realize what you're getting yourself into."

Jo Ann gave her husband a smack to his shoulder and then their fingers intertwined as they held hands.

Charlie reached for Heather's hand and their fingers intertwined.

"I wouldn't have it any other way."

# Epilogue

## *December 16th Seville Quarter Pensacola, Florida.*

The Michaels-Twig wedding at the Seville Quarter complex was a grand affair and the reception was a grander one. Heather decided that she wanted to be married in Pensacola and Charlie, now fully recovered from his wounds didn't object.

Casey Edgars married Charlie and Heather. All of Charlie's fraternity brothers were attendance, along with friends and family of the Twigs. Also in attendance were Heather and Charlie's mutual friends, Isabelle Franks, her husband David and their daughter Tori, Ron Thomas, Mohammad Baghai and President Jennifer, Hays, who had reclaimed the office of the Presidency, after receiving assurances from Speaker Cedric Wrangler that the article of impeachment would die in committee.

Heather looked radiant in her wedding dress and Charlie, equally dapper in a black and gray tuxedo, complete with a white shirt and black bow tie. Charlie asked Ron to be his best man and several of his fraternity brothers as groomsmen. Heather had several friends from school to be her wedding.

Ralph, usually the stoic one, had tears in his eyes as he gave his daughter away.

Charlie and Heather exchanged the traditional wedding vows and wedding bands. Afterwards Edgars instructed Charlie to kiss Heather, but before Charlie kissed his eager new wife he turned his head to the audience and flashed a semi-sinister grin. Heather blushed because she knew that every one of the guests knew exactly what Charlie was thinking. The guests on both sides of the isle broke out in laughter. It was a Kodak moment, which was recorded by a digital movie camera and a paid photographer.

"I guess Charlie has other things on his mind besides the reception," Edgars remarked.

The guests laughed again and Heather's face turned another two shades of red.

"Ladies and gentlemen, it is my privilege to introduce to you for the very first time, Mr. and Mrs. Charlie Michaels," Edgars said.

The reception was catered and with a cash bar. The food disappeared quickly, since college students and free food is a combination very much like fire and gasoline; it doesn't last long.

Heather danced with Charlie and her father, while Charlie danced the Jo Ann. Several of Charlie's fraternity brothers had made dates for jet skiing on the beach with members of Heather's wedding party for later in the day.

Charlie and Heather excused themselves at the appropriate time to change into traveling clothes. Jo Ann left to help Heather, leaving Ralph in the outdoor courtyard.

"Excuse me Mr. Twig?"

"Yes?"

"We haven't met. I am Mohammad Baghai."

Ralph offered his hand to shake, which Mohammad accepted.

"I have sort of a wedding gift for Charlie and your daughter. Would you see that they get it?"

"Certainly Mohammad."

Mohammad removed an envelope containing a million-dollar check, less federal and state taxes, from his coat pocket and handed it to Ralph.

"It's a certified check, that I intended to give to him earlier, but for various reasons was not able to do so."

"I'll see that they get it and that they know who gave it to them. Is an address inside so they can send you a thank you note?"

"Yes there is. You have a beautiful daughter sir."

"Thank you."

Mohammad walked over to a table with Ralph to take a bag of rice and though he wasn't familiar with the custom. What was the adage? 'When in Rome, do what the Romans do.'

After Charlie and Heather left for their honeymoon, a cruise in the Caribbean, where they intended to do some scuba diving as well, which would depart from Miami, Mohammad went and said hello to Isabelle and David, which he had not had the opportunity to do so.

"David! Isabelle! How are both of you?"

Mohammad embraced both of his friends.

"Mohammad, it's great to see you again! I'm glad you could make it."

"I wasn't sure if it would be appropriate for me to come here but Casey called Charlie and the Twigs. They insisted that I come."

"Mohammad, you never have met our daughter Tori," Isabelle said.

"Tori, this is Mr. Baghai. Say hello."

Tori recognized Mohammad.

"Bad guy," she uttered to the horror to her parents.

Mohammad raised his hand to silence Isabelle and David's protests.

"I will explain in a moment David."

Mohammad squatted down to give Tori a hug.

"Not anymore Mary Victoria, not anymore."

LaVergne, TN USA
31 August 2010
195400LV00003B/14/P